LOLA MILES

Strelitzias in Spring

First edition

This book was professionally typeset on Reedsy.
Find out more at reedsy.com

*To everyone who has ever felt they're simultaneously too much
and not enough.*

Contents

Acknowledgement

When I first sat down to write Serena and Wolf's story, I had an entirely different direction in mind. As I'm sure you've figured out from my first two books, *Lilies in Autumn* and *Daffodils in Winter*, I am an instant gratification type of gal; I like the spice hot and heavy within the first 30% of the book. However, I made a promise to myself that I would someday craft an angsty, slow burn romance. Serena and Wolf drew the straw for it.

If you're going into this book expecting instant spice, you'll be disappointed. The emotional journey, the lust, and the strong female friendships are all present from the start, but the sweltering (can I say "sweltering" if I wrote it, or does it come across as self-promoting?) scenes arrive in the second half of the book. I promise, the journey is worth it and you will be squirming when you get there.

As always, thank you to Kat's Literary Services. A very special thank you to Steph White and Vanessa Esquibel for the support, guidance, and help you've both given to me throughout the Marymount University series. Every time I get your notes back, I squeal because I know you're going to help take the weirdness contained within the pages and help me make it palatable.

Thank you to Deb Neri for my gorgeous book cover. You are so incredibly talented and I can't thank you enough for your patience with my madness.

To my BETA readers, Kristi, Lizet, Taylor, and Theresa, your insight, feedback, and critiques helped to fine-tune this story and center the narrative. I am so fortunate to work with all of you.

Thank you to the Author Agency for organizing my release tour, ARC distribution, and reveals. Both Shauna and Becca have helped to promote this book and I would not have the audience or reach without them.

To my husband, who constantly asks, "What are you working on?" just to be given a thirty-minute dissertation on the sex scene I'm trying to nail down (pun intended). Thank you for supporting me and encouraging me to continue. I love you; thank you for being my real-life HEA.

To my parents and siblings, thank you for being the strangest advertising sources for my spicy romance books. Colleagues, hairdressers, random people at work events, women on dating applications; it's an interesting marketing strategy, but I am indebted to you. As always, thank you to my mom and dad for never quelling my love of literature, or telling me that an English degree was useless. I'm here because of your support (though I'm sure you didn't think I'd be writing smut with my MA, but here we are).

And finally, thank you to my children. Though they have no idea what I'm working on while I type away, they grab their little toy laptops and go to "work" with Mommy at six o'clock at night. They give me the motivation to continue, and I hope they always know that I followed my dreams so that they could one day follow theirs.

Strelitzias in Spring

She is chaotic and disorganized, while he thrives on order and control.

Brainiac, freak, nerd: just a few of the names that have been thrown at me since I started college at sixteen. It's not that I liked the designations, but I was used to them and learned to block the jabs out.

But then, the strangest thing happened; I made friends, the fabled "ride or dies" who hold your hair back after too many drinks, cry with you on the sofa when your life implodes, and encourage you to spread your wings. I changed from "nerd" to "Rena," a college student who went to parties and kissed boys.

Everything was great... until it wasn't. And then I met him.

Wolf McCleery is like no man I've ever met before. He's stubborn, artistic, and infamous for his MMA fights. Opposites in every way, there's no reason for our attraction, yet I can't deny that every time I'm in his presence I want him.

But when Wolf becomes my savior, will he be too stubborn to submit, or will he become the big bad wolf who protects me from my demons?

Warnings

For those of you who do not wish to go into this book without the complete trigger and content warning list, please read below. Please note that this book is a work of fiction.

Trigger Warnings: This book contains references to absentee parents, parental abuse, emotional manipulation, violence, and explicit sexual scenes. Please, take care of yourself and your well-being when reading.

Some things to know about *Strelitzias in Spring*:
   Told in dual POVs
   Stubborn and MMA fighter MMC
   Quirky and intelligent FMC
   Slight age gap

Playlist

"The Wolf" – Mumford & Sons
"Dreaming of You" – Selena
"I and Love and You" – The Avett Brothers
"Hot Revolver" – Lil Wayne
"Dive" – Ed Sheeran
"Solo De Mi" – Bad Bunny
"Curiosity" – Bryce Savage
"Something in the Orange" – Zach Bryan
"All I Want" – Kodaline
"Wilder Days" – Morgan Wade
"Earned It" – The Weeknd
"London Calling" – The Clash
"Beggin'" – Måneskin
"Whispers in the Dark" – Mumford & Sons
"Wherefore Art Thou, Elvis?" – The Gaslight Anthem
"Bad Boy" – Brantley Gilbert
"Nobody to Love" – Sigma
"Ride" – SoMo
"Charmer" – Kings of Leon
"Love Galore" – Sza
"It Ain't Me" – Kygo ft. Selena Gomez
"Body" – Loud Luxury ft. brando

Prologue

Serena

Of all the ways I thought I'd lose my virginity, half-dressed in my dad's guest house with socks on was not one of them. I also didn't anticipate that I'd have sex for the first time on the hardwood floor, but here I am: uncomfortable and sweaty. Lying here, knees bent, and wool shirt pushed up to my bra, I can't help but think of all the things I need to do when I get back to my apartment. My plants need a good watering, and I probably should buy some of the plant food for my herb basket. I also need to call the printer for Sigma Tau Delta, the English National Honor Society, and verify that they received the payment for the marketing materials for next month's poetry night.

I feel like I'm forgetting something, but it's hard to concentrate when a two-hundred-pound man is drilling into you like his dick is an electric screwdriver and your vagina is a metal beam.

"Fuck, your wet hole feels so fucking good, Siren," Devin pants above me, and I do everything I can not to cringe at his use of "wet hole." Pussy, cunt, even vagina would have been preferable to "wet hole."

At least he didn't say petals, I reason in my head.

"You like my big dick, Siren? You'll never have better than

this. Fuck," he groans, stilling on top of me and coming into the condom. I haven't seen many penises, but I assume that his length is average while the girth is thin, almost like a Number 2 pencil. Devin plops down next to me and rips the condom off his dick, tying it like a balloon before flinging it across the room.

That's disgusting and highly unsanitary.

"Yep, it was great," I murmur. Other than the slight twinge of discomfort when he first rammed into me, I didn't feel much of anything besides the cold floor digging into my back.

"Fuck, I'm tired. Where's my phone?" Devin muses, getting up and walking toward his discarded pants. Slipping them on, he grabs his phone from the coffee table and releases a sharp breath. "Fuck, Marina texted me. I need to go over there and see what she needs." Marina, my former best friend turned stepsister turned archnemesis and Devin's ex-girlfriend, is a manipulative she-devil who gets everything she wants. However, in this instance, I'm not complaining about her tactics because I need Devin and his pencil dick to leave so that I can scrounge up what's left of my dignity.

"Okay, see you around," I call out from my position on the floor. I reach for my leggings, which Devin tossed haphazardly next to me, and quickly slide them up my legs. I have no idea where my thong is, but that's the least of my concerns.

As soon as I stand up, Devin is on me, shoving his pointy tongue into my mouth and licking into my gums like I'm one of those grape-flavored ice pops he loved as a kid.

"You were so hot, Siren. But"—he plants another sloppy kiss on my mouth before pulling back—"no one can know about this. If I find out you told Marina, I'll kill you." I nod my head at his dramatics. Do I think he'll actually kill me? No. But I do believe that he'll make my life a living hell if Marina somehow finds out about this.

I already regret my weakness and decision to sleep with him. I know it was wrong; I know I shouldn't have done it, even though he told me they were broken up. But I was lonely and upset when he came to the guest house this afternoon, and when he kissed me and called me beautiful, I didn't stop him.

God, I'm such an idiot. And now, I'm the other woman.

My friends, Ava and Celeste, both experienced romance-novel-worthy love as soon as they arrived at college, Ava with Greyson, and Celeste with Dante. And though Celeste has resisted Dante's affections, there's no doubt that their men are obsessed with them. But after impulsively kissing my best friend, Dylan, last week and now this, I'm convinced that there's something fundamentally wrong with me.

When Dylan molded his lips to mine in a sweet, gentle kiss, it felt wrong, almost incestuous. Devin's hip thrusts and tongue-lashing were only nominally better.

"Did you hear me? Or are you ignoring me, Serena?" Devin's words jerk me out of my thoughts, and I look up at his handsome face. Why did he have to be such an asshole? Tall and broad, Devin looks like he stepped out of the pages of a Ralph Lauren catalog. Before puberty, we had been close friends, but when my parents divorced, our time together dwindled until we were reduced to strangers.

"I heard you," I whisper. "I won't say anything."

"You better fucking not," he growls before opening the door and walking down the path to the main house, where Marina is ensconced in my old room, living the life I might have had if my father wasn't a cheating asshole.

1

Serena

It's funny how betrayal feels like an ulcer in my stomach, an undeniable burning radiating from my chest and encompassing every part of my body. I feel sick and hot but also strangely cold, as though my blood is frozen in my veins and refuses to pump in time with the rhythm of my heart.

I know that's scientifically inaccurate, but there's no rationale for the disloyalty I'm facing.

When I came to Greyson, Dante, and Lincoln's house with Dylan to hang out with CeCe and Ava for a movie night, I never anticipated that my poor decisions would cause such irreparable damage. After Devin stormed into the house to find me and fought with Celeste's boyfriend, Dante, the very last thing I expected was for Dylan, my best friend since childhood, to admit to telling Marina that Devin and I slept together.

It's not that I think I didn't do something wrong; I did. I messed up. I should have stayed far away from Devin, and it's something I will regret for the rest of my life.

"You fucked him after we hooked up? You're a fucking

1

whore, just like he said you'd be once you got a taste of dick," Dylan seethes. Shaking my head, I feel the tears roll down my cheeks as I stare at the boy I once thought of as my best friend. His gross exaggeration simultaneously angers and hurts me; Dylan and I kissed, but it never went beyond that point. For him to claim that it was anything more is mortifying. I'm about to open my mouth to defend myself when CeCe approaches him calmly, like a warrior ready for peace negotiations. But instead of diffusing the situation, she lifts her right hand to shove his head back by his forehead and uses her left hand to hit his throat with an open palm. Simultaneously, she hooks her right leg around his foot and moves the hand from Dylan's forehead to his knee, pushing him backward until he crumbles.

Looking down at him, she lifts her leg and positions it over his dick. "Give me one reason why I shouldn't crush your balls for speaking to Serena like that." It's hard to remember that my five-foot-nothing friend is trained in Brazilian jiu-jitsu and can incapacitate a person with little to no effort.

"Fuck you, you fucking bitch," Dylan wheezes, struggling to speak after she karate-chopped his windpipe.

Before CeCe can respond, Ava's voice breaks in. "You suck at kissing. And you," Ava turns to Devin, who's now slumped against the wall from Dante's hits. "You're a selfish lover."

"Vixen," Grey grinds out. "Not fucking helping."

Dante grabs CeCe, wrangling her body behind his and approaching Dylan like an angry wildebeest. Before I can say or do anything, Ava's arms wrap around me in a tight hold.

"We'll kill them for you, Rena. You don't deserve that; you don't deserve any of this," Ava whispers, pressing me tighter

2

against her body.

"Wh-why would he do this? He was my best friend," I choke out, disbelief and sorrow chopping up my words. "I confided in him. I-I told him what happened. I knew he w-was angry, but this?" I say through the tears.

"Serena, are you okay?" Dante asks, coming to stand behind CeCe.

I don't hesitate to respond. "I just want to go home," I murmur, dropping my head so that I don't see the pitying glances on their faces.

"I don't think that's a safe option right now. They both know where your apartment is. Why don't you stay here? Or in my dorm with me?" Celeste asks. Ava responds, probably with something sarcastic, but I tune her out.

"I-I am going to go home. To my mom's house. I can't be here. H-he was my best friend. Why would he do this?" I repeat, barely getting out the words. "I-I'm going to call an Uber."

Ava immediately jumps in, offering to drive me the half hour back home. I protest, but Ava and CeCe keep insisting, and I realize that it's easier for me just to give in. I feel helpless and embarrassed that my friends witnessed Devin and Dylan's treatment toward me, that everyone now knows about the greatest mistake of my life, and that I'm now relying on them for a charity ride back home.

Walking away from the circle Ava, CeCe, and Dante created, I walk to the front door and press my body to the wall, trying to make myself as small and invisible as possible.

—

The ride to my mom's house was silent and tense; not even Ava, who can be clumsy with both her words and her body,

3

attempted to diffuse the tension. But now, less than five minutes from my mom's house, I break the silence.

"Thank you both. I…" I clear my throat, addressing Greyson and Ava. "I appreciate you bringing me back home."

Ava turns in her seat, staring at me with her large, dark eyes. "We're always here for you, Rena. I'm so sorry for what happened back at the house."

Grey puts the car in park and turns to look at me. "I never would have invited Dylan if I knew he was going to pull shit like that tonight. I'm sorry, Serena. That was fucked up, and he had no right to start shit. Devin's a little prick, and I'm not surprised by his reaction, but Dylan? Not fucking cool."

I smile tightly, thankful for their concern but also mortified that I'm on the receiving end of their pity. "It's okay," I offer lamely.

"Hell no, it's not," Ava yells, and I wince at her volume. "Sorry." She lowers her voice. "But it's not okay. He had no right to judge you, let alone spread your business around like he had a right to it."

"I know," I whisper. Reaching for the handle, I open the door. Before I slip out of Grey's Jeep, I lean over the console and grab Ava's shoulder. "Thank you, Aves. It means a lot to me that you and CeCe were there for me and stood up for me. I've never really had that before." I look to Grey. "You, too. Thank you and the guys for defending me."

"Always, Rena. Always." I remove my hand from Ava, hop out of the Grey's lifted monstrosity, and shut the door behind me.

The short walk from the curb to my mom's front door feels like I'm walking the plank in a pirate movie. I look behind me and wave at Grey and Ava, who waited to back out until I made it to the door. Looking forward, I take a deep breath and press down on the handle.

"Mamá," I call out, stepping over the threshold.

"Serena?" my mother's voice rings out from the opposite side of our small house, a mixture of surprise and confusion at my sudden appearance. "What are you doing home? I thought you were coming next week?"

Walking toward her voice, I round the corner and see her sitting at the kitchen island, wine glass in hand while working on her laptop. Before the divorce, my mother was a stay-at-home mom; post-divorce, she used the teaching degree she spent four years on and started teaching history at the local high school. Two years ago, she became the vice principal of that same school. Now, it seems as though she never stops working.

"*Muñeca*, what's wrong?" I smile at the endearment. My mother has called me her "doll" since I was a little girl obsessed with baby dolls.

"Nothing. Why does something have to be wrong for me to come home unexpectedly?"

My mother levels me with an assessing gaze. "Did you forget I raised you? I know you, Serena, and how carefully you plan each move you make. Tell me, what happened?"

"I made a mistake." I wince. "Several mistakes. And n-now everything feels like it's imploding." I release the last of my words with a cry, dissolving into silent tears as I watch my mother set her wineglass down and rise from her stool. Walking toward me, she envelops me in a hug, squeezing me into her petite body.

"Come, talk to me, *hija*." My mom leads me to the living room and all but pushes me onto the couch. "Are you hungry?"

My stomach clenches at the thought of food. "N-no, thank you."

"Serena, what happened?"

Throwing my body against the cushions, I let out a heavy sigh. "I slept with Devin," I state matter-of-factly. "And I made out with Dylan before that."

I chance a look at my mother and see her eyebrows raised to her hairline. "In the same day? Is this one of those 'why choose' things?"

I rear back. "Wait, what? No, of course not. How do you know what those are?"

"I'm forty-five, not dead. Start at the beginning."

"I feel like I'm in an alternate universe." I pause, shaking my head. "You know Dylan and I have always been close. A few weeks ago, we kissed; it felt… off. Just not right. I told him I wasn't interested in anything more than friendship and that I didn't want to risk our relationship for something that wouldn't even work out."

My mom nods. "Okay. How did he take that?"

I think back to our initial conversation. "He was fine with it. Or so it seemed. But that's not where I messed up. If I just kissed Dylan, we could have worked through it without any major issues. But, when I was at Dad's a few weeks ago, Devin came over, and we slept together." I look away from my mother, too ashamed to see her face. My mother has zero tolerance or empathy for adultery, and I'm mortified that I put myself in this position.

Long moments of silence pass before my mom asks, "Are Devin and Marina still together?"

I shake my head. "No, or at least they weren't. They were broken up when it happened, but I'm not stupid. I knew they'd get back together, but I was lonely and angry that I had to be at Dad's house just to be ignored for the entire weekend. I knew it was wrong, knew I shouldn't have done it, but I did."

"You haven't been to your dad's in three weeks. What happened today to upset you?"

I look toward the ceiling and release a sigh. "We were at Ava and CeCe's boyfriends' house; Dylan and a couple of other people were there. We were supposed to have a movie night, but Devin came barging into the house, hurling accusations and insults at me, saying that I had told Marina about us. I had a feeling our night together would get out, but I didn't perpetuate the rumors. I just told Ava and CeCe today.

"Devin and Dante, CeCe's guy, ended up trading punches, and it was a bloody mess. Dylan admitted, in front of everyone, that he told Marina because she had a right to know what happened. H-he said such horrible things, Mom," I say with a sob, burrowing my face in my hands.

"Shh. It's okay, Serena," my mom soothes, rubbing my back as though I'm an eight-year-old with a bellyache and not an eighteen-year-old harlot.

"I-I was the other woman, Mamá."

"No," she says sharply. "You made a bad judgment call, *Muñeca*; I won't lie to you. But you are not the other woman if they were broken up. Should you have slept with that boy? Probably not, but only because he didn't respect you or the gift you gave him."

I'm about to respond when my phone vibrates in quick succession, signaling a phone call. Pulling it from my pocket, I check the caller ID and groan when I see my father's contact information on the screen.

"Serena, do not answer—" I cut my mom off by swiping on

7

the icon and bringing the phone to my ear.

"Hi, Dad."

"Of all the selfish, irresponsible, reckless things you could have done, you did this? You slept with your sister's boyfriend? How could you be so cruel, Serena? Your sister is a goddamn mess because of your actions. Have you no shame?"

"Dad—"

"It's your mother; she poisoned you against your family, and that's why you did this. After everything I've done for you. I provide for everything, including that hobbit hole your mother calls a house. I'm ashamed of you. You need to get over here now and make this right, or I'll—"

My mom yanks the phone out of my hand, preventing me from hearing the rest of my dad's tirade. "How dare you speak to my daughter this way, Stephen. Instead of asking her what happened, checking on *your* daughter to make sure she was safe and well, you verbally attacked her and accused me of poisoning her against you and your disgrace of a family. Your mother would be ashamed of you, Stephen Castillo."

She pauses, listening to his response. Her face quickly morphs from disgust to outrage the longer she listens. "Contigo se confirma la teoría científica de que un humano puedo vivir sin cerebro." *You have confirmed the scientific theory that a human can live without a brain.* "No, I will not put my daughter back on the phone to be subjected to your abuse. How—" My mother is cut off, her lips pinching together. "You and your wife are both assholes that can rot in hell," she yells before hanging up.

I choke on my saliva, a mixture of laughter and tears momentarily halting my speech. "Did you just tell Dad he and

Brandi can rot in hell?"

"Yes. You are not going there, Serena."

I search her face. "What did he say?"

She just shakes her head. "It doesn't matter what he said. He doesn't provide for you, I do. *You* provide for yourself. You have a full-ride scholarship, and your housing is covered through the scholarship. I pay for this house; it's just his stupid name on the mortgage. I will sell this place before I allow him to take one more damn thing from us."

"Mamá," I start, but she shakes her head.

"No, this is not up for discussion. You will not be subjected to his cruelty. You made a mistake, but you are not a bad person. You are his daughter. He seems to have forgotten that." Handing my phone back, she grabs my shoulders and pulls me into her body. "I'm sorry that this happened to you and that you lost people in the process. But remember, *Muñeca*, if they were supposed to be in your life long-term, they wouldn't have done this to you. Isn't it better to find out their true character at your age than in ten, twenty years from now?"

I shrug against her body, sniffling. "I don't care about Devin; he's always been an asshole, and I was just lonely. But Dylan? I-it just hurts. He was my best friend, and now? It's like I-I don't even know him."

"Shhh, he's not worth your tears," my mom soothes.

Pulling back, I look up at my mother's beautiful face. Her warm honey complexion is clear, not a trace of makeup marring her skin, and her dark brown eyes are pained, as though she feels my anguish just as deeply as I do. She offers a sad smile, her full lips barely pulling at the corners.

"Can I ask you something?"

9

"Of course," she answers immediately.

"I didn't feel any spark—any connection—with Dylan *or* Devin. Is it possible I'm defective?" I feel like an idiot for even asking the question. But shouldn't I have at least felt *something*?

My mom tsks, grabbing me again. "Your body just knew what your mind didn't: both of those boys were not worthy of you. One day, you'll meet someone who sees you as their whole world and will make your life, your happiness, their priority."

Despite my mom's wisdom and her reassurance, I can't help but think that she's wrong.

2

Serena

Three weeks later

Life has been shit lately; there is no counterargument or silver lining. Ava almost died because she fell in love, I lost my best friend and my dad's respect, and after listening to CeCe's gut-wrenching sobs, I found out that she had lost her unborn child.

Growing up, my mother always counseled me to "trust in God's plan." But God's plan is utter bullshit, as evidenced by the near-death and heartbreak the three of us have endured. My anger at the universe is how I wound up here, in the parking lot of Ink and Needle, CeCe's cousin's tattoo shop a half hour away from campus. When Ava first suggested we get tattoos, I balked and almost said no to coming. Both Ava and CeCe were supportive when I told them about my hesitation, convincing me to come regardless of whether I received a tattoo or not.

Now, staring at the innocuous brick facade, a feeling of rightness comes over me, as though I'm exactly where I'm supposed to be.

"Come on, Wolf is waiting for us, and if I know anything about my cousin, he's going to be a fucking grump if we make him wait on us," CeCe calls from the back seat of my ancient Toyota Corolla.

Okay, ancient may be a hyperbole, but my cherry red four-door sedan is ten years old and has more scratches and patch-ups than I care to admit. Internally, I scowl because Marina has a newer Mercedes, and I'm driving a car held together with prayers and duct tape.

I'm proud of my car—I bought it with money saved from birthdays, holidays, and tutoring jobs—but it still hurts that my dad claims that he's taken care of my mom and me for the last decade when he's done nothing more than guilt me into going to his house and relegating me to a guest in my childhood home.

The slamming of a door jolts me from my internal musings, and I look up in time to see CeCe and Ava rounding the hood of my car, waiting for me to turn off my engine and get out.

"You coming, Rena?" Ava calls out. My chest warms at the nickname. Before Ava and CeCe, I was always Serena, the child brainiac with too few friends and too many responsibilities. No one had ever shortened my name or given me a nickname that was born from affection, aside from my mother. Devin always mocked me by calling me "Siren," and everyone else has always used my full name. But now I'm Rena, a college student with friends.

It's tragic that it's taken me this long to feel like I finally belong somewhere.

"Yes, sorry. Coming," I respond, hurrying out of the car.

"Hey, what did I say about apologizing? Cut that shit out,"

Ava comments. "Now, let's go get some ink. I call going first."

"Aves, calm your tits; Wolf is going to think you're high on drugs if you run into the shop screaming like a lunatic."

Ava lets out a scoff, not breaking her stride. "Wolf has known me since I was prepubescent; he's used to my personality." Ava throws the door open on the last word, yelling at CeCe. I follow them into the building, surprised by how open and bright the space is.

Gleaming white walls hold framed artwork, a foil to the masculine black furniture spread throughout the open space. On the far side of the room, private rooms with doorways framed in black trim offer privacy to clients and prevent anyone from seeing the art in process. CeCe stops at the reception desk, a smile on her face.

"Hey, Aubrey. How are you?" CeCe greets. Peering over her shoulder, I'm struck by how stunning the woman behind the desk is. With long blonde dreadlocks and mocha skin, tattoos cover her body in vibrant pops of color, complimenting her beauty. She smiles at us, a small ring dangling above her teeth. "Holy shit, did you get a smiley? Did that hurt?"

She laughs at CeCe's outburst, rolling her eyes before answering, "It didn't feel good, but it wasn't too bad. Wolf did it last week." Aubrey looks around CeCe. "Hey, Ava, good seeing you again. And you must be Serena."

"Oh, yes. Hi," I murmur.

She smiles at me, nothing but warmth and kindness radiating from her badass features, and I feel less nervous than I did a few moments ago. "It's great to meet you. CeCe told Wolf that you're on the fence about a tattoo. Do you want to take a look at work samples and stock designs?" She lifts a book, holding it out for me.

13

I carefully take the offered book, clearing my throat. "Yes, that would be great. Thank you."

"Thank fuck you're finally here. I thought you were going to stand me up," a voice sounds behind us, and I feel my stomach immediately clench. The deep timber and rasp wash over me, and I'm surprised by my reaction to a voice. I haven't even seen the owner's face, yet I feel foreign beads of attraction travel up my spine. Turning slowly, my jaw slackens at the sight of a real-life Jamie Fraser, one that's covered in tattoos and muscles.

My mom went through an *Outlander* phase, and I heard the words "Sassenach" and "lass" too many times to count. At one point, she even played the audiobooks on repeat while cooking dinner. It was a weird year.

I'm staring at the Highlander's profile, presumably CeCe's cousin, when he shifts his gaze to me, and I'm greeted by shining green eyes, a sharp jawline with a dimpled chin, and a nose that has definitely been broken more than once. In a word, he's stunning. Breathtaking, intense, and intimidating would also work. My body shivers under his stare, and I feel my nipples pebble against my thick sweatshirt. I'm not cold—the heat in this building is on full blast, and I'm in a sherpa—I'm attracted to him and the cool reception he gave us.

"Are you cold?" he asks, breaking me out of my trance.

I flush, mortified that he saw my full-body reaction to his presence.

"Ah, no. I'm okay," I whisper, averting my eyes. I can feel his gaze linger on me like he's not quite sure what to make of my presence. Unlike Ava and CeCe, who have known each other since childhood, I'm naturally quieter and more introverted.

14

When I first met my two friends, I was shocked to find myself nearly begging for their company and inviting them to my home. I was even more surprised to find that they didn't judge me for my studies, my fucked-up family situation, or the omnipresent self-doubt I harbor.

The weight of his eyes leaves me, and I take a deep breath, sucking in as much oxygen as my lungs can handle. Ava gives me a confused stare, but I just shake my head, willing her not to open her mouth.

"Okay, Wolfie," CeCe begins, excitement in her tone. When CeCe came to my apartment earlier this evening to meet for a girls' dinner with Ava, she collapsed into my arms as soon as I opened my door and told us about her loss; I felt guilt seep into my bones that the altercation with Devin and Dylan somehow contributed to her miscarriage. But her tears have dried, and the melancholy is missing from her voice. "I'm going to go first, then Ava. Serena is still on the fence about getting a tattoo, so we'll give her enough time to decide if she wants one, okay?"

I look at Wolf's face to see him raise one perfectly groomed red eyebrow. "What are you, my scheduler? Aubrey will kill you if you try taking her job."

"If it means she has to deal with your grumpy ass, then she can have it," Aubrey calls out from her seat by the desk.

CeCe turns to Aubrey, smiles, and offers a wink before turning back to Wolf. "Don't be a pain in my ass, Wolfie." Without any more preamble, CeCe walks past her cousin and through the first door on the left, as though she's been here a thousand times and knows her way around the shop.

"After you, Celeste," Wolf grumbles, trailing behind her.

"Okay, my little petunia, what are you thinking about

getting?" Ava asks beside me, stealing my attention.

"Petunia? When have you ever called me that?" I ask, and she just shrugs. Rolling my eyes, I continue, "I'm not entirely sure if I'm getting one."

"Liar, liar. You wouldn't have come if you didn't want a tattoo, so give it up, Rena."

"That's not true; maybe I just wanted to hang out with you and CeCe. It's been a while since we have all been together."

"Well, you're here now, so you may as well participate, right? It's like, we're all bungee jumping, so you should, too."

I narrow my eyes at her, squinting at the rationale. "So you're saying that if you and Celeste jumped off a cliff, I should follow because you're both doing it? Ava, you're describing peer pressure but putting a pretty bow on it and disguising it as friendship."

"Anyway," she scoffs, ignoring my response. "What are you getting?"

I sigh, giving up the pretense that I'm not seriously considering a tattoo. "I have a few ideas, but I want to speak to him"—I tilt my head in the direction of Wolf's station—"before I commit."

"You mean Wolf?"

I nod, feeling my cheeks heat at the mention of his name. Like a seasoned detective, Ava sniffs out my attraction and raises a brow. "Little Rena, do you think Wolf is hot?" she asks, nearly yelling the words.

"Shhh," I hiss. "Lower your damn voice, Ava."

"Oh my God, you do."

I sigh, glancing up to make sure Aubrey isn't paying attention to us before I respond. "He looks like Sam Heughan, just with tattoos and more muscles." Ava's brow furrows, confused by my response. "Jamie Fraser from the *Outlander* series."

Her eyes widen, and her jaw drops. "Holy shit, he does. I can't believe I never saw that before."

I nod and look down, throwing myself into the act of looking through the book Aubrey gave me. The front of the book holds basic drawings and stencils, art that can be placed over and over again and hold a different meaning for each client. Though the images are beautiful, if not simple, I'm struck by the delicate script samples. The deeper I dive into the book, the more intricate and complex the artwork becomes. Gone are the generic roses and banner hearts, and in their place are full-body tattoos and intricate designs that serve as inspiration rather than stencils. My eyes gravitate toward a large man, face cut off, with a massive back tattoo that disappears into boxers before re-emerging on his legs. Though the tattoo holds no color, the artistry is so impressive that it looks as though the dragon, warriors, and flowers are going to climb off this man's skin. The images on the back of the legs complement the scene on the man's back, as it's just a beautiful continuation of cherry blossoms and koi fish.

Ava looks over my shoulder, peering at the image. "Oh, that's Wolf's work. He competed for Tattoo of the Year in a competition a few years ago and used that piece to enter."

"Wow," I reply, not sure what else to say. His talent is undeniable.

"I know. Okay, I'm going to go check on C and see how she's doing back there. Our girl may act tough, but she's a little marshmallow," Ava offers before standing up and walking to the back of the shop. I mull over her words; I don't think anyone besides Ava would describe Celeste as a marshmallow.

I roll my eyes, secretly thankful for Ava's absence so that I can finally think and observe the tattoos in peace.

Though the illustrations and drawings are stunning, I keep flipping back to the samples of handwriting on the front of the album. Like a divine epiphany, I suddenly know what I want permanently inked on my body.

After my parents divorced, my mom would take me to the butterfly gardens in Brooklyn, a welcomed distraction from the chaos in our family. We'd be there for hours, exploring the grounds and taking in the flowers that seemed to attract the most intricately winged butterflies. I remember being struck by how the tiny insects would land on the flowers, stay for a bit, and then take flight, zooming to the next destination in their sights.

There's a sense of freedom with butterflies, almost like they have a home, but they're not tethered there; they land and take off at will or instinct. I've always wanted to be like a butterfly: free but also belonging everywhere. I've never felt that way, not even in my own home.

I must zone out for long minutes, lost in my thoughts, because by the time I refocus, Ava and Celeste are standing before me, bandages on their arms.

"Hi," CeCe says, approaching me slowly as though I'm an animal in the wild. "Have you decided if you're getting a tattoo?"

I clear my throat, nodding my head. "Yes, I think I am."

"Eek!" Ava squeals, sounding like a rusty door hinge. "What are you getting?"

"Let her be, Aves. She'll show us when we get back to her apartment," CeCe reprimands with an eye roll. "Wolf is ready for you; he just finished sanitizing and setting up the station."

18

"Great," I mumble, nerves assaulting my stomach. Taking a deep breath, I make my way to the back of the shop, where Wolf's tattoo room is. From the entry, you can't see into the private rooms, so I'm surprised as I step over the threshold and see dark walls, floor-to-ceiling bookshelves, and hunter-green accents. If the common area of the shop is modern and airy, with gleaming white walls, black trim, and framed artwork, then Wolf's private space is like a nineteenth-century villain's secluded lair. It's simultaneously masculine and feminine—a dichotomy born from attention to detail and a balance of sex and darkness.

I don't think I've ever been turned on by a room before— truthfully, I've barely ever been turned on—but there's something carnal about the space that hints at the personality of the man who designed it.

A throat clears to my right, and I turn quickly, flushing at Wolf's presence. He must notice my embarrassment because he raises one dark red eyebrow before jerking his chin to the tattoo chair in the center of the room.

"Celeste said you were on the fence about a tattoo. I'm assuming you decided?"

"Yeah. Yes, I…" I pause, shaking my head to compose myself. "Yes, I decided. That I want one, that is."

"Okay," he says, drawing out the word like he's waiting for me to add more. When I don't, he lets out a sigh. "And what do you want?"

"Oh, right. The word *mariposa*. It means butterfly in Spanish."

"Got it. I'm going to do a quick look-up to make sure your translation is correct." He walks over to a writing desk and opens a laptop. He glances over his shoulder, taking in my form by the door. "You going to sit, or are you planning on getting a tattoo standing up?" I feel my cheeks heat; my blush is probably deepening from pink to a deep, mortifying red.

"Sitting, of course. I'll just go sit." His eyes follow me as I place my body on the chair, sliding until my back hits the dark leather. I feel his eyes linger on me, an unnerving perusal that leaves my breathing erratic and my nipples pebbling against the fabric of my bra. I thank God that I'm wearing so many layers and can hide my reaction to him. When I look up, I see that he's typing on the computer, the harsh clicks on the keyboard the only sound in the room. I shift on the chair, trying to get comfortable, and his hands flex on the keyboard as though he's affected by my presence.

"So, did you find the translation?" It shouldn't take long to look up the single word, but he's been staring at his computer screen for five minutes.

"Yeah. All set." Taking a notepad and pen, he scribbles something down before coming to his stool beside the tattoo chair. "Where are you thinking placement-wise?"

I swallow thickly as I unzip my jacket and reach for the hem of my shirt. When I saw that both Ava and CeCe got tattoos on their forearms, I immediately ruled the spot out. Lifting my shirt slowly, my heart pounds erratically as I bunch the shirt under my bust. With my free hand, I indicate where I want the word. "I'm thinking here, right below my bra line."

Unable to meet Wolf's gaze, I take in the death grip he has on his notepad and the flex of his arm, like he's physically holding himself back.

Wait, what?

Shifting my eyes up, I see that Wolf's gaze is trained on my bare skin, his jaw set in a tight scowl. I'm not sure if he's turned on by my bare midriff or viscerally offended.

Is it wrong that I think both reactions are hot?

I watch as Wolf works his jaw until his body relaxes, a contradiction to the tense posture he had moments ago. "Do you want me to stencil it or freehand?"

My mind goes back to his portfolio and the skill evident in his work. "I'm fine with freehand. But, uh, could you make it feminine?" I say, wincing at the last part. Amusement takes over his face, and that stupid eyebrow raises again. "I just mean that I saw your work, and it's amazing. So beautiful, but uh, I was thinking that I don't want something bold on my body right now. Just dainty, delicate. Like an ornament on my skin," I rush to clarify.

"Calm down, I wasn't planning on giving you block letters in a heart that says, 'Mom.'" He rolls his eyes, reaching behind him to grab a bottle of antiseptic and paper towels. "Get up for a minute while I adjust the bed, and take your jacket off for me." He uses side buttons to adjust the seat until it's flat. "Alright, go ahead and sit back down. I'm going to sanitize your skin and prep the area. Because it's freehand, I'm going to do a marker to show the placement and the length before I ink it on your skin. Once you're comfortable with the logistics, we'll get started." I follow his directions and work my jacket off, letting it fall behind me on the back of the chair. My shirt lowers in the process, and before I can adjust the hemline, I feel Wolf's fingers. "Can I?" he asks, pulling on the fabric. I nod wordlessly, my eyes trained on his face as he works my shirt up with the efficiency of a man who has taken off innumerable articles of clothing. He preps the area, marking out the size and location of the tattoo, and once I agree, he continues to prep the space before freehanding the word on

21

my body.

Lifting the covered gun, he looks at me before asking, "Ready?" I nod, not trusting myself to verbalize my response. Wolf sets his free hand on my skin, and I gasp. There's nothing sexual about his movements, but the graze of his gloved fingers against my bare skin has me shivering uncontrollably.

Wolf looks up sharply, pausing before bringing the tattoo gun to my skin. "Are you cold?"

"No. I'm good. Fine." I swear I have an above-average IQ and can strum together more than banal platitudes and sentence fragments. Wolf must think I'm a freaking moron with a perpetually frozen body temperature.

I shut my eyes, trying to focus on the sting of the machine and not the presence of the man marking me.

3

Wolf

Looking down at the woman before me, I pause, hovering my tattoo gun over her smooth ribcage. Her body convulses, a shiver working its way down her spine, and I frown, looking up at her before glancing toward the thermostat. It's set to seventy-three degrees and is comfortable, if not a little too warm. The fuck is she shivering for?

"Are you cold?"

"N-no. I'm good. Fine," she responds, shaking her head rapidly. I narrow my eyes and look down, taking in her flat stomach and the way it clenches against my touch. I don't know if she's nervous or turned on, but it's late, and I want to get home. Accepting her words as truth, I lean back down and settle my tattoo gun against her skin.

"It's going to sting a little, but it'll be over quick." Pressing down on the peddle, I start tracing the delicate script, going slowly to make sure there are no blowouts in the cursive lettering. Objectively, she's attractive with her short blonde hair, warm honey skin, and large dark eyes. Her lips are plump in the center, turning down on the sides like her face

23

is set in a perpetual pout.

I'm full of shit- she's more than pretty, but I try to block out her appearance and how good she smells, like cinnamon and cloves and vanilla. She's like a cake laid out before me.

I notice that her diaphragm has stopped moving, and I look up. The poor girl's face is turning red from oxygen deprivation. Don't get me wrong, I like breath play, but not like this when I'm in the middle of working. "Breathe for me. Does it hurt?"

"No."

"Can I keep going?"

"Yes," she answers simply before closing her eyes and cutting off all communication. I press on the peddle and resume, breathing in her scent as she lays like a barely breathing corpse beneath my hands. The process of tattooing is methodical, a release that gives me so much fucking joy that I can't imagine never doing it again. The need to create, to draw permanent art for my clients, is the same reason why I told my coach I was done with MMA; I've been lucky the last few years and haven't suffered any career-ruining injuries to my hands. Straddling both the shop and my commitment to the octagon meant that I couldn't devote all of myself to either, and I'm fucking done. Done with training at dawn and dusk to get my gym hours in and done with running on caffeine and Red Bull to get through my clients. I'm twenty-five, too young to feel this goddamn old.

My gaze travels back to the woman before me. Next to my mammoth body, she looks as dainty as the tattoo she requested. She breathes in deeply, expanding her ribcage before pulling it back in. The unexpected movement causes my line to shake.

"Fuck," I murmur, passing over the line again to thicken the weight. The script on her body was supposed to be a fine line, but I have to compensate for my slip-up.

"Is everything okay?" her soft voice murmurs from above me.

"Yep." I pop the "p," refusing to glance up at the caramel eyes I feel on my profile. I wish I could rush through this shit, but my pride and artistry won't let me. Even if everyone else thought it was a good tattoo, I'd never fuck a client over and make them leave with a half-assed rushed piece, especially not a girl whose flawless skin looks like it needs more of my artwork to accentuate its beauty.

I finish up the minuscule tattoo and finally set my gun down. I look down at the work and regard it critically. Her skin is red, irritated from the ink and gun, but I can already tell that it's going to heal nicely. She shifts in the chair, tilting her head to try and catch a glimpse of the tattoo. As she moves, her shirt rides up, and I catch sight of the underside of her tits. I look away quickly, grabbing the disposable wipes from my station and wiping off the excess ink on her skin.

She's been silent for the last ten minutes, not even a gasp or intake of breath since she asked me if I was okay. It was a quick tattoo, but the ribs are a sensitive spot, and I'm impressed by her pain tolerance. I'm about to commend her when my cousin walks into the room with a large, tattooed guy behind her.

So, this is Dante. I take him in, noticing that he has impressive amounts of ink on his body. His work is good—not as good as mine, but the artistry is solid, and I reason that at least he has good taste.

As soon as I make eye contact with Celeste, she rushes

over to us and places a hand on my shoulder, leaning over to take a look at the work on Serena's body. A low growl sounds off behind me, and I swallow a laugh. I look over to Celeste's boyfriend and barely contain my laughter at the scowl marring his face.

"You cannot be serious," Celeste says, an incredulous tone in her voice.

"I don't like seeing your hands on another man," the fucker says. I have to give him credit; at least he's possessive and protective.

"He's my cousin, you ogre. Don't make this weird." At the same time that Celeste speaks, Serena shifts in my chair, drawing CeCe's eyes down. My cousin's expression softens, and she praises the small artwork. "It looks so beautiful. What does it mean?"

"Butterfly," I offer, and Celeste whips her head to me.

"Since when do you speak Spanish?"

I roll my eyes. She should know that I would never tattoo something without confirming the definition, connotations, and denotations. The last thing I need is for someone to walk out of my shop with a tattoo that means hairy dicks when what they wanted was "from an acorn."

"I don't speak Spanish, but I asked your little siren what it meant and looked it up before I let her ink it on her skin. She could have fucked up and put 'scrotum' under her tit instead of 'butterfly.'"

"Don't call me that," Serena snaps out in a hard voice, and I look up, seeing the strain in her eyes and the set of her jaw. Since she entered my space, she's been nervous but not uncomfortable. Now, it looks like she'd rather be anywhere but here.

26

I'm not going to lie, I'm fucking intrigued by the change and the sudden fire darkening her eyes.

"What?" I ask, making sure I understand her.

"Siren. Don't call me that."

"I—" I start, but my cousin cuts me off, asking about payment.

"You know I'm not accepting your fucking money, Celeste, or that of your friends." I stare at Serena's back. When the fuck did she get off the table? I watch as the girls walk out of the room, heading to the front of the shop, where Ava and Aubrey wait with two guys I've never seen before. I'm about to follow them out when the douchebag's voice cuts in.

"You know, there's something about these girls that will have you serving your balls up on a fucking platter. I can see you noticed Serena." He tilts his head. What the fuck is he talking about? I'm a grown man, and while yeah, she's fucking hot, she's also six years younger than me, and I just fucking met her. I drown him out until I finally see his mouth shut.

"I don't know who the fuck you think you are, frat boy, but don't presume you know me."

We go back and forth until finally, I realize he's fucking gone over my cousin and projecting that shit on me and a woman I just met. Laughing, I tell him, "You're so fucked. Celeste probably already has your balls in a vice." Hitting him on the back just a little too hard, I send his body forward with the force. "Welcome to the family. But if you fuck with her, I'll personally see to your death."

Walking to the front of my shop with my arm around Celeste's man, I'm met with my cousin's wild stare and her accusations that I just bonded with her boyfriend.

"Fuck off, Celeste. You"—I turn to look at Serena—"I didn't

get to go over the aftercare instructions with you. Come back to my station, and we'll go over how to prevent infection."

"It's fine. CeCe and Ava know what to do; they can tell me," Serena says in a terse voice.

"That's not how I do business, princess. So, either walk back into the room and sit your pretty ass on the chair, or I'll drag you there. Your choice." I hear Ava spout some shit about sexual tension behind me, but my eyes don't leave Serena. Annoyed that she's not listening to me, I continue, "If it becomes infected, you have no one to blame but yourself. Don't blame me or my shop for that shit, and don't fucking call me complaining that you messed up your tattoo."

Like a balloon that loses all of its air, Serena's shoulders deflate, and she loses the fire that intrigued me moments ago. Barely meeting my eyes, she nods, acting like a meek little mouse.

I furrow my brows, confused again by the sudden change in her demeanor. In the thirty-minute interaction I've had with her, I've seen three different facets of her personality: timid, angered and defiant, and finally, submissive and dejected. I have fucking whiplash from the shift.

"Alright, well, this has been fun. Thank you, Wolfie," Celeste calls out, forcing her friends to trail after her.

"Well, that was interesting," Aubrey says from the receptionist's desk. "I'm heading home. You want some company?" I glance at one of my closest friends. To some, they may think her question is sexual, but I know better. Aubrey has been in a committed relationship with Trent, another tattooist in the shop, for the last ten years, and our friendship is strictly platonic. She's truly just asking if I'm okay.

"No, go home. Tell Trent I said to fuck off." She laughs and rolls her eyes, shutting down the computer before grabbing her bag and walking out the front door with a wave. I watch her walk across the lit parking lot until she gets into her car and drives off.

Alone with my thoughts, I try not to remember the feel of smooth golden skin beneath my gloves.

4

Serena

There's been no peace in the days following my visit to the tattoo shop. Though my dad swore my betrayal was inexcusable, he will not stop texting me and calling me. My phone buzzes again on my desk at the tutoring center, an annoying staccato that's tempting me to throw my phone out of the window.

Sighing, I reach down and read the texts from my dad.

Dad (11:32 AM): We need to speak. Be at my house for dinner at six.

Dad (1:46 PM): You have not confirmed dinner. Be there.

Dad (2:13 PM): Answer your phone right now. You have a phone for my convenience, not yours. If you continue to ignore me, I will turn your service off.

Shit. Looking at the time on my screen, I sigh in relief when I realize it's only been a few minutes since his latest text.

Serena: Sorry, Dad. I'm in the tutoring center working with students. I haven't had my phone. I'm unable to come tonight. I have class until eight.

Dad: Skip it.

Tears form in my eyes, blurring my vision. Growing up, I was the epitome of a "daddy's girl"; there was nothing I wanted more than to spend time with my dad and be the center of his universe. When my parents first divorced, I was angry and resentful, but my dad still made time for me. Now, the older I get, it's like I'm an inconvenient stranger with shared strands of DNA. Even before I slept with Devin, my presence in his house was an unwelcome occurrence tolerated only because his guilt nagged him to be a semi-present parent.

Clutching my phone, I take a deep breath before typing out another message.

Serena: I have a test today. I can't skip my exam.

Biting my lip, I type out a hasty "I'm sorry," praying that my lie will appease him. Almost instantly, my phone buzzes with another text message.

Dad: Tomorrow, Serena.

The last time I saw my dad, he screamed at me and told me that I was a disappointment, a stain on his family for my actions toward Marina. My mother tried to prevent me from going back to his house, but my anxiety wouldn't let me put off the conversation; I had a gnawing need to know how he would treat me and how his family would treat me at our next interaction.

Needless to say, it was a shit show. My dad's screams, Marina's tears, and the stony silence from Brandi were deafening. I've successfully avoided them for three weeks, but it seems as though my time is up. My mother has made no secret that she'll sell everything she owns, house included, to sever all ties with my father, but the thought of that makes me physically ill. Her home, with its warmth and love, is my sanctuary, the place where I go to decompress and feel

31

at peace. I can't imagine never smelling the cumin, cilantro, and garlic of my mom's *albondigas* simmering on her sleek stove, in the kitchen she designed, or never again watching the sunrise from our back porch.

If agreeing to my father's demands for an audience keeps my mother in the house where we both healed after my father's betrayal, then I'll do it without question or complaint.

I look up from my musings to take in the faded white walls of the tutoring center. As part of my scholarship, I was granted student work, a way for students to work on campus, receiving minimum wage for jobs that should pay significantly more. I would have much preferred sitting behind the reception desk at the student gym, checking ID badges, than tutoring college kids who see me as some kind of freak for starting college so young. I was sixteen when I first started in the center, and the senior I was working with was so uncomfortable that someone six years younger than him had to help with his statistics coursework.

He requested an immediate reassignment.

I don't enjoy tutoring, and I've never fantasized about becoming a teacher or educator. When I enrolled in Marymount at sixteen and declared English, not math, as my major, my father assumed that I'd pursue scholarly research on classic literature and ultimately become a professor. That future sounds about as appealing as eating Tide pods.

Only my mother, Ava, and CeCe know that my dream is to work in film and television as a screenwriter, which is not nearly as prestigious a job as my father expects. I haven't had the opportunity for any classes geared toward that future, but I'm hopeful my senior year will present the opportunity.

"Serena, your next student is here," my supervisor, Jay, calls from his desk. Stashing my phone and my father's bullshit into my bag, I stand and make my way to the reception area to greet my next student.

—

The next three hours pass in a blur of papers, instructions, and critiques. By the time I get to my evening class, I'm exhausted.

I listen as the professor drones on about modernity and twentieth-century social class structure and clench my jaw to stave off the sleep threatening to pull on my eyelids. By the time he introduces Edith Wharton's *House of Mirth*, I'm completely checked out.

Not even pretending to pay attention, my mind wanders to a place it's gone all too frequently recently: Ink and Needle.

Or, more specifically, the *owner* of Ink and Needle.

I bite down on my lip, unable to hold back my reaction to the mental image of Wolf McCleery. I was uncomfortably transfixed by Wolf until he called me Siren, the idiotic nickname that Devin bestowed upon me over five years ago. At thirteen, I existed in two different worlds simultaneously: puberty and high school, and Devin loved to tease me about it. Two years older than me, Devin had just read *The Odyssey* in his English class and found it hysterical that my name was so similar to that of the beautiful women of the sea in the epic poem. My gangly frame and awkward disposition were the ultimate source of humor for him.

Thinking back to my sole encounter with the massive tattooist, I inwardly cringe; I went from quietly awkward to rude and standoffish within minutes. He must think I'm, at best, incredibly weird and, at worst, a bitch.

"I'll see you all next week for our discussion on gender

33

roles in modernist literature. Please read up to chapter nine of *House of Mirth* for our next class." The professor's voice breaks through my thoughts, and I flush, feeling both guilty and chagrined that I let my mind wander so effectively.

I gather my laptop, notebook, and pens and place them carefully into my leather backpack. Throwing my bag over my shoulder, I hurry out of the building and start the walk to my apartment. The longer I walk, the more I think about the demands of my father, his insistence that I skip class just to, what? Be berated in person again, rather than text messages over the phone? By the time I make it inside my apartment, I'm fuming, my earlier heartache transforming into fury.

"What the fuck?" I breathe out, dropping my head into my hands and gripping my hair. "Why is he such..." I pause, looking for the right word, as though my furniture cares about the designation. "A dick," I yell. I release my hold on my scalp, and without thought, my right hand settles over the healing script at my rib. My mind travels back to Wolf, how right his hands felt on my body, but also how free I felt as he permanently marked my skin.

Right now, after my dad's demands, I am craving that sense of freedom, the euphoria that came from deciding for myself, by myself.

I would give anything to feel that way again. Squeezing my eyes shut, I think about the number saved on my phone. When Ava and Celeste came back to my apartment after Ink and Needle, Celeste made me add Wolf's cell number into my phone in case I had any questions about preventing infection.

Those numbers taunt me as I slide down and huddle against my door.

—

I pull my phone out with shaky hands, pacing back and forth through my apartment like an animal about to be let out of its cage. In this scenario, I'm not a lion; I'm the gazelle prancing itself into slaughter.

I've been talking to myself and walking around my apartment for the last—I check the clock on my oven—seventy-eight minutes. If I had a high-tech watch, it would probably tell me that I walked five hundred miles and burned an absurd number of calories thanks to anxiety and indecision.

"I should just call him. He may not even answer the phone. He doesn't have my contact information, and he could be one of those people who refuses to answer from an unfamiliar number," I reason to my furniture. "Or I could block my number so that he can't call me back if he turns me down. He can't call to mock me if he can't get in touch with me."

I wince, remembering that he does, in fact, have my cell number. "God, I'm being such a wimp." I stop my movements and look up, dropping my head back so that I can stare at the ceiling.

Almost two months ago, I made the horrible, inexcusable, idiotic decision to sleep with my neighbor and former love. Crush? Infatuation? I compounded that mistake by telling my best friend about the night I spent with my bad-boy neighbor, and I ended up losing my virginity, my lifeline, and half of my family in one fell swoop.

As far as slip-ups go, mine is major. Maybe I wouldn't feel so much regret if I enjoyed the sex. It felt like a baby carrot was poking me in the vagina; I didn't even have that romance novel-worthy hymen tear that shocks the naïve virgin before she writhes under the rakehell like a brothel owner.

35

No, I had an abysmal experience, and my stepsister accused me of sabotage and subterfuge.

I doubt she even knows what subterfuge means.

Breathing in deeply, I press the call button and bring my phone to my ear before I back out.

He answers on the second ring. "Hello?" his gruff voice sounds over the line, causing goosebumps to erupt over my skin. I can hear the soft rock music in the background, the bass notes dripping with sensuality and carnage.

I clear my throat. "Uhm, hi. This is Serena, my last name is Castillo. My name." I laugh awkwardly. "Right, this is Serena Castillo. I called because I need some help and I was hoping that maybe we could meet at the shop? I'm sorry, I got your number from Celeste. Is that an issue? I'm not sure—"

His deep laugh cuts me off, the sound jarring and beautiful. I suddenly crave hearing it in person. "Calm down, Serena. Yeah, I remember you. What do you need, princess?"

5

Wolf

I was at the bar when Serena called, well on my way to getting fucked up to forget the shitshow of a night at the shop. Like zombies on *The Walking Dead,* idiots kept coming in, asking for artwork that was either a blatant rip-off of someone else's work or the dumbest shit I've ever seen.

When a young kid came in asking for a gang sign tattooed on his neck, I nearly lost my shit. I don't care what other shops do in the name of "business," but I don't fuck with drugs, gangs, or shady deals in the back alley.

Never have, never will. So, when the punk came in asking for a goddamn beetle on his neck to show that he was part of the Bógar crew, the newest gang to form in Forest Valley, I kicked his scrawny ass out of my shop and warned him that if he or his brothers ever came back, I'd beat their asses.

Threats typically work when you're a six-foot-six Scotsman with a temper and red hair. My MMA background probably helps, too.

My phone went off just as I received my third IPA, the unknown number on my screen not phasing me in the least. I was used to promoters, sponsors, and tattoo referrals calling me on my cell and didn't hesitate to pick up. What a fucking mistake that was. As soon as I hit accept and brought the phone to my ear, my cock got hard from the breathing on the other end of the line. The delicate clearing of a throat had me thinking about shoving my cock down someone's fucking throat.

It could be a seven-foot hockey defenseman named Igor on the other end of this line, but fuck if my dick got that memo. My body started to relax as soon as I heard the soft, melodic voice burst through my speaker.

"Uhm, hi. This is Serena, my last name is Castillo. My name—" She paused and let out a self-deprecating laugh. "Right, this is Serena Castillo. I called because I need some help and I was hoping that maybe we could meet at the shop? I'm sorry, I got your number out of Celeste's phone. Is that an issue? I'm not sure—"

"Calm down, Serena. Yeah, I remember you. What do you need, princess?" The endearment slips out of my mouth, and I cringe, pretty fucking sure that I sound like a creep.

"Oh. You remember me? Great. I was hoping to book an appointment to see you. For a tattoo. An appointment for a tattoo. A consultation. Yes." She pauses and releases a long breath. "I want to schedule a tattoo appointment."

"That was a lot of words for a simple sentence. I'm free on Friday. The shop is closed right now but call tomorrow when we open; Aubrey will schedule you an appointment." I hang up on her before she has a chance to respond and drain my beer.

At twenty-five, I've fucked more women than I can remember and have a trail of bad relationships. It's not a brag—it's a recognition of my lifestyle and the choices I've made. I've slowed down the last few months; I'm too tired to beat the shit out of people in the ring, tattoo art for my clients, and then fuck for longer than twenty minutes.

Sitting here, with my empty beer glass and half-hard cock, I reason that the stress of two careers and a depressing social life is the reason why the awkward ramblings of an eighteen-year-old did more for my cock than my ex-girlfriend, Kelly, ever did. Running a hand over my face, I scowl at the excitement and anticipation pounding in my veins over seeing her again.

Fucking hell.

—

"Do you think she's trying to be inconspicuous?" Aubrey whispers beside me as we watch Serena from the windows of the storefront. At four in the afternoon on a Friday, the shop is packed, the buzzing of tattoo guns and the steady beat of rock music the anthem of the afternoon. I don't know why I told her that I was free today or why I instructed Aubrey to book her an appointment in between my clients.

But I fucking did.

"I don't know what she's doing." And it's true, I have no clue what she's doing or why she's dressed like a celebrity undercover. In an oversized beige trench coat, baseball cap, large sunglasses, and holding an umbrella, she looks insane.

It's thirty degrees and sunny; she should be wearing a winter coat, and there's no need for an umbrella.

"Should I go get her?"

I shake my head, too curious to see what she's going to do once she crosses the parking lot and enters the shop. Tugging her jacket lapels, she walks quickly across the lot,

39

head downcast and not looking at her surroundings. I shake my head again, confusion taking over every other thought.

I mean, really, what the fuck is she doing?

I don't realize how tense her shoulders are until she walks through the shop's door and lets out an audible sigh, releasing the tension that kept her shoulders by her ears. The moment she catches Aubrey and me looking at her, she squeaks, sounding like a scared little mouse, before recovering her composure.

"Oh, uh, hi."

I just stare at her, taking in her features swallowed by the ball cap and oversized trench. She looks like an extra in a bank heist movie.

"Are you okay?" Aubrey asks, diverting Serena's gaze from mine. "You looked frazzled out there. Do you need water or to make a phone call or anything?"

Serena clears her throat, shaking her head. "No, I'm fine. Sorry, I must look crazy right now. I sometimes take a pottery-making class on Fridays at the community center in West Helm, and I don't like to wear any of my good clothes, and I couldn't find my old winter coat. I didn't want to be late, so I threw this on." She pauses, taking a breath. Lifting one small hand, she touches the bill of the baseball cap and smiles wryly. "And I'm a dyed blonde, so getting clay in my hair would be a disaster. Hence, the cap. And the umbrella, well, it might rain later."

Aubrey and I just stare at her, the rambling seemingly on par with what I know about Serena. When I first met her, I was struck by how beautiful she was and then puzzled by her switch from silence to wordiness.

"You make pottery? That's cool," Aubrey offers, breaking the awkward silence that descended. Like a match, Serena lights up, her features morphing from self-conscious to excited.

"I love it. I started when I was eight with my great-grandmother, and I started doing it again a few weeks ago. My mom's family is from Mexico, and I became enamored with Cholula designs and the scenes depicted on the pottery. She humored me, and we started to make clay pots and vases," she finishes her explanation and looks down, the excitement draining and embarrassment taking over. "I'm not very good at it, but it's fun," she adds, shrugging.

Aubrey must sense the change in her, too, because she approaches Serena and lays a hand on her arm, squeezing it and offering a wide smile. "That's great, Serena. I understand embracing heritage and your culture; my family is from Nigeria, so I tattooed the national flower on my arm." Aubrey rolls up her sleeve, showcasing the yellow trumpet flowers decorating her skin. I feel my lips twitch at the memory of Aubrey sitting for hours in my chair, cursing my name as I inked from her wrist to her elbow. For having so many tattoos, she's a baby when it comes to pain.

"Aubrey, tell Serena how well you sat for that piece."

Instead of answering me, she just holds up her middle finger. I laugh and walk to the reception desk. Bringing the computer out of idling, I pull up our calendar booking software and mark Serena as "here" before closing the application.

"You ready to head to my station?" I ask, nodding toward the back of the shop.

"Yes. Yep. I'm ready," she responds, her voice squeaking. Again, I bite down on my tongue, holding in the laugh that's threatening to spill out. She's so fucking nervous, it's palpable.

I don't wait for her to start walking; instead, I lead the way

41

to my private room. Pride washes over me the moment I step over the threshold; it's a blessing that I own a successful business and have a long list of clients begging for my ink. I never excelled in school; I preferred fights, sex, and feeding my artistic soul over math and science. As soon as I turned eighteen, I started as an apprentice under my dad's tattoo artist, Skull, and took over a year ago when he decided to sell the shop.

MMA pays well when you win the fights, and I'm grateful for the years I spent in the cage. I'm even more grateful that I'll be retired from that world by twenty-six and have a career that won't break my body down by thirty.

I sense Serena as soon as she steps into my space, the light vanilla fragrance wrapping around us.

"Should I sit in the tattoo chair or over in one of the green chairs, or…?" Serena's voice breaks through my thoughts, jolting me back to where we are and what we're here for.

Clearing my throat, I shake my head and point to the wingback chairs I use for consultations. "Have a seat in one of the chairs. I don't typically take walk-ins, so we'll talk about what you're looking for before we go any further." I watch as she walks to the chair and sits delicately, as though she's afraid the sturdy furniture will break under her slight frame. Her back is rigid, and she looks like she's ready to bolt.

If I wasn't so confused as to why she's here, I'd be laughing my ass off at the proper display she's projecting.

In a fucking tattoo shop.

Settling myself in the chair across from her, I let out a breath. "Alright, Serena, why are you here?"

Her eyes shoot to mine, wide and glowing with unease. Her eyes are like no color I've ever seen before; a traditionalist would call them brown, but they're more golden, a mixture of brown and yellow hues that make the most surreal color. My hand flexes, wishing I had paint or markers or anything nearby to capture their likeness.

"Well, I want a tattoo," she begins, a self-deprecating smile falling from her lips. "A few tattoos, actually." I raise my brow, waiting for her to continue. "On my back. A back piece, I think it's called?"

"I'm familiar with the term," I muse, sarcasm dripping from my tone. "What is your vision?"

"Butterflies. I'd like for them to start at the base of my spine and fly up toward my shoulder. I want them to look like they're in motion, about to jump from my skin."

My eyebrows raise, absorbing the enormity of the piece she's detailing. "You want a butterfly kaleidoscope over your entire back?"

Her brow furrows, and she licks her lips. "Kaleidoscope?"

"A group of butterflies is called a kaleidoscope," I respond, shaking my head. "What you're asking for is going to take multiple sessions, a lot of pain, and time to heal. Are you sure you want to dive into your second tattoo with a piece that big?" Her eyes widen, uncertainty morphing her features.

"I—" she begins, pausing to swallow her reply. "I've thought about this. I'd like this tattoo, I think." She mutters the last part of the sentence, and that's all it takes for me to make up my mind.

I fold my arms across my chest and lean back against my chair, shaking my head as I survey her face. "Listen, the fact that you just said the last part of that sentence tells me that you're not ready for this tattoo, maybe not ready for any more tattoos." I work to keep my voice light and judgment-free.

43

I'm not berating her, but tattoos are permanent, and she should be certain before applying something to her skin.

"But—"

I shake my head, cutting her off. "No, I'm sorry. I can't give you a tattoo when you're not sure. Ethically, I'd be the biggest asshole, and I won't let a client regret a piece they receive from me or my shop. Take time to think about it and give us a call when you figure it out." I stand and move toward the door, indicating the end of the conversation.

Serena unfolds her body and hangs her head, dejection evident from her posture and defeated expression. Guilt unfurls in my stomach; I'm not changing my mind about the tattoo, but I do feel bad that she's upset. Clearing my throat, I mumble, "For what it's worth, it was a cool idea. Maybe in a couple of years, when you're a little more sure, you can get it."

Her head snaps up, heat blazing from her golden irises. If I thought my words would ease some of her disappointment and turn it into acceptance, I was wrong. Instead, annoyance seems to have settled. Twisting her lips in a scowl, she shoots out, "Thanks," though her expression reads she's not the least bit thankful for my comment.

Continuing to walk toward the door, Serena stops when she's right in front of me, and my focus settles on her. She doesn't meet my eyes as I stare down at her; her gaze is trained on the scabs on my left hand.

"What happened?" She reaches out as though she's about to touch my skin before dropping her arm back down to her side.

"Had a fight last weekend." One of the final ones of my career, thank fuck. "Listen, I think you should—" My words are cut off by the sudden pressure of her mouth against

44

mine. I'm too shocked to do anything but stand there for long seconds before I step back, leaning my body against the door frame.

She's over a foot shorter than me, so she either jumped up and levitated to capture my lips, or I was leaning down closer to her than I realized.

Fucking hell.

"Oh my God. I'm so sorry," Serena rushes out, stepping back until she's pressed against the wall opposite me. I take in her face: mortification, shame, and panic are stamped all over her features, and instead of laying into her for kissing a man she barely knows in his fucking business, in an open doorway where any of my clients could see, I just shrug.

Like it's no big fucking deal.

"It's fine. But you need to leave. Now." My tone is harsher than I intended, but the mixture of shock and arousal pisses me off.

"Of course. I'm sorry. I don't know why I did that," she murmurs, pushing off the wall and walking out of my station. I follow her retreating form, telling myself that it's to make sure she leaves the building, and slam into her when she stops short. Whirling around, she pleads, "Please do not tell Celeste about this. She doesn't even know I'm here, and I don't want her to question me. Please?"

I nod sharply. The last thing I want is for my nosy-ass cousin to interrogate me, so there's no way in hell I'm opening my mouth. "I won't say anything."

She releases a breath, her shoulders dropping in relief. "Thank you. And I'm sorry, again." Waving her off, I stay rooted in place as she scurries across the shop like a scared squirrel, shaking my head until her trench coat-clad form is

45

bundled in her beat-up car and driving away.

"What was that about?" Aubrey asks, walking up to me and handing me a mug of tea with lemon. Unlike my cousin, whose body is made up of sixty percent sugary coffee, I can't stand the stuff and drink English Breakfast tea for my caffeine fix.

Shaking my head, I sip the hot liquid before muttering, "You don't want to fucking know."

6

Serena

Of all the imbecilic, idiotic, foolish things I have ever done, sex with Devin included, kissing Wolf in full view of his tattoo shop after he refused to consider taking me on as a client is at the top of the list.

My lips tremble at the memory of his mouth on mine. It was a chaste, juvenile kiss, nothing that screamed sensual or experienced. God, he must think I'm such a moron for throwing myself at him like a desperate schoolgirl with a crush.

Slamming my hand against my steering wheel, I wince at the sound of my horn going off and the middle finger I receive from the car in front of me. Nothing is working out the way I planned. At first, when I arrived at the studio for my pottery class, I was relaxed and hopeful. The methodical practice of molding the clay, coupled with the feel of the silky earthenware between my fingers, was euphoric, and I enjoyed diving back into a hobby long abandoned. That euphoria was eradicated by nerves and butterflies the moment I caught sight of Wolf and Aubrey standing at the window at Ink and

Needle, watching me with amused expressions. I have no idea why I grabbed an umbrella; it's a sunny, balmy, thirty-degree day with no chance of precipitation.

No, that's a lie. I do know why I grabbed the umbrella: it was an added layer of protection against the unnerving stares of the tattoo shop owner and his trusted receptionist.

Pressing down on the gas pedal, I push my old car from forty to forty-five, inching toward the actual speed limit and the highest speed I'll permit my car to travel. Not because I'm afraid of driving but because I'm afraid my car is going to combust if I push her too hard.

It seems to be a theme in my life: taking things slowly until I rush forward and situations blow up in my face. Devin, Dylan, Wolf, and the tattoo. It's like I willingly and knowingly put myself in a position to be either embarrassed or disappointed. And I'm sick of it.

I am so fucking sick of it.

I feel anger start to build in my gut, traveling up until my heart is racing and thoughts and emotions are wrapped around my throat, suffocating me. My mind travels back thirty minutes to the tattoo shop and Wolf's dual denial. Admittedly, I shouldn't have kissed him; it was impulsive and just stupid. My anger isn't directed toward his physical repulsion; no, it's aimed at the arrogant way he turned me away as a client, as though I didn't know what I wanted tattooed on my body. As though I wasn't aware tattoos are painful and virtually irreversible. My social skills may be lacking, but my analytical abilities and deductive reasoning are firmly in place, and they're both telling me that Wolf is an asshole.

A hot, well-built, tall, and imposing asshole, but an asshole nonetheless.

I mentally slap myself for not being more assertive in my consultation and not projecting authority and certainty regarding the design and the size. I have no idea why I said, "I think," or why I dissolved into a mumbling idiot the moment my wants were challenged and questioned. I don't *think* I want butterflies to decorate my back, an illustration of the freedom I'm trying so hard to find. I *know* I want them; I want the pain of the needle, the mental clarity that comes with decisiveness. I need it. And if Wolf's not going to give it to me, someone else will.

My mind moves from Wolf's imposing form and gruff personality to the vitriol spewed by Dylan and Devin, and my anger continues to rise. Not for the first time in the weeks following their verbal assault, my heart aches. These two boys, whom I used to regard as two of my closest friends, have not only disappointed me but discarded me as though I'm damaged goods, useless and used. My dad has continued with his tirades, his accusations that I intentionally hurt my "sister." It's bullshit.

I release a laugh, not able to help the bubble of giggles that break from my throat. Four months ago, I barely ever uttered a curse word or even thought of one in my internal contemplations. Ava and Celeste, and their inventive language and insults, have irrevocably changed that, changed *me*. Though I know that I'll never be as close to them as they are to each other—I'm the late addition third wheel—their friendship has shown me just how kind people can be. How people, other than my mom, can care for me and support me even when I mess up or become so full of self-doubt and shyness.

49

Losing myself in the monotony of driving, stopping, driving, I can't help but think, *next semester is going to be different. I am going to be different.*

If I wasn't so cautious with my driving, I'd be concerned that the forty-minute drive from Ink and Needle back to my apartment passed by too quickly. I was on autopilot as my mind raced through the past few months, mindless as I operated a vehicle on public roadways and could have caused harm not only to myself but also to others.

"Stupid," I mutter, shifting into park and unfastening my seatbelt. Throwing my head against the headrest, I look up to the roof of my car and stare at the staples holding it together. Last year, the adhesive on the fabric lining my interior wore off, causing the gray fabric to fall like a curtain, a veil separating me and my outdated, run-down car from the rest of the world.

Specifically from safety checks at the DMV. To correct the issue myself and not bother my mother with my problems, I had Dylan help me staple the fabric with his dad's staple gun. The memory is tainted, the afternoon spent with my former best friend now bittersweet, and his jokes and taunts cruel rather than funny.

"Asshole," I whisper, filling the sedan with all the anger and resentment I'm feeling. I sought Wolf out to feel better, not ruminate in the memories that hang like a specter haunting its burial ground. Clearly, my voyage was a dismal failure.

Blinking back my tears, I swing my door open and reach behind the driver's seat, grabbing my bags and spare books, before slamming it shut. Readjusting my things, I'm startled by the hand on my shoulder and the chuckle that follows my inadvertent jump.

"Rena, you could qualify for a pole dancing competition with that jump," Ava's voice sings out.

"You mean 'pole vaulting.'" I smile at CeCe's biting tone; her pregnancy, miscarriage, and relationship with her large Italian boyfriend, Dante, have done nothing to mellow out the aggression in her tone.

"Whatever. Now, Rena, tell us why you're late."

Whipping around, I stare at Ava and CeCe in confusion. "Late? We didn't have any plans today."

Ava waves her tattooed arm as though my comment is insignificant. "No, but you're always in your apartment on Fridays by five. It's five-thirty, and you're just parking your cute little car. So tell me, where have you been"—she pauses, looking me over and biting down on her lip—"dressed like Inspector Gadget? Is that dirt in your hair?"

Only Ava would classify the rusted pile of metal as "cute," but dammit, I must have gotten clay in my hair. "No, it's clay. I was at that pottery class I told you about."

CeCe's eyes narrow, smelling the half-truth. "That class ended earlier this afternoon. Where did you go after that?"

"Just ran errands." I clear my throat and swallow down the nerves that tickle my esophagus. "Anyway, what are you both doing here?" I avoid CeCe's gaze, instead focusing on Ava's face, lit in excitement.

"Movie night. Well, a competition night. There's a new series of *The Great British Bake Off* that just dropped, and I need to be surrounded by Paul Hollywood's essence. So, let's freaking go, I have cheeky bakers to watch." Ava doesn't wait for a response, just turns and walks toward the front of my building before stopping abruptly, large fabric bags swinging in her arms. "I brought ingredients to make roasted

51

chicken and an orange olive oil cake. I'm not eating that bullshit cardboard pizza again."

"She is such a food snob," CeCe scoffs. Turning, I see that she's shaking her head, though a small smile is on her face as she watches Ava charge across the parking lot and into my building. Her green eyes meet mine, and she sobers, one red eyebrow rising. "Now that it's just us, what's going on? Are you in trouble?"

"What? No, of course not." I shake my head, emphasizing my rejection of her words. "I was just running errands like I said."

CeCe doesn't answer and continues to look at me with her unnerving stare. Like Jenga blocks, I fall, opening my mouth before I even realize what I'm going to say. "I went to Ink and Needle for a tattoo. I didn't get one. Wolf was there. That's where I was."

Her mouth pops open, the only sign that my words surprised her. "You wanted another tattoo?"

Nodding, I explain, "Ever since I got the tattoo on my ribs, I can't help but remember how freeing it felt to have something permanently etched on my skin, a decision that I made by myself. Since I was a little girl, being jostled back and forth between my parents' houses, schools, and extracurriculars, I have never been in control. It sounds silly to say that a tattoo has given me so much clarity, so much excitement for the first time in so damn long, but I felt like an adult for the first time in my life. I thought that if I went back and explained to your cousin what I was looking for and what I wanted, he'd be able to help me." I pause, shaking my head in frustration. Releasing a sigh, I continue, "But he told me that I didn't know what I wanted, that I seem unsure. So, I left without another appointment." I seal my lips shut, keeping the disastrous kiss to myself. Even now, after his rejection, my lips tingle at the brief pressure I felt, how damn good he smelled as I jumped up like a rocket to capture his mouth.

"Hey," CeCe soothes, her features softening. "I understand what you mean; we've all been through some shit, yeah? I'm sorry that Wolf didn't help you out, but maybe it's for the best. It'll just give you more time to feel certain about your decision before you go through with it. He's a dick, but he does know what he's talking about, sometimes at least."

"Yeah," I choke out, considering her words. "Maybe you're right. Let's get inside before Ava reorganizes my spice cabinet again."

7

Wolf

Why the fuck did I come out here? I wonder to myself for the tenth time since I got to this party. When my trainer, Jedd, invited me to his new gym for the grand opening, I thought there would be sponsors, trainers, and athletes mingling over cheap vodka in the name of celebration. I didn't expect a goddamn rave in the middle of the training center.

Maybe rave is an exaggeration, but blinking neon lights decorate the ceiling like some fucked up Christmas movie, and there's no doubt drugs are being passed out like appetizers. I don't do this shit; I train, fight, and leave my MMA persona in the octagon. My bloody knuckles may follow me out the door, but I leave the lifestyle of partying to people who want to live in that space.

I don't like people; as a rule, I avoid them unless they're a client, an opponent, or one of the five people I trust. Promotional events hold all the appeal of a root canal without lidocaine or being punched in the face by a two-hundred-

54

pound wall of muscle.

I'd rather be home, working on the piece for my client on Sunday, or in the bar down the street from my shop, drinking a locally brewed IPA with Trent and Aubrey. I'd rather be anywhere but here, surrounded by people desperate for fame and money or fighters looking to start some bullshit feud for marketing.

Sipping on my club soda, I lean against the cinder block wall and watch as people form pods, talking over each other in the name of business. My eyes catch on bright pink on the opposite side of the room, and I groan, sinking back into the wall to try and make myself as small as possible. Fucking hell, I should have known she'd be here.

I wince as soon as the beautiful, pink-haired she-devil spots me and practically sprints over to me. If this were a game of hide-and-seek, I'd lose. I struggle to hide my scowl as she approaches, but it's no use. Her dark eyes narrow; eyes I once found captivating but now just bother the shit out of me.

My mom calls them lying eyes, and she's not wrong.

"Hi, Wolf."

I nod. "Kelly."

Her lips turn down, a frown marring her beautiful, vindictive face. "What, no hello?"

I sigh, shaking my head. "You expect me to say hello to you after the shit you put me through? Where's Gage?"

She has the good sense to look sheepish, faux embarrassment dotting her cheeks. Kelly and I dated for two years, and I thought we had a good thing, something that could last. CeCe was wary of Kelly from the start, warning me that she was with me for clout and social media followers. I dismissed that idea like a goddamn fool.

55

As soon as I announced my impending retirement, Kelly left. She packed up the shit in the house we shared—the house I paid for—and immediately started dating Gage, a prick from the gym with a mean right hook and an even shittier attitude. He's predicted to win the welterweight title, and that's all Kelly needed to shift her interest from me to him.

"He's speaking with one of his sponsors. How are you doing?"

"Do you care?"

"Wolf," she gasps. I can't stop my eye roll in response. "You know I care. I just have dreams. Dreams bigger than being a small-town artist's girlfriend."

"I have a two-year-long waitlist and tattoo some of the biggest names in the tri-state area, but fuck me, right?" I murmur, shaking my head. It's the same excuse she gave me when she left. "Someone like me deserves to be seen. I can't support a starving artist on my Instagram sponsorships," she'd told me right before she drove off in her little pink Audi. I would have been upset if her comments hadn't made me so fucking angry.

"Listen, I don't want to fight with you. Have a good night. Say hi to Gage." Pushing off the wall, I down my drink, wishing it was something stronger than carbonated water, and set my glass down on the cocktail table beside me. Without sparing Kelly another glance, I walk to the center of the room where Jedd holds court like a king. Kelly's sputters and unjustified outrage follow me as I walk away from her and the bullshit her presence brings.

I'm stopped in my retreat by a booming voice to my right. "Wolf fucking McCleery, you fucking giant. How you doing?"

"Hey, Johnny," I respond, turning to offer my hand to the

56

energy drink promoter I've known since I began training with Jedd.

"What's this shit I hear? You're retiring? No, man, that's got to be a mistake. Blue Grizzly needs their fucking top athlete to keep selling their shit." Johnny's grip on my hand tightens. He may be strong, but his grip is infantile compared to mine.

"No, man, not a mistake. I need these hands to create my art. You know that's always been my end game." I emphasize my point by squeezing his palm until he winces and finally releases my hand.

"Fucking hell, Wolf. What are you thinking? You've got a shot at the heavyweight title this year, and you're going to throw it away for goddamn tattoos? Did you take one too many hits to the fucking head?"

I feel my jaw clench. I'm so sick of this question. I love MMA, jiu-jitsu, and the financial freedom it's afforded me, but I'm done with the rigorous training, the early mornings and late nights, watching every single piece of food that goes into my mouth. And I don't need Johnny, or anyone else in this room, questioning my decision.

Johnny's face grows red, no doubt concerned at my sudden hostility. Good, prick.

"What I'm thinking is that I'm retiring from this sport and living my life away from assholes who don't know when to quit. Have a good night." Offering a nod, I brush past Johnny, purposely clipping his shoulder with my arm. I smirk as he stumbles back, muttering about "asshole fighters" under his breath as I keep walking.

Finally making it to the center of the room, I throw an arm around Jedd, not giving a shit that I'm interrupting his conversation. The older man looks up, a bright smile decorating his face when he realizes it's me.

"Christ, McCleery, ye gave me a feckin' heart attack," Jedd says in his deep Irish brogue. Originally from Cork, my trainer came to the States in the eighties and has been terrorizing fighters ever since.

"Like anything could kill you, old man." I laugh, shaking my head. "Listen, I'm going to head out. I have some clients in the morning and need to work on their sketches."

"What, club Farrell not good enough for ye?" He pauses to look around at the lights and cocktail tables decorating the walls, wincing slightly when he catches a string of balloons tied to the ropes on one of the rings.

"Feckin' hell, I'm gonna eat Lauren's head for this. I told her this was an event for fighters and promoters, and she's made it into a bloody sweet sixteen."

"She means well, but listen, I need to go before fucking Johnny comes over to talk to me again."

Jedd's face darkens, disgust and contempt written on his features. "A feckin' chancer, he is. Go before ye use his body to wipe the scuff marks off the floor. But listen—" He hesitates, looking back toward the group of men I interrupted. He leans in, lowering his voice until it's barely a whisper. "Come by tomorrow after yer appointments. I need ye to take a look at Gage's form. Something's off with him, but I need yer opinion."

Shaking my head, I try to push away, but his arm is locked tight around my neck. "You know I can't be objective when it comes to him. He throws a punch, and I'm going to say it's shit because he is. Ask someone else."

"No, boy. Yer the best fighter this gym has. I respect the decision to retire. I think it's damn smart to go out on the top of yer career, but I still need yer help. Come by, check his training, and then come for supper upstairs. I know the missus will be happy to see ye."

"For fuck's sake, Jedd. Don't throw Miriam into the mix; you know I can't say no to her."

"She'll make biscuits."

"You play dirty. Fine, I'll be here around five. I need to—" I'm cut off by the vibration of my phone in my pocket. "Let me check this," I tell Jedd before pulling it out and frowning at my cousin's name on the display.

"C, what's wrong? Aren't you in Connecticut this weekend?" Celeste wanted to come with me tonight since she used to train with Jedd, but her asshole of a boyfriend decided to take her to Connecticut with Ava and her equally douchey guy to spend a weekend meeting celebrities or some shit.

I know my cousin loves him, and he seems to respect her and treat her right, but he follows her around like a goddamn stalker. I'd be concerned if she didn't seem to love it.

"Wolf, are you free?" Celeste's voice is panicked, and anger instantly boils beneath my skin.

"What the fuck did he do to you? I swear to God, I'll kill him with my bare hands if he hurt you. Where—"

"Not me, Wolf, Serena. She, she—" CeCe pauses, clearing her throat. "She stayed behind, said she didn't want to be the fifth wheel or impose. Aves and I begged her to come with us, but the sorority she just pledged had a mixer with a fraternity tonight, and she wanted to go. Sh-she promised she would be okay." CeCe's voice breaks, and my anger is pushed aside for fear of what she's going to say next.

"Dylan showed up and said or did something. I don't really know. But something happened, and that little fucking weasel caused it. Her big just called me and told me that Serena locked herself in the bathroom, and no one can get her out. She doesn't know what to do or who else to call to help get Serena to calm down. C-can you go and get her?"

"Send me the address." After trading a few more words with my cousin, I hang up and grip my phone so hard, I'm surprised it doesn't shatter.

"Wolf, everything okay, son?" Looking up, I meet Jedd's eyes and shake my head.

"That was my cousin. Her friend's in trouble and needs some help." I don't know if she's going to come out for me—I met her twice, and though I gave her a delicate little tattoo and had her lips planted against mine for a brief moment, her reaction before leaving was frosty both times. But, if she, or any woman, is in trouble because some punk decided to harass her, then I'll make damn sure she's safe.

"Off with ye then. And don't forget about tomorrow." I nod at Jedd's retreat and take long strides to the entrance of the gym.

No one fucks with an innocent woman and gets away with it.

No one.

8

Serena

"You look like a cupcake."

"Ava Maria, you cannot tell someone that they look like a cupcake."

Sitting at my makeup vanity mirror, FaceTiming with Cece and Ava, I laugh as I listen to them bicker back and forth about Ava's remarks on my outfit. She's not wrong about my appearance; I'm going to a "My Favorite Food" mixer tonight, and my outfit is supposed to emulate a cupcake.

"C, it's okay. Ava's not wrong, I do look like a cupcake, but it's intentional. It's a messy mixer, and we have to dress like food before, well, we get covered in food."

I'm surprised by the silence that follows my explanation. Looking up, I see the confused expressions on my two friends' faces. "What?"

CeCe clears her throat, shaking her head before asking, "Are you saying that they're going to throw food on you at a party? That can't be a real thing."

Gnawing on my lower lip, I try to find the words to explain the party I'm getting ready for. With a three-dimensional candle headband, a red bandeau top with glitter and cream-colored fabric gathered to look like frosting, and a red skirt, I look like a personified red velvet cupcake.

I didn't even dress up for Halloween last year, so a DIY cupcake outfit in February is not something I saw coming.

"It's not exactly food. Well, it's edible, but it's not like they're throwing baked goods or a steak at you when you walk in. Meg told me that the seniors in the fraternity and sorority each get a bottle of syrup and whipped cream and that it gets very messy."

"That sounds unsanitary. Are you sure this is a good idea?" CeCe questions, concern lacing her voice.

"It sounds fun, you old hag. Don't bring Serena down when she's so excited that she's dressed like a limited-edition Hostess cupcake," Ava offers.

Punching Ava in the arm, CeCe murmurs, "Shut up, Ava. Serena—" She pauses, turning her attention back to me and gentling her voice. "I don't want to ruin your good time; I'm just telling you to be careful. It makes me uncomfortable that we're not there with you. We went to the last mixer with you, and everyone was great, but still, if something happens, we're over one hundred miles away. Don't accept drinks from strangers; be cautious. Okay?" Greyson's dad, Greg Jansen, is hosting a charity event this weekend, and Greyson and Dante took Ava and CeCe up to Connecticut to support him. Ava and CeCe tried to get me to come, but I had no desire to be the fifth wheel in the group.

"C, I appreciate your concern, but I'm a big girl, and I can handle myself. Meg is picking me up before we go over to the pre-game." I met Meg, my big and a senior in Alpha Gamma, at the beginning of the semester in my diaspora class, and she convinced me to sign up for Round Robin. Before meeting Meg, Greek life was not something I was interested in, especially after the recruitment party Ava, CeCe, and I attended during the fall semester and one of the sisters, Felicity, displayed erratic and dangerous behavior toward Ava. But Meg convinced me to give it a chance. Though I'm not as active as most of the other sisters, and rarely attend chapter meetings because of my conflicting class schedule, everyone I've met has been welcoming and friendly.

"Make sure you turn your location on. If you need us, call, and I can always send one of my cousins over to help. Or Lincoln, he stayed back, but I think he's working until close at Frankie's restaurant. Just stay in touch with us, okay?"

Thoughts of CeCe's cousins—or, more accurately, *cousin*—have my heart pounding in my chest, and I fight to retain a neutral expression. Adopting one of CeCe's signature moves, I roll my eyes and laugh. "Okay, Mom."

"I'm serious, Rena. As a group, we don't exactly have the greatest experiences at parties. I don't like feeling like we abandoned you, you little shit." I wince because she's not wrong. Starting with the first party that we went to, where I was verbally attacked by Marina and then kicked out of the party by Devin, followed by Ava's encounter with Felicity, the sorority girl who was obsessed with Grey and tried to kill Ava, at the barbecue Grey hosted. Not to mention the Campus Hotties incident at the party on Ava's birthday, where innocent mirror selfies of Ava and CeCe became dirty, distorted images with vile names and their contact information.

My God, we have a bad track record. But that is still not stopping me from going tonight.

Letting out a sigh, I grab my phone from where it rests against my vanity and look directly at the screen. "You didn't abandon me; I told you that I didn't want to come up this weekend because I'd feel like a fifth wheel."

"That's—" Ava starts, but I cut her off.

"No, that's exactly what it would have been. I'm so happy for both of you and that you have great guys in your life. But not everything has to include me, especially when it's a couple's thing. It's starting to feel like I'm a pity invite or an obligation rather than your friend."

"Rena, no. That's not why we invite you." Ava's voice is stern, a tone that rarely accompanies her words. "We invite you and hang out with you because you're our friend, and we love you. So, like CeCe always tells me, stop with that self-deprecating bullshit, my little butterfly and silence those intrusive thoughts that make you question everything." She twists her lips, pausing. "Except drugs, white vans, and alcohol from strangers. Your intrusive thoughts can turn back on for those things. That's important."

CeCe takes the phone from Ava, moving her out of the frame. "Those aren't intrusive thoughts; that's common sense. Rena, we love you; just be safe. Call us if you need anything."

"And you look like a hot piece of ass," Ava calls out, making me blush.

"Thanks, and I love you guys, too. I'll text you tomorrow. Have a great time at the charity event tonight." I hang up quickly, breathing out a long breath as soon as the phone screen goes black. It feels strange having people outside of my mother care about me and my well-being, but I can't say I'm not grateful. Though Dylan was my best friend and confidant, I couldn't rely on him for everything. When I was upset, struggling, or needed advice, I would bypass him and consult my mother or keep my emotions locked up, firmly ensconced inside me.

Having two friends who care so deeply for me feels like a novelty, and while I'm endlessly grateful, I'm also determined to gain independence and experiences that have been denied to me because of my age and academic advancement.

A horn beeps outside my building, followed by my phone screen lighting up with a notification. Grabbing my phone, I swipe to open the latest text.

Meg: Hey! I'm outside. Come down when you're ready :)

Taking one last look in my vanity mirror, I note the subtle changes in my appearance that have made the biggest impact on my psyche. My hair is blonder, brighter, and bolder than it's ever been. I've always kept my hair short and highlighted with caramel streaks, but after everything that happened during the fall semester, I cut it to an asymmetrical bob and added blonde highlights to my face frame. The effect was staggering. My skin looks more illuminated, my brown eyes more golden, and my jawline more pronounced.

For the first time, I don't look like a high school student who got lost during her campus tour and never left. I look like an adult, and more importantly, I feel like one.

Typing out a quick text, I let Meg know I'm on my way down and shut the lights off behind me. Taking a deep breath, I release it slowly, excitement coursing through my veins for the night to come.

—

I am covered in chocolate syrup, my phone is shattered, my jaw is tender from where I took an accidental elbow to the face, and I locked myself in a bathroom after a disastrous encounter with Dylan.

In short, this is the worst night of my life.

"Serena, Little, come out. I'll have one of the sober drivers take us back to the house, and we'll clean up and watch movies in the living room," Meg calls from the other side of the door, concern lacing her voice. I hear grumbling, followed by pounding on the door, and nearly break.

But I am not going back out there. I should have gone to Connecticut with Ava and CeCe or stayed home in the quiet solitude of my apartment. Hell, I would rather watch paint dry than be here right now.

"Serena, I'm calling Celeste. If you won't let me help, then I'm going to find someone who will." I cringe, knowing that though CeCe won't gloat that she was right to be concerned about this party, she will be extra protective of me. I don't bother responding to Meg and instead just drop to the floor, curling in on myself while I replay the last hour in my mind.

When I first got into Meg's car, I couldn't stop laughing at the strawberry costume she wore and how indecent it was. Dressed in a red corset, tiny spandex shorts, and a red headband, she looked more like a lingerie model than an innocuous piece of fruit. In comparison, I felt overdressed.

My feelings changed when we got to the party; I was grateful for the clothing I had on since it provided an extra layer between me and the chocolate syrup that was squirted on us as soon as we stepped through the front door. I barely had a chance to take in the plastic covering the walls of the house like a scene from *Dexter* before a stream of chocolate pelted my skin and clothing like a water gun game at the boardwalk. Meg's scream of surprise was followed by laughter as her boyfriend, Eric, wrapped her in his arms after the assault.

As soon as they started making out, I ran to the basement, where most people were dancing in the middle of the cinderblock room, and migrated toward a makeshift DJ station in the far corner. Syrup and whipped cream flew rampant down there, too, and I found myself knocked on the floor by a bony elbow to the face when I tried to shield myself from the onslaught. My phone dropped as I fell, and before even checking, I knew the screen was smashed.

I should have known that being reduced to a puddle of chocolate and questionable fluids on a concrete slab, along with a broken phone, was an omen of things to come. But instead, I accepted the profuse apologies of the handsome guy who, unknowingly, tried to incapacitate me.

"Shit, I'm so sorry," he said, his voice a mixture of worry and embarrassment. "Are you okay? Do you need some ice for that? Fuck, your phone." Offering his hand, I didn't hesitate to grab it.

Once I was standing, I shook my head and patted myself down to make sure all my body parts were still covered. I tried to emulate Ava, who would brush off the encounter and proceed as though it had never happened. "No, I'm fine. A little sore from your mean jab to the face, though," I teased before looking down at the broken phone in my hand. "And it looks like I'll need to go to the store tomorrow. But hey, you could have broken my jaw, so it could always be worse." I watched as the blood drained from his face. I rushed to add, "Sorry, I didn't mean that. I'm fine. It was an accident, and I can get this fixed. Have a great night." I turned to leave but was stopped by a hand on my wrist. Looking back, I was startled to see the stranger's handsome face still set in a look of worry.

67

"Don't go. Shit, I'm so sorry. Can I pay for your phone? Let me get you a drink, or at least try to make up for the bruise on your face."

"I—" CeCe's words filled my head about not accepting things from strangers, like a DARE commercial from the nineties, and I shook my head. "No, I don't want your money, and I don't need a drink."

"Then wait here while I set mine down. Maybe we can dance, or talk?" He seemed so eager, so desperate for me to say yes, that I couldn't help but nod my head. "Great, don't leave..." He looked at me, a smile breaking out across his face, before continuing, "What's your name, beautiful?"

"Serena."

"Serena. I like it. My name is Jack. Just don't go anywhere." I watched him leave, small butterflies erupting in my stomach at the attention paid to me by a handsome stranger. The butterflies were nowhere near as volatile as when I saw Wolf or had his hands jabbing ink into my skin, but I took the fluttering as a positive sign.

Only seconds passed before I felt warm breath on my neck and powerful arms band around my midsection. Startled by the intimacy, I tried to pull away, but the grip around my waist only tightened, preventing me from moving.

"Let go of me." I struggled, gripping the forearms imprisoning me and trying to break free. A disfigurement on the inside of the thick wrist made me still, freezing me in place as I looked at the decimal mark-like scar.

"Dylan?" As soon as I said his name, the grip holding me in place loosened, and I took the opportunity to spin around, coming face-to-face with my former best friend. "What are you doing? Why are you here?"

68

"What am I doing?" Dylan chuckled darkly. "What are you doing? You don't belong here. What fucking happened to you?"

"I became the person I was always supposed to be," I retorted, taunting him like an idiot instead of disengaging and walking away.

"And you're proud of that? The Serena I knew would be studying like the good little girl she was rather than half-naked in a basement, panting after some guy's dick. Devin was right about you; one taste of cock and you became a fucking slut for it." My slap was so quick, so instinctual, that I didn't even realize I broke free from his hold to deliver it.

I was about to back away when Dylan grabbed ahold of my wrist and squeezed. "Don't you ever put your fucking hands on me again. I don't see your friends here to protect you, and don't forget, I know you, Serena. I know you can't defend yourself for shit, so don't start something you can't finish."

I gasped, shocked and disgusted at his words. "Are you threatening me?"

"No, I'm promising you that you won't get another free shot in."

"Hey man, let go of her." I whipped my head around to see Jack standing beside me, a look of confusion adorning his face. "You're hurting her, let go."

"It's nothing she doesn't deserve," Dylan replied before pushing off me and stepping back, placing much-needed distance between us. "You fucking changed, Serena. You're a goddamn embarrassment."

Jack stepped between us, cutting off Dylan's line of sight. I didn't wait for any more verbal harassment; I just ran out of the basement, up the stairs, and into the nearest open door.

Which happens to be this bathroom, where I'm huddled on the floor and contemplating every decision I've ever made and every word I've ever spoken.

Yelling and crashing erupt outside the bathroom, and I whip my head toward the door. Whoever is out there sounds furious, like a lion trying to break out of a cage. "Where the fuck is she?" a voice growls. Goosebumps travel down my arms, and my body shivers. I know that voice; I've dreamt about that voice.

It's not a lion that's here; it's a wolf.

9

Wolf

"Where the fuck is she?" I seethe, my voice laced with anger. The minute I walked into this hellhole, I had whipped cream sprayed on my face, and strawberry sauce poured down my arm. Normally, I wouldn't be annoyed that a girl squirted in my face—hell, I'd probably pound my chest and feel like the king of the fucking mountain any other time—but in this context, I'm just pissed.

I glare at the girl who ambushed me, no doubt solidifying myself as the big bad wolf in her nightmares, but fuck her and fuck this. These kids have to be at least eighteen—too goddamn old to be playing with food.

"Wh-who?" a voice asks behind me. I turn to see a tall brunette dressed in a red corset leaning against the wall, arms folding over her midsection. She clears her throat as I continue staring. "Did Celeste send you?"

I nod once, running my hands over my freshly buzzed head. "I'm her cousin, Wolf. Where is Serena? C said she was in trouble."

Her gaze moves from me to the door to my right. "She

locked herself in the bathroom. I don't know what happened, just that she ran off after a guy confronted her. Jack, my boyfriend's best friend, intervened after he met Serena and tried to get the guy, Dylan, off her, but he refused to move. I think he came as one of the brothers' plus ones."

I narrow my eyes at her words. "He put his fucking hands on her?"

Corset Girl nods, distress coating her features. "He was pretty worked up, Jack said, and looked like he was going to hurt her in the middle of the basement." She hiccups at the end of her explanation, either from too much alcohol or too much emotion. Maybe a combination of the two.

"She's through this door?" I tilt my head toward the nondescript door. The girl nods, hiccupping again. "Okay, you can go now." Turning, I dismiss her without another thought and take a deep breath, unsure of what I'm going to find on the other side of this door. The thought of a man—any man—putting his hands on a woman pisses me the fuck off, and part of me wants to find the guy that hurt her, seemingly physically and emotionally, and put him in a sleeper hold.

Fucking hell, is she going to be in tears? Rubbing a hand over my face, I let out the breath I was holding and raise my hand, knocking lightly on the wood.

"Serena?" I call, loud enough to be heard over the god-awful pop remix blaring from some unseen speaker.

"No," a small voice responds, barely a whisper, and I have to strain to hear it. I laugh at her denial.

"Yes, Serena. Celeste called me. It's Wolf. Open up for me."

"Everything's fine. Sorry to worry you. I'm going to go home now."

"You'll need to leave the bathroom for that to happen. Are

you planning on coming out, or are you looking for an exit plan through a window?"

I hear mumbled words that sound suspiciously like, "Parasitic, infuriating, disgusting men." I take it as an insult to the fuckface who hurt her and not me, who's an innocent guy just trying to help. So what if I terrify a few college students in the process? They deserve it for the goddamn whipped cream.

Reaching for the door handle and pushing down, I'm surprised to find the door unlocked and the ease with which it opens.

Scowling, I look down at the knob. "Has this been unlocked the entire time?"

"Yes. It's not my fault Meg didn't think to try opening the door. If her deductive reasoning skills aren't available, I'm not sure how much help she'd be to me, anyway."

I look in front of me and see Serena huddled in the corner of the bathroom, her knees drawn up to her chin and her arms wrapped around her legs. She's a small woman, and in this position, she looks like a collapsed marionette doll.

"Deductive reasoning? Don't you mean investigative? For Christ's sake, I would have come anyway because Celeste asked me to make sure you were okay, but don't you think Corset Girl would have wanted to be in here with you? She was a mess outside this door." I shake my head, disappointment and annoyance coursing through my veins.

"'Corset Girl?' That's a new one. And yes, deductive reasoning. As in, all doors have handles. You use the handle to open the door. Therefore, I should try to open the door before I call Celeste. And I didn't ask you to come, Wolf. I don't need your help, anyway."

"Yeah, you seem pretty fucking capable sitting in the fetal

73

position on a bathroom floor that has more piss and jizz than I even want to think about." Her face transforms from a scowl to a disgusted expression, and she quickly stands up, shaking her hands out at her side as though that will remove the germs and bacteria covering her body. It won't; she'll need Bactine or Listerine to get the grime off.

She'll probably need to burn those clothes, too.

I take her in as she stands, and I can't hide my surprise over her appearance. The clothes—or lack of them—don't bother me, especially because I'm used to half-naked men and scantily clad women in the MMA world and exposed bodies when I tattoo. No, I'm shocked because she is covered in chocolate syrup and red marks that are sure to turn into bruises. My eyes settle on the mark on her jaw, a nasty red spot that takes up a majority of the lower right half of her face. Blood trickles down her arms from unseen gashes, and I can see marks on her forearm that look suspiciously like a hand.

A hand that gripped a little too tightly.

"What, don't I look okay?" Serena asks, an inflection in her tone that lets me know she's joking about the blood and bruises on her body.

"No, you don't look okay, goddammit," my voice vibrates with anger. "Who the fuck did this to you?"

I watch closely as Serena sucks in a long breath, like a smoker taking a drag from a cigarette. Her shoulders bunch, and for a minute, it's like she's holding the weight of the world in her chest. Her slow exhale is accompanied by a shake of her dirty hair and a humorless laugh. She walks to the vanity, looking in the mirror before turning and bracing her hip against the counter. "Most of this is an accident or looks worse than it is. I was trying to avoid the chocolate sauce tyrants and walked into an elbow in the process. The hit sent me back, and I skidded my elbows." She twists her arms, showing off the cuts that decorate her skin. "Right now, these don't hurt too bad. Probably because I still have the vestiges of rage and adrenaline in my system. I'll probably want to hide in a hole tomorrow, though." She pauses, tilting her head as though considering her words. "You know, I want to crawl into a hole now. So, I'll want to fade into obscurity tomorrow." She turns her body, giving me her side profile as she turns on the faucet and places her hands beneath the stream of water.

I grunt at her explanation, not missing that she didn't elaborate on the very obvious handprint on her arm. "What happened to your arm, Serena?" She waves me off as though it's not important.

Not fucking happening.

"Serena, I'll give you three seconds to tell me who laid their hands on you so hard that I see the beginnings of a five-finger bruise on your skin." I cross my arms, leaning back against the door, and silently count to three. When she remains quiet, I nod. "Fine, then you won't mind if I tear this party apart until I find the limp-dicked weasel who put his hands on a woman." I uncross my arms and clench my fists, ready to throw a punch or two if it means teaching these idiots to keep their hands to themselves.

Hypocritical? Maybe. But they deserve the lesson.

I move to turn around, but Serena's frantic voice reaches me before I do. "No, just don't kill anyone. Then I'll have death on my conscience, in addition to being an apparent homewrecker and friendship betrayer, and I can't carry the entire load, okay? So just calm down and maybe unclench your fists because if I have one more freak-out and end up

75

rocking on this floor with semen and urine, I'll probably need to throw my entire body into a Lysol bath. I don't think I'll survive that, so just, no." She takes a breath, the first one since her rambling began. "Dylan, my best friend—no, former best friend—did it. He grabbed me from behind, and I thought it was Jack, the guy who elbowed me in the face."

Serena pauses to shake her head, the dried chocolate on her neck flaking off from the movement. "When I tried to get him off me, he gripped me harder, and I couldn't move. I'm not even sure how, but I was finally able to break his hold and slap him. He grabbed my arm after that, and that's where this came from." She motions to her forearm and the marks that seem to get brighter the more I stare.

With her back to me, I'm able to see the lacerations on her elbows and can make out flakes of dirt embedded in her skin. "You need to clean those cuts and disinfect them before you get an infection." I glance from her arms up to her face.

Her eyes meet mine in the mirror, and I realize for the first time how closely we're standing. Somewhere during her explanation and my inspection, I drifted from the door to directly behind her, less than a footstep away. I watch her reflection in the mirror as her eyes go wider and her mouth pops open, like a blow-up doll, before she sucks her lower lip between her teeth. My eyes catch on the movement, and fuck if I can look away from her delicate nibbling.

My chest aches with the realization that this girl is hurt, not just surface level, but to the deepest caverns of her soul. I never went to college, but my fourteen dipshit cousins did, and Celeste, and I know that hiding in a bathroom in the middle of a party is a defense mechanism.

Despite the sugar coating her skin and the bruises that

shouldn't be there, she looks striking, like a siren hidden below the depths of the ocean. I take in the rest of her, the parts camouflaged by the mess, and notice that her hair is shorter than the last time I saw her and blonder. I replay the kiss in my mind, if it can even be called one, and I can't help but wonder how it would feel to have her lips on me now—would she taste like the cinnamon and vanilla perfume I smelled when I tattooed her, or will the chocolate be an overwhelming flavor on her skin?

"Wolf," she breathes, and that's all it takes to break the spell I fell under. Stepping back, I clench my eyes shut and shake the remnants of insanity out of my head.

"We're leaving now. Do you need to get your shit, or do you have everything?"

10

Serena

When I woke up this morning, excited and deliciously anxious to go to a party with my new friends, I didn't think I'd end the day with Wolf McCleery walking me out of a mixer, covered in dessert toppings.

What's the saying? It wasn't on my bingo card.

Though I don't follow professional, semi-professional, or amateur sports, Wolf is a well-known figure, not only because of his athleticism but also because of his art. As we walk down the hallway, through the crowded living room, and toward the front door, I feel eyes on us, probably shocked that a local hero is in our midst.

If I had any desire to fade into the background after tonight, I could forget it.

"Fucking college kids," Wolf mumbles under his breath as flashes start going off, betraying the people who are not so subtly taking pictures of Wolf. And me, since I'm huddled against Wolf's side, trying to make it out of this house without another incident.

I breathe in relief the moment we walk out the front door,

the crisp winter air filling my lungs with a burn that feels like a lifeline. "I'm sorry about the pictures," I murmur, staring at the ground, too embarrassed to look at his face. "If I had never come here, none of this would have happened."

Wolf releases a sigh, the sound both exasperated and sympathetic. "Listen, none of that is your fault. No one— no matter their sex or gender—should put their hands on you without your consent. Going to a party with your friends shouldn't end in you huddled in the corner of a dirty bathroom. Don't apologize for shit you didn't do, princess." I see his mouth twist, annoyance crossing his features, but all I can process are his words and the endearment he keeps using.

Before I can help myself, I ask, "Why do you keep calling me princess?"

Wolf remains quiet as we walk down the sidewalk and turn the corner. Whole minutes pass, and I think he's not going to respond as we approach an imposing motorcycle. "Fuck if I know," he whispers before clearing his throat and raising his voice. "You okay to ride on the back? How much have you had to drink?"

I shake my head, opening and closing my mouth in rapid succession. "I didn't have anything to drink. Meg, or 'Corset Girl,' picked me up for the party and drove me straight to the house since her boyfriend lives there and she was spending the night. I was only there a few minutes when everything happened. But"—I pause, swallowing down the lump in my throat—"is that thing even safe for two people? The seat looks kind of small, and well, you're not small," I finish, wincing at my words.

He lets out a gruff laugh. "It's a Kawasaki Versys 650, and

it's one of the best bikes for taller people. And listen, it's as safe as any other motorcycle." He reaches over the handlebars and grabs a helmet, thrusting it at me. "Here, wear this. I don't have a spare helmet with me since I didn't plan on a co-pilot tonight, but I'd feel better if you wore it."

I look from him to the enormous object in his hand. "And you're sure we're not going to die?"

"Just put the damn helmet on, Serena, and tell me where you live." As though his words hypnotize me, I grab the helmet and fit it over my head, not surprised by how much room I have in the safety gear.

"It's a little roomy in here," I comment and watch as Wolf rolls his eyes and levels me with a stare that says, "Address, now." Clearing my throat, I continue, "Right. So, my address is 155 University Boulevard. It's right by the library. Which you probably don't know how to get to, right? Okay, so, go down this street and make a left at the house that looks like a gothic mansion transplanted to New Jersey. The one with the broken window. Then, make a quick right at the overgrown tree. You have to be sure to stop there because there's a stop sign hidden behind the leaves, but the owners don't seem to care. I think they should probably get fined for that, but what do I know?

"If you drive maybe a football field's length and then make another right turn by the library—the big building that looks like a library—then you'll get to my apartment complex." I swallow the rest of the words bubbling up my throat; word vomit that doesn't need to be voiced. Wolf just continues staring at me before taking out his phone and typing on the screen.

I rise on my tiptoes to see what he's typing out and

80

realize that he has a GPS application open on his screen, the navigation set to my address. I flush, embarrassed to realize all he needed was an address and not my tour guide explanation.

"Sorry, I didn't realize that you were just going to put it in your phone. How can you watch the screen while you drive?" Nerves replace my embarrassment, and suddenly, I'm wondering if he's a safe driver or if tonight is going to end significantly worse than I thought.

At my question, he reaches into his pocket and pulls out a small black case. "I have wireless ear pods so that I can listen to the navigation on my rides." He tilts his head, peering down at me from his high vantage point. "Aren't you a genius or something? Shouldn't your directional skills be better?"

I cough, caught off guard by his question. "Being a 'genius'"—I air quote—"doesn't mean that I have a proficiency for geography or directions. And I'm not a genius; I'm just slightly above average when it comes to test-taking and retaining information."

"Celeste said you're graduating college next year?" I nod, silently confirming his question. "Yeah, you're a genius. Here." He shrugs off the leather jacket he's wearing and drapes it around my shoulders, immediately wrapping me in his woodsy scent. I fight the urge to lift the fabric to my nose and inhale; he'd probably think I was insane if he witnessed me smelling his clothes.

"Put your arms through the sleeves and zip the jacket. Do you need help climbing on the bike?" He throws a leg over his large black motorcycle, straddling the seat, and I shiver, not from the cold or my damp clothing but from how indecent he looks on his bike coupled with the feel of his clothes on my body. I never understood the appeal of a motorcycle club

81

romance, but suddenly, I'm sold.

He holds out a hand to help stabilize me as I throw my leg over the rear part of the seat, a poor imitation of his graceful display. Using my other hand to grab his shoulder, I pray to every god and goddess I've ever read about that I don't fly off the back of this bike and have my vehicular homicide pictures commemorate that I dressed like a red velvet cupcake on my final day on earth.

I smile at that thought; I'm spending too much time with CeCe and Ava if death and falling are at the forefront of my mind.

As soon as I'm situated behind him, Wolf reaches back and grabs my hands, pulling me forward and guiding my arms around his waist. I squeeze instinctually, and I can feel the laughter shake Wolf's body at my movement. I start to loosen my hold, but he stops me, placing his hand on top of mine and squeezing in a silent communication to hold on. He presses a button, and the sound of his bike fills the night just before Wolf kicks off the kickstand, and our bodies jolt forward from his twist on the throttle.

I squeeze my eyes shut, too petrified to watch as we race past trees and houses, road signs and road work. Wind travels over my body, and I press myself close to Wolf, telling myself that it's the cool temperature that has me seeking his body and not the impossible attraction I feel toward him, especially when he's between my legs.

Within minutes, I feel the bike stop and the engine turn off, a silence that's just as deafening as the bike's engine. Peeling open my eyes, I take in the modern façade of my apartment building, seeing it through Wolf's eyes. To him, he probably sees a college living unit where teenagers pretend to be adults and live with an independence both revered and feared.

To me, it's my second favorite sanctuary and a place where I can just be. My dad has never been through the lobby of this building, let alone my apartment, and no memories of him choosing another woman and child over me and my mom plague this building. Aside from my mother and the movers who helped me move in, only Dylan, Ava, and Celeste have been inside my living space. I sigh at the thought of Dylan; our friendship is a ghost that haunts me, forcing me to relive the times when I thought he was a safe space. Tonight and his aggression and manhandling have forced me to reconsider our relationship even more.

"Serena, you can let go of me now." I flush at Wolf's words, realizing that I'm clutching him to my body as though he's still operating the machine between my thighs. I drop my arms immediately.

Clearing my throat, I raise my hands to unstrap the helmet and fumble with the clasp. Somehow, with me still on the back of the bike, Wolf throws his leg over the seat and stands before turning to face me. I'm too concentrated on the clasp to meet his eyes, and I'm surprised when his large, callused hands push mine away and unbuckle the strap with ease.

"Which apartment are you?" he asks as he removes the helmet from my head. I wince at the smell of chocolate that becomes overwhelming; I must have had some in my hair and ruined Wolf's helmet.

"I'm in apartment twelve-J," I tell him, trying to determine how best to get off the overly large motorcycle. Before I can voice a need for help, Wolf grips me by the waist and lifts me off the seat, placing me down gently before him. Though he's easily a foot taller than me, our bodies are so close that we're sharing air; inhales and exhales breed together until there's a single cloud of oxygen between us and not much more.

I'm not sure what Wolf sees on my face, but his eyes narrow, and I can feel their caress like a feather on my skin. Whatever he sees must repel him because he takes a step back and opens his mouth, probably to say good night. But before he can, I ask a question I have never asked of another man.

"Do you want to come up?"

"For what?"

"Tea, maybe. I could use a cup, and I don't want to be alone right now, if you don't mind." I bite my lip, gnawing on my flesh as I wait for his response.

Wolf remains quiet for a beat, weighing my words before asking, "Why don't you call one of your friends? I'm walking you up and will make sure you get in okay, but I don't think staying is a good idea, princess." My stomach flutters at the continual use of the endearment before it sinks as I absorb the remainder of his words.

"Right, it's just other than CeCe and Ava, I don't really have anyone I can call. I just met Meg—Corset Girl—and she's not exactly available right now. But it's fine, forget I asked. You don't need to walk me up. I'll be okay." I pause, taking a deep breath before continuing, "Anyway, thank you for your help tonight. I could have handled it myself, and eventually, I would have left the bathroom to find someone to bring me home, but still, I appreciate it. You're a good guy, Wolf, even though you look like the Terminator."

I pat Wolf on the arm like he's a good little boy who helped the grown-ups and not a grown man saving young women from parties and walk toward the entrance of my building. His groan slices through the air, and I stop.

"Serena, wait." I turn in time to see Wolf walk over to me. When he's beside me, he runs a hand over his buzzed head. "It's not a bad thing to have a small circle; having people I can count on and know that they're not there for the fame and shit has been a lifesaver. So, I get it. Fucking hell, I get it. So yeah, I'll come up for a bit."

I bite back the smile that wants to break out over my face and tilt my head toward the entrance. "Okay, but can we go in now? It's a little cold, and I'm a little wet." His mouth tilts, and a smirk breaks out on his face. I replay my words, and mortification sweeps through me.

"Shit, no, that's not what I meant. I meant I'm soaked." I groan. "God, that sounds even worse. Just come up. I'm going to stop talking now."

Wolf's smirk breaks into a grin, and laughter echoes through the courtyard. It's the first time I've ever heard his laugh, and it's rich, like dark chocolate wrapped in bacon and sprinkled with sea salt. "Come on, princess, let's get you inside."

11

Wolf

I don't know why I agreed to come into the building, follow her up to her apartment, and ride in a metal deathtrap elevator, but here I am, doing shit I never should have agreed to. Not because I don't want to, but because it feels too good to be in this awkward, intelligent, beautiful woman's presence.

I keep reminding myself that I've got too much going on in my life and that she's at the stage where she's figuring her shit out, while I'm in the season of settling down. It doesn't stop me from leaning in and smelling the vanilla perfume that lingers under the sticky-sweet chocolate, nor does it stop me from mapping the freckles on the back of her neck where my jacket meets her skin.

I open my mouth to ask how she's doing after her first bike ride when the elevator doors open, and two guys step inside. They reek of weed and sweat, and I feel Serena press her body against mine, the only place she can go to get further away from their presence and stench.

"Hey, Serena," one of them says with an appreciative look over Serena's form. She moves impossibly closer to me.

"Hi." Her voice is barely a whisper.

"You ever going to come down and hang out with me? We had fun the last time."

"Mhm, yeah. I, uh," she stammers, sounding like she has no idea how to string two words together. "Have you met Wolf? He's a tattoo artist." I jolt back in surprise at her introduction, not just because why the fuck is she introducing me to some random guy, but also because she introduced me as an artist and not an MMA fighter.

Both guys turn to look at me, and I watch as their eyes widen, the realization of who I am slackening their features. "Holy fuck, you're Wolf McCleery," one of the guys says. I don't bother responding because they know who I am, and it's not like there are many other six-foot-six gingers covered in muscles and tattoos.

To deny would be useless, and to confirm would be a waste of words.

"Holy shit, I saw your fight against Guero last year. You were fucking epic. Can I have your autograph, man?" I look down at Serena, whose back is plastered to my chest like a coward, and scowl at the attention she's called to me. The fight against Victor "The Warrior" Guero, a bloodbath that had both Vic and me stitched up and bruised, was the fight that convinced me to retire. I won—barely—but had to cancel all of my tattoo appointments for three weeks while my body recovered from the brutality of the match.

Turning my attention back to the guys who are both annoying and high as fuck, I grumble, "I don't have a pen or sheet of paper, man. Sorry about that." The elevator doors open with another group of people waiting to be let on, and I don't hesitate. Grabbing Serena's hand, I pull her out of the elevator and into the hall.

"Wolf, this isn't my floor," she says behind me, her hand still clasped in mine. I look down at our connection and curse, dropping it like it's burned me.

I won't linger on how soft and delicate her hand felt in mine. And I definitely won't think about how she looks like she's about to fall over in those heels that make her legs look endless.

"What floor are you on?"

"Twelve. This is…" She pauses, peering behind her to read the floor plaque. "This is the sixth floor. We have six floors to go. Should we go back to the elevator or…?" Her voice trails off, uncertainty threaded through her words, and I shake my head, rejecting her question.

"No, we're using the stairs. That moron couldn't decide if he wanted to be a creep to you or beg to suck my cock like an obsessed fan. I'm not in the mood to deal with idolatry tonight. Can you walk?" I don't miss how she wobbles in her shoes or walks with a slow gait as though she can't get her balance.

Red coats her cheeks, and she looks down at her feet. "My ankle hurts a little from when I fell. I don't think I noticed it before because I had so much adrenaline, but now it's a little sore. I'll be fine, though."

Following her gaze, I see that her right ankle and foot are slightly swollen. "I'm going to pick you up. It'll be faster than watching you struggle down the hall and up the stairs."

"No, you don't need to—" Her words are cut off as I bend down to scoop her up and cradle her against my chest. She struggles in my hold. "Wolf, I can walk. Please put me down."

"No." My legs eat up the distance between the hallway and

88

the stairwell door. Lifting my foot, I kick the door and stride up the stairs, practically running up until I reach the door that reads "Twelve."

"Can you get the handle?" I ask Serena, bending my knees until she's able to reach the knob. Once we're through the doorway and stepping onto the stained carpet of the hallway, she speaks up.

"You can let me down now. My apartment is the first door on the left; it's right here." She motions with her hand. "Really, I'm fine. I promise." I grunt in response, not fully believing her, but place her feet gently on the floor before stepping away.

I watch her closely as she hobbles to her door, limping slightly as though she's trying to hide her pain. Without inserting a key, code, or card, she presses her door lever and walks inside.

"Did you just open your door without a key?" I call from behind her, following her into her small apartment and shutting the door behind me. I reach for the lock and twist it, making sure that there's no chance of someone getting in from the outside.

She turns to look at me and furrows her brow. "You look angry."

"Answer the fucking question, princess."

She swallows, an audible gulp that lends sound to the silence of her apartment. "I want to say no, but that would be a lie. And I feel like lying to you would make you madder than the truth, so I'll tell you the truth, even though you'll be mad at that, too."

I shake my head at her words. "Serena, can you just answer the question without adding more syllables than necessary?"

"Oh, right. Okay. Yes, but this apartment building is very safe. There have been no break-ins or robberies. It's fine."

I run a hand down my face, groaning at her response. "For someone who is supposed to be a fucking genius, you're a goddamn idiot if you think leaving your apartment door open in the middle of the night is safe. What kind of bullshit is that?"

"I-I," she starts, looking at the floor and stumbling over her words.

"No, save your excuses; it's fucking stupid. Go wash that shit off your body. I'll wait until you're done, and then I'll head out."

She moves her gaze from the hardwood to my face, biting on her lower lip as she examines me. I feel my body stiffen at her expression, and I clench my jaw to keep the blood from rushing to my groin.

"Can I wash you?" she murmurs, and I cough, sure I didn't hear her correctly.

"What?" I rasp out.

Her eyes widen, the golden irises glowing in the dull lamplight of the apartment. "Oh my God. I meant your clothes. Not you. I don't want to wash you. I mean, if you needed help, I could." She groans, squeezing her eyes shut and shaking her head as though to collect her thoughts. "I mean your sweatshirt. It's covered in chocolate, and I feel bad because you went to that party to help me." She gestures down her body to the syrup smeared all over her torso. Without my permission, my eyes trail over her.

Fucking hell.

"It's fine, I'm going home." The last goddamn thing I need is to be naked in Serena's apartment while she's wet.

"Please, I would feel so much better if you would let me

take care of your clothes. Maybe you can shower first, and I'll hand wash your things and then throw them in the dryer." She stops to look at me with her big, expressive eyes, and I know at this moment that I'm a fucking goner. "Please, Wolf. Let me take care of it."

Bringing my hand to my face, I pinch the bridge of my nose between my thumb and forefinger and close my eyes. There is no question I should say no. I performed my service toward Celeste and made sure Serena left the party and got home safely; nothing and no one is forcing me to stay here.

So, despite the knowledge that I should abso-fucking-lutely go home and finish prepping for my clients this weekend, I find myself saying, "Okay. But I don't need a shower; just give me a washcloth, and I'll wash this shit from my face."

Holding out her hand, Serena steps forward, so close that her cinnamon and vanilla smell invades my senses. "Give me your sweatshirt, and I'll wash it."

"Let me see to your ankle and battle scars first," I respond, gesturing to her myriad of cuts, scrapes, bruises, and swollen body parts.

Her blush is instant, and she backs away as though I'm about to throw her over my shoulder and force first aid down her throat. "It'll just take a minute, and then I'll put some antiseptic on my elbows, but just—" She wriggles her fingers and jerks her arm in a "give me" motion. "Please, just give me your shirt."

"You're letting me do more than put hydrogen peroxide on those lacerations. But fine, you want to wash my sweatshirt so fucking badly, here." Gripping the bottom of my gray sweatshirt, I drag it over my head until I'm left in a T-shirt with my sleeves on full display. I watch her face as I hand

91

her the article of clothing and take notice of the attention she's paying to my forearms. It's early February, the weather is cold, and most people would leave the house in a winter jacket, but I can't have my mobility restricted while riding my bike. Had I known how the night would end, I would have brought my truck to the event tonight.

Diverting her eyes, Serena unzips my leather jacket and shrugs it off before heading into her small kitchen.

"I won't get too much water on the leather, but I want to wipe off the lining and the stains on your jacket. Your sweatshirt doesn't seem too bad, and I don't think the stains set yet, so it shouldn't take long to get it out." I expect her to walk to her sink, but instead, she walks to a small closet and carefully opens the louver door. On one side of the closet is the most disorganized pantry I have ever seen, with cans, bottles, and bags shoved in with no regard to functionality or order. On the other side is a stacked washer and dryer and ironing board that looks like it's about to fall and hit her in the face.

I must be a fucking psychic because as soon as thoughts about the ironing board leave my head, I see the dilapidated piece of shit start to come down.

"For fuck's sake, Serena," I huff out, lifting my arm to catch the board before it hits her on the forehead.

"Thanks, that board won't stay put."

"It's shoved in there, maybe have some organization. Christ, this closet looks like a tornado blew through it." She spins away from me, but not before I see the twist of her lips and the redness bloom on her cheeks.

"'Organized chaos,' my mom calls it. To anyone else, they would see this closet and think that I have no semblance of organization, but I know where everything is. It may look messy, but for me, it's functional. I have the cans of tomatoes next to the rice and canned vegetables and the cereals next to my protein bars. My snacks are thrown in by sweet and savory categories, and the containers of broth are just shoved in wherever they fit because I didn't have much room remaining."

"And the ironing board?"

She huffs, and I watch her shoulders drop. "No one likes a smart ass."

I can't help but laugh as I watch her get to work on cleaning my clothing. Pulling out a spray bottle and a bar that looks like soap and smells like lemons, she sprays the stains and begins scrubbing the fabric with an aggression that concerns me.

"Please, go take care of yourself. This will be done in a minute, and I promise, I feel okay," she tosses over her shoulder, not breaking her cleaning frenzy. "The bathroom is the first door on the right. Towels and washcloths are in the closet inside the bathroom, and there's soap in the shower and another one under the sink in the vanity. If you decide to shower, the water takes a few to heat up, so don't be alarmed that it stays cold for roughly six minutes and thirty-four seconds."

I raise my eyebrow. "Have you timed it?"

She pauses in her ministrations. "Uh, no?"

"I'm not taking a shower. Don't worry if the stains don't come out; I have six sweatshirts that look the same, and I can give two shits if I have to throw this one away." I leave her in the kitchen/laundry room and make my way to the bathroom. Unlike her bizarre directions to her apartment building, these instructions are easy enough to follow, and I find myself locked behind a surprisingly dark bathroom. While the rest of her apartment is a study in bright, light colors mixed with neutrals, the bathroom boasts dark gray walls, a heavy mahogany vanity, and chipped black tiles inside the slim shower stall.

I scowl at the construction, knowing damn well that a man of my size could barely fit one leg and his dick inside that shower without feeling claustrophobic. As it is, bending down in this miniature bathroom makes me feel like a bull in an antique shop, and I have to contort my body not to hit my head or knock anything over on the shelves next to the vanity mirror.

Opening the vanity, I push aside feminine hygiene products, hair shit, and spare rolls of toilet paper. Just like in her pantry, the interior of this cabinet looks like a bomb exploded, and I try not to reorganize the mess that she claims is a form of organization.

But I can't help it; there's no rationale behind the placement of the contents, and my organized brain can't handle the disorder. Within five minutes, I have neat little rows lined up like soldiers beneath the sink and a bullshit first aid kit placed on the Formica countertop. She must have just two band-aids and expired hydrogen peroxide in the way of medical supplies. Shaking my head, I pull out my phone to place an online order for the local pharmacy, stocking up on shit she should have in her home kit: bacitracin, ibuprofen, hydrogen peroxide, gauze, alcohol swabs, and other basic necessities that seem to be unimportant to Serena. I pay extra for expedited delivery and stuff my phone back into my pocket before glancing up at the mirror. I take in my appearance and can't help the scowl

94

that comes to my face.

What the fuck am I doing here, playing doctor with Serena while she plays house with my clothes? I need to get my shit, get the fuck out of here, and forget about the pretty girl with the sad eyes and chaotic categorization. And I still have chocolate syrup on my goddamn face.

"Fucking college," I grunt before turning the faucet on. If my cousin were here, she'd probably tell me I'm acting like an old, grumpy man. But who hosts a party and thinks to themselves, *Let me make every person in my vicinity as uncomfortable and disgusting as possible while wasting as many food products as I can?*

Grabbing the hypoallergenic body wash from the cabinet, I squeeze a drop in my hand and massage until suds form. I use the unscented soap to scrub the stickiness from my skin and sigh in relief when no trace of chocolate remains.

"Wait for her to clean herself up, get the shit from the pharmacy, clean her wounds, and get the fuck home," I mutter. "Get the fuck out of this apartment and stop organizing cabinets and obsessing over the smell of a woman we barely fucking know." Nodding to myself, I grab the band-aids, pull open the bathroom door, and take long strides back to the kitchen. I'm not surprised that Serena is no longer bent over the washing machine, tending to my shirt. But I am surprised to find her clean and dressed in a black tank top and oversized sweatpants. There must be another bathroom in this small apartment, and I must have taken longer to right her cabinets than I thought. She's facing away from me, reaching up to a mess of a cupboard to grab God knows what.

My gaze trails over her back until it gets to the top of the flimsiest fucking shirt I've ever seen. I'm praying that there's

95

some kind of built-in bra in the front because the material looks thin, and I don't think my willpower is strong enough to resist glancing at her tits if her nipples are front and center. My gaze moves from her clothing to her skin, and a sliver of black teases me from the center of her back.

What the hell is that? Leaning closer, I see a small patch of inflamed skin and wonky linework, like an inexperienced apprentice stabbed her back with ink and continued the piece, even after her skin rejected the application. The ink and infection seem too fresh for it to have been an older piece, and I'd bet my ass she got a botched tattoo within the last few days.

"What the fuck is on your back?" I growl, my voice taking on an edge I usually reserve for the cage.

She stops reaching for whatever it is she is searching for and settles back on flat feet. Turning around slowly, I don't miss the wince on her face—either from pain or discomfort at my question—but I'm too angry to care.

From where I'm standing, it looks like a tattoo artist ruined a canvas with no regard for the person—the young, beautiful person—who would have to carry it around like a fucking shackle for the rest of their life.

Serena clears her throat and folds her hands in front of her waist, like a child about to be scolded by the principal. "I got a tattoo."

"No fucking shit, you got a tattoo. Where? When? I saw a piece of the infection and shitty application, so don't even pretend that it's a fucking masterpiece."

"Royal Ink, on Lexington and Fisher Blvd."

I jerk back as if slapped. "You went to a fucking gang parlor for ink? You realize DeSilva provides the initiation tattoos

96

for the Bógar and Killet crews, right? You could have been in there with fucking members who wouldn't think twice about taking advantage of a pretty girl in a vulnerable situation. What were you thinking?"

"I—"

Shaking my head, I cut her off. "Save it. I'm not trying to be a dick, but you put yourself in danger for a tattoo you could have waited for. And from the little I've seen, your impatience wasn't worth it. I fucking told you to call the shop when you decided. Why did you rush it?"

She drops her hands and forms fists at her side like she's getting ready to hit me for my comments.

"Because I didn't want to wait. When you refused—no, you had your chance to speak, do not interrupt me. When you refused, I decided to go elsewhere to have it done. The only shop with availability was Royal Ink, so I made an appointment and went. No, to your asinine question, I had no idea that it was affiliated with gang tattoos. I'm not a moron and would never willingly put myself in danger." She sucks in a breath, shaking her head vehemently. "My God, you act like all tattoo parlors are dens of iniquity and depravity, as though you don't own one yourself. Yes, I went and got a tattoo that I had to stop because of the incredible amount of pain and the sketchiness of the establishment. No, you cannot order me around or dictate to me like you're anything other than my friend's cousin. So kindly see yourself out so that I don't need to kick you out."

My eyes widen at her speech, shocked at her words. Shaking my head, I clear the surprise and order, "No. Turn around."

Her eyes narrow into slits at my words, and she laughs without humor. "'No?' You don't have the right to tell me no.

97

Get the hell out of my apartment."

"No. I'm sorry for being a dick, but I know you're in pain, and I know that your tattoo is a fucking hack job, and both of those things piss me off. Now, turn around and pull up your shirt so that I can take a look at the damage."

She stares at me, her stunning face pinched in a mixture of annoyance and contemplation, before responding to my order. "The only reason I'm doing this is because it hurts, and nothing seems to be helping."

"If you're using the hydrogen peroxide in your hall bathroom, it's water now, so there's no surprise that it didn't do shit."

"Stop being a jerk—" Her voice cuts off at the sound of her doorbell. Her brows furrow as she asks, "Did you order something?"

Pulling out my phone, I check the delivery app to make sure that the items I ordered arrived. "Yeah, shit for your first aid kit because you have less useful things than in a kid's doctor bag." I leave her silently fuming in the kitchen and go to the front door to retrieve my purchase. Walking back into the kitchen, I hold the bag up and lift my other hand, twisting my fingers for her to turn around.

"Insufferable jabroni," she mumbles but follows my silent command and turns until her back is facing me. Grasping the hem of her shirt, I open my mouth to tell her she doesn't need to take her top off but clench my jaw when I see the fucked-up wings of butterflies from her right hip to the center of her back as she whips her shirt off. There aren't many insects on her body, but what's there is fucking terrible. Her skin is puckered and red, and obvious infection aside, the tattoo looks like shit. The lines of each butterfly are shaky, and I can spot more than one blowout among the four illustrations.

"Fucking hell, princess. What did they do to you?"

She goes quiet at my words, no longer mumbling insults at me. "I know," she breathes out so quietly that I almost don't hear it. I drop the bag on her peninsula island and walk up to her, taking a closer look at the redness covering her skin.

"My shop can fix the work, but we need to get you healed first. Let me take care of your open wounds right now, and then I'll see how I can help with the healing process for the infection. I'm warning you, Serena..." I reach out and grab her jaw, turning her face until her profile is in view, and she can look up to meet my eyes. Her expression is pained, and I grind my teeth, anger bleeding into my motions. Tightening my hand on her jaw slightly, I continue, "If these don't heal with topical ointment, you will need to go to the doctor and get an antibiotic. I don't know how much I'll be able to help, but you need to take care of this before it worsens. Do not wear tight clothes, keep the areas of infections clean and free of harsh chemicals, and do not use anything abrasive."

She nods, dropping her eyes.

"Hey," I whisper, gently squeezing her jaw until her eyes meet mine again. "I'm sorry I raised my voice. I'll fix this."

"It's okay. You were right; I shouldn't have gone to that place. I knew that it was a bad idea, but, well..." She pauses to shrug. "I wanted the tattoo, and the original artist I found wouldn't cooperate." She bites her lip, drawing my attention down to the plump flesh. I swallow, steeling myself against the wave of lust that rolls through me at the action.

"So your botched tattoo is my fault, princess? That seems like a stretch."

She shrugs again, a dainty hitch of her shoulders. "I

99

wouldn't have gone to a dangerous part of town without your refusal to work with me on a design I very much wanted. So, the way I see it, my blood is on your hands, Wolf."

12

Serena

Being touched by someone with so much obvious strength is a heady experience, especially when they're doing all they can to maintain a gentleness that doesn't seem to come naturally to them. Wolf is cradling my jaw like it's the most precious thing in the world while simultaneously scolding me and telling me what a bad decision I made, as though I'm not fully aware that the piece on my back was a mistake of epic proportions.

I've already established that I'm not an idiot, so it's not as though I'm ignorant of my current predicament. I just chose to ignore it for the last seventy-two hours.

"I'm going to take a look at your elbows and clean them up. I also got you some butter for the bruise on your jaw."

"Butter? Why would I eat butter for my jaw?" I ask.

"You don't eat it; you rub it on top of the bruise. My first trainer, Wojotek, was from Poland, and he swore by rubbing butter on bruises to help break up the blood clots and increase the flow of blood to the injured area. I've been doing it for years, and it seems to help. Some people use diluted apple

101

cider vinegar or arnica cream, but I can't stand the smell of either."

He removes the supplies from the reusable bag as he speaks, lining things up first in height and then alphabetical order as he proceeds. I watch him arrange the labels so that they all face forward, a perfect arrangement of orderliness and functionality.

"My cabinets must have given you a coronary."

His gaze cuts to me, and he offers a wry smile. "I rearranged your sink cabinet. Your shit pissed me off, and I couldn't leave it like that."

"Wh-what?" I sputter with a laugh. "You reorganized my bathroom?"

"That's what I said." He turns his attention back to the medical supplies and grabs a container of cotton pads. "Where would I find a small bowl?"

I point toward the sink. "The cabinet next to the sink has all my bowls and dishes. It's better organized, I promise," I tease. He grunts in response and moves in the direction I indicated. Turning on the faucet, he washes his hands before he opens my cabinet and grabs one of my cereal bowls. He quickly fills it with warm water and returns to my side.

He grabs a small bottle from his lineup, and I peer over my shoulder, careful not to turn my torso, to inspect his next steps. He must sense my interest because he holds up the container in his hand so that I can read the label of a brand I don't recognize.

"What's that?"

"A gentle soap. It's the best to clean lacerations with." He squirts the soap into the bowl and mixes it with a swirl of the bowl. "Stay still, I'm going to clean these cuts, and I don't

102

want your bony ass elbow getting me in the face."

He makes quick work of cleaning out the wound, his fingers gentle as they wash out the dirt and grime that remained even after my shower. He's soon finished and applying a topical ointment to my scrapes.

"Alright, I'm going to need to touch your back." I swallow, shivering slightly at the thought of his touch over the expanse of my skin. For Wolf, I know that he's seen and felt plenty of naked body parts before as a result of his career, but it still makes tingles race up my spine.

Not in dread, though it should be, but in excitement.

"Wait," he cuts in as soon as I lean forward to give him better access. "Go lie down on the couch, you're shivering. I should have realized you were cold; I'm sorry. Give me a minute to turn around." I shake my head but don't bother correcting him that I'm shivering in anticipation, not because I'm cold. "Okay, you can go to the couch now."

I spin around, taking in his broad form and the tattoos that snake down from his neck to his fingertips like armor. I may have googled pictures of Wolf and videos of previous matches, so I know that eighty percent of his body is covered in detailed artwork. The black and gray pieces, mostly animal and hunter-themed, look like they're three-dimensional and about to leap from his skin. In one video, the huge wolf head on his back has eyes so vibrant, so well-done, that it looked like it was watching you as he moved through the cage. I move my eyes back up to his neck, taking in the buzzed hair that was significantly longer two months ago. My hands flex with thoughts of running my fingers over his scalp and the faint lines I see on the back of his skull. I squint, trying to make out the circular triangle design, but can't figure out what it is.

103

"You done staring at me?" I jolt in surprise, meeting his gaze in the hall mirror that hangs across from where we stand. From this vantage point, he can see everything: my breasts, naked stomach, and the attention I paid to his body. I flush, bringing up my hands to cover myself. "It's a Triquetra."

I draw my brows together, unsure of what he's talking about. "What?"

"The symbol on the back of my head that you were studying. It's a Triquetra, or Trinity Knot, a Scottish symbol for the Father, Son, and Holy Spirit."

"Are you religious?" I ask, as though I'm not standing in front of him half-naked and covering my nipples with a dainty forearm.

"Not particularly, but I'm not dead yet, even though I risk my life inside a cage and get beat up by men my size or larger. So, someone's got to be looking out for me. Now, get on the couch so I can tend to your back." I risk a glance back up at his face, only to see his eyes squeezed shut and his jaw clenched.

"Right, sorry." I hurry to the couch and fling my body down, wincing at the graze on my jaw. I am going to have a nasty bruise in a few days, there is no doubt about that. "Okay, I'm decent."

Wolf mumbles, and I hear something that sounds suspiciously like "Not likely" come from his direction. Turning my head, I rest it so that I'm looking out toward my living room and can see Wolf's progress as he stalks to the kitchen island to grab supplies. Once he has everything he needs, he comes to my side and kneels on the floor beside me.

Just like before, Wolf narrates what his process is. "I'm going to clean the area with the soap and warm water mixture, and then I'll apply a coat of A&D ointment."

104

I look up at him, frowning. "I don't have A&D."

"I ordered it." Wolf dips a clean cotton pad into the water and begins dabbing my skin, gently cleansing the irritated flesh on my back. I squirm under his ministrations, unable to stay still as he takes care of me.

"Stop moving, Serena," Wolf admonishes beside me as he grabs a paper towel and blots the water from my skin. I don't follow his command, instead moving more under his attention thanks to the sensitive areas of my body. "For fuck's sake, Serena, stay still."

"I can't; I'm ticklish," I rasp, breathing in a deep pull of air.

He stills, his hand on my lower back as he absorbs my words. "That so, princess?" His voice is deeper, more sensual than before, and I look up, watching his green eyes as they rake over my back. He drops the paper towel on the couch and brings his hand back to my skin, grazing it with the tips of his fingers. Unlike his previous clinical touches, this feels like more: more intimate, more personal, more important, and my mouth grows dry.

His fingers dance over the uninfected parts of my back as though he's trying to determine the spots that make me squirm in discomfort and writhe in pleasure. He's so focused that his eyes narrow into slits, and his mouth pops open, his tongue peeking out from his concentration. His fingers browse a sensitive spot, and I can't help the gasp that breaks from my mouth.

"Wolf," I whisper and start to turn to face him. My voice breaks Wolf of whatever spell he was under, and he bolts upright, banging into my ottoman before grabbing the decorative throw blanket and tossing it over my body. Before I can even ask if he's okay, he's speed walking into my kitchen and grabbing his still-damp sweatshirt and jacket.

"Your clothes are still wet; you'll catch a cold if you put them on and then ride home like that," I say, coming behind him while clutching the throw blanket over my body like a shawl.

"I've had worse," he grunts out beneath the fabric. Once his face breaks free, I can see the panic stamped across his features. I don't bother saying another word, knowing that any additional protests will come off as begging, and I refuse to put myself in that position again tonight. It's bad enough that I had to petition him to let me wash his clothes; I won't force him to stay in my home if he's desperate to run out.

Following him to the front door, I huddle into my blanket and jump back when his voice fills the apartment. "Do not come to the door without a shirt on, for fuck's sake. Who the hell knows who will be outside your door."

I roll my eyes and do everything I can to keep the annoyance from my voice. "I'm completely covered, and no one will be out there. It's too early for most people to come back from a party and too late for those who stayed in to be out."

"Pain in my ass," he grumbles. Reaching for the door handle, Wolf stills before turning his head, giving me his disgustingly handsome profile. "Make sure you keep all your wounds clean and wear loose, baggy clothing for at least a week or until the infection clears up on your back. If the infection doesn't go away in a day or so on its own, or if you develop a fever, you need to go to the urgent care or your primary care physician for an antibiotic, probably penicillin. As soon as you're all cleared up, give the shop a call, and Aubrey will schedule you with one of my artists for a consultation for a cover-up. There's no fucking way you're walking around with that shit

106

for the rest of your life."

"You won't do the piece?" I ask, surprised that he mentioned another artist.

He shakes his head once. "I have too many clients and too long of a waitlist to add a cover-up into the mix right now. It takes planning, color theory, and a shit-ton of work to make sure the original is completely camouflaged or incorporated into the new piece."

"Oh. Right, of course."

"Don't worry, all of my artists are highly skilled and can out-tattoo any other shop in the tri-state area. And that's not me being cocky; most, if not all, my artists have won or placed in national competitions and are recognized as some of the best in their respective styles. I think you'll like Sloan—she does both watercolors and photorealism and could make a real nice piece for you."

"What's your specialty?"

"Fine line and Japanese. Listen, I need to go. Don't forget what I told you, and make sure you take care of your bruises, too. Rub some butter on your jaw before you go to bed; it should help to reduce the swelling and inflammation."

"I will."

"And lock up behind me. So help me God, do not leave this door open at night."

"I will," I repeat, transferring both edges of the blanket to one hand.

"And—"

I cut Wolf off, placing my free hand on his forearm. Rising on my toes, I place a delicate, chaste kiss on the underside of Wolf's jaw, the highest point I'm able to reach due to our size difference. He sucks in a breath as though shocked by my actions. "Thank you, Wolf. For picking me up tonight, making sure I was safe, and taking care of me afterward. I know you didn't have to and only did it as a favor to Celeste, but thank you anyway."

Releasing a long exhale, Wolf turns his head and unlatches the door, throwing it open before tossing words over his shoulder. "Stop fucking kissing me, princess. And lock the goddamn door."

He slams the door behind him, and I quickly turn the lock and the deadbolt, severing our connection. My mind nags at me to look through the peephole, and I raise my eye to watch the hallway. Wolf didn't storm away, as I expected, but instead, he's standing in front of my door, hanging his head and looking like a defeated man. I continue to observe him as he runs a hand over his buzzed head and scowls. Though I can't hear him, his mouth moves, and I can make out the words departing his lips, "Fucking hell, princess."

I watch as his form disappears through the peephole, holding my breath until I'm sure he's out of the hallway and through the stairwell door. Releasing it slowly, I drop my head to my door and laugh, unable to contain my absolute confusion about how my night ended with me here: bruised, bloody, and drained. I'm grateful, annoyed, and unfairly turned on by Wolf's appearance tonight; I shudder to think of what could have happened if I needed to walk through that party alone after hiding in the bathroom.

Dropping my shoulders, I drop my grip on the blanket and let it fall until it's nothing more than a pool of fabric at my feet. Walking across the room, I turn off the lights and make my way to the hall bathroom Wolf used earlier.

His smell assaults me as soon as I step through the door and

I inhale deeply, savoring the scent that envelops me.

"God, he smells like a freaking forest." I sigh into the room. Grabbing the glass door of the shower, I pry it open and switch the water to hot. Even though I showered less than an hour ago in my primary bathroom, and had Wolf rubbing ointment on my back, I feel sticky and needy. I reason that I'll reapply whatever Wolf did, even if I have to contort my body to do so. While the water runs, I check on the vanity cabinet and bite my lip at the color-coded rows. Wolf lined up each product in vertical lines according to color and height order, giving me a perfect view of every item in my cabinet.

Steam starts to fill the bathroom and I yank the shower door open, stepping into the stall carefully before closing the door. Somehow, Wolf's scent is magnified by the scalding water, so strong that it feels like he's in this tiny bathroom with me. Closing my eyes, I let myself imagine a world where Wolf doesn't view me as helpless and impulsive, but beautiful and desirable. Trailing my hands up my body, I trace the droplets of water until my fingers meet my nipples, pulling at them until they stand erect and wanting. I don't swallow the moan that builds in my throat, sharing it with the chipped black tile.

In my mind, it's not my slim fingers on my chest, but Wolf's thick, scarred hands pulling at my nipples until they're red and puffy. Dragging one hand down my body, I don't stop until my fingers meet my clit, strumming against it in hard, sure strokes. The dual stimulation causes my knees to buckle as an orgasm whips through me with little warning.

"Shit," I gasp, moving one hand to brace myself against the wall. Wolf's face still clouds my vision, and his smell still consumes me as I suck in a lungful of air.

I allow myself a few moments to feel the aftershock of my

109

climax and the water beating my back before I push myself up,
finish my shower, and leave all remnants of the night behind.

13

Serena

"What do you mean you're selling the house?" I yell into my phone. "You told me that you could buy Dad out if you needed to."

"Lower your voice, *Muñeca*; getting loud with me will not change my decision." My mom pauses, taking a breath so deep that I can hear it through the phone. "We came to this house to heal—you, me, and your grandmother—and it gave us beautiful years and memories that we can cherish. But it's just a house, Serena, and no matter what it looks like to you, this house will always have a part of your father connected to it. When I couldn't get a mortgage, I needed your father to sign as the primary lender; he has held that over my head for the last eleven years. Even if he agreed to refinancing—which he won't—the walls of the place would still be haunted by his presence. We need a fresh start, one where he can't hold the literal roof over our heads.

"I'm done, Serena. I cannot communicate with him anymore, not after he verbally and emotionally abused you for making a mistake that most young people make: trusting someone who was not worthy. *You* are his daughter, not Marina. While you may have made a poor decision because that boy wasn't good to *you*, your father has no right to act as though you killed someone or broke a family apart. I will not condone his behavior toward you, and if that means selling this house, good. I don't want it anymore. I've told you we have the money for a fresh start without your father's influence."

Tears splash on the counter, and I can't hold back the choking sobs that overtake me. "B-but it's our home, Mamá."

"No, it's a house, Serena. Memories transfer; they're not contained in wood or brick and mortar. I know you love this house, but it's time. This house served its purpose and will be good to the next family."

"I'm sorry. I feel like this is my fault."

My mom lets out a sigh, and though I can't see her, I can feel her shaking her head. "Stop apologizing for being a young adult. Your father is an asshole. And, while you're the best thing to ever happen to me, marrying your father was the worst decision I ever made. I should have left him the moment I found out I was pregnant."

"Mom—" I start, but she cuts me off.

"No, Serena. I chose to stay with him, knowing what he was capable of, knowing that remaining faithful to one woman was too much for him. I don't regret meeting him because it gave me you, but I regret giving him the power to hurt you. He and his money can go fuck off. We don't need him, not anymore."

"Are you sure about this, Mom?" I wipe the tears away with the back of my hand and bite down on my lower lip. I called my mom to tell her about the party on Friday night and the

112

botched tattoo; I never expected her to answer the phone with a confession of speaking with real estate agents to sell our sanctuary. Though she won't say it, I know that my father and his manipulations are behind this.

"It's time, *Muñeca*. Now, what did you have to tell me?"

I cough, a watery splattering of saliva and tears that land on my once-clean countertops. "After this revelation, I hardly think I have anything else to add. My brain is short-circuiting."

My mom gentles her voice, using a tone she reserves for babies and toddlers. "It's going to be okay, Serena. There's nothing for you to do except take care of yourself, be with your friends, and continue to excel in school. I just want you to be happy, baby. I'm asking you—no, begging you—to please let this be. I am at peace with the decision to sell, and I need you to accept it."

There is no way that I'm accepting it, but I also won't let my mother harbor any guilt for doing something that I'm almost positive my father is forcing.

"Okay." My voice is resigned, but my will is anything but. I refuse to let this go without a fight, even if it's futile.

My mom's voice is relieved when she says, "Thank you, baby. I need to run; I have a date tonight with the baseball coach, and I need to start getting ready."

I cringe at my mom's mention of a date. Though she hasn't been in a serious relationship since divorcing my dad, my mother is not shy when it comes to insignificant dates. "Say less, Mom. I'm going to hang up now." We say our goodbyes and disconnect. The moment the line goes dead, I go to my contacts and dial my father's number.

"Serena," he answers, not bothering to give me a "hello" or

113

a "how are you?"

"How could you?"

"Excuse me?" My father's tone is short, almost like he's annoyed I bothered to call him.

"Why are you doing this? You could buy and sell our house a million times over, yet you insist on making Mom's and my life as difficult as possible."

My dad is silent as he takes in my words, and I can feel him seething through the phone. After long moments of silence, he finally says, "Brandi and I decided that we can no longer support you when you continue to hurt Marina and our family. We won't have anything harm the well-being of those in our household."

I rear back as if struck. "Are you listening to yourself right now? You realize that you are not Marina's father, right? You didn't impregnate Brandi; your DNA is not in Marina. What the fuck do you not get about that?"

My sperm donor has the audacity to scoff. "Marina is more of a daughter to me than you, at this point, Serena. You dare to call me, questioning my generosity through the years when I housed and footed the bill for you and your disgrace of a mother? After all she's done to poison my own child against me? No." He laughs. "Until you show me the respect that your sister does, you will not get a single dime out of me."

"Respect? Why would I show you respect when you're the one who broke up our family? You're the one who cheated, not Mom. Even your own mother couldn't stand the sight of you and moved in with me and Mom to get away from you." My grandmother, Abuela Pia, immigrated from Mexico City in the early sixties with her parents and married my grandfather, an American Command Sergeant Major. My

114

grandfather died when I was a baby, and my grandmother immediately moved into her only child's home with his family. My mother's family lives in Puebla, Mexico, and though we see them every summer, Abuela Pia was a staple in my life.

It says a lot about my father's actions that his mother disowned him after cheating on my mom and marrying Brandi.

"Watch your mouth, Serena. My mother was a senile woman who was lied to by your mother."

It's my turn to scoff. "Senile? She had more sense in her pinky toe than most people. Abuela was fully coherent; she died of a heart attack." I pause, swallowing down the rest of the vile words I want to say to the man who is fifty percent responsible for giving me life. Releasing a breath, I gentle my voice. "Dad, if you do this, I will never forgive you."

"I neither want nor need forgiveness from you. Stop acting like a child and grow up." He hangs up, not giving me a chance to respond. I stare at my phone, stunned by his words and the vehemence behind them. For my entire life, my mother has done nothing to pollute or discourage my relationship with my father; if anything, she encouraged me to foster our relationship. That is until Marina assumed the role of daughter and pushed me into a guest role in my childhood home.

I look down at my phone, debating whether or not I should call him back and demand that he listen to me. I weigh the option of getting in my beat-up car, driving to his affluent neighborhood, and staining his doorstep with my presence until he sees reason and leaves my childhood home—my sanctuary—alone. But I know, as sure as I know that the hands of a clock always move forward, that my father will

115

never be rational. At least, not about this.

A knock on the door disrupts my musings, and I throw my phone on the couch before making my way to the peephole. Part of me hopes that it's Wolf, that he didn't mean his parting comment of, "Stop kissing me," and has come back to ravage me and stake his claim. I may be smart, but a girl can daydream, even if it's about something as probable as tigers dancing in the ballet.

Looking through the glass hole, I'm surprised to see Ava and Celeste on the other side of my door, holding a tray of coffee and bags from JJ's Diner, the restaurant on campus that serves breakfast all day and boasts New Jersey staples like pork roll and omelets with fresh tomatoes. I unlatch the door and am instantly enveloped in a large hug.

I breathe in Ava's soft scent, finding comfort in my friend's arms. "This is quite a reception."

"If you ever give me a scare like that again, I will force Celeste on you and chain you to my ankle for the rest of your damn life, Serena. What the fuck happened on Friday?" Ava asks, squeezing me tighter until there's barely any space left between our bodies.

"Ava, you're suffocating me," I choke out.

"Suck it up, you owe me this."

"Okay, crazy, release Rena and take a step back," CeCe orders.

"Fine." Ava sulks, unlatching her arms from my body. "But you," she says, pointing at me. "You better start talking while I eat this pork roll, egg, and cheese. I don't want to hear anything but the sound of your voice until I'm satisfied with your explanation."

I shake my head but laugh. "Can we do this inside the

apartment and not in the hallway? I don't want my neighbors to overhear our entire conversation." I grab the bag from CeCe's hand and step to the side, allowing them enough room to enter my apartment. As soon as I shut the door, Celeste whirls around to face me.

"Give me that bag. You are not going to distract us by playing host."

"That's not what I was doing," I grumble, clutching the bag closer to my body and skirting around them toward the kitchen.

"Nope, not happening. Hand it over."

With a sigh, I hand the bag back to Celeste, watch her walk to the kitchen table, and set it down.

"This is the part where you start talking, Rena," Ava mock whispers beside me.

I shrug, downplaying the events on Friday. "Not much happened. Now, what did you get me from JJ's?"

"Oh, no you don't. If I were to call my cousin right now, would he tell me the same story? Or would there be a different recollection of events?" At the mention of Wolf, my insides go liquid, and a kaleidoscope of butterflies erupts in my stomach. My mind travels back to his hands on my back, my jaw, and my elbows, cleaning me up while teasing me for my lack of organization. "See that look. That look on your face tells me that something happened. So, spill it, princess."

"Don't call me that," I mumble, not liking the nickname in any voice other than Wolf's. What the hell is wrong with me? "Friday night did not go as planned." I pause, sighing at the reminder. "I told you; Meg picked me up, and it was a 'messy mixer,' which, yes"—I cut a glare at Ava—"I know is gross, but it sounded like fun when she described it. When we got

117

there, I went to the basement and got an elbow to the face, followed by scraped elbows." I twist my arms to show the bandages. "These were an accident from one of the brothers in the fraternity, Jack. He felt horrible and tried to make it up to me, even offering to pay for my phone, which cracked. I went to the store and had it fixed yesterday, so that wasn't an issue. But after Jack asked me to dance and left to get a drink or put a drink down, or whatever exactly it was that he was supposed to do, Dylan came."

"What?" "I'll fucking kill that gerbil," Ava and Celeste yell simultaneously.

I shake my head, dismissing their question and comment. "I didn't realize it was him—he wasn't supposed to be there, anyway; it was a closed party, but when I spoke to Meg yesterday, she said he came as a guest of one of the brothers. I thought Jack was getting a little too comfortable because when arms grabbed my hips and pulled me back, I felt so uncomfortable and violated. It wasn't until I saw a unique scar on Dylan's wrist and heard his voice that I realized who it was.

"I tried to pry him off as he spewed mean words at me, but I wasn't able to at first. But then I was consumed by so much rage after he called me a slut, that I broke his hold and slapped him across the face. He became irate after that, and Jack tried to step in and diffuse the situation; he even yelled at Dylan. But I was so upset that I ran away and closed myself in the bathroom. I ran by Meg on my way upstairs, and she followed me. I assume Jack told her about what happened, which is why she called you when I didn't come out when she knocked."

"You locked yourself in a dirty bathroom? Why didn't you

have one of the sober drivers take you home?"

I shrug, releasing a long breath. "It was closer than the front door, and I didn't lock myself in. I closed the door but never engaged the lock; it's not my fault Meg didn't try the handle."

"And Wolf?"

I can't hold back the small smile that pulls on my lips. "Wolf was like a wrecking ball. He terrorized half the party just by showing up there, and he was covered in syrup. I think that if I wasn't so shaken up, he would have called the cops to shut it down; he kept murmuring about 'goddamn college kids playing with food.' But he got me out of there and brought me back here."

"He just dropped you off? He didn't make sure you were okay?"

I clear my throat, shifting my weight on my feet as I decide how best to answer. "Ah, not exactly. He came up to the apartment after and cleaned my scrapes with supplies he ordered from the pharmacy. He wasn't too happy with me, but he made sure I was okay before he left." I leave out the touches, the tension, and the tangible need I had to climb his body like a tree.

"God, Rena, I wish I could twist that dick's balls off and feed them to piranhas," CeCe seethes, crinkling the paper bag in her grip. "The next time I see him, I'm going to put him in a Kimura hold and not release him until he's unconscious. Then, I'll shave off his eyebrows and feed him the hair."

Ava and I look at each other before turning our gazes to Celeste, who looks like a bloodthirsty witch from *Macbeth*. "Calm down, C, you sound deranged."

"Calm down? Aves, Serena was assaulted in front of a basement full of people by her 'best friend,' and you're telling

119

me to calm my tits?" Celeste releases the bag long enough to provide air quotes around the words *best friend*. As though I need any further confirmation that Dylan is a horrible person.

"Nope, I heard it, too. But you're taking indignation to a whole other level, so simmer down before you pop a blood vessel in your eye again." Ava stops talking and turns to me. "In high school, the red-headed monster over there got so mad when some idiot on the football team started a rumor about Seraphina, my sister, that she screamed in the bathroom until her eyes turned red. I'll never forget the look on the douchebag's face when she confronted him like a harpy in the middle of the cafeteria. C, didn't he choke on his Frito when you whispered your threat to him? What was it again?"

"I told him that if he didn't stop insinuating that Seraphina was anything less than an intelligent young lady, I would chop off his dick with a rusty kitchen knife and shove it down his throat so that he could choke on his stupidity. It would have been poetic justice."

"There is something so wrong with the two of you," I whisper, shaking my head.

"Yes, but you love us. Back to the points at hand: Dylan is an asshole, and CeCe shouldn't be allowed near him until she cools down."

"No, it's a point, singular: Dylan deserves explosive diarrhea for the rest of his pitiful life."

"Okay, and we're done. Celeste, stop manhandling that bag and pass the food over here." I walk to the table and move the food out of her reach, finally prying open the brown paper held together by staples. The smell of grease and herbs fill the room, and my stomach grumbles, silencing any protests Celeste planned on making.

I read the labels on the containers: pork roll, egg and cheese with no roll, two cereal-coated French toasts, and a container of fruit. I push the meat toward Ava and grab one of the sweet meals for myself. As with every meal, Ava's self-prescribed food rules dictate what she eats. Though I've known her for a handful of months, she's been exercising more freedom recently, thanks to the encouragement of her boyfriend, Greyson, and her therapist.

"Thanks for this, by the way. I was planning on making myself a sandwich, but this is much better."

"No problem. Did anything else happen with Wolf?" CeCe asks, and I choke on the bite I just put in my mouth.

Coughing through the food lodged in my throat, I grab a coffee from the holder and take a small sip, savoring the richness of the brew before I cut another bite of my food. "What makes you ask that?" I ask tentatively, worried that Wolf mentioned something to Celeste about the charged moment where I bared my skin to his eyes and fingers.

"He has been ignoring my calls, and I'm stopping by the shop once we're done here. Ask Dante, the only thing I hate more than being bothered is being ignored."

"Speaking of being bothered"—I toss a look at both Ava and CeCe—"weren't the two of you supposed to be in Connecticut until tomorrow?" While the main reason for my refusal was not wanting to feel like a fifth wheel in their group, another reason was the timeline and my eight o'clock class on Monday morning.

"We made Grey and Dante bring us home right after the event yesterday. There was no way in hell we were going to delay getting to you more than necessary if you needed us." My body warms, and my lungs compress, emotion clogging

121

my being. I've never had this level of friendship.

Never.

"You didn't have to do that."

"Yes, we abso-fucking-lutely did. Now, eat your French toast. I have to get going soon."

I look down at the piece of sweetened, fried bread on my fork and wince. If she's going to Wolf's shop after this, there's a very real possibility that he'll mention the tattoo on my back and the need for a cover-up. "Right, so in the spirit of friendship and in an effort to be transparent, there may be one other thing that happened. It's minuscule, microscopic, really. But worth mentioning, all the same." I feel Ava and Celeste's eyes on me as I continue to avoid their gazes. "So, I may have gotten a tattoo on my back at Royal Ink, and well, it may have come out bad. Like, grotesque, and Wolf may have seen it."

It's silent when I bring my eyes up; the shock and confusion on both their faces force me to continue my explanation. "It's not that I didn't want to tell you both that I got a tattoo, but it was something I wanted to do myself and then show you the finished product. CeCe…" I bite my lip, finally making eye contact with my friend. "Remember when I told you that I went to see Wolf about the tattoo, and he turned me away? Well, I found someone else to do it, except they didn't have a great stencil, or technique, or anything, and so I had to stop the piece before it really took shape, and now I have a bit of a sore spot on my back."

"I have so many questions, and I have no idea where to even begin," Ava whispers, abandoning her food.

"I'll start," CeCe speaks up. "How did Wolf come to see your tattoo?" Her eyes narrow as though she's waiting for a

122

confession that won't be given.

"The top I wore on Friday night; a little piece was sticking out since it's on the center of my back, and he saw the irritated skin and pressed me until I admitted what happened. He took a look at it and gave me instructions on how to properly care for it. It's better already; I don't think I'll need antibiotics. But I'm telling you because he offered one of his tattoo artists to take a look at the piece and do a cover-up so that I don't have to live with the ugliness on my skin for the rest of my life."

CeCe softens at my explanation, her posture losing its rigidity. "Good. I wanted to make sure he didn't take advantage of you."

"I don't think Wolf is capable of taking advantage of a woman." *Not that he has to*, I add silently in my head.

"You're right. Sorry."

"Did they draw a bunch of dicks on your back? Oh, or a bag of dildos?"

I whip my head to Ava and don't bother holding back the laugh that bubbles out of my throat. "What? No. I went in for butterflies to travel up my back, almost like they are in flight, but what I got is closer to a blob. There's no definition on the butterflies, and the artist kept jabbing my skin, even when the irritation became too much. When I walked out, I was told never to show my face there again."

"Can we see it?"

"Do you have to?"

"Of course not," CeCe responds immediately. "If it makes you uncomfortable, we'll never ask again." Setting my jaw, I place my fork down and stand up, turning so that my back is facing both CeCe and Ava.

Resolved to show them the extent of the damage, I brace

123

them for what they're about to see. "Don't be alarmed, I know it's bad, okay? Just look without saying anything." I lift my shirt, giving them a full view of the mess that was made on my back. Unlike a couple of days ago, the redness and swelling have gone down some, and it's no longer physically painful.

Just emotionally traumatizing.

I suck in a breath, holding it while I hear footsteps approach, examining my skin closer. Though I asked them to remain quiet, I know my friends, and I know that neither one of them has a filter on their thoughts or words. I'm not sure which one will break first, but I'm waiting for the comments regardless.

After long minutes exposing my back to them, and my nipples to the kitchen appliances, I hear Ava murmur, "Rena, they gave you four flying dicks on your back."

14

Wolf

"Fuck, man. This looks sick," my client Anthony says, pulling me in for one of those awkward-as-fuck hugs between two men with too significant of a size difference. I lightly pat him on the back, trying not to break his body.

"Glad you like it. I'll walk with you up to Aubrey, and she'll get you checked out. Remember the aftercare instructions. If anything happens, give me a call." The piece I just did, a Sailor Jerry cocktail pinup girl, is bold and bright, standing out against his pale skin. Pinups aren't my favorite thing to draw, but this one came out cool as shit.

Once we reach the receptionist's desk, I nod at Anthony and leave him with Aubrey to take care of his final payment. Like most men who come into the shop, Anthony's eyes take on an appreciative gleam the moment Aubrey's dark skin, colorful tattoos, and bright blonde dreadlocks come into view. It's almost funny when Trent growls at the guys who get a little too flirty with his fiancée.

"Hey, beautiful. How's it going?" Anthony comments, his voice taking on a grating tone. "Is that a new tattoo?" He waves toward her body, offering up a bullshit excuse for checking her chest out.

"Nope, still the same sternum tattoo you commented on last time, Tony. You owe five-fifty for today. How are you planning on paying?" Though Aubrey's voice is sweet, her eyes communicate that she will disembowel him if he makes another comment about her or her appearance.

"Are you sure? It looks—"

"Eh, Tony. Keep your eyes off her body, you fuck," Trent calls out, cutting him off mid-sentence.

"I've got it covered, Trenton," Aubrey sighs, though there's no annoyance behind her words.

"I know, baby, but you shouldn't have to. Fucking pigs," Trent murmurs loud enough for the rest of the shop to hear him. While the tattoo stations are set up in private rooms, some of the artists use the consultation tables and illuminated drafting tables in the center of the shop to meet with clients or draw out their work. Though Trent is my right-hand man, second only to Aubrey, and has a good setup in his private room, he likes keeping an eye on Aubs.

Unlike Trent, who can't seem to help himself when it comes to defending his woman's honor, I don't step in unless Aubrey asks me to. Not because I don't value her safety or protection but because I've seen Aubrey flay a man's pride with an effortless combination of words, and I trust her to de-escalate a situation. Plus, I trained her on self-defense, so she could easily kick someone's ass if they get out of line.

Anthony must sense that he's on the verge of a takedown and on the fringes of both Aubrey and Trent's shit lists because he thrusts his card out at her and throws a wad of cash at me before running out of the shop.

126

"God, watching them shit themselves never gets old." Trent laughs, shaking his head like it's the funniest shit he's ever witnessed.

"Trenton Phillips, stop bothering me when I'm with clients. I swear to you, I will tell your mother that you are being a jackass."

"Baby, he was ogling you like a fucking piece of meat. You wanted me to sit on my ass while he sexualized my fiancée?"

"I am capable of handling the occasional pervert that comes in here without losing the shop clients. If I need help, I'll ask for it, but I'm not weak, and I'm not a damsel, so don't treat me like one."

I bite the inside of my cheek, holding back the laugh that threatens to break out at Aubrey's chastising.

"Oh, don't look so smug over there, you redheaded pussy. I saw you inching closer to that twat."

"Don't know what you're talking about, man; don't bring me into your shit."

"Fuck off. You used to do the same shit with that harpy, Kelly."

I sober real fucking quick at the mention of my ex-girlfriend and the memory of our encounter on Friday night. I've had so much other shit on my mind since Friday that I almost forgot about the training session with Gage and Jedd. I shouldn't have been surprised that Kelly was there, filming the entire session for her dumbass social media followers and giving away all of Gage's weaknesses.

Honestly, that shit made my day when he realized she was live streaming his instruction and giving his opponent an advantage for his upcoming fight.

"I don't want to talk about her."

"She still with that prick, Gage?"

"What fucking part of 'I don't want to talk about her' don't you get?"

"Dude, calm down. You seem a little frazzled. When's the last time you had some company?" Trent wiggles his eyebrows before wincing as a tape dispenser is thrown across the shop, right at his head.

"We have clients here, you imbecile," Aubrey hisses, looking around to determine if anyone heard Trent. "God, I am marrying a man-child."

"Thanks for defending my honor, Aubs. I don't think anyone overheard him, not that you should be concerned with my sex life, you freak." I glare at him. "I'm your boss."

"Go. Outside, now," Aubrey orders, pointing to the side door of the shop, where employees take their smoke breaks and breathers when shit gets too heavy inside.

"Fine, I need a smoke anyway." Trent walks over to Aubrey and plants a kiss on her cheek before turning toward the door. "Come on, you grizzly. Let's give Aubrey time to recover from her heart attack."

"Not funny, Trenton," Aubrey grumbles, turning back to the computer and pressing down on the keys in a furious rhythm.

"She loves me, I swear," Trent whispers as he walks past me, clapping me on the back as he goes. Unlike with my clients, I don't bother curtailing my strength, and I punch him on the arm as I turn to the back door. "Ow, fuck, you beast. You're lucky that's not my drawing arm."

"C'mon, let's go before Audrey tries to fire you." In my head, I add *again* because Aubrey's favorite pastime is firing Trent and forcing him to make it up to her. It's a weird game of foreplay, but it seems to work for their relationship. Who

128

the fuck am I to judge? My only relationships have ended in breakups or her leaving me for another guy on my team.

I follow Trent through the side door and sit on the picnic bench while he lights up.

"So, where were you on Friday night?"

I clear my throat, surprised by the question. "I had Jedd's promotional shit."

He pulls in a drag from his cigarette and holds it in, releasing the smoke slowly so it wafts around him. Trent's eyes are on me when he takes another long inhale. "And after?"

My jaw locks, and I debate how much I should tell him. "I had to help my cousin out. How did you know I did something after?"

"Aubs and I stopped by, figured you'd need some friends there since that viper and lug nut would be at the party. Jedd told us you went to help some girl."

Some girl? Calling Serena a girl would be a disservice; she may be six years younger than me, but she has an eerie maturity, a wry sense of humor, and a face that deserves to be painted and hung in a fucking museum.

"C's friend had a problem and needed someone to get her. It was no big deal," I lie as a montage of our interactions plays in my head. I see her bare back and the bruises and scrapes on her body. The mental image of her abused form reignites the anger that had dulled to a simmer. "She got manhandled by some asshole at a party and closed herself in the bathroom. I checked to make sure she wasn't harmed and brought her back to her place."

Trent's eyes narrow at my words. "Someone put his hands on this chick? Did you fuck him up?"

"Don't call her a 'chick.' And no, she asked me to take her

129

home, and I never got the chance to see him."

"Fuck, McCleery, you should have beat his ass."

"And traumatize a house full of college students and a woman who needed to get out of that shithole as quickly as possible? Nah, as much as I would have liked to beat his ass, her needing to leave was more important." I don't mention how I nearly broke down the fucking door to get inside because I was petrified of what I'd find in that bathroom. I also don't mention how good her skin felt beneath my hands or how the feel of her lips lingered on my skin for a goddamn day.

"You're going soft, you—oh, shit." Trent drops his cigarette and stubs it out with his foot, grinding it down until the filter separates from the paper. I follow his line of sight and grimace as Celeste and her boyfriend approach the shop. Celeste doesn't realize we're out here until Dante nudges her arm and points in my direction.

"Why the hell are you outside? It's like five degrees out here," she yells from across the lot.

"Celeste, it's forty degrees."

"I am not talking to you outside in the arctic tundra, Wolf. We'll meet you inside," she says before disappearing into the shop.

"Man, let's go inside before she tries to shank me," Trent murmurs, shivering as he pulls his leather jacket closed. "She threatened to shove cigarettes down my throat if I kept smoking, and I'm scared she's going to do it."

"Fucking wimp. She's five feet."

"She's terrifying," he mutters over his shoulder as he opens the door and heads back into the warmth of the building. Instead of heading back to the drafting table where his work-in-progress sits, he waves hello to my cousin and power walks to his room like a fitness instructor from the eighties.

"I told you he was scared of you." Aubrey laughs, following the path Trent took to his room.

Celeste shrugs off Aubrey's words as though they don't phase her. "It's not my fault I have bigger balls than him."

"Red, trust me, you don't have balls. I would have seen them. Now, a pretty little—" Celeste covers his mouth before he can continue, and I'm grateful. I would have had to lay him out if he had said a single word about my cousin's fucking anatomy.

"Dante Nicholas Camaro, watch your freaking mouth," she scolds in a voice that is both annoyed and amused.

Dante mumbles against her hand, and I don't even want to know what shit he's saying. "Yeah, watch your fucking mouth, Camaro, or I'll kill you with my bare hands."

"Hey, no threatening my boyfriend, Wolfie. Besides, people are starting to stare. Can both of you keep your voices down before they start filming?"

"I threaten him when he says stupid shit," I grumble before surveying the floor. Celeste is right, and I take in the people staring at us like we're performers giving a show. "Fine. C, fuckhead, let's continue this in my room." I turn on my heel and walk across the floor, waving at a few of the artists as I pass.

Once I step over the threshold of my private room, I go to my drawing table and sit, allowing the green wingback chairs to remain available for Celeste and Dante. Dante seems to realize my intent because he walks to the corner of the room and settles in one of the oversized chairs, eying me warily as Celeste paces across the hardwood.

"Why are you pacing, Red?" Dante asks. "You're going to

give me motion sickness if I have to keep whipping my head back and forth to look at your ass."

"Watch it," I growl at the same time that Celeste's footsteps falter. She glares at her boyfriend, mumbling obscenities under her breath before turning back to me. "I'm pacing because I want to know everything that happened on Friday night, but I also want to thank you for going to make sure Serena was okay. I'm just trying to prioritize my thoughts so that I say and ask the right things."

I roll my eyes. "Sit, C," I command and wait for Celeste to sit before continuing. "Nothing happened on Friday other than I went to that stupid-as-fuck party, picked up Serena, and drove her home."

Her finger darts out, pointing at me like a nun with a ruler in Sunday school. "See, I knew you would lie."

I raise my hand, running it over my head, and wish that I had hair to pull onto so that I could vent my frustrations. "I'm not lying."

"You are. You went into her apartment. You cleaned her scrapes." Celeste pauses, lowering her voice until I have to lean forward to hear her. "You saw the flying dicks on her back and offered to have someone fix them for her."

I scowl at the reminder of the busted tattoo on her skin and the images that mar the perfection of her back.

I shudder at that thought; the perfection of her back? What the fuck am I even thinking?

"What was I supposed to do, drop her at her apartment door while she was bleeding and bruised after pretending to lock herself in a goddamn bathroom? I may be a fighter, but I'm not a fucking monster. Of course I helped, and thank fuck I did because that girl had expired hydrogen peroxide from

2019 in her cabinet and probably would have used it to treat her wounds."

"Woman," C says gently.

"What?"

"You called her a girl. She's not a girl; she's a woman. You have this idea in your head that she's a child, but she isn't."

"I know she's not a fucking child, Celeste. Fucking hell, one look at her is all you need to know she isn't a child."

"So, what you're saying is, you think she's pretty?" Dante asks from the corner like a moron.

"I swear to God, I will kill him if he doesn't stop talking."

"No, you won't. All that is fine, but the part I don't understand is how you saw her back tattoo or how you came to offer her a difficult-to-get, highly coveted appointment with one of your artists when you have a yearslong waitlist for each tattooist."

I sigh, done with this conversation and the line of questioning. "Because I couldn't leave a beautiful *woman*," I emphasize, "with a tattoo of flying cocks for the rest of her life. Because the only thing that should grace her skin is a beautiful piece designed with care and consideration, not one stabbed out like a prison tat in exchange for ramen noodles." Shaking my head, I continue, "What do you want from me, C? The end result is the same because I know damn well that the moment you saw the monstrosity on her back, you would have called me up and asked for a favor to fix your friend. I got in front of it and offered up my team's skills on my terms, provided that she's fully healed and mentally ready for a cover-up."

C stands from the chair and walks toward me, slowly approaching like I'm a caged animal, and she's a trainer worried about getting bit. "Wolf, I have to ask you a question."

133

"What, Celeste?" My voice sounds resigned.

"Do you like her?"

I choke on the saliva in my throat. Like her? I don't fucking know her other than how she smells like an unorthodox combination of serenity and sin, has a fire buried underneath her adherence to societal expectations and social pressure, and looks disgustingly like the Sailor Jerry pinup I just did on Anthony.

I didn't intend for the drawing to look like Serena, but it happened and unnerved me the entire goddamn time.

"I don't know her, and she's got too much left to figure out."

"I forgot how old you are, you troll," C comments, rolling her eyes to accentuate her annoyance. "You're less than six years older than us. Stop acting like you grew up in a different generation."

"What do you want me to say, C?" I shrug, holding out my hands in defeat. "You want me to sit here and say that I don't think she's beautiful when we both know that's a lie? I'm not ignorant, nor am I blind. But nothing is happening, so stop pushing your matchmaking agenda on me when I neither want nor need your interference."

"She is an adult."

"Okay," I agree. "That still doesn't change anything."

"So, you view her the same way you do Ava and her sisters?"

I rear back, disgusted by the comparison. I've known Ava and her sisters since they were knobby-kneed kids who raised hell on the playground. They're my de facto cousins through Celeste, and I see them as an extension of my family. To view them as anything else feels incestuous. "Fuck no, I don't view Serena the same as Ava. I've known Ava since she was five. It's two unrelated views."

134

Celeste's expression transforms from contemplative to sly, and I cringe at the smirk that breaks out on her face. "Whatever you say, Wolfie. But a word to the wise: if you hurt her, I'll put you in a headlock and laugh as you lose oxygen."

"Did you not hear a single word I just said?"

"Oh, she heard it, McCleery. But all the same, you're fucked." Dante laughs, shaking his head like it's the funniest thing he's ever heard.

Fucking prick.

15

Serena

Unknown: Hey, how are you?

I glance at my phone, confused by the unknown number and question that arrives in the middle of my linguistic theory class. The class, which is one of the most intensive I have ever taken, requires my full attention, and I have more notebooks dedicated to the structural properties of human language and the principles of universal grammar than I care to admit. And we're not even at mid-term yet.

What I should do is put my phone back in my bag and devote my attention to the instruction on phonemes, graphemes, and morphemes. But, while I may be book smart, I am abundantly curious and can't resist finding out who the sender is.

Serena: Who is this? How did you get my number?

I bite down on my lip, waiting for the response. Minutes pass as I drown out the droll lesson and stare at my phone in anticipation. I'm just about to put it away when an incoming message pops up on my screen.

Unknown: It's Wolf McCleery. You didn't save my number?

I squeak, dropping my phone in my surprise, and feel the incinerating stare of my seatmate as I try to right myself.

"Are you okay?" Heather, another junior, whispers, handing me the pen I knocked over.

"Yep," I yelp, my voice so high-pitched that it's unrecognizable.

"Well, keep it together; the last thing I want is Forester paying us more attention than necessary. She's like a predator hunting for prey, and I'd rather not be on her radar." I nod my agreement because she isn't wrong. Dr. Susan Forester is a leader in the linguistics field and the most terrifying person I have ever met. But she's terrifying in a subtle way, like a shark mistaken for a dolphin in the Atlantic Ocean. She looks like everyone's favorite brooch-wearing grandma: tiny and unassuming, but the minute she opens her mouth, you know you are in the presence of extreme genius. She's kind, ridiculously smart, and takes no bullshit or interruptions in her class. The fact that my phone is out during her lecture hall is enough for Miss Manners to pen an entire article about my lack of professionalism.

Glancing back at my phone, I type eight different messages, continuously deleting the words until I settle on a simple update on how I feel. I ignore his question about saving his number; I deleted his contact information after my solo visit to Ink & Needle.

Serena: I feel fine, thanks.

Certain that there's no more expected conversation, I shove my phone into my backpack and return my attention to the front of the room, where Forester continues to speak as though my entire being hasn't just been shaken from the impact of two short text messages.

With my phone in my bag and complicated subject matter, it's easy to throw myself into her words and compartmentalize the last five minutes.

"Who can tell me what a phoneme is?" Forester asks, looking around the room at the sea of hands, all desperate to impress her.

A girl three rows in front of me, Bethany, waves her hand so violently that I think she might fall out of her seat if she isn't called on within the next two seconds.

"Bethany, yes?"

"A phoneme is the smallest unit of sound. Like a syllable."

I cringe at what I'm about to do, but the academic in me can't help it. Also, Bethany is a jerk who asked if I was in the right place on my first day of freshman year. In every class I've had with her, she's never failed to make me feel like a freak because of my age. I raise my hand.

Dr. Forester nods her head at me, a silent gesture for me to respond. "It's the smallest unit of sound to make a meaningful difference to a word. The word 'cat,' for example, has three separate phonemes, /k/-/a/-/t/, though it only has one syllable. The two aren't mutually exclusive."

I blush as soon as the words leave my mouth and sink in my chair, embarrassed at the attention the room is now paying to me and the glare that Bethany shoots. I'm not trying to be a know-it-all, but sometimes I just can't help it.

"Thank you, Ms. Castillo. Now, who can tell me what a morpheme is?" Dr. Forester continues, not paying my flushed cheeks any attention. I look up and see Bethany eyeing me with disgust, a snarl on her face.

"You've done it now, Serena," Heather whispers, leaning over to speak directly into my ear. "Maybe don't eviscerate

138

the queen bee during class next time."

"I didn't eviscerate her; I just corrected her. It's not my fault she was wrong. If it wasn't me, Forester would have said something."

The lesson continues in the same manner, with Dr. Forester asking us questions to assess our knowledge and verify that we read the assigned chapters in the book. As soon as she wraps up the lecture, with external assignments tossed like confetti, and dismisses the class, I run out of the hall, intent to avoid every person who was just in that class. Once I step into the hallway, reality crashes back into me, and I grip my bag, eager to check my phone. I make it out of the building before I pause long enough to pull the device out of my backpack. I'm surprised to see not one but three texts from Wolf in the last hour I've been occupied with class.

Wolf (1:34 PM): Good. Happy to hear it.

Wolf (1:47 PM): How are the cuts on your elbows doing? Did they get infected? What about your back? Is that monstrosity feeling any better?

Wolf (2:32 PM): Fuck, sorry, you must be sleeping or something.

I shake my head at his last text, confused at his assumption. Ignoring the cold February air, I quickly type out a reply.

Serena: Sorry, I was in a class and needed to focus. It's almost three in the afternoon on a Tuesday. Why would you assume that I'm sleeping?

I hit send and start my walk across campus, keeping my head down and arms crossed as I hurry against the cold wind biting my face. My phone vibrates minutes later, and I resist the urge to check it until I'm back in the sanctuary of my apartment.

I'm not watching where I'm going, walking on autopilot and so engrossed in the message burning my phone that I'm shocked when I slam into a body and stumble back. Thankfully, I regain my footing before I fall. Glancing up, I'm shocked to see two familiar faces looking at me.

"Serena, we need to stop meeting like this," Jack murmurs, reaching out a hand to steady me. I offer a tight smile before turning to face my stepsister. "Oh, this is my lab partner, Marina. She's a freshman but wickedly smart."

"Hi."

"Hi, sis," Marina says slyly, a smirk breaking out along her features. I bite my tongue, bracing myself for what she's about to do or say.

Jack looks back and forth between me and Marina, trying to figure out what he just inadvertently stepped into. "You two know each other?"

I open my mouth to respond, but Marina's voice rings out. "She's from my dad's other family."

I roll my eyes at her explanation and scoff. "I think you mean I'm your stepfather's biological daughter from his first marriage, Marina. Anyway, good seeing you both." Dipping my head down, I walk around them, moving my legs as fast as I can in the direction of my apartment building.

The sound of rapid footsteps and a shouted, "Serena, hey, wait up," makes me stop in my tracks. Turning, I see Jack approaching and stop walking. At this point, hypothermia is sure to set in. "I'm sorry about that. I didn't realize you two were stepsisters."

I shrug, making it seem as though it's not a big deal. I barely know this man; he doesn't deserve to know anything about my personal life.

140

"I asked Meg for your number, but she said she needed to speak with you before giving it to me. How are you feeling? How are your bruises? Do you, uh, think maybe you'd want to hang out sometime?"

I jerk back in surprise at the rapid-fire questions he just asked and move my gaze from Jack's face to Marina's scowl. It shouldn't make me happy to see her so annoyed, but I am. "What about Marina?"

"Marina?" Jack questions, shaking his head. "She's just my lab partner, and we're walking from our practical to class. I think she's dating someone in one of the other fraternities. So, what do you say?"

I gnaw on my bottom lip, taking in his handsome face and sandy brown hair, before lowering my eyes to the rest of his body. Though he's bundled in a coat, I know that he's lean and muscular from our encounter last weekend.

"I'll let Meg know that she can give you my number," I whisper against the cold. "It was nice seeing you, Jack." The smile that erupts on Jack's face is sweet, and I feel the same fluttering that I felt on Friday night low in my stomach. It's not the same rampage as when Wolf pays attention to me, but it's a simmer, something that could maybe be coaxed into a boil.

"That's good, Serena. Real good. I'll talk to you later then?" I nod and turn around, resuming my trek through the cold to my apartment. The quick walk has my mind reeling over Marina, Jack, and the message from Wolf that I have yet to read.

—

Once I step through the lobby, I relax my shoulders and breathe in the warmth of the building. In almost no time, I'm out of the elevator and walking through my front door, peeling off my coat and throwing it on the back of an accent chair on my way to the kitchen.

When the electric tea kettle is on and my tea mug is prepped, I unlock my phone and read Wolf's latest message.

Wolf: I don't know. Isn't that what college kids do? I've never been to college, but I imagine it's just people getting fucked up, sleeping until one in the afternoon, and buying Costco-sized boxes of condoms.

I snort at his description of college life, snapping a picture and attaching it to my message.

Serena: <attachment> This is my current "college life" setup. On my third cup of mint tea today after walking in the cold.

Wolf: <attachment> I'm on Earl Grey with lemon. Try not to get too crazy over there, princess.

I begin to type out a response when another text comes through from Wolf.

Wolf: But you didn't answer my question. How are your elbows and back? Healing well?

I roll my eyes and huff, annoyed at the big brother feel this conversation is taking.

Serena: I'm fine. Both are healing, and my back doesn't hurt anymore; no antibiotics needed.

Wolf: You sure about that? It was pretty bad when I saw it on Friday night.

"You've got to be kidding me," I mumble to myself, pressing down hard on my screen as the water starts to boil inside the kettle.

142

Serena: Should I send you a picture to show I'm not lying?

Text bubbles appear and disappear on the phone before a message comes through.

Wolf: I'm going to pretend like you didn't just ask me that shit. I want you in the shop by Saturday so that I can take a look at your back and have Sloan meet with you.

Furrowing my brow, I puzzle over why he seemed annoyed with me in his last text and why it took him so long to respond. Reading back my words, I'm horrified by the insinuation of what I just asked.

"Why can't I just be a functional human being when speaking to a man, God? Why do you hate me so freaking much?" I ask.

Serena: That's not what I meant, and you know it. But fine, sir. I'll call Aubrey tomorrow and set up something for the cover-up.

Wolf: Call now.

I roll my eyes at his authoritative text. I may be deeply mortified by my undeniable skill at putting my foot in my mouth, but he is the grumpiest human being I have ever encountered. And I'm friends with his cousin, so that's saying a lot.

Serena: Yes, sir.

His response is immediate.

Wolf: You're skating on thin fucking ice, princess.

Swiping up from our chat, I set my phone down and pour the hot water over the fresh mint leaves I picked from my small window box. I may not have any grass, but there are some things I refuse to buy, like mint and chamomile, since I drink herbal tea so frequently.

Setting my mug aside to steep, I google Ink and Needle and

143

click on the phone number, placing it on speakerphone before I set it down next to my mug.

"Ink and Needle, Aubrey speaking."

I clear my throat, suddenly nervous at the prospect of this conversation. "Yes, hi, Aubrey. This is Serena Castillo, Celeste Downing's friend. Wolf asked me to call and—"

Aubrey cuts me off with a gentle laugh. "Hi Serena, I was expecting your call. Just give me a minute to pull up Wolf and Sloan's schedule for the rest of this week, okay?" I hear clicking in the background, the sound calming me down. "Alright, do you have a day or time that works best?"

"Uh, I guess Friday afternoon or Saturday morning? My schedule is pretty heavy with classes and coursework during the week, so those probably work best for me if their schedules can accommodate it."

"Alright, let me see," Aubrey mumbles, though I suspect that it's more to herself than to me. "Okay, they can fit you in on Friday at seven. Does that sound good?"

"Yes, yes, that sounds good." I pause, clearing my throat. "That works well."

Aubrey laughs again, a light, tinkling sound that seems to emit genuine joy. "Great, we'll see you then. Oh, and Serena," she says, "I'm happy you're coming back. Wolf is the best at what he does, and if something needs to be fixed or covered up, no one is more talented than him."

"Oh, no. He's not doing the piece, just inspecting it to make sure it's healing. That's why I'm meeting with Sloan, too."

There's no sound on the other end, and I glance down at my phone to make sure I didn't somehow hang up. Tapping on the screen, I see that the call is still connected.

"Sure, sure," she finally responds. "See you on Friday, Serena.

I'm really looking forward to it."

I hang up, puzzled by her parting comments.

Wolf:

Sir. She called me fucking sir, and my dick got hard like a fucking loser getting a boner over some girl he met on the internet who claims she's a five-foot-nine blonde with fake tits, but in actuality is some guy named Chad living in his mom's basement. I'm disgusted with myself and more than a little turned on at the images in my head that a title like "sir" is accompanied by.

Sick, twisted, perverted old man.

But, like a glutton for punishment, I can't help but reach out to her again after I see her name pop up in my appointment calendar.

Wolf: I saw you made the appointment. Good.

Serena: Like you gave me any choice?

A small laugh escapes my mouth at her words. She's right; I didn't give her a choice. But then again, she didn't fight too hard. I guess neither one of us wants her to walk around with dicks on her back for the rest of her life.

Wolf: I'm a professional. I know when something is wrong or poorly executed, and it's my job to fix it.

Her reply comes minutes later, and I can feel her quiet, understated sass seeping through the phone. Unlike the overt pain-in-the-ass qualities my cousin and Ava possess, Serena is nearly soundless in her sarcasm and humor, a foil to my cousin and her best friend that probably serves to ground them when they initially seek murder and mayhem. I'll never tell it to Celeste, but the first thing I noticed about Serena

145

when she walked into the shop with the two of them was how little space she took up and the force of her small presence. She's an anchor, a calming agent, a fucking balm.

I look at the message Serena just sent, and another laugh breaks free. Add funny to the list of her attributes, too.

Serena: You're not an officer, doctor, or lawyer. So, no. You're a nosy artist who can't take no for an answer.

Wolf: You're right. And you're a woman with a fucked-up tattoo who needs my team's help. Don't be late on Friday.

16

Serena

The days leading up to today have been a lesson in patience and anxiety. It's not that I'm nervous to go to the tattoo shop and see a certain red-headed giant; I'm excited. And that excitement is making me anxious because I know I shouldn't be excited about it since he has told me, in no uncertain terms, that he is not interested in me and to keep my distance.

I'm sick of looking desperate, and before I even exit my car, I resolve that I will not pay attention to Wolf outside of the normal client-artist relationship. Squaring my shoulders, I slam my car door with a loud squeak and make a note to myself to bring it into the shop to be looked at. Unlike my second visit, I don't have post-pottery attire on, choosing instead to skip my class and look presentable instead of like a fugitive on the run.

Stepping into the brightly lit shop, I'm immediately greeted by Aubrey and her contagious smile.

"Serena, hey. It's great to see you. How is everything?" Aubrey rounds the receptionist's desk and pulls me into a hug like we're longtime friends and not acquaintances who have met twice.

"Hi, Aubrey. I'm well, how are you?" I reply, returning her embrace.

"I'm great. I know you're here for a cover-up piece, and though I have no idea what ink you need camouflaged, just know that our team is the best at what they do. I promise you, whatever needs fixing will be fixed."

"Thanks, Aubrey."

"Call me 'Aubs,' all my friends do." She pauses, winking at me, before continuing, "Okay, first, give me your coat; I'll hang it in the employee closet. Wolf is waiting for you with Sloan in his room. You know the one, right? You can just head on back there and give me a yell if you need anything."

I slip off my jacket and smile at Aubrey's encouragement and easygoing nature. From what little CeCe has told me, Aubrey is friendly unless you get on her bad side, and I can believe it. I think the power behind her hug squished some of my organs together.

I approach Wolf's space slowly as though there's something to fear on the other side of the threshold. Wolf must sense my approach because, suddenly, he's standing before me with his arms crossed and a raised eyebrow.

"Why are you dragging ass across the shop floor?"

Clearing my throat, I shake my head, feigning ignorance. "I don't know what you're talking about."

"Sure, you don't."

I swallow against the surge of attraction that bubbles in my stomach at his appearance. In a black Henley with his sleeves rolled up to expose his tattooed arms, black jeans, and heavy black Doc Martens, he looks lethal. I've never been into the *Dog the Bounty Hunter* look before, but there's a first time for everything, I guess.

Don't act like a moron, Serena, I remind myself. Mentally slapping my face, I skirt around him and perch myself on one of the wingback chairs next to the bookshelf. "I don't."

In the opposite corner of the room, standing next to his drafting table is one of the most badass-looking women I have ever seen. Draped in a black leather jacket, cut-out black jeans, and a backward ball cap, the woman is, I assume, Sloan, and I am immediately intimidated. If Wolf's presence sends shock waves of lust through my system, this woman looks like she could kick my ass and make me apologize for the inconvenience.

I take in the swirls of black and gray ink on her neck and am mesmerized by the dichotomy of masculinity and femininity that she presents; her makeup is simple, just a swipe of mascara and fire-engine red lipstick, and her hair is silvery blonde. Her chunky boots and black leather cuffs around her wrists look like she took all normative gender ideologies and repurposed them to fit her aesthetic. She looks so cool—an adjective that barely grazes her vibe. Coupled with an obvious confidence that I can only hope to one day obtain, I think I have a girl crush on her.

"Hey, you must be Serena," she supplies, her voice a deep rasp that further cements her appeal.

"Yes, uhm, hi. You must be Sloan."

She offers a wide smile and nods, instantly setting me at ease. "I am. Wolf said you have a tattoo that needs some covering up. Do you mind if we take a look?"

"Wolf is right here and can speak for himself," Wolf grumbles, sounding like a petulant child unused to being cast aside. "I want to make sure that her skin is fully healed first before

149

we start with anything."

"Sorry, boss. You know I get excited for cover-ups." She turns to me and winks. "I love getting my hands on pretty skin and making it even hotter."

"Oh, I, uhm. Right." I stumble over my words, unsure how to respond.

"Alright, Sloan, calm down. Serena hasn't agreed to anything just yet."

Sloan doesn't answer him, just rolls her eyes. "Anyway, why don't you lay down on your stomach so we can take a look at what you've got going on back there?" She gestures toward the tattoo table, already flat and prepped for my mortification.

I look between Sloan, Wolf, and the table and grimace, knowing that they won't like what they're about to find under my shirt. Even though Wolf has seen the tattoo, it's not pretty, a blemish that showcases my impulse and stupidity and an endless source of embarrassment. Clearing my throat, I look at Sloan before explaining, "Just don't be alarmed, okay? I know it doesn't look good, and it's nowhere near ready for more work, but"—I cut my gaze to Wolf—"it is better than it was, so it's healing. Slowly, but it's healing."

"It's fine, Serena; I've seen it all in my time here. Whatever it is, we'll help you make it beautiful," Sloan offers, softening her voice from a sexy rasp to a deep, placating tone. I return her smile and walk to the tattoo bench, easing down until my body is flat. Reaching down, I grip the hem of my shirt and inch it up my body, exposing the skin of my back slowly, like a strip tease, except there's nothing sexy or alluring about this.

"Oh shit," Sloan whispers, and I wince.

"Shut up, Sloan."

"Sorry, boss, but—"

"Enough," Wolf commands, cutting her off before she can continue verbalizing her thoughts.

I squeeze my eyes shut and will their words not to affect me, continuing to expose my skin until my shirt is bunched under my bra. I refuse to turn my head; instead, I burrow my face into the cool leather of the table and breathe in the antiseptic that lingers in the room. But even though I'm not looking, I can feel their presence behind me and the warmth of their bodies as they approach.

"Your skin is better than it was, but you still have a way to go, Serena."

"I know," I mumble into the leather, mentally flipping off Wolf for stating the obvious.

"Did you see a doctor?"

"No."

"Are you going to?"

I pause for a moment, considering his question. "Probably not."

"Fucking hell," he murmurs, and I can picture him dragging a hand through his buzzed hair, emphasizing his frustration. Though, I'm not sure if he's frustrated with me, the tattoo, or the slowness of the healing.

Metaphorically pulling up my big girl panties, I turn my face to look at them. Sloan's expression is, in a word, comical; with her lip between her teeth, she's smeared her bright red lipstick over her teeth.

Wolf just looks livid. However, he always looks livid.

"Do you mind if I take a picture of your back? It'll help with the sketch," Sloan asks as she pulls out her phone.

"No problem."

I lie still, allowing the click of the phone's camera to fill the silence of the room.

"Okay, perfect. I've gotten what I need. I'm going to head out now. It was great meeting you, Serena. I'm so excited to get started."

"Me, too. Thank you, Sloan."

With that, she leaves, softly sliding the door closed behind her, leaving me alone with Wolf.

17

Wolf

"Why didn't you fucking tell me that you were still red and swollen," I seethe, pissed that she came into this shop with a red and splotchy back, as though she was fucking ready to be worked on.

"You told me to come, basically demanded it, so I came. My God, you give me whiplash with your questions," she retorts, sounding as exasperated as I feel.

"No, you don't get to have an attitude with me, princess. I'm not the one who fucked up your back or convinced you that a back full of flying cocks would look good. I'm the fucker set on fixing this shit."

"I didn't ask you to," she erupts, sitting up and sliding her legs over the side of the table until she's seated before me, indignant and beautiful. "Listen, I appreciate the help you gave me the other night, and I'm thankful for your hyper-fixation on my tattoo, but do not, for a single second, think that you bossing me around or treating me like a child is okay, Wolf. I may be younger than you, but I'm not an idiot. Your warped belief of age as a sign of maturity is inaccurate and baseless. I may be nineteen, but I have lived a thousand lives, and I won't allow you to make me feel as though I owe *you* a favor when you're the one insistent on me being here and invading each other's space. This entire thing is your fault because you refused to listen to me when I came into this room and asked for the tattoo I received at Royal Ink. Albeit it's an ugly tattoo, but at least they attempted it."

I stare at her in disbelief, processing her words. "Oh, fuck no, you're not going to blame me for the cocks floating on your back. You were unsure and undecided when you came into 'this room' and asked for butterflies on your back, and I don't fucking tattoo people who aren't sure of what they want. So fine, paint me as the fucking villain, but know that you are the one who went to a shit-hole shop for a tattoo. You're lucky you didn't get hepatitis from the fucking needle."

"Stop being vulgar."

"Vulgar? You haven't seen vulgar," I growl, leaning forward until I'm in her space, speaking directly into her face. I would never put myself in this position, a giant looming over a woman in my shop, but Serena is my goddamn downfall.

"You know what? I'm leaving." She pushes against my body with her dainty hand, and I allow it, moving as she exerts pressure on my chest. "And don't you dare think about stopping me."

"Fine."

"Fine," she grinds out, pulling down on her shirt as she moves past me. "When you get the stick out of your ass, I'll be back. And if you never do? Well, then I'll find someone else to fix this because I sure as hell won't ask you." She pulls open the pocket door with an aggression that threatens to tear the wood from the hinges. She shudders at the sound of

154

the wood rattling against the frame.

I watch her as she storms out, stomping across the shop and pulling the door open like it's done her a personal injustice.

"Fucking hell," I murmur, not for the first time tonight.

"That looks like it went well," sounds from next to me, and I turn to see Aubrey watching Serena pull out of the parking lot in her piece of shit car.

"She's fucking unreasonable. I asked her why she didn't tell me that her tattoo was still infected, and she lost it."

"Did you ask or demand? Because it's a big difference, Wolf."

"Same shit," I mumble, knowing that my delivery probably wasn't the greatest.

"Oh, Wolf. There is much to teach you."

"Go schedule some clients, Aubrey. I don't have time for this shit." Her laughter follows me as I turn my back on her and walk into my private space, sliding the door shut behind me.

"What the fuck," I say into the space, glancing down at the table Serena just occupied. I try not to reminisce on the smooth, golden skin that framed the infected tattoo or the fullness of her lips as she yelled at me for dictating to her, an accusation I strongly fucking disagree with.

What a goddamn shit show.

A knock on my door breaks me from my musings, and I turn to see Sloan sauntering in.

"Hey, boss, have a minute?" She doesn't pause before continuing, "So, I was thinking, I can take the flying penises and transform them into a bunch of cool watercolor hot air balloons flying through the air. I think that if I pair it with some background—"

"No," I cut her off. "I'm doing the tattoo."

155

"Wait, what?"

"I'm doing the cover-up," I repeat, slowing down my words to cement their meaning.

I'm met with silence. Looking up, I see Sloan twisting her lips as though she's debating if she should verbalize her next words.

"Just fucking say it." I sigh, waiting for the accusation that I know is coming.

"Fine. If you knew you were just going to do it yourself, why would you bring me in in the first place? It seems unnecessary and kind of mean, boss."

"I made the decision five minutes ago, Sloan. I'm not letting you put fucking hot air balloons on that woman's body."

"They would have been sick as fuck."

"I'm sure, but you're still not doing it."

"Wet blanket," Sloan mutters under her breath.

"Go before I fire you."

"I'm your best artist; you'd never."

Sighing, I don't bother correcting her statement because she's right; Sloan is my most versatile and consistent artist and can tattoo watercolor, new school, and American traditional as though she's a founder of each technique. She must know that she's got me by the dick because she turns and runs off, sliding the door closed behind her.

Glancing up at the clock, I note that it's been thirty minutes since Serena left; she should be home by now. Pulling out my phone, I shoot off a text before I'm able to second-guess it.

Wolf: You make it home okay?

It's lame, but watching her walk out of my shop and drive with rage in her eyes is something I never want to fucking repeat. My phone buzzes in my hand, and I glance down,

156

smirking as I read Serena's text.

Serena: Are you stalking me? I just walked through my apartment doors, and I have the sudden need to call a security guard or ADT.

Wolf: No, but I'm decent at math, so I figured you'd be home by now.

Bubbles appear on the screen before they fall away, and I curse myself for the words I said to her before she left. Long minutes pass without a reply, and I mentally say, *Fuck it,* and decide to double-text her.

Wolf: Listen, I'm sorry I pissed you off, but I need to fix the piece on your back. Why don't you come in tomorrow so that I can see how we can incorporate a cover-up on your skin.

I bring my thumb up to my lip, biting on my nail as I wait for Serena's reply.

Serena: Fine. But just so we're clear, Sloan is doing my tattoo, correct?

I look past the question she asked, not willing to lie to her but also not willing to tell the truth and risk her saying, "Fuck you," and never coming back to my shop. I settle on a happy, vague medium.

Wolf: Sounds good. See you tomorrow around eleven.

Serena: I have work until two. I can be there at three.

Three it is.

18

Serena

In my former life, I must have been a terrible person because that is the only reason why I felt compelled to agree to meet with Wolf the day after he pissed me off.

I worked in the tutoring center from nine until two, and following up my day spent correcting grammar and comma splices with Wolf's shitty attitude seems like a unique form of torture. Truthfully, I'm not sure why I keep putting myself in this position, especially since he barely seems to tolerate my presence.

My phone vibrates in my cup holder, and I pick it up, smiling to myself when I see a notification for my group chat with Ava and CeCe, then frowning when I spot the text from Meg. Meg has reached out to me a few times since last weekend, but I've placated her questions with brief, vague answers that don't do much except communicate, "Leave me alone."

What happened last weekend isn't her fault; hell, it's no one's fault except for Dylan's. But I can't help but associate her with the event since she's so deeply ingrained in all of my sorority experiences. It makes me a really shitty friend.

Swiping her message, I read it quickly.

Meg: Hey, Little! Let's get lunch next week? We have a lot to catch up on. I ran into Jack at the house this morning, and he mentioned that he had seen you. Is it okay to give him your number?

I bite down on my lower lip, considering her question. On the one hand, Jack is handsome, came to my defense, and seems to be genuinely interested in me. Glancing toward the tattoo shop, I think about how different it feels when I see Wolf, like a hoard of butterflies diving and dipping and dancing beneath my skin.

But whatever I feel for Wolf, whatever attraction there is, is misplaced.

Making a decision that I'm sure I'll regret, I respond to Meg.

Serena: Hey, I'd love to get lunch next week. Yes, I ran into Jack; you can give him my number.

Swiping out of the conversation as soon as the message is sent, I open the group chat.

Ava: Serena, I have two questions. First and foremost, what are your thoughts on organ meat? A hard no or down to try? Secondly, when will you be home, and can I use your kitchen to test out a recipe for my international foods class? I'd try it at Grey's house, but he's pissing me off, and I may pull a Celeste if I have to suffer in his presence for another minute.

CeCe: Pull a Celeste?

Ava: You know, threaten to cause bodily harm to my boyfriend because he pissed me off. Not everyone can look like a cute Cabbage Patch kid when angered.

CeCe: Sod off.

Serena: C, are you watching Masterpiece Theatre again?

159

CeCe: I started watching a show on ITV. It's bloody brilliant.

Ava: Good God, you are not British.

Serena: …Anyway, as long as you don't make liver and onions, it's fine. But just a disclaimer: I probably won't eat it.

Ava: Fair enough. Does tomorrow work?

I confirm with Ava, letting both her and CeCe know that they could come at anytime tomorrow before shoving my phone in my bag and twisting my key to pull it out of the ignition. In the silence of the car, I give myself a mental pep talk that *no*, this will not result in another heated argument, and no, I will not let my temper ignite if Wolf says something stupid.

I correct myself; it's not *if* he says something stupid, but when.

"Okay, let's do this," I mutter to myself and push open my door. I have a profound sense of déjà vu as I step out of my car and look at the front of the building. Each time I've been here, I've had to mentally corral my emotions, like I'm herding a bunch of cats out of a room with wallpaper.

I don't dwell on those butterflies I'm feeling, nor do I call upon the residual anger I'm harboring from yesterday. Instead, I breathe in a deep breath and center myself, focusing on remaining calm before I start the walk across the parking lot to the entrance of the tattoo parlor.

I don't pause when I reach the door. Yanking it open, I step over the threshold like I've been here plenty of times before—which, at this point, is true enough. Aubrey pauses in her assistance of a client and furrows her brow, looking at me with confusion. "Am I hallucinating right now? Weren't you here yesterday?"

"Your boss made me come in again."

Looking from me to the customer in front of her, she holds up her hand, telling them that she'll be with them in one minute as she makes her way over to me. "So, you're the reason why he's had such a pissy attitude all day. It's all starting to make so much sense."

I shake my head, denying her words. "No, maybe he has indigestion or a stick lodged so firmly up his ass that he can't sit properly. I think those are more plausible explanations for his attitude."

"What was that about a stick up my ass, princess?"

Dammit.

"Nothing. I didn't say that," I respond before turning around and gasping at the split skin and swollenness surrounding his eye. "What happened to you?"

He arches an eyebrow and smirks his stupidly full lips. "What, you're the only one who can wear bruises on your body?"

"Spare me. Seriously, are you okay?" I reach out to touch his face before remembering where we are and who we are and dropping it back to my side. I'm no detective, but he had no marred features last night when I saw him, so something had to have occurred sometime between the time I left the shop and before I arrived.

"I'm fine, Serena. I went to the gym this morning to help my coach train one of the guys, and he got a good hit on me," he says with disgust in his voice, like he's pissed someone dared to hit him while sparring.

"Fucking Gage," Aubrey mutters behind me. "Was Kelly there again?"

"Aubrey," Wolf lashes out, whipping her name out like a

161

strike. "Don't go there."

"What? Don't talk shit about the guy your girlfriend left you for, and your coach is forcing you to help train, even though you're retiring. Don't talk about that?"

My eyes widen at her words, and though shock must be stamped across my features, Wolf looks ready to throttle Aubrey. "Ex-girlfriend and Jedd is more than a coach, and you know it, so don't talk shit about him, Aubs. Now, are you done airing my fucking secrets, or do you want to give Serena my social security number and blood type, too?"

He doesn't wait for Aubrey to respond and instead starts walking toward the back of the shop, not bothering to pause when he shouts, "Let's go, Serena," over his shoulder.

I glance over at Aubrey and note her bemused expression, as though she finds it amusing that she got under Wolf's skin enough to force him to flee her presence. "Told you he was in a pissy mood."

"It's safe to say I'm not the cause." Shaking my head, I offer Aubrey a wave and follow Wolf's path. When I enter the room, I stop just inside the door and cross my arms, waiting for him to look over to me.

"Are you going to come in or just stare at me from across the room?"

"Are you going to be nice to me, or should I walk back to the lobby to let you cool down?"

He rolls his eyes at my quip. "I'm always nice, princess. You just might not like what I have to say."

Unfolding my arms, I let them hang by my side and mutter loud enough for him to hear, "Well, your delivery sucks." I walk further into the room and stop by one of the oversized chairs, sinking until my back hits the chair.

162

"Whatever." He moves past me and grabs the hidden handle of his pocket door, sliding it closed. My heart rate picks up at the solitude we've found ourselves in, though I shouldn't be surprised. With the door open to the rest of the shop and its customers, I could pretend that my being here didn't affect me and had no bearing on my mental state. But with that slide of the door, he's wrecked that belief.

The worst part is that he has no idea that he's set me so off-kilter if his calm expression is anything to go by.

"Okay, Serena, I'm going to need you to take off your shirt, lay face down on the tattoo bench, and show me your back. I want to take a closer look at how the skin is healing and if there's going to be any problem areas with the cover-up. I didn't get a good look at it yesterday."

My mind stutters at the beginning of his statement, grasping onto his instruction to "take off your shirt." That is the absolute last thing I should be doing right now.

"I could just bunch my shirt up like yesterday," I say.

Before I finish my sentence, he's shaking his head. I scowl.

"Sorry, princess, but I need a good look at your skin, and the shirt will slip, fall, and obstruct my ability to see everything we're working with. I've seen plenty of backs, and I closed the door to give you some privacy."

"Fine," I sigh, standing up and quickly whipping the long-sleeved cotton shirt I'm wearing over my head, leaving myself in just a black lace demitasse bra, my jeans, and a pair of Air Forces.

Wolf's throat clears, and I turn my attention to him. "I could have turned around first before you started stripping," Wolf murmurs, running a hand over his face as he looks anywhere but at me.

163

"Right, shit. Sorry," I apologize, mortified that my common sense also seems to have failed me.

"It's fine, just… just get on the table," Wolf nearly growls, still averting his eyes. I have the burning need to cover my chest with my hands, even though it's irrational, and I'm as covered up, if not more, than a woman on the beach. Forcing myself to move at a slow pace, I walk to the flat table and lay down, turning my head toward Wolf's form.

I watch as he takes long, deep breaths like he's trying to rein himself in. Wiping his face with his hand, he clutches his throat and looks up toward the ceiling. Whatever prayer or internal monologue he says must do the trick because he finally drops his hand and settles his gaze on me. Our eyes meet, and a tight smile breaks out on his face. "Ready?" he asks, as though I haven't been watching him have a silent freak-out for the last five minutes while I've been topless on his tattoo table.

"Mhmm."

His eyes narrow, but instead of responding, he walks over to me and rolls his stool over to my right side. Seating himself on the rolling furniture that looks like it'll snap under his weight, he reaches above me and turns on a spotlight, blinding me. I squint and squeeze my eyes shut.

"Stop moving," Wolf orders, his command sharp and leaving no room for argument.

"Sorry."

"I don't want an apology. Just stop squirming." Wolf says this as he places a hand on my back, lightly touching the tattoo and my surrounding skin. The moment his skin makes contact with mine, I feel my body shiver.

"Serena." That's it, just my name. Three goddamn syllables

164

said in Wolf's deep voice with a commanding tone, and I'm putty. No, I'm worse than moldable, malleable putty. I'm water, a fluid that will take the shape of anything Wolf wants to put me in.

Wolf's hand continues to coast up and down my back, taking entirely too long for the task at hand. His fingers graze a sensitive spot, and I bite my lip to keep in the laughter that's threatening to push past my lips.

"I forgot how ticklish you are," Wolf whispers in a voice so low I'd think I imagined hearing it if it weren't for the increased pressure he's exerting on the spot that's making me squirm.

"Wolf!" I shout and move to get out of his reach until I've shifted so much that I'm about to roll off the narrow table. Wolf's arms band around me, pulling me back until I'm cradled in his arms and staring into his deep green eyes. He holds me to him, and I can't help but stare at his perfectly flawed face: the slightly crooked nose, the dark red stubble that adorns his cheeks, the thick eyelashes that are unfairly blessed on his face. My heart pounds so hard in my chest that I imagine it looks like one of those cartoon hearts, beating so violently that it pops out of my chest cavity until my tendons suck it back in.

Wolf tightens his hold on my body for a moment. The move presses my semi-bare chest into his, and he studies me just as closely as I study him before he places me back down on the table. "Be careful, princess. I don't need an insurance claim for a good deed." I bristle at his words, as though I'm a charity case that requires his aid rather than a forced participant in this cover-up.

"I fully intend to pay for—"

165

"No. I'm not accepting your fucking money, so don't bother offering it," he cuts me off. He nudges my shoulder, silently encouraging me to lie on my stomach.

"You're impossibly frustrating."

"Thanks. Now, I need you to stay still. Your skin seems to be healing well enough, but I want to do a hand sketch on stencil paper of your back to see how a piece could lay to cover up the areas that need to be hidden."

"Sloan's not going to just fix the butterflies?"

"*The flying cocks*," he emphasizes. "No one's going to fix the flying cocks on your back. There's no salvaging them. Besides, an artist never wants to correct someone else's work; they'd rather cover it up and show how badass the piece can be without the shit that weighed it down."

"Right. Okay. But what is Sloan thinking?"

Ignoring my question, he continues, "But I need you to stay still. One move, and you'll move the marker, alter the linework, and change the entire piece. Do you understand?"

I nod as best I can while lying down and looking up at him.

"Let me hear you say it, princess."

"Yes. I won't move." *Much*, I tack on in my head.

Seemingly satisfied, Wolf reaches behind him and pulls out a long sheet of paper and a sleeve of markers. Covering my back with the paper, he presses it down before taking a marker out. He puts it between his teeth before pulling the bottom out, revealing a black felt tip.

"If Sloan is doing the piece, why are you sketching?"

"Because I can't fucking help myself," he mumbles around the cap before putting it on the back of the marker. I'm not entirely sure about the sanitation protocols, but something seems off.

166

"Shouldn't you be wearing gloves?"

"We're not breaking any skin, and you have no open wounds on your back, just some redness and irritation. Besides, I'm not sketching on your skin, just tracing the shape of your back and the existing tattoo. We're fine," he mumbles, though I don't miss the wince on his face at my observation.

Despite the thin paper that separates Wolf's hand from my skin, I feel each move like a caress against my bare skin. Unlike the featherlight strokes of his finger earlier, the movement of the marker is sure and purposeful. There's intention behind each lash, and my mind tries to piece together what all the lines would reveal once completed.

"What are you drawing? I ask after thirty minutes of silence.

"None of your business."

"What?" I laugh out, surprised but also not by the gruffness of his answer.

"Fuck," he mutters before raising his voice. "I need you to pull your pants down."

"What?" I repeat, but this time with an entirely different tone. "First my shirt and now my pants? Jesus, Wolf, if you wanted me naked, you could have just stayed at my apartment on Friday."

"For fuck's sake, Serena. I need to continue the sketch lower, but the waistband of your jeans is blocking me. I have a sheet that you can put over yourself if you feel uncomfortable."

I turn my head and consider him, taking in the slashes of his eyebrows and the stern set to his jaw.

"Fine, but hand me the sheet." Putting my hands by my chest, I push up until I'm able to rest on my knees and pop the button on my straight-leg jeans. I silently curse myself that I didn't wear leggings or sweatpants, where the waistband could have just been rolled down to accommodate Wolf's demand.

Shimmying the denim down, I let the jeans rest against my thighs and grab the paper covering from Wolf's outstretched hand. Like a misguided gentleman, Wolf's eyes remain averted, giving me the semblance of privacy as I strip to near-indecency.

Laying back down, I drape the sheet over my lower back. "Is this from a gynecologist's office? It feels like the coverings I use when I go for my annual check-up. I'm decent, by the way. You can look now." I watch as Wolf turns his attention back to me, his eyes immediately catching on the sheet covering my lower half.

"Can I tuck this into your underwear? It's still too high."

"Fine." As soon as the words leave my mouth, Wolf's hands are on me, rolling the edges of the sheet into the modest boy shorts I chose for today. In romance novels and movies, the women are always depicted in matching lingerie sets, perfect pairings that make them look like seductresses ready to pounce. Me? My black lace demitasse bra may be cute, but my boy shorts are covered in donuts with the words "Bite Me" across my ass.

"Nice panties," Wolf chuckles.

"Shut up," I mumble. Wolf's low laughter fills the room as he continues to tuck the sheet inside my underwear.

"To answer your question, they're from the hospital. I get them for the people who don't want or aren't comfortable with being fully exposed when getting a tattoo in a location that requires the removal of clothing or undergarments. Mostly women use these, but I've had a few men cover up their dicks when I give them an upper thigh tattoo," Wolf explains. "I pick them up from my aunt, Celeste's mom. She's my mom's sister, so we've always been pretty close."

I absorb his words, silently touched by the care he shows his clients in preserving their modesty if they wish.

"Alright, you're all set. I'm going to start drawing again, so just stay still, the same as before. Okay?" I don't say anything, letting my silence act as an affirmative while he places the paper back on my skin. Shifting it around, I assume that he's trying to match up the lines of the drawing before he resumes. His hands still, pressing down on my back before I feel one hand lift, replaced by the smooth caresses of the marker. I close my eyes, letting Wolf's steady strokes and smell lull me into sleep.

—

"Fuck, it's perfect." I wake with a start at Wolf's whispered words. "I see you're up, but stay still for a minute, princess."

Ignoring his directive, I glance at the clock and see that it's after five, and I've been lying on this table for over two hours. My limbs ache with the need to stretch, and I'm in desperate need of a glass of water. I shift on the bench but halt my movements at Wolf's growl.

"Serena, how many times do I have to ask you to stop moving?"

Gulping down my apology, I remain silent and fight the urge to continue moving. I pay attention to the flickers of pressure I feel as Wolf finishes mapping out whatever he needs on my back. I count the seconds until, finally, he eases back and caps his marker with a loud click. "Alright, I'm set."

Clearing my throat, I nod my head into the black leather. "I just need a minute."

"Take what you need. I'm going to get this cleaned up." I

169

can feel him getting up from his stool, and the loss of his body heat next to me. "My back is to you; you can get dressed." Glancing toward the direction of his voice, I verify that he's facing away before I get up to redress.

Drawing in a long breath, I reach down and grab the waist of my jeans, sliding them back up until they're sitting on my hips and hiding the embarrassing panties Wolf commented on. Walking to my bag and coat, I grab my shirt as soon as I'm in proximity to my things. It takes no time to slip the fabric over my head and run a hand over my hair, hopefully smoothing it out to the point that it looks artfully messy and not chaotic.

Reaching into my bag, I pull out my cell phone and wince at the number of notifications that fill my screen. Unlocking the phone and reading through the messages and missed calls, my hold on the phone gradually tightens until I'm worried it'll shatter in my palm. Seemingly endless messages and calls from my father are interwoven with texts from Marina and my friends.

Dad (3:56 PM): I will be calling you in thirty minutes. Be sure to answer your phone.

I check and see there's a missed call from him at the exact time he said he'd call. Toggling back to my messages, I continue reading.

Dad (4:27 PM): Answer your phone. I'm calling again.

Dad (4:29 PM): This is unacceptable. Your continued tantrums are an embarrassment.

Dad (4:32 PM): Serena, when I tell you that I'm calling, answer your phone. Do we need to go through the exercise of shutting off your line again to get you to comply?

I roll my eyes at his statement. After the last time he

threatened to turn my phone off, I transferred to my mother's phone plan. He must have never realized his phone bill had changed because a line was dropped on his account.

Dad (5:09 PM): Fine, you want to be a child, I will treat you as such. The home I have provided to you for the last decade has been sold. Your mother will need to be out of the house by the end of March. I am disappointed in you, Serena, and the lack of respect you've continued to show me. If you cannot respect my wife and daughter, then you do not have a place in our lives. I don't know what you were doing that has you too busy to pick up the phone for the man who provides you with your livelihood, but I will not stand for it. I am cutting you off.

Swiping out of his text thread, I click on the unread message from Marina.

Marina: Heard you're homeless now. I'm sure all the guys you're sleeping with wouldn't have a problem paying you for your time.

"For fuck's sake," I mumble, running a hand through my hair and gripping the short ends until I can pull on it. A myriad of emotions run through me: despair at the sale of the only real home my mother and I ever shared, anger at the callousness of my father and the stupidity of Marina, and disgust over his words and accusations. Not giving a thought to my surroundings, the time, or the company I'm in, I click on my dad's name and bring the phone to my ear. The ringing on the phone mimics the ringing in my ear.

"Serena, are you okay?" I hear Wolf ask, but his voice sounds like it's coming to me through a tunnel, and I hold up my hand, silencing him.

The call goes to voicemail, and I snap. "How could you be

such an uncaring, cruel asshole? For nineteen years, I have done everything you have ever asked of me: graduated early, started college at sixteen, smiled, and looked like a pretty bauble for your business associates as you showed off your new family. I am done. You have taken the only thing that has ever mattered to me outside of my mother, and you have thrown it away. I am done pretending like I care about you. Even your mother despised you for what you did.

"The fact that you are so ignorant to think that I have taken a single penny from you, outside of the mandated child support you were required to give, is laughable. Turn off my phone? I have a plan with Mom. You have done nothing but break my fucking heart since you cheated on Mom. You want Marina to be your perfect daughter? Fine, you can keep her, keep Brandi, and keep the house that will collapse in on you from your hubris and self-importance. I am done." I end the call and select Marina's name, opening the conversation to respond.

Serena: Can you get a life instead of trying to steal mine? Don't worry about who I'm with, where I live, or what I'm doing. It's fucking weird.

I hit send and drop my hand, barely resisting the urge to throw my phone across the room and scream.

The sale of the house doesn't come as a surprise; my mother told me that it was being listed and that she was looking for a new place, one that doesn't bear the stench of my father's influence. But seeing his words and listening to his voicemail cemented the truth: he has forced us out of our home. It doesn't matter that I all but moved out once I started college; it was my home, my mother's home.

With one final inhale and exhale, I grab the rest of my things and drape them over my arm before turning back to Wolf.

Even in my haze of anger, it strikes me that it's unfair for a person to be as outwardly handsome, artistically gifted, and physically strong as he is; it's like all of his genes got together in utero and said, "You know Superman? Let's see if we can one-up him."

"Is everything okay, Serena?" Wolf repeats, drawing me out of my observation of his form.

"Yes. Great," I lie. "But I'm going to, uh, go now." I hold up my things, a visible sign that I'm leaving, and walk toward the pocket door. I reach out to unlatch the lock holding it shut when Wolf's voice rings out behind me.

"Wait." His hand shoots out, caging me in from behind. "I can't let you drive when you're visibly upset."

"I'm fine, Wolf," I sigh, the fight I just had in me draining, replaced by exhaustion and annoyance.

"You're not fine, Serena. I'm not trying to be an asshole, but I've seen your car, and it looks like it's held together with duct tape and chewing gum. I'll be fucking sick with worry if you get behind that death trap right now. So just leave the car here, and I'll bring you home."

"Wolf," I start, drawing out his name.

"Serena," he responds, mimicking my tone. "You shouldn't drive, not after what I just heard. I have a few more things I need to do around the shop, and then I'll drive you to your apartment. Okay?"

He disguises his statement by tacking on a question at the end, giving the pretense that I have a say in the matter when, in reality, he's dictating me. I shake my head, offering a compromise. "First, don't talk about my car. I worked hard for her. You don't need to bring me home, but I will wait for a minute before I drive." I pull on the door, ignoring the hand

173

holding it closed. I tug on the handle until Wolf finally moves his hand, letting the door slide open with a bang.

At almost six on a Saturday, the shop is busy, the hum of tattoo guns infiltrating the bubble Wolf and I found ourselves in for the last few hours. I walk across the shop floor, ignoring the eyes on me as I make my way toward Aubrey's desk. Settling myself in one of the chairs against the windows, I drop my bag on the floor and lean back, getting comfortable while I wait for Wolf to finish whatever it is he needs to do and let me leave.

Aubrey walks through a hidden door, stopping short when she sees me. "Oh no. You need a drink."

I shake my head, opening my mouth to deny the offer, but Aubrey holds up her hand. "Nope, don't thank me. You need whiskey."

19

Wolf

I watch Serena glide through my shop before perching on a chair. Though I may call her that stupid name of "princess," she looks more like a dejected queen overseeing a kingdom. It doesn't take long for Aubrey to spot her, and I settle, comfortable that my closest friend is taking care of the woman who's blindsided me.

I run through the words she shouted into her phone, and fuck if her frustration and anger don't make my chest physically hurt. Based on my interactions with Serena, I've seen her chameleon personality: shy and quiet, feisty and passionate, angry and explosive. It's not mood swings but how she reacts to situations and processes them. I don't know much about her family life, but I think back to the warning Dante gave me and the insinuation that people have hurt her; it pisses me off more than any cheap shot black eye from Gage.

"She's cute." Trent's voice breaks me out of my thoughts. I grunt, not giving him any ammunition. "Isn't that Celeste's friend?"

Another grunt confirms his question.

"Okay, you silent fucker, I see that you're being a little gremlin about this shit. If that's Celeste's friend, then Sloan is doing her back piece. But Sloan's not here, so want to tell me what's going on with you that has you ready to bite everyone's fucking head off? Because if it's a matter of needing to get laid, I know a few of Aubrey's friends that will volunteer as tribute."

"Stop with your *Hunger Games* references." Trent may be a dipshit, but he's a dystopian movie and book fanatic. It doesn't matter when it was made, Trent has consumed it and then memorialized it on his body. For *1984*, he has the eyes of Big Brother; for *Brave New World*, he has tiny pills meant to represent soma, the "happy pills" in the book. He has the Mockingjay tattoo, a silhouette of a red robe for *The Handmaid's Tale*, divisions from *Divergent*, and a mask from *The Purge*. He's a walking conglomerate of symbolism, but his reference does nothing but annoy me. "I don't need to get laid." A lie.

"Fine. Back to the other question. If Sloan is doing the tattoo, why is she here?" He nods toward Serena.

"Because Sloan isn't doing her tattoo."

"You're mumbling. Say that one more time."

I look over at him and see the shit-eating grin on his face. It takes a lot of willpower not to jab him in the nose. "Asshole. You heard what I said."

"I fucking knew it. Sloan owes me twenty bucks; I told her you'd never let her touch Serena."

"She wanted to put hot air balloons," I offer by way of an explanation, as though a design that I don't like is the reason why I don't want Sloan handling the cover-up.

176

"Which sounds cool as fuck, especially with her watercolor designs. I don't think anyone would complain about art by Sloan."

"She's not putting hot air balloons on Serena's back. Does she fucking look like the type of person who would want flying balloons all over their back? She's butterflies and rainbows and flowers, not The QuickChek New Jersey Festival of Ballooning."

Trent rolls his eyes at me. "You sound like an idiot. Did you even ask her what she wanted, or did you just decide?"

I glower at him, not correcting his assumption because he's right, and we both know it. "I'm doing the tattoo, and I'm giving her something that she'll love."

Trent just laughs, clapping me on the back before walking to the front of the shop, where Aubrey and Serena sit with glasses partially filled with brown liquid. I squint my eyes, trying to identify the liquid sloshing around in the glass; I wouldn't be surprised if Aubrey poured my O.F.C Vintage 1994 Kentucky Straight Bourbon Whiskey into each of those glasses. Never mind that the bottle costs over six thousand dollars and I receive it each year from one of my high-profile clients as a Christmas gift, but I'm acutely aware that Serena needs to drive home, is underaged, and drinking in the front of my shop, on display for everyone to see.

I take in the expression on her face; she looks like she's grimacing, though whether it's from the taste of the expensive alcohol or Aubrey's words is anyone's guess.

I should go over there, take the glass from her hand, and force her to wait for me in solitude. I watch as Serena takes a small sip, coughs, and puts the drink down on the side table next to where she's seated. She says something that has both

Aubrey and Trent laughing before Trent takes the glass Serena just put down and tilts it to his lips. I can tell from here that he's savoring the flavor and has no designs to give the glass back, which is both a relief and annoying.

"Fuckers," I mumble under my breath and turn to the large photocopier I keep in an alcove in the back of the shop. I have another printer in my room, but it's smaller, and I need something that will capture the entire sheet. Scanning the paper, I make several copies so that I can play around with the design I'm envisioning. The paper maps out the dimensions of her back and the placement of the supposed "butterflies," and though I did a rough placement of the image I have in my head, it's light enough that I can rework the art to better fit the shape of her back.

Taking in the stem and the petals on the flower I drafted, I pick apart the areas where I can add or change elements to make it a better-looking, sexier piece. I know I want to follow the curve of her spine while simultaneously camouflaging the preexisting artwork. She loves butterflies, evidenced by the small script tattoo I drew on her and her latest request. I'll incorporate them, somehow, so that she has at least a semblance of what she initially wanted.

Turning off the copier, I run back into my room and deposit the original drawing and two of the copies on my desk, stuffing the rest of the prints into a folder and putting them in my leather motor bag. Placing the bag on my stool, I start to sanitize all surfaces and prep for my first client tomorrow. I keep all my equipment in their places and cases, but I take out the plastic coverings, paper towels, and squirt bottle and place them on the tray beside my station. I do a final wipe down of the counters before grabbing the trash bag in the waste basket and tying up the ends to place it just inside the door of the room.

A cleaning company comes each night to clean the general areas, vacuum, mop, and replenish the refreshment station at the front of the shop. Though we have them, I maintain a clean space and mandate that all my artists aren't assholes who take advantage of the team that comes in after closing. That means they must sanitize their stations, clean up their shit, and tie off their trash bags before they leave the shop. I'm no exception; I follow the same rules I set for the people I employ.

Casting a glance, I make sure that my space is together before I shut the light and walk through the door. Be it fate, God, or the fucking universe, this is one of the few nights I have free from both the gym and clients. After Serena left last night, I went to the gym and did a few late-night rounds with Jedd, a standard for Friday evenings, even though my MMA career has dwindled to just one more fight in three weeks. This morning, I helped him by being the fuckwit's sparring partner to help Jedd address issues with Gage's form. At the end of the session, he got stupid and hit me in the eye when I dropped the focus pads.

Kelly, who has become a permanent fixture at these sessions, let out a horrified gasp as though the under-two-hundred-pound piece of shit could do real damage to me. My eye looks worse than it is and should heal within the next few days. However, my anger and annoyance at Gage are omnipresent; they aren't going away any time soon.

Approaching Trent, Aubrey, and Serena, I catch the tail end of Serena's words.

"... they've always been important to me; they symbolize

179

growth and change, beauty and freedom, luck and persever-
ance. I've always loved them."

"I hate that they messed it up for you. I should report them
to the Better Business Bureau."

Serena shrugs, looking at her hands as she answers. "It
doesn't matter; I knew better than to go into that shop and
had a horrible feeling the moment the artist started. I didn't
stop it when I saw the sketch, nor did I stop it the minute he
put his tattoo gun on my back and started digging into my
skin. I have a lot of regrets, but they're self-imposed. I doubt
reporting them is going to do anything."

"Serena, you ready to head out?" I cut in, halting the path
of this conversation. I can see she's uncomfortable; her
body language is closed off, and she's refusing to make eye
contact, telling me that she's both embarrassed and upset.
Her emotions seep into the atmosphere, and I need her out
of here before I do something stupid, like grab her in front of
everyone in here and try to console her.

She nods her head and offers a small wave to Aubrey and
Trent. "It was great seeing you both again. Aubrey, should I
schedule something with Sloan now or...?" She lets her voice
trail off, leaving the question open.

Aubrey's eyes widen, and she looks at me before responding,
"Uhm—"

"Let's wait until you're fully healed, then we'll put you in the
books. Okay?" I cut in again, raising an eyebrow at Aubrey
and Trent. Neither one of them says anything, but both have
wary expressions on their faces.

"Of course. Well..." She pauses, standing and wiping
imaginary dust from her body. "I'll see you guys."

She starts to walk to the door, but I lightly grab her forearm, stilling her movement. "Are you sure you're okay to drive?"

She nods, still not looking at my face. "I'm fine, I promise."

I survey her, taking in how closed off her body language reads. "Okay. Send me a text or call to let me know you made it home safe."

She looks up, offering a tight smile, before she walks to the door and slips outside. My eyes trail her form as she makes her way to her car, and part of me wants to follow her home. Stealing myself against emotions I don't want to name, I turn from the wall of windows, trying to expel all thoughts of Serena and her outburst from my mind.

20

Serena

I don't turn on the radio on my ride home. I don't plug in my phone to connect my music on my ride, either. And I don't think of anything other than the disgust I feel over my father's words and actions.

My hands are tense on the steering wheel as I crawl home, unbothered by the honks I receive for my slow speed and for not shifting out of the left lane. It's an asshole move, one I would typically never practice, but the blaring horns roll off my skin like they're nothing more than persistent flies. I slowly eat the miles between Wolf's shop and campus, pulling into my apartment's parking lot in a daze.

Throwing the car into park, I don't bother zipping my jacket, instead letting the cool evening air seep into my bones; at least I know I'm capable of feeling something other than anger and numbness, even if it's just the cold.

Once I'm through the glass doors, I bypass the elevator and take the stairs, hoping that the burn of the climb will settle me before I enter my apartment; it doesn't. Instead of being calmer when I walk through my front door, I'm winded and more annoyed that I thought physical exertion would help. I throw my bag and jacket on the hook by the front door and climb onto my couch, sinking into the cushions and letting the vanilla infuser on my coffee table lull me into a sense of false calm. I should probably text Wolf and let him know I made it home safely, but despite his orders, he probably doesn't care.

Releasing a sigh, I reach forward and grab the remote, turning on the television to block out the outside world.

—

Knocking on my front door rips me out of the 2005 *Pride & Prejudice* adaptation. I have no right to be annoyed since I've seen it no less than one hundred times, but Elizabeth was just denying Darcy in an epic manner, and that scene should never be interrupted.

Pausing the movie, I walk to my front door and rip it open; I realize that I should have looked through the peephole before opening the door. I also should have put a bra on under the white tank I'm wearing.

"What are you doing here?" I ask, confused by my visitor's presence.

"You never let me know you made it home safe," Wolf explains, giving me a once-over that warms my insides and has my nipples standing at attention.

"So, you decided to show up at my apartment? Most people would have called."

"I did call." He holds up his phone. "And texted several times. But you never answered. I wasn't sure if you were dead or what the fuck was going on. Now that I see you're alive and well, are you going to invite me in?"

"Dammit, I left my phone in my bag." I rush over to my bag,

sifting through it until I grip my phone. Just like Wolf said, I have missed calls and texts from the last few hours. "Sorry, I just wanted to block out everything that happened tonight."

"I got it," he consoles at the same time my door clicks shut. "What were you watching?" He motions to the television.

"Oh, nothing," I rush out.

I watch as Wolf's eyes squint, taking in the actors on my screen. "Is that Tom Wambsgan from *Succession*? I fucking love that show."

"It's definitely not *Succession*," I mumble under my breath. Raising my voice, I tell him, "It's *Pride & Prejudice*—the 2005 version, which is the only version that matters. But yes, Matthew MacFadyen is the actor who plays Tom."

"Cool." Wolf sinks onto my couch, toeing off his shoes before sitting back into the cushions.

"What are you doing?"

"Watching a movie. You can go ahead and play it?"

"But, why—" I break off, unable to finish my thoughts.

He glances over at me, offering a small smile. "Why am I here, and why am I staying?" I nod, not trusting myself to respond verbally. "Because you're upset, and no one should be alone when they purposely avoid their phone and the outside world. Start the damn movie, princess, and stop talking."

—

The credits roll, and I look at Wolf, whose face is set in a confused glare. Furrowed eyebrows, clenched jaw, and shaking head, I take him in and laugh at his reaction to the movie.

"That bad?"

He looks at me, smoothing out his features. "No, they just spoke like they were from a different time. Thanks for turning

184

on the subtitles."

I shrug, not phased by his observation. "The movie is set in the late eighteenth century, during the Regency era, so it takes a while to get used to the idiosyncrasies." I turn toward him, angling my body closer to his. I'm in sweatpants and white tank top—sans bra—but it's dark in the room, so I doubt he can see much of anything. The television provides just enough illumination to bathe his face in light, displaying his perfectly formed lips. I can't help my eyes as I stare at his mouth; I blame the romantic movie we just watched, but I'm smart enough to know that Wolf's presence just affects me.

I keep my eyes trained on his lips, and he licks them, moistening his flesh before pulling his tongue back inside his mouth. I'm embarrassed—but not surprised—that my mouth pops open at the same time his closes.

"Do you want me to take the decision out of your hands?" I look up, startled by Wolf's question.

"What?"

He levels me with a look, and I flush under his gaze. "You're trying to figure out if you should kiss me, whether it's a stupid decision or a good idea. But before you do something or ask something of me that can't be taken back, you need to know where I'm at." I swallow, otherwise immobile, as the words tumble out of his mouth. "I'm not looking for a relationship, and I'm not your fairytale happy ending. You're young—and I'm not saying that as an insult. You have a whole life ahead of you, mistakes and decisions to be made, and I'm at a different point in my life. And you're hurting, so tonight would be a balm to your soul more than anything. So, if you ask me to kiss you right now, it won't stop there; I will strip you down, get my hands and tongue all over your body, and then I'll

185

leave. Because for you, I'm a good time, a distraction, a one night, not a forever. Do you understand?"

Absorbing his words, I nod my head, decision made. "I'm not looking for forever, Wolf. I have enough to deal with without adding the pressure of expectation to the list. I'm not going to wait around for you to call me. I'm not going to obsess over what you're doing or who you're with. But for tonight, can you just make me feel something?"

I'm not lying when I say that I'm not interested in anything more than what Wolf is offering; the drama with Dylan and Devin, my dad's betrayal, and the events of last semester have drained me to the point where if it weren't for my mom and Ava and CeCe, I would be numb and desensitized to the world around me, going with the current simply because I'm on autopilot. I have no desire to add someone else's emotions and feelings into my life.

Since losing my virginity to Devin, I made the mistake of sleeping with one other guy—a resident of my apartment complex. Ironically, he was in the elevator the first night Wolf came up to my apartment. It was transactional and deeply unsatisfying. Something tells me that any sexual experience with Wolf would be the antithesis of the laughable experience I claim. And I'm eager to know what it feels like to come on the hands of a man savage enough to rip someone apart but artistic enough to create beauty on skin.

"So, I guess the only thing I have left to say is, Wolf, will you kiss me?"

Wolf:

I stare at her, letting her words fuel the hard-on that's pressing against my pants and the precum that's starting to leak in my briefs.

"You sure about this, princess?" If I need to verify with her six goddamn times before I press my lips against hers and fuck the ever-loving shit out of her, I will. I don't play with consent, and I won't allow her to feel pressured into something she doesn't want.

"Yes."

I watch her for another minute, meeting her unflinching gaze, and nod my approval. Standing from the couch, I walk across the room and flick on the lights, bathing us both in the artificial glow so that I can see every inch of her body. Her brows draw down, and she opens her mouth to speak, but I move fast.

21

Serena

"Wolf—" His name barely leaves my mouth before Wolf rushes in, grabbing the bottom of my thighs and hoisting me up, forcing me to wrap my legs around his waist and hold on for dear life. His mouth crashes to mine, greeting me in an open-mouthed kiss that betrays all the need, all of the desire, that he harbors. I meet each lash of his tongue, battling for dominance in a kiss that takes me by surprise.

Just when I'm getting used to the cadence of the kiss, he changes it; the thrust of his tongue softens to a caress, and the harshness becomes gentle, like he's savoring the taste of my mouth, drinking me in.

Wolf breaks from my lips, kissing a path from my mouth, along my jawline, and down my throat. Stopping at my pulse, he nips my skin before sucking on the bite, leaving a mark that will be more permanent than his position in my bed.

"Goddamn, princess. You taste like a fucking dream," he murmurs, drawing my skin back into his mouth and giving me another mark.

"Wolf!" I scream out his name, equal parts scolding and

pleasure. "You're bruising me."

"Suck it the fuck up." He descends again, biting my throat a third time before soothing my flesh with his lips and tongue.

I'm so lost in the ministrations he's paying against my neck that I don't realize we're moving until my back is pressed against my wall, supporting my weight as Wolf pins me against it, trapping me so that I'm barely mobile. The hands that were at my thighs coast up my body, grazing my waist, molding to my chest until they reach under my arms. Exerting pressure on my joints, Wolf lifts my arms above my head and captures my wrists in one hand.

I'm fully supported by Wolf and the wall in this position, unable to move as he squeezes my wrists tighter. "You're going to drop me," I breathe out, my lips moving against the side of his head as he presses a kiss right below my ear.

A chuckle travels through Wolf's body at my words. "You're as light as those butterflies you love so much."

"I—"

"Shh. The only words I want to hear out of your mouth are, 'Yes,' 'Stop,' or, 'Wolf.'" He says the words against my ear, finishing his statement with a hard bite to my earlobe.

"Oh my God," I murmur, shivers wracking my body.

"I'll allow that one, too."

The hand not gripping my wrists in a vice trails up my waist, pushing my shirt up to reveal my script tattoo. Wolf bends his legs, making my hold shift from his waist to his upper abdomen, and he leans in, kissing my ribs and using his tongue to trace the *Mariposa* etched on my body.

"I like seeing my artwork on this golden skin, princess. It's giving me all kinds of ideas of what else I can give you." He stands back up, shifting my body so that my legs are locked against him. The moment my ankles meet, I feel the outline of his erection right where I need him most. Unable to stop myself, I grind my pelvis against him, groaning at the heady mix of pain and pleasure his concealed cock is giving me.

"Please," I mutter, continuing to shift against him, arching my back as best I can to get the most contact. I'm under no illusion; I know the only reason that I'm able to move, able to grind against him, is because he's allowing me to do so.

His hand snakes around my body and grips my back at the same time he steps forward, pressing our bodies flush against each other and halting my movements. "I'm going to release your hands now. I need you to grab onto my shoulders, princess. Do you understand?"

"Wolf."

"No. I'm asking if you understand. Otherwise, I'll stay in this position all fucking night and watch your body grind against my cock, giving you a little relief but nowhere near what you need to come. So, I'll ask you one more fucking time, do you understand?"

"Yes."

"Good girl." He releases my wrists, and just like he said, I drop my hands to his shoulders and hold on, desperate to see what his next move will be. Tomorrow I'll chastise and mentally slap myself for giving into the whims of a man, *this* man, so damn easily. But tonight, I'll let myself be immersed in the fantasy he's presenting, one that I never knew I wanted to live out.

Moving to my couch, he holds me like I weigh nothing and lowers. His hands move to my face, cupping my jaw with a reverence that makes this encounter seem more intimate than it is.

190

"Goddamn, you're beautiful," he sighs, annoyance seeping into his words as though my appearance is a detriment to him. The words seem to set him off because as soon as they settle between us, he leans forward, taking my bottom lip between his. I open instinctually, giving him access to my tongue and inviting him in, physically begging him to get lost in the kiss with me. He doesn't disappoint, treating my mouth with the same rough treatment that he gave me at the shop and when I opened my front door. I meet each of his bites with one of my own, drawing his bottom lip into my mouth and sucking on his flesh.

Wolf is the first to break the kiss, pulling back while simultaneously moving my body away. I open my mouth to complain, but the look he gives me, one that's somehow both feral and passionate, renders me silent.

"Stand up and strip."

"What?"

"That's not one of the words, Serena."

"Wolf," I rasp, unable to keep the surprise out of my voice.

"I said, stand up and strip." His eyebrow raises, a perfectly masculine brow that has a scar slicing it in half. I stare at the division and twist my lips as I realize that his eyebrows are a metaphor for how whatever decision I make right now— listen to his bossy commands or tell him to stop and throw his ass out of my apartment—will be a critical turning point in my life.

The decision is an easy one.

Climbing from his lap, I stand on wobbly legs and walk across the room, standing close to the wall opposite my couch. I don't hesitate to make quick work of my shoes and sweatpants, slipping them off with a haste I've never experienced before. With Devin, I remained partially clothed and fully mortified before and after the encounter.

With Wolf, I'm finding his authoritative tone and bossiness intoxicating rather than annoying, and his words addicting.

When I'm standing in front of Wolf in just my tank top and ridiculous underwear, I pause, slowing down the frenzy that overtook me.

"The shirt, too. Keep the panties on," he orders, leaning back on my couch and spreading his legs wide. His position has his cock straining against his pants, and I zero in on the bulge. "Eyes up here, princess."

I jerk my gaze back to his face. He wears a smirk like he's used to women ogling his penis as he orders them around. I tilt my head, considering that he probably is used to women standing before him, in various states of undress, and doing whatever he says as quickly as he says it. Jealousy courses through my veins at all of the women before me and all who will be after me; I know it's irrational, and while my mind understands that I have no right and no claim to this man, the idea of him with someone else makes my skin crawl and my ire rise.

"Would you rather I cut it off you and tie you to your bed, princess? Because I'm about three seconds from going into your disorganized-as-fuck kitchen cabinets and finding a knife to slice that shit off your body."

"I just cleaned," I grumble.

I watch Wolf's face as I work the thick straps down my arms and step out of the shirt, feeling powerful when his jaw clenches and his hand flexes like he's physically restraining himself from breaking his control. Leveling him with a stare, I bite down on my lip, worrying my flesh between my teeth

192

as I stand before him—almost completely naked except for the fabric covering my pussy.

The silence is deafening, and his stare is a weight pressing against my stomach, a boulder that seems to amplify the tension swarming us in the room. His eyes are trained on my body, drinking in my near-nakedness with a neutral expression, as though he's not affected in the least.

Annoyance skates over me, and I hold onto it like a life preserver. Here I am, on display, and he doesn't even have the decency to look affected or interested. Setting my jaw, any apprehension I had fades away, and I grit my teeth, steeling my spine for the very bold, very un-Serena-like thing I'm about to do. Like the siren he claimed me to be when I first met him, I raise my hands until I'll cupping my boobs and pushing them together, an offering on display for Wolf to take. He leans forward, resting his elbows on his knees as he watches me.

"Pinch your nipples."

I follow his order, not necessarily because he told me to; I was already planning on paying attention to the nipples that pebble against the coldness of the room and the warmth from his stare. Readjusting my grip, I glide my forefingers, middle fingers, and pointer fingers from the swell of my breasts to the tips of my nipples and let my thumbs rest at the top of my chest while my pinkies remain along the bottom curve. In this position, my hands and fingers create a frame, simultaneously plumping and pushing my boobs out while also operating as nipple clamps.

Pressing my forefingers and ring fingers against my areolas, I let my middle finger rest against the tip of my nipple, rubbing gently while I exert more pressure against the sensitive flesh.

193

Lost to the sensation, I throw my head back, not paying attention to Wolf's reaction or how he's processing my display. Running my fingers in circles, I pinch harder, relishing the pain mixed with the light stimulation.

A moan slips into the room, and I'm startled to realize it's mine; the sound is erotic and loud, needy and impatient, adjectives I've never used to describe myself. I don't wait for Wolf to bark out more orders; keeping one hand on my chest, I let the other trail down, losing myself in the sensation of my hands on my body and the performance I'm giving as a byproduct of my annoyance. I inch my fingers closer to the waistband of my panties, letting my pinky rub across the seam in gentle, unhurried strokes before I allow myself to dip my fingers under the fabric and edge them down my legs, kicking them across the room in my haste to be rid of all clothing. I allow my fingers to glide across the smooth skin between my thighs, reveling in how soft my flesh feels.

Closing my eyes, I block out everything other than the pinching, caressing, and attention I'm paying to myself, letting Wolf and any wants he may have fade into the background. I doubt I would even hear him if he spoke—or demanded— anything at this moment.

"God," I mutter, unable to keep the word in when my fingers make contact with the wetness between my thighs. I've been turned on before—hell, I've masturbated and given myself orgasms, so I know what arousal feels like. But this? This is different. It's like a valve is loose, and I'm leaking. I don't know if I should be mortified or proud, but I can't find it in me to care.

I plunge one finger inside my opening, spearing myself with just the tip to get used to the intrusion. I sway back, catching

194

myself against the wall and leaning into it, using it to hold my weight as I dive deeper, fingering myself until my third knuckle is buried inside my pussy.

My single, slim finger isn't enough, and I add a second, scissoring the digits and stretching myself until the intrusion is almost uncomfortable, on the precipice between pleasure and pain. I increase my speed, tweaking my nipple in time to the thrust of my fingers, and I'm so close. So fucking close that all I need is to rub against my clit, and I'll be coming, going off like a—

Rough hands pull my fingers out and my hand away from my breast, throwing them against the wall and holding them in place.

My eyes pop open, and I look down, stunned to see Wolf on his knees in front of me.

"Wolf."

"That's fucking right, 'Wolf.' Fuck your fingers tomorrow night; tonight, you're coming on my tongue." Wolf lowers his face, leaning in until his nose is at the apex of my thighs, breathing in my scent like a sommelier nosing wine. "You smell fucking delicious," he speaks into my flesh, and his lips graze the insides of my thighs, sending tingles up my spine. I open my mouth to speak, to ask what he's going to do, when his mouth descends, halting every question on my mind.

With his hands still caging my arms against the wall, he uses his jaw to work my legs open, twisting his head until he's situated fully between my legs, and sits on his heels. He laps at me with his tongue, licking up my wetness with noises that can only be described as audible feasting.

Writhing against him, I grind into his mouth as his tongue flattens, applying pressure against my clit before sucking it

195

between his lips. He pulls on it, taking it between his teeth and nipping at it; a burn breaks out in my core before he releases it, soothing the sting with a slow lick that seems to hit every nerve in my vagina.

Wolf pulls back, and I can't help but look down; the wetness on his lips and jaw a testament to how turned on I am. Meeting my eyes, he licks his lips like he just ate the most decadent dessert and is savoring the lingering flavor. "Fucking delicious."

"Wolf, I—"

"... need to come on my tongue. You're right, princess." He dives back in, giving me another long, slow lick before his tongue settles on my opening. My eyes widen as I feel his tongue delve inside, spearing in and out like he's fucking me with his mouth. His nose hits against my clit, giving me the friction I need as his tongue continues to drive in and out of me.

Unable to stop myself, I ride his tongue, grinding against it as though it was his cock inside of me. My hands clench into fists and fight the urge to pull against his hold, even though I want to drive my hands into his short hair and pull him close, fight him for control, and come on his bruised face.

He must sense my need because, without breaking his rhythm, he releases my wrists and grips my hips, guiding me as I ride his face. I give into temptation and grab his head, pulling him impossibly closer until I feel the start of the eruption.

I don't come daintily; no, I come wildly. My body thrashes against Wolf's face, convulsions that can't be contained as the inferno spreads from the center of my body and through every extremity. I feel light and heavy, bright and dimmed, like the entire center of my world was focused on Wolf's impressive tongue, and the minute he delivered my only non-self-induced orgasm, my world got a little darker, a little seedier.

"Holy fucking shit."

"I know, princess." He pauses, licking a path from my inner thigh up to my vagina, collecting all the cum he missed. "You ready to ride my cock now?"

22

Wolf

Whenever I hear people compare pussy to flowers, food, or a drink, I think they sound like fucking morons. Pussy tastes like pussy; the anatomy is the same in each one, and there's no such thing as "petal" pussy lips or a delicate rosette of an asshole. Anatomically speaking, every pussy has a clitoris, clitoral hood, labia, urethral opening, and vulva, followed by a vaginal opening and then the anus.

I've enjoyed every encounter I've had, with every pussy I've tasted; before tonight, I would even go as far as saying that there were no real distinguishable tastes between partners.

I'm humbled as I lick Serena's cunt, trying to drown myself in her cum. She's like nothing I've ever had or tasted before, an ambrosia that makes me sound like a goddamn idiot, but it's addicting all the same.

The hesitation in her eyes when I told her to strip was unmistakable, and I was half-convinced that she'd kick me out of her apartment and tell me to fuck off. I was even more surprised when her eyes narrowed right before she started fucking herself, putting on a show that every cam girl wishes they could pull off. I watched, dumbfounded and hard, as her small hands glided over her rib cage, over that pretty little tattoo, and up to her nipples, where they squeezed and pinched the flesh the way I was dying to.

I settled into her couch, watching the show as she fell back into her wall and performed for herself, with me as a casualty in the room. I was so entranced by the way her fingers glided through her opening that I almost let her come on her fingers, moments away from a self-induced climax that wasn't hers to give.

If I get her one time, for one night, I'm sure as fuck not allowing her to get herself off, even though images of her finger-fucking herself will play like a loop in my mind for longer than I care to admit.

Ripping her hands from her pussy and her perky tit, I grab each wrist in a soft hold and press her palms against the wall. She moans my name, and I can't help the sharp words that come out of my mouth, "That's fucking right, 'Wolf.' Fuck your fingers tomorrow night; tonight, you're coming on my tongue." I dive in, smelling her pussy and nearly drowning in the scent before I start lapping at her, working my head between her thighs until she's almost seated on my face. Looking up her body, I eat at her, savoring the flavor of her arousal until it's all I can focus on, all I can sense, the need for her to come on my tongue fucking palpable.

Changing my speed and pressure, I capture her clit between my lips and suck, pulling on the bundle of nerves before biting down lightly, giving her the pain she so obviously craves as an accompaniment to her pleasure. Her body stills, her thigh muscles going rigid around my ears, and I release, soothing the sting with a long, slow lick that's intended to give her a light pressure to contrast the burn.

"Fucking delicious," I murmur into her skin, looking back up her body until I meet her eyes. Her pupils are blown out, and her skin is flushed, making her golden complexion look like it's fucking glowing against the sterile white walls of her apartment. She looks like a goddess, a fucking siren sent from the gods to be the end of mortal men.

"I—" she starts, her voice breathy and low, but I cut her off, needing to feel her come over my face before I find my release inside her.

"Need to come on my tongue. You're right, princess," I finish for her, wasting no time licking from her pussy to her asshole and back again, circling her opening with my tongue and diving back inside. Spearing my tongue, I tense my muscle and open my jaw as wide as I can, trying to see how much of her pussy I can fit in my mouth as I fuck her with my tongue. Her hips start to meet my thrusts, slowly at first, until her movements become frantic and uncontrolled, as a testament to how close she is to climax.

I feel her wrists pull against my hold, and though I fucking hate the idea of not being in control, I hate the idea of Serena's hands not being on me even more. Releasing my grip, I go fucking crazy as her fingers grab at my hair, pulling me closer as her hips continue to fuck my face. Gripping her hips, I help her ride my tongue, nearly coming in my pants when her pussy starts to contract against my tongue, and her cum covers my mouth, drenching me in the sweetness that is inherently Serena.

Softening my hold and my tongue, I let her body sink back against the wall, though I don't fully release her. Keeping my face level with her cunt, I'm fucking transfixed as her cum

200

starts dripping out of her, dripping down her inner thigh like melting ice cream, and I can't help myself from capturing the droplets with my tongue.

She mutters profanities, and I savor how the smell of sex lingers on her skin, turning her usually light scent musky. Casting my eyes to her couch, I consider the logistics of what we're about to do.

I can delay our satisfaction and have her take me to her bedroom, I can fuck her from behind, letting her body fall over the arm of the couch as I take her soaked cunt in hard thrusts, or I can let her ride me and set the pace. All three options have my cock dripping more precum in my briefs, but only one gives me access to the tits she was playing with before I got my mouth on her. I look back at her face and pride myself on the blissed-out look on her features.

"You ready to ride my cock now?" I ask, and her eyes widen, the brown irises bright with interest and surprise. Not giving her a chance to answer, I unfold my body from the floor and stand up, letting my hands trail up her outer thighs and waist as I rise. Looming before her, I reach down, cupping her perky ass, and lift, letting her legs fold around my torso once again. I resist the urge to drive into her and dry hump her like a pimple-faced teenager with his first taste of pussy.

Walking around the coffee table, I sit on the couch. Grabbing her calves, I unlock them from around my waist and rest them on the deep-seated couch so that she's able to place weight on her knees. Leaning back, I rake my hands over her thighs, up her waist, and settle them on her face, guiding her down until her lips are centimeters away from mine.

"Taste yourself, princess." I eradicate the distance between us and take her lips, seizing her mouth and working it open with my tongue. She lets out a gasp, and I take advantage, stealing my tongue inside so that she can taste how goddamn intoxicating she is. Her tongue battles with mine, tangling together until our mouths are fused so completely, so expertly, it's like we've done this before.

Pulling back, I break the kiss. "Rise up on your knees, Serena." She follows my instructions, allowing me access to unbutton my jeans. "Take my cock out, princess."

Drawing her lip into her mouth, she bites down, hesitating for a minute before lowering her hands from my shoulders and grabbing my briefs, tugging down until my dick springs free, standing at attention before her.

"Wow," she whispers, sounding like a cross between reverent and horrified. I'm not surprised; I don't have the longest dick; it's average-sized, maybe an inch above, and there are no crazy hooks, bends, or piercings that characterize it. However, while my length is average, I'm thick, and I doubt her fingertips will overlap if she holds it in her hand. I stopped bothering with blowjobs years ago because women couldn't fit past the head between their lips without risking lockjaw.

I watch her as she surveys my dick, resting between us like a tent pole. The attention she's giving to it makes me want to line up her pussy and drill into her, but as much as she worked herself up and as explosive as her orgasm was on my tongue, I know from experience that I need to work myself inside, little by little.

"Can I...?" she starts, gesturing toward my cock like it's going to bite her.

Raising an eyebrow, I try to keep the humor out of my voice. "Can you what, princess?"

She clears her throat, throwing her shoulders back before

202

she continues, "Touch it. Can I touch it?" I nod, staying still as she places her hand on top of my dick. I stifle a groan at the contrast in our skin; Serena's touch is warm and golden, while my skin is pale and perpetually cold to the touch. With a feather-light touch, she traces the veins on the underside of my dick like an explorer uncovering unchartered territory. I clench my jaw, willing myself to remain still as she glides her nails across my sensitive skin.

"If you don't want me to come on your hand, you should probably stop," I council, half joking, because if she keeps touching my cock like it's the eighth wonder of the world, I'm going to spurt ropes of cum all over her hand and tits.

"Oh," she squeaks, quickly releasing me like my skin burned her. "Sorry."

"You never have to apologize for touching my dick, princess."

The flush that takes over her skin is satisfying and sweet as fuck, but I need more. "Reach into my pocket and grab my wallet; I have a condom inside." I shut my eyes as she reaches into my pocket and pulls out my wallet, finding the condom easily before discarding the leather billfold on the cushion beside us. She holds the wrapper between us, pinching it tightly between her fingers and surveying the words on the Double Ecstasy package.

"A warming lubricant?" she asks, referencing the warming lubricant on the outside of the condom's skin, a feature with this brand. "Will that burn?"

I shake my head, plucking the package from her fingers. "No; it's cooling on the inside for me, warming on the outside for you. But I don't get them for the lubricant. They're the only condoms that fit without me having to worry the latex is going to rip." She glances down at my cock again, still standing tall between us.

"I'm wider than most men, princess. I don't know who you've been with, and I honestly don't give a shit." I rip open the foil and extract the condom from the package, throwing the wrapper in the same direction Serena tossed my wallet. Rolling the latex down my cock, I pinch the tip to make sure it's on correctly, ensuring that there's enough room at the top so that it doesn't burst when I come.

I can feel Serena's eyes on me during the entire process, a caress that seems to physically touch me, even though her hands hang at her sides, and she's propped on her knees.

That won't fucking do.

Dropping my cock, I bring one hand to Serena's inner thigh and walk my fingers up until they meet the wetness between her thighs. Without warning, I impale her with two fingers, sighing in relief when they are met with minimal resistance as my palm brushes against her clit. She gasps, rocking into my fingers despite her surprise at the invasion.

"This good, princess?" I ask, waiting for her to tell me that she's okay, even though I can physically see how she responds. I want her words—no, I *need* her words—for me to keep going.

"God, yes," she cries out, undulating against the minute thrusts I open her up with.

"Do you think you can take a third?" She nods frantically, widening her stance in my lap to give me more room to work with as I spear her with a third finger. It's a tighter fit, and I watch her face closely, taking in the slight wince that's proceeded by Serena throwing her head back and sinking down, helping me enter her deeper and harder in preparation for my cock. We stay like this for long minutes, simulating a fucking that will inevitably change both of us: me because I've never been with one of my clients nor one of Celeste's friends, and Serena because she's about to have her cunt wrecked.

Her pussy grows wetter, giving me more lubricant to move my fingers, and I scissor them, opening her from the inside to ease any potential pain she may feel when I enter her.

"You ready, Serena?"

She brings her head down, meeting my eyes and nodding erratically like she can't wait one more minute until I'm fully seated inside her. I pull my fingers out and stick them in my mouth, licking at the taste of her and relishing the moan she lets out as she watches me savor her cum.

Dropping my hands to her outer thighs, I level her with a look. "I'll let you set the pace, say, 'Stop' or stop moving if it gets to be too painful."

"Okay," she says, right before she lifts, just to sink back down, taking my cock halfway.

23

Serena

I'm not sure that dropping down and stabbing myself with Wolf's dick was the smartest thing I've ever done, especially considering that it looks like a soda can, but I can confirm that I feel incredibly full. Glancing down, I'm shocked to realize that I'm only halfway seated, no more than three inches inside me.

"For fuck's sake, Serena. I told you to set the pace so that you can go slow, not split yourself in half," Wolf grunts out, sounding pained below me. I move my gaze from where we're joined to his face and note his strained features and the set of his jaw. He looks like he's holding himself back, and while I appreciate his effort, it's not what I need right now.

"I can take more," I pant, shifting against him. The move has his dick rubbing against my inner walls, and I clench, the sensation simultaneously foreign and amazing.

"Clench one more time, and I'm going to come before we get to the good part," he warns, squeezing my hips to still my movements. I don't listen to him; instead, I contract my muscles again and enjoy the feeling of his cock inside me.

"Serena, enough."

This time, I don't ignore his words.

"I'm going to work myself in deeper. Tell me if it gets to be too much." His words are considerate, but his tone is harsh, a lashing against my skin. Does it make me sick that I feel myself growing wetter at his gruffness, more turned on by his intensity?

Wolf starts rocking my hips gently, shifting his left hand until it's splayed over my stomach, his thumb rubbing against my clit. The dual sensations of fullness and his rubbing against my clit have my movements growing less controlled, more erratic, and fighting against the rhythm he sets. With each thrust, each swipe of his thumb, I feel my body loosening more, accommodating his girth in a way I would never have thought possible. It doesn't take long until there's only an inch separating our pelvic bones, and then he's buried inside of me so deep, I'm not sure if I'll be able to get him out.

Fighting against his hold, I lean back, gripping his knees to give myself leverage as I move against him, pushing myself up and down while his thumb continues to rub circles.

"So fucking tight," Wolf mutters, more to himself than to me, as though he can't believe how damn good this feels, either.

Determined to remove the last bit of distance between us, I push up one last time before dropping down in a hard thrust, pinning him beneath my hips and sealing us together.

"Oh," I say at the same time he grinds out, "Fuck."

If I thought I felt full before, that's nothing compared to having him fully seated inside of me. Refusing to move off of him, I release his thighs and lean forward, plastering my naked chest against his clothed one, and grind our bodies together, effectively trapping his hand between us to give me extra friction.

What feels like seconds pass before I feel tingles erupt along my spine, traveling until I feel like a livewire on the verge of exploding. I clench against him, drawing him inside deeper until my orgasm hits me with a ferocity I've never experienced before.

"That's it, ride my cock, princess. Fuck, I can feel you coming around me." Wolf drives into me from below, fucking me until his body stills, and he releases a loud curse. I collapse against his chest, breathing hard as I attempt to catch my breath. Wolf releases my hip and extracts his hand from between our bodies. I start to move up, assuming that he is getting ready to pull away when his hands wrap around me, catching me by surprise when he hugs me closer to his body, keeping us molded together in a way that screams intimacy despite our earlier agreement.

I don't fight his hold, and when a heavy hand touches the back of my head, threading fingers through the short strands and giving my head a soft scalp massage, I feel myself pulling under. I succumb to the exhaustion of the day, the depletion of energy both from sex with Wolf and the anger over my dad and Marina's texts earlier in the evening.

Closing my eyes, I tell myself it's only for a minute, that the safety I feel in Wolf's arms is false, temporary, and the least permanent thing in my life.

—

The room is dark when I wake up, and I startle, disorientated by my surroundings for a minute until I reach over and flick on the lamp by my bedside table. The night comes rushing back to me: the tattoo shop, the texts, Wolf's thick dick. There's a soreness between my thighs that tells me I didn't imagine the last part, even though there's no evidence of Wolf in my space. I look down, surprised to find myself in an oversized T-shirt when I know damn well that I passed out on top of Wolf with not a stitch of clothing on. Either I sleepwalked, opened my dresser drawer, and slipped on one of my cotton shirts, or Wolf rummaged through my things and made sure I was covered before leaving.

I look to the other side of my bed, though I'm not delusional enough to imagine that he'll be there or that there would be an indent or indication of his presence. I take in the perfectly folded sheets and sigh at the thought that there would be some sign of him in this room.

Flinging the covers back, I walk barefoot into my living room, surprised that the smell of sex doesn't permeate the air. Walking through the space, I grab a glass and fill it with water, leaning against the counter as I stare at the couch where I rode Wolf like he was a stallion and I was a champion jockey. Maybe I should be embarrassed, but the two orgasms he gave me eclipse any other thought I have.

My eyes move from the couch to my door, where the lock is suspiciously in place, though the deadbolt remains unlatched. I cut across the apartment and turn the deadbolt, providing an extra layer of unnecessary protection between me and whatever is outside of my apartment.

I'm not sure how Wolf managed to leave and lock my door, but I'm grateful that I wasn't left vulnerable and unconscious in my apartment. I ignore the sting in my chest that Wolf didn't linger until I woke up, scolding myself for having any ill-conceived thoughts that this was anything other than a one-night stand.

Walking back into my bedroom, I grab my phone from

my nightstand—another indication that Wolf was here—and cycle through the text messages that have come through since I've been home. It's the middle of the night, so I'm not surprised I have a few unread messages awaiting me. My eyes snag on one from Wolf, confused as to why he'd text me if he was just here.

Wolf: Turn the deadbolt when you wake up. Call Aubrey next week to schedule your appointment; your back should be healed and tattooable by the end of the month. I'll shift shit around to book your first appointment.

My brows furrow at his text; up until this moment, we were all in agreement that Sloan was doing my tattoo, and I was prepared to sit with her to fix the monstrosity on my back. There's been no mention, no utterance, that Wolf would be the one spending hours on my piece. My hands fly over my phone as I text him back.

Serena: Thanks for locking up, but what do you mean, "I'll shift shit around?" I thought Sloan was doing my tattoo.

Three dots pop up on my screen, and I watch for his reply. My brows furrow as soon as it comes in.

Wolf: I didn't like the direction she was headed, and I have something in mind. I'll see you in a few weeks for your appointment. Don't forget to lock up.

"Dick," I mumble, clicking out of his thread.

Going back to my messages, I see that Ava and Celeste have blown up our group chat once again. I scroll through the thread until I arrive at the beginning of the conversation.

CeCe (8:29 PM): Wolf's final fight is on the twenty-fourth. Ava, Grey, and Lincoln are coming with us. Serena, are you in?

Ava (8:32 PM): Of course she's in. The last time we

abandoned her, she was assaulted by that asshat. Speaking of, have you heard from the double-D assholes lately?

Ava (9:15 PM): Are you ignoring us, my little butterfly?

CeCe (10:54 PM): Okay, now I'm starting to get worried. I'm not above driving to your apartment to make sure you're not dead.

I hastily type out a reply, musing that Wolf's final fight must be why he has availability at the end of this month. He's never spoken to me about it, but I can imagine that training for a fight is intense and requires copious amounts of hours in the gym. I've only seen the artistic side of Wolf, never the side that battles against other men in a cage.

Serena (12:59 AM): Sorry, I had a long day and fell asleep on my couch; I just woke up. Sure, that sounds fun, though I don't know much about MMA. And no, I haven't heard from Dylan or Devin. Marina did text me earlier today, though.

CeCe: Jesus. We were about to drive over to break into your place. I'll kill her. What the hell were you doing to tire you out?

Serena: No one.

"Dammit." I wince, annoyed with myself for how I just answered that question.

Ava: I'm trying hard not to say what we all know I'm thinking.

CeCe: It's fine, I'll say it. What were you up to, Serena? Don't even try bullshitting us because you lie like shit.

Scrunching my nose, I grow increasingly annoyed at my friends' good-natured but nosy texts.

Serena: It's a text message. You can't detect a lie from a text.

CeCe: Can't I?

211

Letting out a sigh, I shake my head before typing out my response.

Serena: Just drop it. I'll be there on the twenty-fourth. I have tutoring and will be in the library all day tomorrow, so I won't make brunch. I'm also scheduled for tutoring sessions next Saturday and Sunday, but I'm free both afternoons if you want to move our weekly breakfast to lunch.

Since the beginning of the semester, Ava, CeCe, and I have met weekly for breakfast, typically on the weekends but sometimes during the week, too. This will be the first week where my schedule is too busy to allow me the girl time I've missed out on for most of my adolescence and teenage years.

CeCe: Do you want me to drop off a French toast? I feel bad that you're missing out on brunch.

I can't help the smile that breaks out on my face at CeCe's question. Even when Dylan and I were on good terms, he was never thoughtful in a way that communicated he truly cared about me or my well-being. Just like when I had the flashback to stapling the fabric of my car, the memories of our friendship are tinted with an unflattering hue.

Serena: No, thank you, though. I'll talk to you guys tomorrow. XX

Swiping out of that conversation, I take a look at the last unread messages on my phone: one from a random number and the other from my big, Meg.

With the knowledge that I spoke to Meg yesterday about giving Jack my number, I have a strong feeling that I know the owner of the unknown number. Without delaying, I open the text.

Unknown: Hi, beautiful. It's Jack. How are you? Meg finally gave me your number. It was great seeing you.

212

The choppy sentences of his text make me feel like I just read the intrusive thoughts of a dog. Gnawing on the skin of my thumb, I consider the fact that I have one man's saliva and bite marks covering my body, who couldn't be less interested in me, while another seems wildly interested despite my reservations.

Serena: Hi, Jack. It was nice seeing you yesterday, too.

I don't have to wait for his response; it's almost instant.

Jack: I had no idea you were related to Marina. That must be cool to have a friend turned sister. I have two brothers.

Furrowing my brow, I think back to our encounter yesterday; I'm not sure if Jack is just trying to make conversation or if he's so obtuse that he didn't pick up on the obvious dislike Marina and I harbor for each other. I'm pretty sure I was blatant in my distaste.

Serena: We're not friends.

Jack: Right, right. So, uh, anyway, would you want to go to dinner sometime? I'd love to take you out and get to know you better.

Serena: I'm not sure. I have a lot going on right now.

Jack: Come on, just one dinner, beautiful. Please. I promise if you want me to leave you alone after, I will.

Jack: Just give me a shot, beautiful.

Releasing a breath, I look at the texts, his obvious eagerness, and feel like there's a rock in the pit of my stomach. For some inexplicable, stupid reason, Wolf's face flashes in my mind when I think about going to dinner with Jack; in my vision, it's not Jack's slender form sitting across from me, it's Wolf's hulking one.

That image is like ice water soaking my veins, breaking me from any delusions I may harbor. We had sex, amazing,

213

wild sex, but there's nothing more to it. Pushing my shoulders back, I expel any thoughts of Wolf from my mind and respond to Jack.

Serena: Okay. I'm free on Thursday.

Jack: Hell yeah :) I'll pick you up around seven.

I like the message before moving to the last unread message on my phone.

Meg: Hey, Little! I just spoke to Jack, he's so into you, holy shit. He's going to text you tonight and ask you out!!!

Yeah, no shit, Meg.

—

I passed out last night after responding to the ungodly amount of messages on my phone. Despite my initial annoyance with Meg, we ended up speaking for a while and confirmed plans for lunch on Tuesday in the Student Center. Though I'm not as close to Meg as I am to CeCe and Ava, I can't deny that she's been a good friend to me despite my distance in recent weeks.

This morning, I have a full schedule of tutoring followed by my coursework. At the end of class last week, Dr. Forester assigned us a write-up on morphological awareness, or how prefixes and suffixes can be utilized to alter the meaning or intent of a word. Unlike other assignments I've received in my English courses, Dr. Forester assigned us only that phrase and told us to come up with a discussion or argument around it.

I decided to focus on how morphological awareness can help increase literacy rates and vocabulary comprehension. How I'll craft that argument, I'm not entirely sure, but I know that I'll need to scour through multiple sources and lexicon

214

to achieve something presentable.

I'm so lost in my thoughts that I don't register the footsteps that follow me to the private rooms until my backpack is tugged, pulling me backward until my body hits the wall. Startled, I look up and meet the eyes of Marina.

"God, you look like you're homeless already."

"Shut up, Marina." Rolling my eyes, I pull myself out of her hold and step back, placing much-needed distance between us. "What are you even doing here; you know it's a library—where people study, right?" I draw out my words, speaking slowly as though she has difficulty comprehending it.

"Why Daddy even cares about you is anyone's guess, you freak. I'm warning you, stay away from Jack. He's not for you."

I can't hold back the laugh that bubbles out of me. "Stay away from Jack? Marina, are you listening to yourself right now? He's not even interested in you, and you have no say on who I do or do not spend time with."

"He's not interested in me *yet*. You already stole Devin away from me; don't be a homewrecker again."

Looking to the ceiling and calling on deep-buried patience, I release a long sigh before looking into Marina's face. "Marina, I mean this with everything in me: leave me the hell alone. I told *my* dad last night—" I emphasize the possessive pronoun—"I want nothing to do with him, with you, or with your mother. I don't need his money, my mom doesn't need it, and I am so damn sick of you, Dylan, and my dad trying to bully me when I am anything other than the good little forgotten daughter. All of you can fuck right off, okay?"

Marina stares at me, clearly stunned over my outburst. In the past, I would take her jibes, internalize my sadness,

215

and then remove myself from the situation. Maybe it's the influence of CeCe and Ava, or maybe it's me just acquiring a backbone at nineteen, but I am so done with them and their treatment of me.

"Have a nice day, asshole," I mutter, lowering my voice now that my tirade is over, and walk past her, pushing into her shoulder so that she gets the hell away from me.

"Yeah, well. Stay away from my big, too."

Unable to help myself, I turn my head, pausing in my steps. "Who is your big?"

"Bethany." I can hear the self-satisfied smirk in her voice and internally groan.

"Of course she is." Shaking my head, I walk away, disgusted and annoyed by Marina, which really isn't anything new.

24

Serena

Seeing Marina on Sunday put everything out of alignment; she's like a walking Mercury in retrograde, a human-sized ball of gas that just messes up everyone's moods and feelings. I tried to put her words and presence out of my mind while I worked with my tutoring clients, but her jabs kept prodding me long after her exit.

I even went as far as cramming ear pods into my ears and blasting The Gaslight Anthem as I worked on my paper, despite typically needing silence and quiet to concentrate.

Casting her from my mind, I ordered a pottery kiln for my apartment last night, which was an extremely impulsive and messy decision. I'm looking forward to having it come this week, just to see if spinning clay in my apartment is the dumbest thing I've ever considered doing. There's something about the clay oozing between my fingers as I create bowls and vases that look more like a Picasso imitation than anything usable that calms my soul.

Shaking my head, I force myself to pay attention to my surroundings as I walk across campus and toward the diner, where I'm meeting Ava and CeCe for lunch before my class with Dr. Forester.

My phone rings just as I step over the threshold of the diner, and I frown at my mom's picture and name on the screen. My mom rarely uses her phone while working, reserving it only for emergencies and her lunch hour—if she decides to take one. If she's calling me at one in the afternoon on a Tuesday, something is wrong. Stepping back outside, I answer the call.

"Mamá?"

"*Muñeca*, hi. Everything is fine," she hurries to say as if she knows that my thoughts immediately went somewhere bad.

"Thank God. Why are you calling; aren't you in school?"

"Yes, but I wanted to call to tell you something before I forgot and let it slip my mind." She pauses, and I can hear the breath on her end of the phone. "I'll be out of the house by the beginning of next month, and I packed up most of the main areas of the house and basement. I'm packing up your room at the end of the month once I get back from my conference in D.C. If you're not too busy, can you come home to sort through your room? I'd like to donate whatever you're not attached to since we'll be downsizing a bit."

I swallow against the lump in my throat, keeping as much emotion out of my voice as I possibly can. "Of course, Mom. Whatever you need, I'll be there. I'm sorry I didn't help more."

"No, baby. You have school and a life; I didn't call you to make you feel bad. I just want to make sure that I don't donate anything you need or want to hold on to. You'll have your room in the condo, but the layout isn't as open as the house, and I don't want to make the space feel cluttered."

I nod as though she can see me. "No, I understand. I'll be there."

"Okay, great. Let me get back to work. I have an interview coming in for the varsity volleyball coach position."

Gritting my teeth, I close my eyes, allowing myself a minute of anger before I get on with my life and get over it. The disdain I have for my father has morphed into hatred.

"Rena!" I open my eyes and turn my head in the direction of my name.

"Hey, guys." CeCe and Ava approach, clutching their jackets against the wind.

"Oh no, what's wrong? Are you okay?"

I offer a weak smile; it feels brittle on my face, and I'm sure I look upset. "I'm fine. Want to head inside? It's chilly out here."

I nod toward the entrance, and they both follow my lead, though I know the inquisition will start as soon as we're seated. I pretend to study my menu as soon as we sit down, though I have no appetite after the call with my mother.

"Okay, time to spill. What's going on?"

I shake my head, looking away from her. "I'm going out with Jack Thursday night," I offer, not in the mood to further dissect my shitty homelife.

CeCe's eyes go wide, and Ava opens her mouth, a squawk-like sound coming out.

"What sound was that?" I can't help but laugh.

"Honestly? I'm not sure. But holy shit. Tell us everything. Where are you going?" Ava leans forward and grabs my hands, tugging them toward her.

I try to pull my hands away, but she is deceptively strong and has a tight hold. "He said a tavern in Millsbrook? I'm not sure which one."

"It must be Starbound. They have decent food and live

music; Grey's brought me a few times for their pizza. Are you excited?" She finally drops my hands, and I hide them in my lap, away from her tentacles.

"I guess. I'm not sure what to expect."

Ava's brows furrow and CeCe tilts her head at me, confusion marring her features. "What do you mean?"

"He's a nice guy, but I'm not interested in him." I shrug, feigning nonchalance, though inside, I'm shouting that this date feels like a horrible idea.

"Do you want me to call him and pretend that you broke your wrist in a stationary bike accident?"

"That was... weirdly specific."

"It happened to me once. I'll never forgive Amanda Betts for watching as I fell on a pile of rocks."

"Why was there a stationary bike next to a pile of rocks?" I am so confused.

Ava starts to answer, but CeCe cuts her off, "She just means that the bike wasn't moving. She was standing next to a regular bicycle and fell over onto a pile of rocks."

"You never cease to amaze me, Ava," I laugh out, unable to help the mirth that swallows the rest of my words. When Meg texted me last night, canceling our lunch because she got a stomach bug, I felt horrible that she was sick and asked if I could bring her anything, like soup or ginger ale. She declined, opting to go home for the rest of the week instead of staying in West Helm.

After Meg canceled our lunch plans, I texted Ava and CeCe to see if they wanted to meet for lunch. It may make me a shitty friend, but I was relieved that the three of us were able to get together.

"Okay, back to Jack. Are you taking your own car or driving

there together?"

"He said he would pick me up around seven. I wanted to
tell him that I would meet him there, but I didn't want to be
rude."

"Fuck that," CeCe provides. "If you don't feel comfortable
driving with him, then you take your car or Uber."

"C and I could drive you in your car and wait inside
the restaurant if you'd feel more comfortable." Though
she doesn't elaborate, I have a feeling that Ava's version of
"waiting" would include watching us from the next table.

Shaking my head, I reject her offer. "No, it's okay. If
anything, maybe I'll leave my car keys with you, and you
can pick me up if things get weird?"

"Of course. But I'll drive. Celeste has road rage."

Celeste casts Ava a death glare before picking up a menu.
"What are you both getting?" We fall into a deliberation of
eggs versus pancakes versus French toast, though our orders
are always the same: French toast for me and CeCe and eggs
for Ava. The waitress appears soon after we close our menus
and leaves with the promise to return with coffee. Not even
a minute later, she returns with three mugs and creamer.

I busy myself making my coffee and take a long sip, savoring
the flavors. Even though it's technically lunchtime, there's
something about a Jersey diner that makes you want breakfast
at all hours of the day.

"So, how's the tattoo coming along?" CeCe asks, pushing
her mug to the side.

"Uh, well..." I clear my throat, images of Wolf at my apartment filter through my mind: him watching me, pleasuring
me on his knees, feeling him under me. I feel my cheeks burn,
and I duck my head, picking up my mug to buy myself a few

221

moments to weigh my response. Taking a sip, I settle my thoughts and look back up at CeCe and Ava's waiting faces. "I have to wait until my back is a little more healed. I think Wolf mentioned that the first session will be at the end of this month."

They accept my answer, though I can feel CeCe's green gaze, so much like her cousin's, on me. It's unnerving and slightly annoying, and as soon as my French toast arrives, I dive in, keeping my mouth too full to speak.

—

"Do you want us to come by on Thursday to help you get ready?"

I roll my eyes at Ava's question and walk ahead of her, racing down the steps and toward the path that will lead me to my afternoon class. "I think I can put on a pair of jeans by myself, but thank you."

"Hey." She stops her walk, grabbing my arm to still me. "You don't seem excited about this. You know you don't have to go, right? If you decide to cancel on him, there's nothing wrong with that."

"I know, Aves. And it's not that I'm not excited, I promise. I just don't want to get my hopes up with, well, everything. Romantically, I don't think I'm interested in Jack, but this is my first real date. Everything with my parents and the house has just been a lot, so my emotions are all over the place, and I'm trying to make sense of it all."

Her face softens. "I'm sorry; it's easy to forget about douchebag Dylan and dickwad Devin. Even Marina fades into the background sometimes. But what you want, who you are, is important, too, okay? I know you're close with

222

your mom, and you have the sorority now, but don't forget that we're here for you, too, okay?"

"Thanks, Aves," I choke out, emotion clogging my throat.

"And don't tell C that you have a crush on her cousin," she whispers.

"W-what? What are you talking about?" I cut my gaze to Celeste, who's walking behind us, engrossed in her phone.

"Oh my God, you should see your face. I'm kidding. Wolf is an asshole, always grumbling or complaining about something."

"It's not like Grey is sunshine and rainbows."

Ava sighs, a wistful look crossing her face. "No, he's a bag of dicks, but Jesus, he knows how to use them."

"And that's my cue to go." I pull Ava and CeCe in for separate hugs, giving them my car key before I head to class, just in case I need either one of them to rescue me.

However, if I needed help, neither one of them would show up without their boyfriends, and the idea of seeing Greyson or Dante in my dilapidated car is humorous. The key is effectively useless but symbolic of the trust I have in both of them to be there for me when I need it.

25

Wolf

"Yer gettin' soft in yer old age, McCleery," Jedd taunts as I land another combination against the sparring gloves. We've been at this for an hour: quick combinations and footwork to prepare me for the last fight of my career. While I may be done with the MMA circuit, there's no fucking way I'm leaving the cage without a win.

"Fuck off, old man," I grunt out around my mouthguard, moving through the uppercut hook movement with a little more force than necessary.

"Feckin' shite, save it fer the cage, ye animal."

I smirk but continue to do the work my trainer demands of me.

"Alright, drop yer hands. Yer going to do cool down stretches before I kick your sorry arse out of my gym."

I spit the mouthguard into my hand, working my jaw to loosen the muscles in my face. "You'll be sobbing on the twenty-fourth like a little baby."

"I'll miss havin' ye around, McCleery, make no mistake. But yer priorities are changin'."

Nodding, I focus on unwrapping the protective tape from around my knuckles. "I'll stop by, and you know you're always welcome at the shop. We need to get those dumbass Irish tats replaced by something more masculine, like the saltire or the Royal Banner of Scotland." I motion toward his Ireland-themed tattoos.

"Feck off. Yer half Irish, and yer mam would hit ye with a damn shovel if she heard you disrespecting yer heritage."

"Ladies love Highlanders; I think I'll claim just that part from now on," I tease.

"Did I say stretches? I meant sprint intervals on the treadmill."

Flipping him off, I ignore his last words and step down from the training platform, running right into my worst goddamn nightmare.

"Oh, Wolf, I didn't realize you were training today," the woman cloaked in pink yells over the music blaring out of the speakers.

I nod, walking past my ex-girlfriend and toward the yoga mats rolled up in the back of the gym. I hear footsteps following me, and I grit my teeth, praying to every god up there that Kelly changes her direction.

"So, how have you been? I saw your work on that Jets player."

I've got no fucking luck. I nod again and unroll a mat in front of the mirror.

"So, how's the shop? How's Aubrey? I need to call her for lunch, maybe get together."

I can't help the laugh that rockets out of me. "The fuck are you talking about? You and Aubs hate each other. And why the hell would you call her?"

"No, we're friends." She crosses her arms, popping a hip out in a stubborn display.

"The fuck are you on about, Kelly?"

"I just, I thought maybe you and I, you know? Maybe we should give it another try?"

My jaw drops, and I stare at her through the mirror. "Kelly, I mean this with no disrespect, but getting back together with you sounds like torture. I would rather pluck every eyelash out of my left eye than talk to you, and the idea of fucking you?" I shudder, not hiding my revulsion. "You're with Gage, be happy with him."

Kelly's face breaks into a scowl before smoothing out, a veneer moving over her features to hide the ugliness inside. "Wolfie, you don't mean that. Don't you ever think about us?"

"Only when I want to make myself throw up."

"Wolf." Her voice is sharp, a reprimand for being honest.

"Kelly," I sigh, tired of her shit, even though I've only been in her presence for a few minutes. "I'm not trying to be a dick, but can you just leave me alone? We're not together, and we probably never should have been in the first place. Gage is a loose cannon, but he's art in the cage. Let him take care of you, be that trophy wife you've always dreamed of 'cause you sure as shit aren't going to be anything to me ever again." Bending, I grab the mat I just placed down and move to another part of the gym, keeping my back to Kelly.

"She's a feral one," Jedd murmurs, sneaking up beside me as I start on my agility stretches.

"She's batshit crazy. And if she thinks I'm still interested, she's delusional, too." All thoughts of Kelly, all feelings, fled when I realized how opportunistic she was. Instead of dwelling on what could have been my life, lately—as in the

226

past two months—my mind conjures up images of a blonde bob and warm skin, a heart-shaped face, and eyes that seem to glow the longer they stare.

My one night with Serena was supposed to quell the idiotic attraction I can't help but feel when she's in front of me or on my mind. Instead, it seems to have done the opposite, making her a constant fixture, a perpetual presence that won't go the fuck away.

"Ye got somethin' on yer brain, McCleery?" Jedd eyes me skeptically in the mirror, loosening the hold Serena has on my mind.

"No," I respond, meeting his gaze in the mirror. "Nothing important."

—

I felt Kelly's eyes on me up until I walked out of the gym, a persistent, annoying gnat that refused to go away. When she broke up with me, I was devastated; I was gutted when I found out she started dating someone else from my gym. But when I took a step back and looked at it, with Aubrey, Trent, and a shit ton of whiskey, I realized that it was the best damn thing to happen to me.

Life with Kelly would have been constant stress, isolation, and fights; no one, from my mother to my employees, liked her; they just tolerated her for my sake, though I didn't find that out until later.

Climbing off my bike, I pull my helmet off and clip it to the handlebar at the same time my phone vibrates in my pocket, signaling a call. Without looking at the screen, I lift it to my ear.

"Yeah."

A soft scoff sounds off, and I smile, knowing immediately that my mother is on the other end of the line. "Is that any way to speak to the woman who gave birth to you?"

"Hey, Ma."

"Oh, so you do remember that you have a mother. It's been so long that I wasn't sure if my child decided to emancipate himself."

"I'm twenty-five; I'm already emancipated." Unlike my science and math-minded aunts and uncles, my mother is a high school drama teacher and makes everything a production. CeCe and I are probably so close because she reminds me of my mother with her theatrics.

"Such a smartass. Are you ready for the game at the end of the month?"

"Fight, Mom, not a game."

"Whatever it is. Are you ready? Are you nervous? How do you feel?"

"I'm good, as ready as I can be."

"Have I mentioned how happy I am that you're stopping your matches? I hate seeing black eyes on my baby." I don't correct her use of the term matches; after this next fight, I'm retiring.

"So you remind me every time we speak."

"Watch your tone, Wolfric Magnus McCleery. Anyway, Celeste called me last night and let me know she, her boyfriend, and their friends were coming to the spectacle. I haven't spoken to Aunt Donna or Aunt Fiona yet, but I assume your other cousins are coming, as well?"

I swallow against the wave of lust that just attacked my cock at the mention of my cousin's friends. I could give two shits about the guys, and Ava is more like a cousin than anything else, but my mind stutters at the thought of the deceptively serene hellcat. Serena has seen me as an artist, never as a fighter, and I don't know if I even like the idea of exposing her to that side of my life. It feels too intimate, too personal, and I balk at the idea that she'll know every fucking facet of who I am.

I don't want the knowledge that Serena has ridden my cock like a champ, has my artwork on her body, and will see me beat a man to a pulp to turn me on. But fuck me, it does. Shaking my head, I think, *She's not for me*, before I ask my mom, "How's Dad?"

"Okay, I see we're not talking about Celeste or your other cousins. He bought a pickleball membership, said a few of the guys at the club were talking about playing pickleball, and, of course, he is easily influenced. Peer pressure works on him every damn time."

I bite my lip to keep from laughing. "Let him be; it's better than drugs." I glance up at the bar sign; Starbound Tavern is a hole-in-the-wall bar with great food, live music, and a decent beer list. I shouldn't indulge with a fight so close, but after the shit Kelly pulled today, I need a beer.

"Listen, Ma, I'm about to get something to eat. Can I call you back tomorrow?"

"Oh sure, call me back because your mother is just going to wait by the phone for when you deign to grace me with your verbal presence."

"Mom," I huff out.

"Fine. I love you, get home safe. Call me in the morning, or else I'm showing up at your house."

"Love you too, Mom." I pocket my phone and open the door to the bar.

229

I'm not surprised that the place is busy tonight; less than an hour from the city and bordering the college town of West Helm, there are a lot of bankers, professors, and families who live in Millsbrook. I nod my head at the bartender, Lance, and take a seat at the far corner of the bar, away from anyone who may want to talk to me but in a good position to see anyone who comes into the bar.

All I need is one look at Kelly or Gage, and I'll run out the back door, get my ass on my bike, and head back home.

"Hey man, good to see you. It's been a while."

"Hey, Lance. Training and clients are kicking my ass."

He nods, setting down a menu as a formality, though I already know what I'm getting.

"I'll do a Dog's Run IPA and a burger, medium, American cheese, and extra pickles."

"I'll have the kitchen start on that, boss."

Lance reaches down to grab a chilled glass and pours the beer expertly, leaving just enough foam at the top to give it a good head that doesn't need to settle before I take a sip. When I'm driving or on the back of my bike, I rarely indulge in alcohol, and if I do, then only a single beer—not willing to put myself or anyone else at risk from overconsumption or drunk driving.

I lift the glass to take a sip when a horrifying black wig enters the room, attached to the head of a face I know entirely too well, one that looks shockingly similar to mine. Following is a woman with discount store lavender synthetic hair and three men. I watch as they make their way across the bar and settle into a booth, my cousin and Ava sitting facing the door, being as inconspicuous as two wig-wearing women can be while Dante and two other guys sit across from them.

230

A waiter approaches almost instantly, presumably asking for ID. My cousin and Ava have the good sense to shake their heads while Dante and the other guys hand over their IDs.

Dropping my beer back down, I push myself out of the barstool but stop as honey-blonde hair captures my attention from the corner of my eye. Turning, I see Serena enter, wearing jeans that should be illegal and a short black puffer jacket. Her short hair is artfully messy, like she styled it that way, and her skin fucking emits light, a beacon in a bar that prides itself on dimness.

My jaw hardens as a tall, slim-as-shit guy walks in after her and places his hand on the small of her back as though he has a right to touch her. I can't hear their conversation, and I'm not a goddamn lip reader, but based on his free hand motioning toward the booths along the back wall, it's obvious his intent. Serena's smile is straining, and satisfaction ripples over my body when she discreetly steps out of his hold, one that I should punch myself in the face for feeling.

I don't have ownership or possession over Serena; she has the autonomy and self-governance to do what she wants with her body, when she wants, and with whom. We fucked one time—singular. I'm going to fix the flying dicks on her back and resign myself to awkward run-ins for the rest of my life since she's become one of Celeste's close friends. But I don't have any claim over her. I tell myself I don't want one, either, though it feels like a lie.

However, something sets me on edge as I see them; he looks too clean, too nice, too straight-edge for me to take seriously. He's probably a perfectly nice, respectable guy, earning a business degree to work as a recruiter or outside sales consultant.

Needless to say, I fucking hate him.

Serena's eyes remain downcast, not noticing me at the bar or the scene across the room, where Celeste and Ava practically stand up on the bench seat to get a better look at their friend on a date. Serena slides into the booth, conveniently facing my direction, and I see the surprise on her face when the idiot slides in next to her, nudging her body over until she's plastered against the wall.

"The fuck—"

"Here you go. Do you need ketchup or anything?" Lance places my burger in front of me, sliding it until it's nearly falling from the bar. I catch the plate and shake my head, silently dismissing him so that I can see what happens next.

Just like with my cousin's table, a waiter materializes and grabs the guy's ID, while Serena offers a tight smile and a shake of her head. I get that if you're in a committed relationship, maybe you bring your not-yet-twenty-one-year-old partner to a bar so that you can enjoy a drink. But on what appears to be a first, maybe second date? What's he going to do, get trashed and make her DD home? Fucking tool.

Before I know what I'm doing, I'm across the dining area and standing in front of my cousin's table, arms crossed and scowl stamped on my face. "What the fuck is going on?"

"Ah shit, here we go," I hear Dante mumble, taking a sip of his beer as he eyes my cousin warily.

"Get down, you oversized giant," my cousin hisses, grabbing my arm and pulling me with her surprising strength into the booth next to her.

"Celeste, what the hell are you doing? Let go of my arm."

"Stop calling attention to us. We're here to make sure that Serena's date with Jack goes okay." Of course, his name is an

232

all-American boy name.

"You called attention to us the minute you walked into this bar with Dollar Tree wigs on. Do you honestly think Serena hasn't noticed you yet?"

"I told you the wigs were a bad idea, Ava."

"In my defense, I ordered them from an online store that had significantly better pictures than what showed up. Besides, my soulless one, your hair stands out too much."

Ava's boyfriend scoffs. "Vixen, and you think purple hair isn't going to stand out?"

"Shut up, Greyson."

"Anyway," Celeste says. "Why are you here? You never drink before a fight."

"Kelly," I mumble, the name containing all the explanation needed as to why I'm here.

"Or to check out Rena?" Dante asks, looking like a smug bastard as he levels me with a look. If he ever thought we'd be friends, he just ruined his chances by being a little shit-stirrer.

"No, you dick. How would I know Serena was going to be here or that you five would show up looking like you're on the run from law enforcement? I wanted to drink a beer and eat my fucking burger in peace, but that's been ruined." I sound like I'm pouting, and part of me is. I was desperate for a low-key night to wallow in my memories from last weekend before I passed out for the night.

"Shhhh, I'm trying to read their lips."

"What the fuck? Vixen, you brought binoculars?" I look over to see Ava holding up a child-size pair of binoculars like it's the most normal thing in the world to have bird-watching equipment in a bar.

"What? Too obvious? I have these, too." She reaches into

her bag and pulls out opera glasses, holding them out for show-and-tell. "These are more inconspicuous."

"Oh, good idea. Let me try them." Celeste holds out her hand and grabs them, bringing them to her eyes like she's watching *Les Mis* and not Serena's interactions with some twat.

"Red, you think we could borrow those for later? It might be a good idea to get a closer look at—"

"Whatever you're about to fucking say, don't, or else I'll have to kill you," I warn, cutting off Dante's words. "And you." I turn to my cousin. "Give me those. You're at a goddamn bar, not the ballet. Stay and make sure she's safe, but don't treat this like a goddamn sport."

Celeste glares at me, and I wouldn't be surprised if she starts growling, based on the annoyance I read in her features. "You don't get it, Wolf. Serena's been hurt by people she trusted, and she was nervous to come tonight. We told her to cancel if she didn't feel comfortable and offered to come here to wait until her date was over, just in case it didn't go well, but she declined. Obviously, we didn't listen. We're here because we love her, and we want to make sure that this guy isn't someone who will bring her any harm or treat her with disrespect.

"We know she can take care of herself, but..." She pauses, shrugging. "We just want to be sure. After what Dylan and Devin put her through this winter—one of the reasons why you went to that party to get her—we don't want her to feel as though she's alone if she needs help."

"What did they do to her?" My voice is tense, and I don't doubt that I have a murderous expression on my face, preparing for the worst.

"It's not my story to tell, but they betrayed her. Two people who have known her since she was a child betrayed her trust and her heart."

I mull it over, working my jaw until I rationalize that what they're doing—minus the dumbass binoculars—is a good thing.

"Make some room," I grind out, gently pushing my cousin further into Ava's side so that I can get more comfortable in the booth. I'm happy that the three men are sitting together in the long booth so that I don't have to sit on that fucker Dante's lap.

"Wolf," Celeste clears her throat. "You know Ava and Dante, but this is Greyson, Ava's boyfriend, and Lincoln, Dante and Grey's roommate." I look over at the two guys, a blonde with long hair and tattoos on one arm, and the other with caramel skin, a buzzed head, and light eyes. All of his visible skin is covered in ink, and he has a scowl that makes him look like he's miserable being here.

Fucking same.

I nod at both of them, receiving the same greeting in return.

"Linc, I'm shocked you had the night off," Ava comments before turning to me. "Lincoln works in the kitchen at *Garganello's*, Dante's sister's restaurant. He's also a culinary student." The tattoos make more sense now; most chefs are covered in them.

Lincoln grunts at Ava's words and Greyson turns his head to glare at his roommate. "You're not going to answer her?"

The tattooed fucker rolls his eyes at Greyson's comment but turns back to Ava. "Frankie gave me the night off," he pauses, seemingly considering his next words as his mouth twists. "How's your sister Seraphina?"

Ava's face falls. "She's still with Mitch."

235

Before Lincoln can put words to the thunderous expression on his face, Celeste claps, interrupting their conversation. "Shhh, guys, look at how Jack is looking at Serena."

The menu covers Serena's face, but it's not difficult to see the look on her date's face: he looks infatuated by her. As she lowers her menu, his head whips forward, concealing his admiration from her eyes, though she probably felt his stare like a thousand ants crawling on her skin.

"He looks like an obsessed stalker."

"As someone who has dealt with an obsessed stalker, I can assure you that is not what it looks like." Ava looks up at her boyfriend, offering him a sweet smile like she knows he needs it.

"I should drag your ass over here, vixen. I don't like you this far away."

"Curb the caveman for now, Grey. Anyway"—she looks back over to Serena—"if anything, he looks smitten."

"He looks like a jackass."

Dante leans forward, lowering his voice until it's barely above a whisper, "Your jealousy is showing."

I scowl but don't respond.

"Oh my God. Look. I think he's trying to kiss her." I adjust my head in time to see Jackass lean in, further crowding Serena against the wall. Serena's body tenses like she's preparing for an assault, and I've had enough.

"Absolutely fucking not." I'm out of the booth and across the bar faster than any man my size has the right to move.

"Serena, I need to speak with you." Both of their heads turn at the sound of my voice. Serena's face looks stunned—and stunning—while Jack looks like I pissed on his Cheerios and forced him to eat a spoonful.

"Wolf? Am I seeing things?" She waves a hand in front of her, testing to make sure I don't disappear. When I remain standing, arms crossed, she shakes her head. "What are you doing here?"

"My gym is a few blocks away, and I stopped by after training. Now, can we speak for a minute?"

"Holy shit. You're Wolf McCleery. Man, I follow all your socials. Your work is sick."

"Thanks. Serena?" I raise a brow, waiting to see how long it's going to take her to get up.

"We're in the middle of something here."

"It'll just take a minute."

She stares at me, contemplation flitting across her face before she lets out a sigh. "Fine. Jack, can you let me out?"

"We're about to order, Ser."

I cringe at the nickname, not hiding my distaste. "Like I said, it'll only take a minute."

"Jack." Her tone is cutting, brokering no argument. I smirk at her assertiveness and keep my eyes on her as she slides out of the booth, striding past Jack to stand in front of me. "Well?"

"Watch the tone, princess," I lower my voice, whispering the words so that only she can hear. Clearing my throat, I nod my head and place my hand on the center of her back, right where the tattoo I designed is going. "There's a hallway in the back. It's private."

"Oh good, exactly what I want. To be in private with the man who fucked me last week, left like he was embarrassed, and then interrupted my date. Sign me up." I stop mid-step, looking over at her tight expression.

"We said it was one time," I say softly, trying to lessen the sting.

237

"I know. I'm not looking for more, but a goodbye would have been nice."

"Sorry," I offer, surprised to hear the hurt in her voice.

"Fine, fine." Serena walks ahead of me, giving me a view of her silhouette. While I can appreciate that she's hot and looks even better without clothes on, that's not the sole reason why I can't help letting my eyes wander over the curves and lines of her body, a walking work of art. She's grace personified; it's in the movement of her hips as she walks, the curve of her neck as she observes. She reaches the hallway before I do and spins on her heel, glaring at me. "Now, what do you want?"

"Are you oblivious or just a good actress?"

"Huh?" Her face scrunches, genuine confusion marring her features.

"I'll ask you again. Are you oblivious? Did you not see Ava and Celeste sitting in the corner with Dante, Greyson, and Lincoln, dressed like cabaret dancers?"

She rears back. "They're here? I told them not to come."

"And you believed that they would listen?"

"Well, I mean. I don't know. I thought, maybe. I—" She breaks off, shaking her head at the news I just dropped on her. "How long have they been here? How long have you been here?"

"I got here thirty minutes ago and haven't been able to drink my goddamn beer since the Muppets got here right before you came."

"Oh."

"Yeah, 'Oh.' Now, I asked you back here because I saw that slimy fucker try to kiss you. You backed away."

"Very observant," she mumbles, averting her face so that I can't see her eyes.

238

"Hey, look at me." I cup her chin and turn her face toward me, tilting it up until her neck is arched and she's straining against my light hold. "Did you want his lips on you?"

"No."

"Join us. Don't be alone with him."

"We're on a date."

"Make it a group fucking hang. Make him understand that you're not letting his hands on your body."

"Wolf, I—"

"Nope. You don't like him."

"He's a nice guy," she argues, making my insides burn.

"He's not a nice guy if he tries to attack your mouth while you're reading about the goddamn spinach and artichoke dip."

"You can't make decisions for me, Wolf. If I decide to go back to my table with Jack, that's my prerogative."

"You're right; I can't make decisions for you. But if he's already trying to skirt around your boundaries when every vibe I've seen is closed off and disinterested, then he's an asshole. I'm not trying to be a dick, but I'm worried about you and don't like the idea of you alone with that prick."

She stares at me, squinting her eyes as though she's peering through my soul. "Are you jealous?"

I clench my jaw, leaning back against the wall. "No. I'm trying to be the good guy here."

"Jack is a good guy, maybe not reading the room well, but he's a nice person overall. But I can tell you're not letting this go, and I have no romantic interest in Jack, so fine, I'll bite."

She leaves, walking straight to Jack and leaning over until she's whispering in his ear. I almost feel bad for the guy as she breaks the news that her friends are here; his face falls, and he looks dejected. I shouldn't feel happiness at his disappointment, but I do.

I'll analyze that later. For now, I smile as Serena grabs her shit and walks toward Celeste and Ava.

26

Serena

When Wolf said that CeCe and Ava were in the bar, donning wig disguises, I almost didn't believe him. I absolutely should have seen them, right? Wrong. And when Wolf said that they looked like cabaret dancers, he wasn't entirely off the mark.

"Of all the weird things you two have done, this may take the top spot," I comment wryly as I approach their booth. Glancing back, I check to make sure Jack has followed and isn't still upset. When I told him that my friends were here and that I wanted to join them, he looked crestfallen, and I felt guilty about delivering the change in plans. However, I wasn't lying when I told Wolf that I had zero romantic interest in Jack, especially after spending one-on-one time with him.

He didn't necessarily do anything wrong—besides trying to kiss me in the middle of a crowded bar—but despite the flutters I felt when I first met him, there's nothing romantic between us. He's kind, smart, charming, and attractive, but my stomach doesn't erupt in butterflies. At least, not in the way that it does for someone else also hovering behind me.

Celeste and Ava have the decency to look embarrassed,

while Dante looks like he's holding back laughter, and Greyson is staring at Ava with unconcealed desire. Lincoln looks like he'd rather be anywhere other than here, and I can't say I blame him. It's lucky for all of us that Ava isn't sitting next to her boyfriend because I have a feeling he would be doing very illicit things in the middle of the bar if she was physically within reach.

"Coming here was a joint decision, but Ava ordered the wigs."

"We were trying to be subtle," Ava offers with a grimace.

"Aves." My eyes widen, and a laugh breaks free. "You're wearing a purple wig in a dive bar. I'm not sure how I didn't see you before, but there is no missing you now." I shake my head, enjoying the embarrassed looks on my friends' faces. "Anyway, this is Jack. Jack, this is Celeste, her boyfriend Dante, Ava, and her boyfriend Greyson, their roommate, Lincoln, and then you met Wolf, Celeste's cousin." Wolf grunts, clearly not pleased at his designation.

Jack clears his throat and lifts a hand, waving at the small group. "Hey, nice to meet you."

"Sorry for crashing your date," Celeste offers, smiling slightly as his cheeks redden. "We needed to make sure that you weren't going to kill her and stuff her body into your trunk before disposing the body in the Navesink."

"Red, why does it always go back to murder? I swear to God, we're detoxing you from the true crime podcasts and documentaries."

"You can pry the remote out of my cold, dead hands. Is there room over there for me and Ava? We'll let Serena and Jack sit over here, and Wolf, you can pull a chair up at the head. Or go back to the bar."

242

I don't have to look at Wolf's face to know that he's scowling at CeCe's dismissal of him. With surprising speed, Ava and Celeste play musical chairs and shift the seating arrangements. Greyson's body is angled in the corner, allowing Ava to sit between his legs; he looks the most relaxed I've seen him look in the last ten minutes. Celeste is seated in the middle of the bench, next to Lincoln and plastered to Dante's side; they look cozy, if not squished.

Thankful that I don't need to press my body against Jack's in an overcrowded booth, I slide inside and watch Wolf as he grabs a chair from a nearby table and places it at the head.

"So, how did you two meet?" Dante asks, grabbing his beer to take a long sip.

"I walked into Jack at a mixer. He lives with Meg's boyfriend."

"Walked into me? Ser, I'm pretty sure we collided. You got some pretty nasty cuts from that and broke your phone, if I remember correctly." I watch, horrified and slightly turned on by how rigid Wolf's posture becomes at the reminder of his rescue mission.

"That was you?"

"Uh, well. I—"

"Not entirely," I cut in. "Jack tried to stop Dylan, who was the real asshole of the night. Jack and I walking into each other was just an accident."

"A happy one?" Jack asks, looking directly at me.

"You were bruised and bloody. That's not a happy accident, and Dylan is a fucking asshole."

I cut my eyes to Wolf and let out a sigh. Before I can respond, CeCe beats me to it. "God, Wolf. You sound like Jack intentionally hurt Rena; I can't disagree with you on Dylan,

243

though. But dial down the big brother act." My cheeks flame at the thought of Wolf harboring any sort of brotherly or familial feelings toward me. Wolf grunts, probably thinking the same thoughts as me.

I should be focused on Jack right now, but all I can see from my peripheral is Wolf, his jaw tense and his arms crossed. My stomach riots as memories of our time together at my apartment play in my mind, like one of those picture glasses at an old school county fair, where you click on the lever, and images swirl around you, capturing your attention and stealing your breath.

I can confirm that the very last thing I feel for him is sisterly affection.

—

"Shit," Jack mutters, glancing down at his phone while conversation buzzes around us.

"Is everything okay?" We've been here for over an hour, eating appetizers and listening to Ava and Celeste go at it like a well-rehearsed comedy routine. While the women at the table are all underage and won't be served, Jack, Lincoln, Dante, and Greyson have been drinking beers. Apparently, Ava is driving Greyson's Jeep back to the guys' place, and I think everyone is a little on edge.

Wolf hasn't consumed a single thing since he sat down at the head of the table, watching over us like a sentry. His beer and burger sat untouched on the bar until a waitress dropped off the flat brew and cold food to our table.

"I need to head back to the house. There's an issue with the electric, and the control panel is in my closet." I tilt my head, digesting his words. He must sense my confusion because he elaborates, "I locked my bedroom door before I left. The guys were having people over, and I didn't want anyone going into my bedroom."

"Oh, of course."

"Do you want to come back with me? I know there are a few girls from the sorority there. It could be fun." He offers a shy smile like he's anticipating my refusal.

"I think I'd like to just head home if you don't mind."

His expression falls, but he recovers quickly, replacing the hopeful expression with an understanding grin. "Of course. But I need to go straight to the house to unlock the door and flip the breaker. I can bring you home after?"

"I'll bring her home." Jack and I shift our gazes to Wolf, who seems to be listening to the conversation with keen interest. "You can get to your little party."

I roll my eyes at Wolf and turn my attention back to Jack. "It's fine; either Ava and Celeste or Wolf will drive me home. Do you mind if I walk you out?"

"Are you sure? I don't mind bringing you back to your place after I stop by the house."

"I promise, it's no problem." I follow Jack out of the booth, sliding until my feet hit the sticky wood floor in front of the table. Needing something to do with my hands, I clasp them in front of my waist and walk to the door, feeling Jack close at my heels.

As soon as we reach the entrance, I pause and look over at Jack's handsome face.

"You don't have to say it."

"What?"

He smiles ruefully, shaking his head. "You don't need to say what's on your mind; I already know. I think you're a

245

great girl, Serena, and you're beautiful as hell. But I know when I'm competing against someone I can't beat, and I'm not delusional enough to think you're interested in me. So, friends?"

I stare at him in surprise before a smile breaks out across my face. "Friends." Reaching out, I throw my arms around Jack's waist and squeeze lightly, attempting to put all my relief in the gentle embrace. "Thanks for being a good guy, Jack. But just so you know, you're not competing against anyone."

His laugh moves the strands of hair at the top of my head. "Tell that to McCleery. That man is built like Mount Everest and looks like he can kill me with a poke to the chest. The entire time we were in that booth, I felt him glaring at me."

I swallow, unable to respond, and nod at his words. Releasing my hold, I step back and watch as he walks through the door, disappearing into the inky night.

Dragging in a deep breath, I steel myself for the inevitable inquisition that I know I'm going to face the minute I return to the table. Spinning on my heel, I slam into a broad chest boasting a woodsy scent.

"Wolf." I sound breathless, even to my ears. "What are you doing?"

"I got your jacket and bag. You ready to head out? We settled the bill, and the girls are in the bathroom."

"Right, how much do I owe?"

Wolf scoffs, disgust lacing his tone. "That guy couldn't even throw in a few dollars for his shitty beer. Don't insult me by offering to pay; you know your money's no good to me."

"Wolf…"

"No. Get your jacket on, and then we're heading out. I need to stop somewhere before I bring you back to your

246

apartment."

"Yes, sir."

"Princess," he growls.

I tell myself that it's indigestion from the hot wings we ordered that's making my stomach flutter. Because there is no way that I'm stupid enough to fall into bed—or a couch or a wall—with Wolf McCleery again.

27

Wolf

"What is this place?" Serena shakes her hair out as she places her helmet on the handle of my bike.

"Best taco place in Jersey." I nod toward the food truck I discovered three years ago. If it were brick and mortar, I'd describe it as a "hole-in-the-wall," but since it's mobile and leaves every night at ten, I'll call it a hidden gem. She eyes me skeptically, disbelief warring with excitement over my statement.

"The best tacos I've had in this state are from *Ranchero*." She pauses, looking at her surroundings as we stand in line at *Comida de Los Vivos*, or Comida for short. I was starving after a gym session one night and in no mood to go to Starbound or some other bar in the area, so I stopped by the food truck with historically long lines. One bite was all it took for me to realize that any other tacos I've eaten in the past paled in comparison.

"Just trust me, okay?"

She looks at me, tilting her head in consideration before shrugging and staring at the menu on the side of the truck.

I watch her closely, taking in her features as she reads the offerings. Just like every time I'm in her presence, the quiet, understated grace and beauty she exudes astound me.

"Oh, they have *pozole*. I haven't had that since I visited my grandparents before COVID."

"That's the stew, right?"

"Soup or stew, depending on whom you ask. My *abuela* tops it with a lot of cabbage, radishes, and avocado. I'm excited to try this one."

"Where do your grandparents live?"

"Mexico. My mom moved to the United States for school, but her family is in Puebla. My dad was born in the States, but his mother is from Mexico City. His dad was American and in the military; they met shortly after my Abuela Pia immigrated with her parents in the sixties. His family was Spanish, from Spain. That's where my last name comes from."

I nod, listening to her as she talks about her heritage and background. We spend the twenty minutes in line talking about her summers spent in Mexico before she started to take on more school responsibilities, and I tell her about my love of jiu-jitsu, how Celeste and I started in karate before transitioning to grappling, and then MMA.

"If you don't mind me asking, why are you walking away from MMA? I don't know much about it, but aren't you, well, good at it?"

I look away from her face, letting the bittersweet emotions crash over me as I think about the end of my fighting career. "Tattooing, art, it's my life. Jiu-jitsu was always an outlet, and I used to love to train with Celeste and a few of my other buddies at my original gym. When Jedd, my coach, recruited me for MMA, I did it solely for the purses; you can win a shit ton of money in the circuit, and I always knew that one day, I'd own the shop. MMA made it a reality I was able to achieve. But if I had to choose between MMA and tattooing—which I did—I'd choose my art every damn time. I can't tattoo if my hands are busted or if I'm in so much pain that sitting in a chair for thirty minutes, hunched over a client, is an impossibility. I knew I had to get out, and luckily, I haven't had much pushback from my coach. My parents are relieved that their only child will stop beating the shit out of men in the cage, and I don't have to feel like my body is a weapon anymore."

"I—" she begins but stops as the person in front of us finishes their order and steps aside, putting us at the head of the line.

"Hi, what can I get you?"

"Hola. *Yo quiero un pozole por favor. ¿Y tienes tostones?*" Serena asks, the Spanish sounding soft and lyrical in her voice.

"*Sí.*"

"*Excelente. ¿Puedo tener esos también?*" Turning to me, she asks, "Wolf, what do you want?"

I clear my throat, surprised that she's trying to order for me. Gently, so that she doesn't think that she's in charge but also doesn't get offended or think that I'm dismissing her, I grab her arm and pull her to my side, effectively tucking her under my arm. "Hi. Can I have two carne asada tacos and a barbacoa? The name is Wolf for the order." I offer my credit card and stuff money in the tip jar next to the window.

"Thank you. *Gracias,*" the woman calls out, looking past us to the onslaught of new customers who have arrived for late-night Mexican street food. I lead Serena over to my bike and lean against it as she paces back and forth.

"You good, princess?"

250

"Just a little cold," she offers, sheepishly rubbing her arms in explanation. Shrugging off my leather jacket, I hold it out to her, nodding toward the fabric wordlessly. "Oh, no. I have a jacket; you'll just be in a sweatshirt, and I can't make you go cold a second time. The party was bad enough."

"Princess, take the goddamn jacket. I'll be fine, but you look like you're shaking." Her shoulders drop, and she reaches out, grabbing the jacket and quickly putting it over her frame. She huddles into the coat as though it's offering her a hug and inhales deeply. "You smelling my coat?" I tease, savoring the redness of her cheeks as she reacts to my jibe.

"Wolf!" Looking past Serena, the woman who took our order calls out my name and holds up a bag containing our food. Pushing from the bike, I walk to the front of the line and grab the bag before circling back to Serena. Despite the late hour, there are no available picnic tables in the lot.

I weigh our options: eat standing up or go to someplace with a table. Taking in Serena's body dwarfed by my jacket and her obvious discomfort from the cold, I rule out eating outside.

"Put your arms through the sleeves. We've got a ten-minute ride. Will you be okay?"

"Where are we going?"

I shake my head, not answering her question. "That's not what I asked. Will you be okay, or do I need to call a car service?"

She rolls her eyes and slips her arms into the sleeves of my jacket. "Don't be dramatic. I'll be fine. I'd feel bad about making you ride without a jacket, but you're the one who prevented me from driving home in a nice, warm car, so I guess this is payback."

251

Scoffing, I stow the food in the hidden storage compart-
ment, grab my spare helmet, and pull it over her head. "You
mean a car, to a party, to a car, to your apartment with a guy
who wants to fuck you?"

"Jack and I discussed that we are just friends, thank you
very much. Stop painting him out to be a bad guy."

"And if I weren't there tonight to stop his advances?"

Her eyes are hidden by the visor of the helmet, but I can
almost feel the anger in her glare. "We would have arrived at
the same conclusion. You're under the misconception that
I needed you to swoop in; I was handling Jack fine, and we
were having a nice conversation before you stormed over like
a disgruntled bear."

"Just get on the bike, Serena." She huffs but throws a leg
over the seat and slides back, getting into position on the back
of my bike like a seasoned old lady. It disorients me how good
she looks with the metal between her legs and how right it
feels to have her there.

Whenever I would ride with Kelly, I felt itchy and claustrophobic despite the open air surrounding us. Her hold was
always too tight, her posture too rigid to make it comfortable.
With Serena, none of the discomfort I expected is there,
and the reasons why I'm holding myself back—our different
seasons in life and the fact that she's Celeste's friend—seem
like convenient excuses. Something about seeing Serena with
another man tonight pissed me off. I'm trying hard to identify
the feelings as something other than jealousy, but I'm coming
up short. When Jack leaned over her in that shitty booth, I
wanted it to be me pressing against her. When she walked him
out of the bar and hugged him goodbye, I wanted it to be me
whom she wrapped her arms around. Somehow, this woman

has embedded herself under my skin, and it both annoys and excites me.

Taking one last survey of her form, I clip my helmet into place and straddle the bike. I let out a breath I didn't know I was holding when her slim arms wrap around my stomach. Without thought, I glide one hand over her thigh, just above her knee, and squeeze. I can feel Serena's body shudder against me and tighten my hold, silently warning her to stop moving.

Kicking up the stand, I twist the throttle and slowly pull out of the lot and onto the main highway. I'm a careful rider and cautious driver; all too often, there are stories of deaths due to motorcycle collisions and unsafe operation of bikes. But with Serena on the back, I take extra care, going slower than I typically would and signaling my turns earlier than necessary.

The ten-minute ride turns into twenty with my measured speed, and by the time we pull up to my house, a modest but modern bi-level, I'm fucking frozen. Tapping on the garage door opener attached to my left handlebar, I pull into my garage before kicking the stand and shutting off the engine.

In the absence of my bike's engine, the silence between me and Serena is deafening. Unlatching my helmet, I pull it off and hang it over the handle before standing up and turning to her.

"You going to get up, princess, or are you planning on sitting there for the rest of the night?"

"Wolf," she stops, pulling her helmet off and holding it between us like a life preserver. "Where are we?"

"My house."

"Why would you bring me to your house?" Her brows are furrowed, and she looks genuinely confused.

"You showed me yours, so I figured I'd show you mine."

"That's not funny, Wolf."

I shake my head, reach for the helmet, and tug it from her hands. "I'm not trying to be. Now get your ass up; I want to eat my tacos before they get too cold."

"Wolf."

"Fuck it," I mutter when she still doesn't move. Tossing the helmet on the bench by the door that leads to my kitchen, I circle her waist and throw her over my shoulder, leaving her legs dangling by my torso and my jacket drooping over her head. Keeping one hand on the back of her thighs, I lift the seat to reveal the hidden storage where I stowed the food and grab it.

With long strides, I reach the door and throw it open, pausing to close the garage before I kick my shoes off. The entire time I walk, Serena beats at my back, demanding that I let her down and stop manhandling her.

Walking into the kitchen, I bend down and deposit Serena on the counter, clenching my jaw to keep from laughing at her red face and furious expression.

"I told you to get up."

"You could have given me a freaking minute, Wolf."

"Sure, and then another minute and another. You were taking too long, and no amount of overthinking is going to change the outcome that you're here, in my house, and we're about to eat Mexican food I paid for. Call it a date, call it a consultation for your tattoo; I don't give a shit. But I'm hungry, I'm tired, and the only thing I want to do is eat a fucking taco. So—" I pause, stepping back from the counter. "I'm going to eat my food. If you want to join me, you're more than welcome to, but if you want to sulk on my countertop

254

because I carried you into this room like the princess that you are, then have at it."

Skirting around the kitchen island, I pull out one of my stools and sit before pulling out the contents of the bag. Setting Serena's food in front of the second stool, I dig into my food, savoring the way the meat, onions, and cilantro melt against the tortilla. "Fuck, that's good," broadcasting my enjoyment by taking another large bite. Part of my behavior is performative, an enticement to have Serena share a meal with me, but a larger part is because I'm truly enjoying the food. I'm about to take another bite when she slides off the counter and stomps to the vacant seat.

"I am not a princess," is all she offers before she sits and peels the lid off her stew. My eyes lock on her mouth as she blows on the still-hot liquid before taking a careful sip of the broth. She swallows the mouthful, and I have to tear my eyes away from the column of her throat and the way her muscles move.

It's fucking pathetic.

"Mm, this is good." She repeats the process over and over again, blowing on the steam before placing the spoon inside her mouth until her container is half-empty. "I am going to eat this entire thing."

I hear her words but can't formulate a response; a bead of liquid lands on the corner of her mouth, and she licks it, pulling her tongue back into her mouth before she sucks on her lower lip.

Her eyes shift from her plastic container to my eyes, then to my lips, until finally settling on a point over my shoulder.

"On second thought, I can pack this up and call an Uber now."

"You can," I agree, taking another bite of my food. I chew slowly, considering my next words. "Or you can eat it while it's still hot."

She nods, looking back down at her food. "Don't tell my mother, but this might be better than my abuela's."

"Will that get you kicked out of the Castillo household?" I tease.

"I think I'm already disowned by them," she responds with a shrug. "I've been on the outs with them since I was twelve, I think." If I wasn't watching her closely, I'd think she was unaffected by her words, but I am watching her closely. I don't miss the quiver in her jaw or the way she draws in her bottom lip like she's holding back more words.

Before I can think better of it, I place a hand on her forearm, still drowning in my leather jacket, and squeeze through the fabric in a show of understanding. I haven't forgotten how she went off on her father's voicemail when she was in the shop or the visceral reaction she had at his messages. It's none of my business, but for some reason, the thought of this woman upset makes me see red.

"You okay, princess?" I ask, a bullshit question when she's very obviously not okay.

Her head tilts down, letting her hair cover the side of her face, and she nods frantically. "I-I'm fine. I should get going now."

"Probably." My voice is soft, barely a release of breath and sound, but that's all it takes to set Serena off. Soft whimpers escape her mouth, and she twists on the stool, bringing one hand up to muffle the sounds.

"Hey, princess, it's okay." Abandoning my food, I push off the stool and walk around her body until her face is level with my upper abdomen. "Shh, it's okay, Serena, I got you," I murmur, pulling her into my arms and letting her tears soak the front of my shirt.

Standing in my kitchen, surrounded by food and the soft sobs of the beautiful woman who's been a reoccurring presence in my thoughts, I know I am absolutely fucked because, at this moment, there's nothing that I wouldn't do to destroy the fucker who hurt her.

28

Serena

When I pictured how my evening would play out, I envisioned a semi-awkward dinner with Jack, an explanation of, "It's not you, it's me," when he dropped me off, and to be showered and in bed by nine-thirty.

If I wanted to get crazy, maybe I would drink a cup of herbal tea and catch up on *Jeopardy!* before finally calling it a night at eleven.

But what I did not see was having my date interrupted by Wolf and my friends, getting tacos on the side of the road, or crying in the middle of Wolf's kitchen while he was feeding me. Technically, he wasn't *feeding* me but making sure I was fed, but it's virtually the same thing. Still, none of that was anticipated when I threw on my loosest jeans and a plain long-sleeved T-shirt. Had I known that I was going to have a run-in with Wolf, I probably would have taken more time on my appearance, which sounds sad considering I had a date with another man tonight.

My appearance doesn't matter now, though, since mascara is undoubtedly streaked down my face, and my hair probably looks like a helmet from the ride.

"Shh, it's okay, Serena, I got you," Wolf breathes down, his words hitting my ear as he hunches over me.

"Serena, are you okay?"

"I don't w-want to talk about my dad," I grind out, forcing myself to calm down and break up the sobs.

"So then don't." Wolf's hold tightens, dragging my body further to the edge of the stool and into his chest.

I feel selfish taking the comfort Wolf is offering; he can't be comfortable in this position with our height difference and the stool I'm perched on. But despite the fact that I should push him away, order a car, and never, ever, ever see him again, I know I won't do that. Instead, I do the one thing I've been dying to do since I found out he left me alone in my house last weekend.

Pulling back, I let Wolf's arms fall from my side and look up at his imperfectly handsome face. His nose is crooked, his jaw is set, and his lips are almost too full for a man, making them nearly feminine in their plumpness. Individually, none of the features work, but together, he looks like a Highlander sent from another time to protect and pillage.

"Why did you leave?" I ask, cutting him off for once.

"You know why I left."

"Because we said one time?"

He stares at me, running his tongue along the inside of his jaw. I track the movement inside his mouth, wishing that it was *my* tongue making those indents in his cheeks. I'm so lost in my observation of his face that when his fingers land on my neck, pushing my head back, I jolt in surprise.

"Tell me why I left, princess."

"Because we said one time," I repeat, swallowing against the

259

grazes to my neck.

"You know that wasn't why. Now say it," he orders, flattening his hand and applying light pressure, just enough to feel the embers of panic without a full-fledged meltdown.

"Because you wanted it to be more than one time."

He nods, emphasizing his agreement with a squeeze. "Good girl. Now tell me why you wanted me to stay."

I meet his eyes, looking directly into the green orbs as I whisper, "Because I wanted it to be more than once."

"Hmm," he mutters, bringing his free hand up to wipe at the remnants of tears on my face. "We seem to be at an impasse then." His fingers slide up and down my neck, never venturing lower than my exposed collarbone, and I can't stop the shiver that overtakes my body. Still clothed in my shirt, puffer, and Wolf's thick leather jacket, I shouldn't feel anything other than the warmth of the fabrics. But somehow, Wolf's touch defies logic, and instead of leaving trails of heat with his touch, I feel cold and in need of his body heat to warm me up.

"Wolf," I whisper his name, though it sounds more like a plea. A plea for more, for less, for something other than the torture of his scent wrapped around my body and his fingers playing with my airflow.

"Just one more time, princess? Is that what you want to ask me?" I nod my head, but he scowls, disgust on his face. My eyes widen, and I start to pull back, but he stills me with his grip. "You think I can have you one more time, and then, what? Forget about it? We tried that, but it didn't fucking work." Both hands move to cup my cheeks, and his expression softens. "Princess, Serena, if I have you again, it's not going to be a one-time thing. I have thought of you every fucking second of every goddamn day since I left your apartment.

Seeing you tonight with that skinny fucker? I damn near lost my mind. I don't know what this means or where this will go. But I'm a selfish bastard, and I don't think I can stand by and watch as you find another man."

"Jack's a nice guy, he—"

"Serena, I suggest you stop talking about Jack."

"Why, are you jealous that I think he's nice?"

"As fuck."

"Wolf," I sigh, straining against his hold. "What does this mean?"

"We see where this goes; that's what this means."

"And what about Celeste? What am I supposed to tell her?"

Wolf quirks a brow at the mention of his cousin, a sardonic smile ripping across his lips. "Are you afraid of my little cousin, princess?"

Truthful answer: yes. The answer I give is, "Of course not."

Wolf laughs, rolling his eyes at my lie. "She'll survive."

"Yeah, but I may not," I mutter, unable to keep the words inside.

"I'm going to kiss you now, princess. If you don't want it, don't want this, tell me now."

"I thought you said to stop kissing you," I challenge, throwing his previous words against him. A deep chuckle is the only warning I get before his lips claim mine.

His kiss is soft, a caress that melts all pretense, all resistance out of me. I throw myself into the kiss, meeting each pull, each bite with one of my own. Wolf kisses like it's a fight, a battle for dominion and an opportunity to dominate. I don't let him lead or dictate how the kiss will progress. When he captures my bottom lip between his teeth, I lick out my tongue, hooking his top lip until I'm able to draw him into my mouth.

Food forgotten, long minutes pass as I vent out all of my frustration in this kiss. Throwing my arms around Wolf's neck, I hug him closer, pulling him down further until his body is pressed against mine, pushing me back into the seat.

Wolf's hands drift from my face, removing both of my jackets, and traveling until one wraps around my back and the other grips my thigh, guiding it until it's wrapped against his waist. Breaking the kiss, Wolf's mouth travels from the outer corner of my lips down to the pulse at my throat, sucking the skin into his mouth.

"Wolf," I pant. "The bruises just faded from my neck." It took five days, ice, and a soft bristle brush to work the marks out of my skin.

"Good, then you need more." I gasp as his mouth attacks my skin, drinking at my pulse like a vampire hungry for his next meal. His teeth bite my flesh, lapping at the sting before repeating the process over and over again, making my head spin by the pain, the pleasure, and the wetness pooling between my thighs.

"Oh my God," I moan, raising my hands to press him more firmly into my neck. I may have complained about the marks he's leaving on my skin, like a tattoo of ownership, but I can't deny that they feel good as he gives them.

He breaks from my neck, breathing heavily as he stares down at me. "I'm not your God. I'm your Wolf, and I'm going to fucking swallow you whole." Without warning, he reaches for both thighs and lifts, plastering me to the front of his body as he weaves out of the kitchen and through his house.

"Wolf!" I yelp. "I can walk. You don't need to carry me everywhere."

262

My words must piss him off because a grunt is the only reply I receive until my back is pressed against a hard wall, and his mouth attacks me, drawing my lower lip inside and biting down hard until he soothes the pain with gentle suction. I fall into the kiss, not gracefully like the kiss from minutes ago, but in surrender. My proverbial white flag waves, and I follow his mouth as he licks into me, opening as wide as I can to have him infiltrate every part of me.

We start to move again, our mouths still connected. The hands on my thighs travel, one moving to the curve of my ass and the other to my neck, angling my head so that he can dive deeper. The hand at my bottom shifts and grabs one cheek in a rough squeeze before releasing. His fingers coast lower, grazing the inside swell of my cheek before resting them just next to my pussy. Even through layers of clothes, I can feel the heat and pressure from his fingers, a promise of what's to come.

I try to shift, to gain friction and relief against his hold, but he squeezes tighter, preventing any movement.

"I keep telling you to stop squirming, princess."

"I need more, Wolf." My voice sounds whiny, needy, almost annoying.

Wolf's answering chuckle and lack of action are frustrating, so I try to grind on him again, gaining a little bit of movement before he stops my progress.

"You'll get more when I say you can, Serena. Stop rushing me." He walks us through a doorway and touches a switch, bathing us in artificial light. Taking in his space, I'm not surprised to see how tidy everything is, based on the rest of the house and his shop. A large black bed rests in the center of the room, made with a black comforter and matching pillows. The walls are also black, with the wall directly behind his bed done in textured paneling to give the image of one large headboard. The rest of his walls are filled with various tattoo-style art, similar to that in his shop. Black and gray, color, surrealism, neo-traditional, new school, and American traditional drawings are displayed thoughtfully, like a high-end gallery in New York.

The artwork is almost enough for me to forget that I have Wolf's hand on my clothed pussy and his other on my neck. Almost, but not quite.

Looking away from the artwork, I take in the television mounted on the wall and the black media console below. He has two nightstands, a tall dresser, and not much else in the space. The only offensive item to his perfectly put-together room is a framed print of bright flowers leaning against the wall. The orange, purple, yellow, and green art pops against the white matte and black frame.

I never thought that the color black could be warm and inviting, simultaneously comforting and sensual, but he's somehow achieved it.

"Your art is amazing," I comment, still staring at the floral print. "What kind of flowers are those?"

Wolf's gaze travels from the drawing to my face, and I can feel his intensity, even from the corner of my eye. Shifting my gaze, I raise a brow. "What?"

He stares at me for a beat before asking, "Do you like it?"

Nodding, I tell him the truth, "I love it."

"Good, it's yours."

Rearing, my brows furrow in confusion. "What do you mean it's mine? You want me to take it?"

A smirk breaks out on his face, making it both kissable and

punchable. "No, you're not taking that. It's your tattoo."

"What?" I screech, turning my head back to the print. "That's my tattoo?"

"That's what I said."

Casting a glare from the corner of my eye, I mentally flip him off. "Put me down. I want to see it." He complies, placing me gently on my feet. He doesn't step back, doesn't give me any additional space, so I skirt around him and bend over in front of the frame, taking in the precise lines and artistry. "Wolf, it's stunning. When did you do this?"

"I started the draft when I mapped your back and butterfly dick placement last weekend. It took a few tries to get it right and to make sure that the original work would be covered. I may still have to alter a few of the flower placements, but that's what the template looks like."

"I—" I break off, shaking my head in amazement. "Wolf, it's more than anything I could have imagined. What types of flowers are those?"

"Strelitzias, or bird of paradise."

Looking over my shoulder, I see Wolf's hands tucked into his pockets like he's proud of his work but trying to maintain a shred of humility.

"What happened to Sloan's piece?"

"She wanted to do hot air balloons." His face twists, a disgusted sneer morphing his features.

"Oh." I tilt my head, considering hot air balloons on my back for the rest of my life. While I don't hate the idea, I also don't feel connected to it. "What do they symbolize?"

Wolf looks to the ceiling like he's reading a script on the black paint. "Hope, love, adventure."

"And Strelitzias?"

He looks back down, meeting my eyes. "Freedom."

"Oh." My throat works, swallowing down the emotion attempting to choke me. "I think I like that better."

He shrugs like it's no big deal. "You wanted butterflies for the same reason. I'll try to incorporate a few freehanded ones, but I wanted your tattoo to have the same meaning as what you originally intended. I wasn't going to let Sloane put a romantic balloon on your back when you wanted something to symbolize breaking free." He shakes his head, raising his arms to cross his chest. "I couldn't do that to you."

"Th-thank you." I feel tears prick at the corner of my eyes, and I wipe my face, praying that Wolf doesn't notice I'm crying again. "That was considerate."

He shrugs again, not voicing a response.

"What about the rest of this art?" I wave my hands, gesturing to the walls.

"Some are pieces I've done; others are commissions from my artists or ones from other shops whose work I admire." I nod, taking a closer look at each of the prints on display.

Turning back to the rendering of my tattoo, I smile. "They're all beautiful, but I like this one best."

"Me too." His voice comes from behind, closer than it was a minute ago, and I stand, straightening to my full height. Not a second passes before his front is pressed against my back, and his arms are around my waist, adhering to my body. Keeping one hand wrapped around my abdomen, the other dances up, over the valley between my breasts, over the ridges of my collar bone, and to the peak of my jaw. Applying gentle pressure, Wolf turns my head and tilts it toward his lowering face.

I close my eyes, anticipating another kiss, but it never comes.

Snapping them open, I see Wolf's mouth inches from mine, like he's giving me the air I need to breathe. "What—"

"I'm going to fuck you now, princess. And I'm not going to be gentle this time."

My eyebrows lift to my hairline, and I sputter a laugh. "You were gentle last time?"

"As gentle as I could be."

With my head at this angle, I'm able to see everything that transpires within his eyes: desire, skepticism, need, and I'm sure his emotions are mirrored in my own. Erasing the distance between us, I ease up on my toes and press my mouth to his, initiating a soft kiss. Easing his lips open, I lick into his mouth and let my tongue dance lazily with his. He seems inclined to let me lead and set the pace because he doesn't fight for control or turn our kiss into a battle.

Pulling back, I tip my head up and smirk. "What was that about gentle?"

An eyebrow quirk is the only warning I receive before Wolf scoops me into his arms, bridal style, and strides to the bed, throwing me toward the center. Wolf grabs the back of his shirt, pulling it off in one fluid motion.

In clothes, Wolf's body is impressive; the way his form fills out jeans is nearly sinful, and his shoulders stretch out a shirt indecently. But shirtless? His body is a master class in art and kinesiology, a reflection of the perfect human form if scars and body modifications were normative. I stare at him wordlessly as he strips off his jeans and boxers, leaving him completely bare. His cock is hard, so red, that it looks like it physically hurts to remain untouched. As though he's reading my mind, he grips the base of his cock, squeezing before jerking his hand up and down, spreading the precum over himself.

Shaking myself out of my trance, I move my hands to the hem of my shirt and start to raise it over my ribs.

"Stop." I halt my progress at his voice, leaving the shirt bunched at my waist. "Get on your hands and knees and come to the edge of the bed."

"Are you planning on ordering me around all night?" I ask.

"Yes. Now get on your hands and knees, princess. Don't make me ask a third time."

"What'll happen if you do?"

"Something you probably won't like," he supplies, quickening his speed as he continues to stroke himself.

"I'm tempted to find out," I tease but rise on my knees before dropping to my hands and crawling over to the edge of the bed. Though I'm listening to Wolf's commands and following instructions, I'm doing it because it's what *I* want to do. I know that whatever Wolf is about to do to me will cause me optimal pleasure, and I'm determined to be selfish for once in my life.

Thoughts of my family, the failed dating experience, and every previous sexual encounter that didn't include Wolf fade away until I'm left fully clothed, on my hands and knees, waiting to service the man I never thought I'd have.

29

Wolf

Serena's ass sways as she crawls over to me, a temptress in denim on a sea of black sheets and blankets. I stopped her when she tried to undress because I knew the moment I saw her naked body, I'd be a fucking goner. She reaches the edge and sits back on her heels, folding her hands in her lap like a seasoned courtesan playing at demure. Except with her, it's no act. A heady cocktail of inexperience and sensuality oozes from Serena's pores; even just sitting there, fully covered, she looks like sin incarnate.

"Open your mouth," I rasp, squeezing the tip of my dick to stave off the waves of lust crashing into me. One insolent eyebrow raises, but she continues to follow my instructions, opening her mouth wide, not moving any other part of her body.

Stepping forward, I place the tip of my dick on her tongue. Precum gathers at the head, and I watch, entranced, as the droplets blend with her saliva and settle on her tongue. I'm too big for her to take, and already my dick looks like a fucking monster against her mouth. She must not realize that there's a logistical issue because the minx tries to widen her mouth before closing it around the head of my cock.

"Fuck," I grunt, unable to keep the chill from my spine. "Princess, as much as I wish you could deepthroat me, you'll split your mouth open, and my dick will have teeth marks if we try." If I weren't watching her closely, I'd miss the gleam in her eyes, like she's picking up the gauntlet of a challenge she doesn't want to lose. Pulling her head back, she releases me from her mouth, saliva trailing her release.

In a move I don't anticipate, Serena grabs my dick and pulls me forward like a dog on a leash; I have no choice but to follow her silent command. Her delicate fingers circle my cock and tilt it forward until her mouth is mere centimeters away. With all the prior women I've been with, my size and girth have been much appreciated for the pleasure it can provide, but very rarely has anyone tried to give me head or even a hand job. After my first girlfriend in high school compared it to a fucking Yeti, I knew that anything resembling a blowjob was off the table for me.

Serena doesn't seem intimidated by my size, or maybe it's the scholar in her treating my cock like a hypothesis she needs to test. Leaning closer, Serena's tongue peeks out, giving me a long, slow lick from the base to the tip before circling the head and lapping at the precum. She repeats the movement on the top of my shaft, tilting her head so that her tongue is able to taste the entire length.

"Goddamn, princess," I rasp, tunneling my hands into her hair to help her glide her tongue around my cock. She hums to herself like she's eating an ice cream cone on the boardwalk in the middle of August and is savoring the flavor. Not dictating her movements, I gather her hair up and hold it above her

270

head in a makeshift ponytail, giving me a prime view of how much she's enjoying herself. "You like the taste of my cock, princess? You're lapping at it like it's the best thing you've ever tasted."

She looks up beneath her lashes, and I nearly come at the need I see reflected in them. "You look so fucking pretty like this," I tell her, unable to keep my admiration contained. Like I'm getting a reward for my words, Serena moves to the head of my dick and runs a circle around it with her tongue before bringing the tip into her mouth and sucking hard. Pulling at her hair, I ease her back.

"I wasn't done," she pouts, moving forward once again. Shifting my hips out of her reach, I clench my hand in her hair and still her movements.

"I don't know where you learned to suck cock—or lick cock—like that, but I was about to come all over your shirt." Getting down on my knees, I can't help the chuckle that comes out of me when I see that we're at eye level with her on the bed and me on my knees. "Goddamn, you're short."

Her face twists into a sneer. "I'm the tallest of my friends. You're just abnormally large everywhere."

"Five feet four inches is not tall." I raise an eyebrow at the angry expression on her face.

"I'm almost five foot six. Again, you're just aberrantly tall."

"Tell me, princess, how did it feel to have an 'aberrantly' tall man nearly fall to his knees by that smart mouth of yours? Did it make your cunt nice and wet knowing that you had power over me just by using your lips and tongue?"

"I—uhm. Yes?" she responds, though it sounds more like a question. The minx from moments ago is gone, replaced by a woman unsure. My eyes narrow on her blown pupils and heaving chest; maybe it's not so much unsure as it is turned on and needy.

Grabbing the ankles tucked beneath her, I pull them and gently lower her legs to the floor. My sudden movement causes her upper body to fall back, and she lands awkwardly on my comforter. Not wasting any time, I pop the button on her jeans and slide them and her underwear down her thighs. Her shoes prevent me from removing her pants, so I slide each one off and throw them over my shoulder, not giving a shit as they sound against the wall. Her jeans and panties follow until she's left half-naked on my bed.

Grabbing the hem of her shirt, I push the fabric up and lean over to lick every inch of exposed skin. I've tasted her before, had her pussy writhing over my face while I fucked her with my tongue, but the thrill of tasting her again is potent. I don't stop my progress until the shirt is pushed over her bra, framing her tits like a pretty picture that deserves to be hung in a museum of natural wonders.

Running my hands up her sides, I cup her tits and squeeze. "Did you wear this for him?"

She looks down, confusion taking over her face before understanding graces her features. "I wore this for me."

"Good, princess. Because I'd have to tear it from your fucking body if you wore this in the hopes another man would see it." Spreading my fingers, I let my pointers dip beneath the fabric, grazing the top curve of her areola as I stroke my fingers back and forth over the swells. Her breathing becomes shallow, barely sucking in air as her eyes track my movements. Hooking each finger, I drag the bra down until both tits are resting on top of the cups.

My mouth waters at the display, but I drag my gaze and

hands away.

"What are you doing?"

"Feasting." I grab each of her legs and drape them over my shoulders like the prettiest fucking earmuffs I've ever owned. "Now, be quiet while I eat." Leaving my hands around her thighs, I dive in, capturing her clit and sucking it between my lips in a hard pull. Her sharp gasp fills the room, and I suckle, drowning in the taste of her cunt. Releasing her, I flatten my tongue and lick, tasting the wetness that's already drenching her pussy.

"Jesus, Wolf," she cries, her tone sharp as I move to bite against her flesh before soothing it with my tongue. I continue lapping at her, alternating between bites and soothing caresses, suction, and fast flicks of my tongue.

Serena's hands find their way to my head, clutching at the buzzed strands to pull me closer, a wordless invitation to gorge myself on her cum. The action makes me go feral. Pulling her thighs wider, I spear my tongue inside her tight opening and tongue her cunt, letting my nose rub against her clit with each grind of her hips. Moments drowning in her pussy is all it takes for her breathing to become heavier, her hold tighter, and the shaking in her legs to pull them closed, cutting off any ability to move away from the space between her legs.

Like I'd fucking move, anyway.

"Wolf," she whispers, my name reverberating through her entire body like a recoil. I don't stop, don't give her time to catch her breath, just keep fucking her pussy until all she can do is spasm against my mouth as I capture her cum.

"Wolf, please. No more." The breathless sound of her voice breaks me from my frenzy, and I pull my tongue out, flattening it against her clit and giving one more lick before meeting her gaze.

She opens her legs, letting me out from the heaven between her thighs. Sitting up, I grab her hips and drag her off the bed, letting her fall into my lap. Even after an orgasm and partially clothed, she's graceful. As though we've been in this position a thousand times, her legs cradle my hips, and my cock strains between us, precum beading at the tip in desperate need to sink inside her.

Shifting my hold, I let one of my hands rest against her ass and reach for my discarded jeans behind me. Catching a leg, I drag them over and fish inside my pocket for the condom housed in my wallet. Ripping the foil open, I use one hand to drag the latex down my cock.

"Unless you tell me otherwise, either take my cock, or I'm going to drop you down. Lady's choice."

Serena swallows, her throat bobbing with the force, and she grabs onto my shoulders, inching closer until my cock is rubbing against her folds. Lifting herself, she silently positions her hips over me. Keeping my eyes locked on her face, I watch the emotions play over her features as she lowers, taking just the tip and wincing slightly before continuing.

"Princess," I squeeze the hand resting on her hip, stilling her motion. "Go slow if you need to."

She nods, rocking against me and slipping down a little further, the fit a little tighter, and I bite back the groan at the feel of her pussy. She continues rocking, minutely easing herself down until I'm sweating and seeing fucking stars in the heat surrounding me. With one last rock, I'm buried inside Serena's cunt.

The dichotomy between the two of us is captivating: her

274

gentle exhale and my curses, my pale skin and her golden limbs, my size and her slender frame. She pulls up before dropping back down, erasing all thoughts outside of *more, faster,* and *come.*

Trailing my hand up her back, I grip the base of her neck and help guide her movement, setting the pace as I meet each of her downward thrusts with one of my own. Looking down at her face, I note that her eyes are closed and feel an immediate desperation to have them pinned on me, the same way I'm pinned beneath her.

"Open your eyes." She snaps them open, looking at me as she grinds against me, switching her motions to rub her clit along my pelvic bone. "That's right, Serena, take what you need." I promised her I'd fuck her hard, nearly lost my fucking head over the thought of slamming into her cunt and taking us both to the edge, but the subtle shifts and grinds of Serena's body are more erotic than any hard fuck I had planned.

With her eyes glued to me, I dip my head into the curve of her neck, sucking at her pulse as her body writhes against mine. Her head falls back, giving me more access to the skin on her neck. Serena's hand moves from my shoulder to my head, and she presses down, the same as she did when I worshipped between her thighs, and, just like then, I lose control.

Tightening my grip, I bend my knees and press my feet to the floor, pumping into her until I feel her pussy grip me, fluttering and squeezing against me until I can't hold back and come inside her, filling the condom with a litany of curse words.

"Fucking shit, goddamn, Serena."

Her body slumps, exhaustion and sweat covering her like a

275

blanket, and I feel my own body start to give out. Falling back, I lean against the edge of the bed, easing her off my deflating dick before cradling Serena closer to my body.

"That was—" she starts, pausing mid-sentence to shake her head. "That was something."

"Give me a few minutes, and I'll be ready for another round."

The laughter that flows out of her is surprised and lyrical, a relaxed expression of joy that does something to my chest. "I think I'll need to sit that round out."

I nod against her head, smirking to myself at the joke. "I'm an old man; it'll take me longer than a few minutes to recover." Her body turns stiff, energy suddenly zapping through her, and she pulls back, staring up at me with a hard expression on her face.

"Why do you keep doing that?"

"Doing what?" I play dumb like I don't know what she's referring to.

"Referencing our age. I'm six years younger than you; we've established that. But don't make this into some strange illicit affair. It's demeaning and, quite frankly, gross."

"I'm not—"

She shakes her head, cutting me off. "You are. I can tell it bothers you, and that's fine. If it's something you can't get over, a fact you can't move past, then I'll end this now. I've said this to you before, and I'll say it again: I won't be treated as less than or undervalued. I know what I bring to the table. I know that someday, someone is going to see me and think, 'Her, she's the one I want.' And if that person isn't you, then thank you for the orgasms and the tattoo, and have a nice life." She applies pressure on her knees, shifting her weight to lift off my body, but it's my turn to cut her off.

"Serena, stop." I take in a long breath, looking at my ceiling before casting my gaze down on her face. "Yes, okay, it bothers me. I feel like an old man lusting after a woman too young, too good, with too much potential for a man like me. I know six years isn't a large age gap in the grand scheme of things, but you are still in college, figuring out your life, and that's not something I can ignore. But tonight, when I saw you with Jake or Jack or whatever the hell his name was, I lost it. It felt wrong. It felt fucking disgusting. His hands on you? His mouth hovering like he had a right to your body? No, fuck that," I seethe, shaking my head. "So yeah, maybe I need to reprogram my thoughts on your age to make me feel like I'm not an asshole for craving every single thing about you, but here we are. Okay? That's what I fucking got."

She greets my words with silence, staring at me with assessing eyes and a contemplative look. I lift my hand from her body, raking it through my buzz cut until she finally opens her mouth.

"Okay."

"Okay?"

"Yeah. Okay."

"Good. Now let's go to bed. I'm exhausted, princess."

30

Serena

It's still dark out when I wake up, either early morning or late night, and I startle at my surroundings. The first thing I notice is that I'm not in my bed, nestled in my crisp white sheets and heavy comforter. The second thing I notice is that there is a staggering amount of heat coming from beneath me, like a furnace has been placed in the bed and is warming me from the outside in. And the third and most obvious thing I notice as I slowly drift into the world of the living is that there is a very thick erection pressed against my thigh and an extraordinarily skilled finger dancing between my legs.

"Oh," I breathe out, hitting Wolf with my morning breath as he delves into me, taking one digit and burying it in my pussy. His motions are lazy and unhurried like he has all the time in the world to play my body like his favorite instrument. I wasn't sure what I would get this morning, the stoic version of Wolf or the side of him that's more open to exploring the possibility of us. Last night, he said a lot of things, a lot of words that made me believe that he is slowly accepting facts we cannot change. Facts like our ages, our experiences, and

278

the undeniable chemistry we have. I have no idea where this will go, if this is something viable, or if this is just a fling to round out the end of my collegiate years, but I'm determined to enjoy it while it lasts.

Wolf adds another finger, stretching me wider before scissoring his fingers inside me and rubbing against my walls. Laying half on top of him with my leg hitched up around his waist, I don't have much leverage to move or add friction to my clit, something I desperately need to come. He must sense my agitation because he holds me tighter, pinning me to his body in a vice that prevents any small movements I would have made.

"Wolf," I groan, sliding one hand down from where it rests on his chest and trying to worm it between our bodies.

"Stop rushing, princess. Let me take care of you." Wolf's voice halts my progress, and I turn my face up, glaring at him through my lashes.

"You woke me up with your finger inside of me. How did you expect me to respond?"

"Exactly like this." He pauses, a deep chuckle breaking from his mouth. "I like seeing you desperate for my cock, Serena. It's fucking hot."

"Yeah, well, good for you," I mumble, squeezing my muscles together and gripping the fingers playing between my legs.

"So impatient," he clucks, resuming his leisurely caress. I'm about to scream in frustration when he finally pulls out and lifts me off of him. Looking over, I see him reach for the condoms in his nightstand drawer, tearing one of the tiny foil packets from the strip.

He tears the wrapper and rolls it on, taking no more than two seconds to sheathe himself. I move to my back, expecting

279

him to climb on top of me, but instead, he reaches for me and deposits me on top of him, facing away in a reverse cowgirl position.

"You don't want to get on top?" I ask, pressing back against him.

"You like the clit stimulation," he explains, lifting my hips until I'm hovering above him.

Looking over my shoulder, I furrow my brows. "How did you—"

"How did I know that you come when I rub against your clit? The wetness between your thighs is a good indicator, princess. Plus, you make these breathy moans every time you come."

No other man has paid attention to the needs or cues of my body before; granted, my other sexual experiences were never intimate, almost sterile in their execution. With Wolf, I'm slowly learning that he's both observant and considerate, though his outward appearance screams brutality and fierceness.

Guiding my hips down, Wolf helps me lower myself onto his cock, slowly easing himself inside until he's buried and hitting nerve receptors that I never knew existed. He shifts behind me, and suddenly, I feel his chest against my back, filling me with his scent, his presence, and his cock.

"Lean into me, princess. Let me do the work this time," he orders softly, making the statement sound more like a question, though I'm not deceived. I relax against him, letting my body go pliant.

The hold on my hips is gentle, his fingers gripping only as hard as he needs to, and he controls each press and pull of our bodies. Tilting my head back, I sink further into him, the fullness of his cock a welcome intrusion as he continues to stretch me and move us in a lazy rocking motion, back and forth, back and forth, until one of the hands at my hips sneaks to my clit, rubbing it in tandem with his thrusts.

"Yes, Wolf," I moan, gripping the hand at my hip.

"Come on my cock, Serena. Let me feel you break apart, princess."

"Faster," I pant, my voice barely audible over the blood rushing to my head. "Please, faster, Wolf." He doesn't hesitate to give me what I ask for and starts moving me faster, rubbing my clit in hard, firm circles until an orgasm crashes into me, forcing me to spasm above him. Like a detonator, my release triggers Wolf, and he stills my body, forcing my hips down as his cock jerks into me, emptying inside the condom until we're both sweaty and spent.

I try to roll off him to catch my breath and my bearings, but he pulls out and clutches me tighter, turning us until we're on our sides and he's spooning me from behind. Maybe it's the exhaustion from three orgasms, or maybe it's how comfortable I feel wrapped in his arms, but I close my eyes and surrender to the sleep that tugs on me.

Wolf:

"Shit, shit, shit. Wolf, wake up. We need to go."

It's too early for this shit. "Go back to bed, Serena." I roll over, grab a pillow, and put it over my head. As soon as it's in place, Serena yanks it out of my hold and throws it down. "Serena, what the hell?"

"I have a tutoring session in an hour. I need to get home, get changed, and then meet my student in the library."

"For fuck's sake. Why would you schedule a session on a

281

Friday morning?"

"Because it's my job and I needed to fit it in before class. Now, up. You need to drive me home now. Do you have an extra toothbrush? You know what? It's fine. I'll use my finger."

"Under the sink," I grumble, running a hand over my face to wipe the sleep from my eyes. Grabbing my phone from the nightstand, I look at the time and scowl at the hour. "It's six in the morning.

"I have an appointment at seven-thirty," she calls out, sounding disgustingly awake. She walks back into my room, shoes in hand, and leans over to slip them on. "Don't yell at me; you're reminding me a lot of Celeste right now."

"I'm nothing like my cousin."

She pauses in her motions and lifts her head, tilting it up at me with an amused expression on her face. "You are exactly like your cousin, especially, it seems, when it comes to sleeping. The first time I woke her up, I thought she was going to attack me with some jiu-jitsu move."

"Don't be dramatic."

"I'm not. Now get up, seriously. I need to go."

Hauling myself up, I shake my head and make my way into the bathroom, the scowl still on my face as I go. I rush through my morning routine, not bothering with a shower and instead opting for cool water on my face and a quick brush of my teeth. I'm back in my bedroom and dressing in a fresh pair of jeans and hoodie within five minutes, though, with Serena, you'd think I spent an hour primping myself in the bathroom. Her foot taps anxiously against the floor, and I feel her anxiety seeping into my bones.

"Would you calm down? It's been five minutes."

"I haven't said anything."

I roll my eyes, unable to stop myself. "You're tapping your foot like you're timing me. I'm ready. Let's go." Standing up, I slip into my sneakers and walk toward Serena. Before I let her walk through my door, I cage her against the wall, pressing my body against hers. "You need to learn patience, princess."

"Yeah, well, you need to learn how to hurry up." Leaning down, I capture her lips in a light kiss and trail my hand down her side, squeezing her ass before pushing off the wall.

"Come on. I've been waiting for you."

She sputters, her face going red at the taunt. "Asshole," she mutters before slipping past me and stomping to the door.

—

The drive to Serena's place is quick, taking less than thirty minutes to deliver her to the front of her building.

"Thank you for bringing me home. I'll text you later. Okay, bye," she rushes out, swinging the door open and hopping out of the cab of my truck before I'm able to string two words together. Shaking my head, I get out of my truck and round the front, eating up the distance between her fleeing form and mine.

Grabbing her hand, I stop her mid-jog. "You can thank me properly, Serena."

"Wolf, I don't have time for this," she huffs, pulling at my hold.

"You're wasting more time, princess. Kiss me goodbye."

"Did you get a personality transplant overnight? I distinctly remember you telling me to stop kissing you not too long ago."

"Serena," I growl.

"Fine." She throws herself at me, pulling my neck down at

283

the same time she leans up to press her lips against mine. It's a quick kiss, but anytime her lips are on mine, it's fucking euphoric.

"Good girl. I'll call you later. I'm not going to be able to see you much before the fight; I have training and clients in between. We'll plan for your tattoo the first week of March, okay? You should be fully healed by then."

She steps back, releasing her hold on my neck and nods, looking a little unsteady. "Okay, that's no problem."

"Hey," I start, stepping forward to grip her chin and tilt her face up. "I'll see you at my fight, right?"

She nods, her head guiding my hand up and down. "Of course. I'll be there with Celeste, Ava, and the guys."

"Good. Make sure you stay with them while I'm in the cage. My parents and other cousins will be there, too. So will Trent and Aubs."

"Oh, your parents?"

I smile at the nervousness that flits across her face. "Yeah, my parents. That a problem for you, sweetheart?"

This time, she shakes her head, moving my hand from side to side. "Of course not. But Wolf, I really need to go."

"Okay." I lean down, grazing her lips one final time before stepping back and dropping my hand from her chin. "Call me tonight."

"Bye, Wolf."

I watch her spin and run across the pavement; something in my chest shifts at her retreat. I don't analyze it too closely, but I do know that I can't fucking wait to see her again.

284

31

Serena

Two weeks later

"Serena, is everything okay?" I glance up, looking at Meg's concerned face over my plate of French toast at JJ's. It's been two weeks since I've seen Wolf, and honestly, I am such a riot of emotion that I don't quite know how to respond.

On the one hand, I'm happy for the forced distance between us and the conversations that have transpired as a result. Both through call and text, Wolf and I speak every day, multiple times a day, and I've learned so much about his wants, dreams, and views. In turn, I've told him about my screenwriter dreams, the trouble with my dad and his family, and even the events at the end of last semester with Dylan and Devin. When I told him how they showed up at Greyson, Dante, and Lincoln's house, only for Dante to punch Devin and Celeste to incapacitate Dylan, I thought Wolf would drive to my apartment to check that I was okay before finding my former best friend and neighbor and killing them.

Not figuratively, but literally, in cold blood. It was the first time that I had thought about the incident in a few weeks. I've been so busy, so distracted, that I haven't had time to dwell on anything other than my coursework and my relationships with my friends, my mom, and Wolf. Even the stress of my father has taken a backseat since I haven't heard from him in two weeks.

"I'm good," I finally respond, taking a bite of my food and smiling around the sweet bread. Swallowing, I pat my mouth with a napkin and look at Meg. "I'm happy we were able to get together. I feel like it's been a while since we saw each other." My relationship with Meg may be much different, less effortless, than my relationship with Celeste and Ava, but I value her friendship, and I feel lucky that I met her.

"I know. Me too, Little. Are you going to the mixer this weekend? I know you haven't gone to one since the messy mixer. It's with Sig Phi, the business fraternity; they're co-ed." Immediately, I shake my head and watch as Meg's face falls. "Oh. Do you have other plans?"

"Yeah, I have plans with C and Ava on Saturday night."

Meg nods her head, considering her words before asking, "Are you happy, Serena? Being in the sorority, I mean. You haven't come to much since rush and pledging."

Looking away, I think about how best to respond. "I am happy, and I like all the women in the sorority, you especially." I pause, smiling at her. "But aside from you, I don't feel connected to the other girls, probably because I have classes during chapter, work weekends, and have commitments with other organizations, too." I reflect on STD, the English Honor Society, and how my role continually changes. "Things aren't too busy with STD, but I know they'll pick up once the weather gets nicer, and I'm relishing whatever free time I

286

have before things get too hectic. I should make more of an effort; I know that."

"Just maybe come by the house, hang out with us, and get to know everyone a bit. You don't need to go to the mixers or rush events if you really can't or don't like them. I know they say you have to do certain things, but no one is going to force you, especially if you're paying your dues. And if you decide to disaffiliate, we can still be friends; it's not like I'll kick you out of my life just because the chapter isn't the right fit." Meg reaches over and squeezes my hand, showing me with both her words and actions that she supports me.

"Thanks, Meg." I smile, but she rolls her eyes.

"Would it kill you to call me 'Big?'"

Returning her eye roll, I tease, "Probably."

I'm about to cut off another piece of French toast when Meg asks, "So, how's everything with Jack?"

"Nothing is going on between me and Jack."

"Your date didn't go well?"

Shaking my head, I drop my fork and reach for the glass of water, taking a generous sip before telling her about the shitshow of a date. Meg is practically rolling on the floor by the time I describe Ava and Celeste's wigs.

"So let me get this straight: Jack picks you up, brings you to a tavern for pizza, tries to kiss you but gets interrupted by Celeste's cousin, who just so happens to be there. Your two best friends are dressed like international spies, and then Jack abandons you without paying the bill?" When I nod, not bothering to correct a single thing she said because there's no lie detected, she howls with laughter. "My God, Jack needs to fix his game. No wonder he's still single."

"He's a nice guy," I grumble, feeling protective of him even

287

though there's no romantic feeling there.

"Nice? Sure, but incredibly stupid. So, tell me about this guy, Wolf."

Grabbing my fork, I slice a piece of toast and pop it into my mouth, chewing slowly. "He's Celeste's cousin."

"Serena." Her voice sounds like a teacher scolding a kindergartener.

Clearing my throat, I offer, "We're seeing each other. He's the guy from the party, the one that came to pick me up, you know."

Meg's eyes widen at the realization. "Holy shit. That huge redhead that looks like he could bench press a tree?"

"Yeah, that's the one."

"Damn, good for you. No wonder why you aren't interested in Jack."

Laughing, I'm about to respond when I see familiar blonde hair out of the corner of my eye. Sobering immediately, I turn my head and watch as Marina and Bethany walk into JJ's and slide into a booth on the opposite side of the room. It's far enough away that I'm not forced to interact with them, but it's directly in my line of sight. They both see me, and their pretty faces transform with the ugly sneers plastered on them.

"What's wrong?" Meg asks, instantly recognizing that something is off. Spinning around, she follows my gaze and turns back to me, a frown marking her face. "Isn't that your stepsister?"

"Yep, and her big, Bethany. She's a senior in my linguistics class. I think she hates me as much as Marina does."

Meg's nose scrunches at my explanation. "She's probably annoyed she's not at the top of the class. Let me guess, you answer every question correctly?"

"I may have corrected her once or twice."

"Ah, no one likes a know-it-all," Meg teases, her face smoothing at the taunt.

"Shut up. I couldn't help it."

"Forget them. We're done anyway, right?" she asks, glancing down at our almost-empty plates. Nodding my agreement, she pulls out a couple of twenties and lays them on the table. "Let's go, my treat today."

"Wait, let me pay you back. I'll send you the money." Pulling out my phone, I swipe over the unopened texts and click on my banking application.

"Serena, it's fine. You pay next time."

Sighing, I drop my arm. "Thanks, Meg. I appreciate it." We both slip on our coats and rise from the booth. I don't look over my shoulder toward the table on the opposite side of the restaurant, but I can feel the prickles of their attention like jabs from barbed wire.

—

After hugging Meg goodbye, I hurry into Beans & Things to grab a drink before Dr. Forester's class. It's been a challenge keeping up with her reading and assignments, but I've found that I genuinely enjoy learning about linguistics, especially how she teaches it. The line isn't long, but I find myself scrolling through the texts on my phone as I wait to reach the barista. Clicking on the unread messages from my mom, I read through her texts.

Mom (11:36 AM): Hi *Muñeca*, just reminding you that I need some help on Sunday if you're still available.

Mom (11:42 AM): You must be in class. Call me this

afternoon; I'm off today to finish packing, so I'm able to answer your call.

Reminders of the move make my heart plummet, but I click on my mother's contact information and dial her number. Unsurprisingly, she picks up on the second ring.

My mom's voice greets me instantly. *"Muñeca*, how are you? How are your classes?"

"Hi, Mom. I'm doing well. Classes are fine; I just got done having lunch with Meg."

My mom hums her approval. She's never made any secret that she was worried about me starting college so early, but my father was the driving force behind me not only starting college at sixteen but also moving out and living on my own at such a young age. To say my mother is relieved that I've finally found friends and formed strong bonds would be an understatement. "That's wonderful, honey. How is she doing? How are Celeste and Ava?"

"Everyone is well. But yes, I'll be there on Sunday. Do you need any boxes or anything?"

"No, I have it all. I just need you to go through your things. I'll be up early, so come whenever you'd like. I can't wait to see you."

I smile into the phone. "Me too." Movement in front of me catches my attention, and I see that I'm next in line. "I'm at the coffee shop, and I'm about to order. I'll call you later, okay?"

"Don't drink too much coffee, *hija*. I love you. Call me tomorrow."

"I know; I'm getting tea. Love you, too." Hanging up, I walk to the counter and place an order for a mint tea. The barista swipes my student ID in exchange for a boiling cup of tea, and less than ten minutes after I entered the shop, I'm already on my way out.

I take my time walking to Forester's class, letting myself enjoy the crisp weather outside before I'm stuffed in a classroom for almost two hours. Transferring my tea to my left hand, I fish inside my bag for my phone and pull open Wolf's texts. We spoke a little this morning, but he had to rush to get to the gym before a full day of clients. I decide to text him, just on the off chance that he's available.

Serena: Hey, how's your day going?

My phone vibrates seconds after sending the message, and I laugh at the incoming call. "I thought you were busy today."

"Busy as fuck, but I have a few minutes between clients. How are you, princess?"

"Full. I just finished eating lunch with my friend, Meg. She's the one you scared half to death at that party."

"Ah, the one who didn't realize she should try to open the door instead of just pounding on it."

Nodding my head as though he can see it, I laugh. "Yep, the same."

"Hmm." His hum flows over me. "You on your way to class now?"

Clearing my throat, I nod again. Anyone watching me probably thinks I'm impersonating a bobblehead. "Yes, I have class in a few minutes."

"You still coming this weekend?" There's a note of worry in his voice, like he thinks I might have changed my mind.

"Of course. I told you I would be there. I'm excited to see you fight." Excited is not exactly the right word—terrified, apprehensive, and strangely aroused would all fit better.

"I'm excited to see you. Wait for me after the fight. I'll bring

291

you home."

"Okay." I stop in front of the door to the building where Forester's class is held. "Listen, I'm about to walk inside the building for class. I'll talk to you tonight?"

"No problem. Be good, princess."

"I'm always good," I comment wryly before hanging up on him. Replaying our conversation in my head, I walk through the building and into class in a daze. Sliding into my usual seat, I shift through my bag and begin placing my things on my desk to prepare for the lecture.

At the sound of Heather sliding into her seat beside me, I sit up to say hello. Except, when I look over, it's not Heather occupying the seat, but Bethany with a mocking smile.

"Hello, Serena."

"What do you want, Bethany?" I sigh, already over the conversation.

"What, I can't say hello to my little's sister?"

Scoffing, I let my disgust bleed into my voice. "Marina and I aren't sisters; we're not even friends. Can't you just leave me alone? Both of you. She won; she got the family. And anyway, aren't you graduating this semester? Aren't you too old for the bullying trope?"

"Aren't you a little young to be a homewrecker?" she replies, but instead of sounding vicious, she just sounds confused.

Rolling my eyes, I shake my head. "Just let it go, Bethany. I get it, Marina is your friend. That's great. But truthfully, I don't want to be anywhere near either of you. If you've come over here to warn me away from Jack, let her know I'm not interested. I'd tell her, except I don't care about what either of you want. So, go back to your seat, study your notes for the quiz we're probably going to have, and stay far away from me." Turning forward, I avert my face so that she's not in my peripheral view.

Though, just because I can't see her doesn't mean I can't hear her. Bethany huffs and mumbles, "Bitch," under her breath before standing from Heather's seat and walking down the aisle toward the front of the room. Relaxing once she's no longer next to me, I watch as Heather slides into her seat and offer her a small smile.

Forester steps to the podium not a second later, greeting us before telling us all to clear our desks for the pop quiz. Bethany looks back at me and scowls.

I shouldn't feel so satisfied that I was right about the quiz or about telling her to fuck off. But there's no denying that it felt good.

—

Two hours, a pop quiz, and a hand cramp later from typing fast enough to keep up with Forester's lesson, I'm relieved to walk out the doors of the lecture hall. That relief quickly morphs into dread at the sight of Dylan leaning against the wall opposite me. Stopping in the middle of the hallway, I welcome the grumblings of my classmates as their bodies collide with mine to sneak past me; at least it makes me feel something other than absolute dread at his presence.

"Stop blocking the hallway, bitch," Bethany mumbles under her breath as she shoves me aside. Her comment is all I need to jolt myself out of my haze and start my movement, letting my legs take quick strides toward the exit and away from my former best friend.

"Serena, wait," Dylan calls from behind. Three, four months ago, I would have listened to his command; hell, I would have been overjoyed to see him and would have hugged him the moment I realized his presence. Now? My body, mind, and heart are repulsed by the thought of any form of contact with him. I pick up speed, breaking into a light jog as I weave through the crowd walking through the doors.

"Sorry, excuse me. Whoops, sorry about that," I mumble as I elbow, side-step, and stomp on the people in my way, all to avoid Dylan. I don't breathe until I'm yards away from the building, certain that I've placed enough distance between us that a run-in is impossible. Stopping to catch my breath, I draw in a long exhale and jump at the haunted voice behind me.

"Serena, please. Can we talk?"

Whipping around, I take in Dylan's disheveled appearance; he's always been vain, consumed by his presentation and outward appearance. The rumpled clothing, bags under his eyes, and paleness of his skin are almost enough to make me feel bad for him. Almost, but not quite.

"You're joking, right? No, we cannot talk. As Celeste would say, get fucked." Turning, I step forward to continue my walk across campus but stop when Dylan's hand reaches out to grip my shoulder. His hold is light, but a flashback to the party assaults me and my body stiffens. "Get your hand off me. *Now.*"

His touch is immediately lifted. "I'm sorry. Please, Serena. Just give me five minutes."

Keeping my back to him, I clench my fists. "You don't get five minutes. You don't get another minute of my time, Dylan. You were my best friend, my rock, for years, and you betrayed my trust out of what? Jealousy? You know that our kiss was wrong; it was like kissing a cousin or a brother. You were just mad that you couldn't have me all to yourself anymore, that I

294

wasn't yours and yours alone. I made other friends, I had sex with someone, and you lashed out like a child because you couldn't control me. And then, you put your hands on me, bruised me, and whispered vile things. What fucking right do you have to come up to me, demanding we speak?

"Following me, as though you have the privilege to be in my presence? You don't. I never want to see you again. I never want to speak to you again." I've had time to analyze why Dylan did what he did, and all theories point to the same conclusion: he wanted control.

A strangled sound comes from behind me, but I have no sympathy, no shred of compassion. "Serena, I'm sorry. I'm so fucking sorry. I found out you were in Bethany's class and knew I needed to speak to you, apologize for what I did. I miss you; I miss us. Please, look at me."

Shaking my head, I'm surprised by the lack of tears in my eyes as I say, "You should be sorry for acting like a monster, but that doesn't mean I forgive you or want to speak with you. Get your shit together and have a good life."

I don't let his sorrow stop my progress forward and resume my walk back to my apartment. Maybe this is a good thing, though I never felt I needed closure after he put his hands on me. To be honest, I'm pissed that I had to see him at all. I'm sure some would romanticize his tracking me down, but I'm disgusted that he forced me to see his face after what he did. Maybe I'm a bad person, or maybe I just refuse to be subjected to cruel behavior by someone I trusted and cared for, but in either case, I have no desire to see or speak to Dylan again.

"Asshole," I mutter under my breath as I pull my cell phone out to let Ava and Celeste know what just happened.

295

32

Wolf

Mumford & Son's *The Wolf* flows over me, hyping me up as I get my hands wrapped by Jedd before the final fight of my career. I mouth along to the lyrics of my entrance song, the same song I play on repeat before every fight I've ever had.

Sheltered, you better keep back from the door
He wanders ever closer every night
And how he waits, begging for blood

"Ye'd think, after all this time, ye'd be sick of this song," Jedd murmurs. He's always a pain in the ass, but the emotion behind this being our final pre-fight ritual is hitting both of us hard. While I'm happy as fuck to stop the physical abuse to my body, I'll miss seeing my coach regularly. Though, if I know Jedd, he will guilt me into coming back to the gym frequently.

"You going to start crying, old man?"

"Oh, feck off, pissant." Jedd cuts off the end of the wrap, securing it to my hand. Holding up the roll, he shows me that it's nearly finished. "Ye got any more in that bag?"

"Shit, no. I thought I had enough."

"Fecker. I'll swipe from Gage." Jedd ambles out of the room, leaving me to my thoughts. I spoke with Serena again this afternoon and confirmed that she would be in the crowd with my cousin, Ava, and the rest of my family. She seemed calmer about it than she did earlier in the week, but based on the conversations we've had over the last couple of weeks, I know that she gets anxious easily.

The door to the room opens, and I look up, expecting to see Jedd striding over to me with a roll of tape in his hand. Instead, Kelly enters the room.

"Kelly, what the fuck are you doing here?" I look at the clock above the door and note the time—Gage should be entering the cage soon, and she has no reason to be in my room when she's with him.

"I wanted to wish you luck," she offers with a sultry smile. Six months ago, my cock would have gotten hard at the promise in her voice and what she's so obviously offering. Now, I feel nothing except pity and disgust.

"Where's your boyfriend?"

She shakes her head, and I know before she even says the words what's about to come out of her mouth. "We broke up. I realized I made a mistake, Wolfie." Her voice takes on a whiny tone, one that grates on every sensibility I have.

Looking to the ceiling, I step back as Kelly approaches, moving as far away from her as fast as I can. "Kelly, go back to Gage."

"But—"

"No," I cut her off. "Go back to Gage. There's nothing left here. Just fucking go."

"I love you. Please, just let's try."

"Kelly," I lower my voice, gentling it as much as I can despite

297

my irritation. "You left me for another man. I'm sorry it didn't work out for you. But me? I'm happy. So please, go back to Gage, or don't. Be by yourself, find happiness, or find it with someone else. But leave me alone. I'm done."

"Okay, ye overgrown horse's arse, let's feckin' get this on— oh, Kelly—" Jedd stops short, looking from me to Kelly, then back to me. "Gage is almost up. Shouldn't ye be over there?"

She grinds her teeth, an angry habit I became familiar with during our relationship, before nodding to Jedd and walking out of the room. We both watch her go, not speaking until she's cleared the door, and it clicks silently behind her.

"The feck she want?"

"Nothing. Let's get this wrap on." Jedd eyes me, suspicion on his face, but he doesn't say anything. Wrapping my remaining hand with a speed and dexterity that belies his experience. When he finishes and snaps off the remaining piece, I nod, silently thanking him.

"Alright, I won't give ye any pointers since ye won't follow them anyway. So, get the job done, McCleery."

Clapping him on the back, I tug on my black sweatshirt with a large, embossed wolf head and zip it before tossing the hood up. I had the sweatshirt custom-made when I first started fighting, and I've worn it for every entrance since. Jedd disappears behind the door for a minute, giving me a semblance of privacy, before he reemerges with three of the other guys on my team. Gage's fight must be finished already if they're all back here, except that doesn't explain why Jedd never left my side.

"Did you watch Gage's fight?" As a coach, Jedd typically stays with each fighter on the side of the cage, yelling out encouragement, observations, and instructions. It just hit me

298

that he didn't perform that task with Gage.

"No. Caleb handled it."

My eyes narrow on my trainer and friend. "Why?"

"Because the fecker is switching gyms, and he's a gobshite, that's why."

"Oh fuck. He's going to another gym?"

"Feckin' eejit." I can't disagree; Gage is a goddamn fool for leaving Jedd, especially since there have been whispers about more endorsements coming his way based on his performance. To have any real shot, he needs Jedd, not just because of skill but also because of the discipline Jedd mandates of all his fighters. Shaking my head, I expel all outside thoughts: Kelly, Gage, and even Serena, and focus on what matters right now: getting out of the cage with as minimal pain as possible and closing this chapter of my life.

Serena:

"I'm so nervous, I think I'm going to throw up," Ava shouts, causing an infinite amount of heads to swivel in our direction. We've been here for two hours, watching men from all different weight classes pummel each other until the main event.

I don't know how to feel about what I've seen tonight, but I do know that Ava throwing up on me will not help matters.

"Please don't, Aves."

"God, where is Greyson? He went to the bathroom thirty minutes ago."

"Ava." I turn to look at my friend, taking in the lines of worry on her face. "Why are you freaking out right now?"

She stops her frantic search for her boyfriend and turns to look at me, her eyes pleading but somehow embarrassed

299

at the same time. "Wolf's like an annoying big cousin, you know? I've only come to one other fight, but it was bloody and ended dangerously. I don't love violence like C, and I hate the thought of someone I care about getting hurt, especially this close to retirement."

Swallowing back my nerves, I offer Ava a small smile. "I don't think C loves violence, but she is pretty good at it, isn't she?" A laugh bubbles out of Ava's throat, and I breathe out a sigh of relief. "It's going to be okay, Aves." Pausing, I point to the doorway. "Look, there's Greyson, Dante, Lincoln, and Celeste. Who's that with them?" Trailing behind Celeste is a middle-aged couple that wasn't part of the Downing or Ink and Needle clans I met earlier tonight. Aubrey painstakingly introduced me to everyone from the tattoo shop, though I already knew Trent and Sloan from my previous appointments.

"Is that Wolf's mom with CeCe, Ava?" Ava doesn't have a chance to answer as Greyson scoops her into his arms, pulling her tight to his chest and giving her a hard kiss. I look over at Dante, who tries to pull Celeste into the same passionate embrace, but she gives him a hard look that promises pain if he even attempts it. I don't need to be a lip-reader to know that Dante responded with, "Don't tempt me with a good time, Red," since he yelled it loud enough for the entire section to hear. Celeste's answering hit is not a surprise.

"Celeste Lauren Downing," the woman next to her, presumably Wolf's mother, chastises her. "Stop hitting your boyfriend."

"Aunt Glynnie," Celeste whines, sounding like a petulant child who just got caught stealing a cookie.

"No, now introduce me to your friends, you insolent little

beauty." The way she says it, it sounds like she's putting on a performance, one intent on displaying the maximum amount of emotions to her audience.

"Fine. You know Ava"—she gestures toward Ava and Greyson—"and that's her boyfriend, Grey. Next to her is Serena, our friend from school."

"Hi, Mrs. McCleery, Mr. McCleery." Ava greets her and her husband with a wide smile, wrapping Mrs. McCleery in a hug before falling back into Greyson's embrace. Greyson offers a hand to both of Wolf's parents before returning it to Ava's waist.

Clearing my throat, I step forward, offering my hand in the same manner Greyson did. "Oh no, young lady. You give me a hug; I'm too young to be so formal."

"Oh," I squeak as Wolf's mom throws her arms around my shoulders and pulls me in for a tight hug. I feel like my organs are about to burst from the pressure when she finally releases me, stepping back but keeping a hold on my shoulders. I'm not sure what I expected, but it definitely wasn't a pint-sized tyrant with death-gripping hugs.

"I've heard so much about you, Serena. I'm so happy you're here. This is my husband, Lachlan. Lock, say hi," she commands, nudging her husband forward. Mr. McCleery offers a hand and smiles, greeting me in a silent hello that is the polar opposite of his wife's display. "He doesn't say much."

"Aye, because ye speak enough for the both of us, woman," Mr. McCleery teases in a light Scottish accent, glancing at his wife with affection. "It's lovely to meet ye, Serena. Wolf's told us much about ye."

"He did?" CeCe and I ask in unison, though my voice sounds confused, and hers sounds excited. Cutting my gaze to her, I narrow my eyes at her outburst, but she just tucks her lower lip beneath her top lip and acts like she can't see my questioning glare.

"Yes, sweetheart. I am so excited to get to know you. I'm sure we'll become great friends," Mrs. McCleery responds.

I smile at her, sure that it looks more like a wince than anything resembling enthusiasm. "Great. Sounds good."

"Wolf and CeCe have always been the closest of the bunch, you know," Mrs. McCleery says beside me. "And I've always viewed her like my daughter, especially since my little sister has all the emotional output of a broom. Celeste doesn't let many people in, so the fact that you have befriended her and Ava in such a short time tells me all I need to know."

"They've become my best friends," I answer truthfully. "I don't know what I would have done without them the last few months."

The hands holding my shoulders pull me back in for another tight hug before releasing me. "That's good, honey. Now, tell me about yourself."

"Oh, there's not much to tell. I'm a junior at Marymount in the English program."

"'That is part of the beauty of all literature. You discover that your longings are universal longings, that you're not lonely and isolated from anyone. You belong.'"

I pause for a moment, reflecting on her words and where I've heard them before. "Fitzgerald?"

Mrs. McCleery smiles, pleasure lighting up her face. "Good girl. Are you a Gatsby fan?"

Shaking my head, I wince. "Not really. If I'm reading anything from that period, it's Wharton or Eliot, maybe Hurston. But I'm not a huge fan of Fitzgerald. Daisy annoyed me."

"Well, we can't all be perfect, can we, my dear?" she says with a wink. She opens her mouth to add something else to the conversation when a high-pitched voice calls out to her.

"Oh my goodness, Glynnie. How are you?" Slender arms wrap around Mrs. McCleery's neck and pull her in. From my viewpoint, it looks like this new pink-haired woman is trying to suffocate her with her embrace.

"Kelly, how lovely," Mrs. McCleery responds, sounding like the words tasted like sawdust on her tongue. I look past her to see Mr. McCleery scowling at the woman who just joined us.

"You look amazing. Have you lost weight?"

"No." Kelly's smile falters at Wolf's mother's flat tone, but she doesn't seem deterred. "New haircut then?"

"No, same style I've had for the last fifteen years."

"Then—"

"Kelly, nothing's changed. How is Gage?"

Kelly's smile becomes brittle. "Oh, Wolf didn't tell you? We're not together anymore. You know Wolf and I were talking earlier; we think we deserve to give it another chance. There's so much love between—"

"Have you met Wolf's girlfriend, Serena?" Mrs. McCleery interrupts, shocking both Kelly and me if my sputter and Kelly's icy stare are any indications.

"Mrs. McCleery," I start, shaking my head emphatically. The last thing I need is for Wolf to think I'm telling his friends and family that I'm his girlfriend.

"Glynnie, dear. Remember?" No, I don't remember.

"I—"

"... am so modest. But tell Kelly how you two met." Raising

303

her voice, she explains, "Wolf gave her a tattoo. Isn't that romantic? And she's one of Celeste's best friends. And you know how discerning our CeCe is when it comes to character."

Giving me the attention she didn't think I was warranted when she first interrupted us, Kelly surveys my form, dragging her eyes from the tip of my black sneakers, up my baggy jeans, and to the tight, off-the-shoulder top I'm wearing. Though my shoulders are on display, I'm a lot more conservatively dressed than some of the other women here, Kelly included. In her pink minidress and heels, we look like we're going to two different events.

"Hmm. Anyway, Glynnie, it was so good catching up. Lunch soon? I'll tell Wolf to set it up." Her words show her dismissal, her analysis that whatever Wolf and I are, it's no competition for her.

"I'm with my son's girlfriend, Kelly. I don't believe Wolf will be inclined to set anything up. It was nice seeing you. Say hi to Gage for me." Mrs. McCleery turns from her, pulling me with her to hide within the crowd we're with.

Once Kelly is out of earshot, Mrs. McCleery releases my arm and offers me an eye roll. "I hate rooting against women, you know? I'm all for empowerment, going after what you want, and being the maker of your destiny. But that girl, my goodness, what a viper." Shaking her head, she shivers before continuing, "When Wolf told me they broke up, I felt bad for him, but I was so relieved she would be out of our lives, especially after he told me what she did."

Furrowing my brow, I can't help but ask, "What did she do?"

Mrs. McCleery scoffs, not hiding her distaste. "She left

him, practically in the middle of the night, for one of his teammates, or training mates, whatever the hell it's called. Wolfric is retiring after this game. Kelly was against it and tried to convince him to postpone his retirement."

"I think it's called a fight. And Wolfric? That's his real name?"

"Yes, I went through an Old English phase for a while. He was almost Ultread, but my husband wouldn't allow it."

"Thank God," I mutter. "No offense."

"None taken."

"Mrs. McCleery—Glynnie—I'm sorry to disappoint you, but I'm not Wolf's girlfriend."

She shrugs like it's of no consequence. "Yet, but I'm sure you will be. Now, shh, I hear Wolf's entrance song." She turns, giving me her back and effectively ending the conversation. I feel like I have whiplash from the amount of information I learned in the last fifteen minutes.

"Told you she was fiery," Ava whispers into my ear. "But you and Wolfie, huh? Freaking knew it." She holds up her hand in an invitation to high-five me.

"I am not giving you a high-five," I grumble, earning laughs from both her and Greyson. We sober as soon as we hear a loud wolf howl, followed by the opening chords of Mumford & Son's *The Wolf*. The lights dim, casting us all in shadows as a spotlight shines on the mouth of the entrance. "Ava, I thought Wolf was an amateur fighter?"

CeCe butts in, answering my question. "He's not, technically. He got his start in jiu-jitsu championships, then worked his way into the MMA world."

I nod, feigning understanding. I could ask more questions, but I stand enraptured by the hooded figure walking out to the

305

lyrics about a wolf on the hunt for blood. His journey to the cage is timed perfectly with the song and the lyrics; he walks through the crowd as the song croons, *You have been weighed, you have been found wanting.* He steps up to the platform as the singer taunts, *You better keep the wolf back from the door.* And finally, he arrives at his corner of the mat with the lyrics, *I promised you everything would be fine.*

Howls and claps usher him in, sealing his control over the crowd. I don't pay attention as his opponent's song begins, nor do I give the same focus to the coordination of their entrance song and their arrival in the cage. My eyes are trained on Wolf as he strips to a tight pair of shorts and his tattoos.

The other fighter strips quickly, and a man in a referee shirt walks into the middle of the cage, announcing the rules to Wolf and his opponent before ordering them to shake hands and retreat into their corners. A sound like sticks breaking goes off, and then Wolf sprints.

For someone of his size, I never would have expected the speed with which he can move, but he charges at the other fighter so quickly, in such a blur, that the punch combination he lands takes him down immediately. As soon as his opponent drops, Wolf is on him, giving one final blow until the ref rushes out, stopping Wolf's punches and signaling the end of the fight.

The crowd becomes pandemonium; frantic energy seeping out of everyone's pores as we collectively process what the hell just happened and how, not even eight seconds into the fight, Wolf laid that man out. The ref holds Wolf's arm up, declaring him the winner as his team storms the stage. In the brightness surrounding him, I doubt he can see me, but I scream, cheering for the man who just ended his career so viciously that there's no doubt his fight will be remembered.

Mrs. McCleery grips my arm, squeezing so tightly that I'm worried I'm going to be the next one down for the count. "Mrs. McCleery—"

"Aunt Glynnie, Rena, come on. We need to go back to the family section and wait for him before this place becomes a madhouse." Keeping my forearm in her grasp, Wolf's mother clutches her husband's hand and leads us through the crowd. I'm thankful for the anchor she's providing as we weave through the crowd, giving me direction as my emotions riot inside.

We break through the hoard and slip through a doorway, bringing us to a large hallway filled with all of the fighters' family and close friends. Easing through a door, we're deposited into a large room to wait.

Mrs. McCleery finally eases her grip off me, letting me go with a sharp gasp as Wolf enters the room thirty minutes later. I thought it would have taken longer for Wolf to bask in the adoration of his fans one last time, but one look at his face tells me that he's ready to get out of here.

"Hey, Ma." Wolf pulls his mom into a hug, dwarfing her with his size. Looking up, Wolf grabs his dad and pulls him in, too, embracing both of his parents in a sweet gesture that seems so out of place in the brutality of the night, yet still strangely right. I hang back, stepping next to Ava as Celeste runs at Wolf, throwing her arms around his waist.

"Holy shit, what a combo," she rushes out, bouncing on her heels in excitement. "What a way to go, Wolfie. You annihilated him."

"Yeah, he's okay though, in case you were wondering, killer," Wolf replies dryly, easing Celeste's arms from around his body.

He nods at Dante before making his way around the room. He thanks each cousin, each friend, and each person from his gym for their support, giving hugs, handshakes, and backslaps as necessary before making his way over to me. Though I'm the last person he approached, I feel the weight of everyone's eyes intimately and shrink back, blushing furiously at the attention. Wolf sees what I'm trying to do and mumbles under his breath, "Don't think so, princess," and hauls me forward, crushing me against his body.

"I fucking knew it," Celeste calls out behind me, and I blush deeper as I push against Wolf's hold.

"Wolf," I mutter, putting distance between us so that I can look into his face. "That fight was—" I pause, shaking my head to find the right word but coming up short. "Incredible." The word doesn't feel like it has enough currency to fully describe my thoughts, but it's the best I have.

"Thanks, princess. You ready to get out of here?"

I furrow my brow, shaking my head at his question. "But, what about everyone here? They all came for you."

"They're going to the bar; my parents are probably going home. I just need some time to decompress. You game, princess?"

Swallowing down the denial lodged in my throat, my guilt at taking him away from the people who want to celebrate him is pushed aside, and I slip my hand into his. "Sure."

33

Wolf

"You rode your bike to an MMA fight? What if you were hurt?" Serena doesn't hide the incredulity in her voice, and I laugh at her disbelief.

"I knew I'd be fine."

"That is the worst explanation for idiotic behavior. You can't know that, especially not when your sole purpose was to hit and be hit." I shrug, handing her the spare helmet. She huffs but slides it over her head and secures the chin strap. She grabs onto my shoulder as she slides behind me, molding her front to my back and circling her arms around my waist. The heat from her body seeps into my back, and the hard-on I get from the feel of her delicate hands around my body is embarrassing.

Reaching for her hands, I squeeze them before donning my helmet and easing the bike out of the lot. Her grip tightens on my abdomen when I start to pick up speed, driving us deeper into the pine barrens as we edge toward central Jersey. The further I drive, the harder she grips me, and the more convinced I am that I'm not going to make it home before the need to fuck her becomes unbearable. After a fight, I'm always riddled with adrenaline and a need that was usually slaked by whatever woman I was seeing or a random hook-up at a bar or party afterward. But there is something about knowing Serena was in the seats for me that makes the lust harder than normal to control.

The event center where the fight was held is an hour away from my house and forty minutes from Marymount University and Serena's apartment, a drive through the Pinelands of New Jersey. When I was younger and first got my driver's license, Trent and I used to explore the woods over here, hunting for the fabled Jersey Devil and swearing that the old cabin foundations we'd come across belonged to Mother Leeds.

Now, I'm jaded enough to realize that the stories and sightings were probably nothing more than a lone sighting of a great blue heron, but something about the drive through the desolate pines is eerie yet seductive. Making a quick decision, I drive onto the shoulder and then onto a path that's obscured from the road and bring the bike a few yards into the tree line, where I know that no passing cars can see. Switching off the engine, I engage the kickstand and let the sound of the woods fill the air as I unlatch my helmet and stand from the bike.

"What are we doing here?"

I respond by unclipping her helmet and hanging it next to mine on the handlebar. Reaching for her, I lift her off the seat and guide her legs around my waist, securing them by locking her ankles behind me. Maneuvering my leg back over the seat, I sit with Serena straddling my lap and holding on to me for dear life.

"Wolf?"

"Princess, I'm fucking high on adrenaline—the natural kind—and don't think I can go another minute before sinking into your cunt." Snaking my hand between our bodies, I pop the button on her jeans and reach my hand inside, pleased as shit to find her panties soaked and the jeans loose enough to allow my hand and wrist to fit inside comfortably. Even without sight, my fingers find her clit immediately, like a beacon calling to them, and strum the nerves once, twice, before moving down to sink into her pussy.

Serena's answering moans fuel me, and I lean forward, burying my head in the curve of her neck, lapping at the spot where her shoulder and neck meet. Using my free hand to lower the shoulders of her jacket, I slowly expose her skin, which seems to glow in the moonlight.

"Fucking beautiful," I murmur. Biting down on the skin, I mimic the speed of my fingers with my mouth, pressing open-mouthed kisses against her flesh until I feel her body grind against my fingers.

"That's right, princess, fuck my fingers." I push into her harder, curling my fingers and rubbing against her inner walls. Her hips gyrate faster, grinding her pussy against my hand like she'd die without my fingers inside her. "You're so fucking wet, Serena. I can't wait to feel you come around my cock." I stuff a third finger inside, stretching her in preparation for my cock.

"You want to come, princess?"

"Wolf, please."

Leaning down, I capture her mouth, drawing her in for a hungry kiss before leaning back. "Tell me how fucking bad you want it, Serena. Tell me how badly you want me to stuff my fat cock inside you, how much you need to come all over

311

my dick. Let me hear you say it."

"Please. Faster." Chuckling to myself, I pull out, keeping my fingers hooked to catch her wetness. Bringing my fingers to my mouth, I lick her juices off my hand and feel like a goddamn king when I hear her whimpering protests from my retreat.

"That wasn't what I wanted to hear, princess." With my clean hand, I grasp the base of her neck, letting my fingers glide through her short blonde strands, and drag her head back. Exposing her throat, I trail my tongue from her jaw down to her clavicle, devoting attention to each inch of exposed skin.

"Take my cock out," I murmur against her shoulder. With deft hands, Serena reaches for me, unzipping my jeans and reaching inside to pull me out. Her hands flutter around my shaft, and I have to bite my lip to keep from coming from her light touch. Working my way back over her collarbone, up her neck, and to her mouth, I capture her bottom lip, grasping it lightly between my teeth. Her hands move faster, spreading the precum all over my cock as she jerks me off with both hands. "Fuck," I groan against her mouth, releasing her lip before working my tongue inside to tangle against hers. I lick into her, fucking her mouth with the same all-consuming focus I'd eat her pussy.

Breaking away, I shake my head to clear my thoughts. "There's a condom in my wallet." She pretends not to hear me, or maybe she's so focused on my cock that she's unable to comprehend anything else. Releasing my hold on her neck, I still her hands, stopping her movements until we're both cradling my dick in our hands. "Princess, grab the wallet out of my pocket and get the condom. I want to watch you roll it on me."

She swallows, the sound audible in the otherwise quiet night. Tomorrow, I'll thank God that no cars or other riders have gone down this stretch of highway since we detoured, but now, all I care about is getting inside Serena.

Like the good girl she is, Serena reaches a hand inside my pocket and pulls out my wallet, quickly finding the condom and returning the leather binding inside my jeans. With shaking hands, she rips the foil and discards the packet into my pocket. Lowering her hands, I help her by grabbing the base and tilting it forward, away from my stomach. Her fingers are unsteady and slow as she places the latex on the tip and rolls it down, and fuck me, why is that a turn-on? When it's finally secure, she rips her hands away and places them on my shoulders as though she's trying to get off my lap.

"What are you doing?"

She stutters in her movements, confusion crossing her features. "I need to take my pants off, don't I?" Unwilling to delay, I slam her hips back down until her ass hits my thighs.

Pinching the fabric, I test the durability of the denim and ask, "Do you have an emotional attachment to these jeans?" The quick shake of her head is all the encouragement I need to grab each side of her zipper and pull until the sound of denim ripping fills the quiet night. "Ride my cock, princess. I'm not going to last long."

"Did you—did you just rip my fucking pants?"

"Yes." I guide her hips forward, positioning her until the head of my cock is sheathed inside her cunt. "Fuck," I groan, pulling her body slowly until I'm buried inside of her. Serena's body is ready for me, stretched to accommodate my size, and I

313

slide into her with little resistance. Shifting the hand between us, I move from the base of my cock to her clit, strumming the nerves until she starts to move against me, grinding back and forth in a rhythm that pulls my cock out an inch before disappearing back inside.

"Just like that, princess. Ride my cock." I punctuate my words by moving a freehand around her hips, slapping her ass at the same time she pulls me back inside. Her answering moan is sinful, telling me everything I need to know about how much she likes pain on the side of her pleasure, and I do it again, wishing that I could see the handprint I'm leaving on her ass as I split her apart.

"Wolf, I'm coming. Oh my God," she whispers, tossing her head back as the orgasm overtakes her.

I feel feral, and it's the only excuse I have when I grab her face and press her lips up to mine, drinking in her moans and cries like an elixir meant to give me life. My possession causes another wave to hit Serena, jolting her body forward and squeezing my cock until I explode inside her, wishing that my cum was painting the inside walls of her pussy.

I ease my mouth off of her, though I keep my lips hovering about hers. "We need to go, Serena." With each word, my lips brush against hers.

Serena licks her lips, licking mine, too, thanks to our proximity. "How am I supposed to ride on this thing with crotchless pants?"

Smirking, I glance down at her torn jeans and the bright pink thong concealing her pussy. "You'll be pressed against me, and the jacket will cover it."

She shakes her head and sighs, tugging her jacket over her shoulders. "You owe me a pair of pants."

"Hey," I start, cupping her cheek to tilt her face up. "Thank you for coming tonight."

The annoyed expression melts off her face, and she offers a tiny smile. "You're welcome, though I never need to see you beat someone else ever again." Casting her eyes down, she looks at the hand resting in her lap. "How are your hands? Do you need to ice them or something?"

"They're fine. But I'm happy that I won't be in the octagon again." Lifting her off my lap, I swing my leg off the bike and stand, depositing her back on the seat as soon as my feet hit the ground. Yanking off the condom, I tie it off and shove it in my front pocket to dispose of later and pull my jeans up. Grabbing our helmets, I hold one out to her and watch her slip it over her head and fasten the chin strap. Securing my helmet, I get on the bike and wait for her to wrap her arms around me before reversing out of the woods and back onto the highway.

34

Serena

My journey to consciousness is soft, nothing more than a hand caressing my back and my eyes lifting like a weighted blanket is pressing down on me. It's slow, like the sizzle of pancake batter on a hot skillet. And it's hard like a six-foot-six man beneath you, dragging you into the land of the living after the best sleep of your life.

"Wolf, let me sleep," I grumble, trying to twist out of his hold. When we got to his house last night, I took off my destroyed jeans and slipped into one of his shirts. Thanks to Wolf's breadth and our height difference, the shirt came to my calves, and I looked like a child playing dress-up with her father's clothes.

It didn't help that Wolf laughed at me as soon as he saw my appearance. I told him to fuck off, but that just made him laugh harder. Asshole.

His hand continues running over my back, stroking me like a cat, and, at this point, I've given up on sleep altogether. "Fine, I'm up. What are you even doing up this early? Shouldn't you still be hibernating?" I raise my head to look up at him, noting the quirked eyebrow and smirk on his face.

"You woke me up, princess. I was sleeping, but you started clutching my arms, and then you climbed on top of me like you were climbing a mountain. Far be it from me to stop you from reaching your dreams."

My face turns red, and I duck my head into his chest, cutting off our eye contact. I've always been an active sleeper, so I'm not necessarily surprised that I moved in my sleep. However, I am embarrassed that I seemed to have orchestrated climbing on top of him in my subconscious. "Sorry," I mumble against his bare, tattooed chest, speaking into the endless lines decorating his body.

"You think I mind?" He flexes his hips, pressing them into me to show his obvious arousal. I wince at the thought of him entering me again; while it's been the best sex I've ever had, I can't deny that I'm sore.

My body language must betray my thoughts because he chuckles and relaxes into the mattress. "Sore?"

"A little," I offer, looking back up at him and offering a small smile. "Are you relieved to be officially retired?"

"Mmm," he hums, his hand stilling at my neck. "I'm relieved it's over. I'm grateful for what MMA has afforded me, but I can't say I'm sad to close that chapter." His fingers knead into my skin, lightly massaging my muscles. "How were the last two weeks for you?"

I tense at his question, debating how best to respond. Sensing my dilemma, his fingers stop their movement and skate to my jaw, tilting my head up to meet his eyes. "What happened, princess?"

Swallowing my nerves, I offer, "I ran into Dylan."

"That dick who put his hands on you?" Wolf's eyes turn

glacial, betraying all of the anger he must harbor at my omission. "What the fuck did he want?"

"To apologize, but I refused to speak to him. I haven't seen him since."

His eyes survey my face, pinging between my eyes until he accepts my answer and nods. "Will you let me know if he bothers you again?"

"Yes," I reply, pressing a kiss against his chest. "I need to get going. I have to go to my mom's to help her finish packing up my room before she moves today."

"Where is she moving?"

I swallow down the fury that always accompanies thoughts of my mom's forced move. Though she swears she's fine, happy even, that my dad will no longer be a presence in any part of our lives unless I choose for him to be, anger, guilt, and disgust war for the primary emotion. "She's moving to a condo in Frog Tree."

"You don't sound too happy about that."

"I'm not. My dad is a dick."

I can feel Wolf's confusion. "But aren't they divorced?"

"Yeah, because he's a cheating asshole who couldn't keep it in his pants. But he was the main signer on the mortgage because my mom didn't have great credit when they divorced. After everything that happened with Devin and Marina, my dad decided to torpedo every part of my life where he still had some semblance of involvement. My mom never said, but from the conversations I've had with my dad, he all but demanded she move out or buy him out. My mom has never been one for games or theatrics, so she listed the house herself and told him to fuck off." Shaking my head against his chest, I feel the tears start to come down, not in sorrow but

SERENA

frustration. "You know the worst part? I begged my dad, cried to him to reconsider doing this. That house was our sanctuary after the divorce. It's where I learned to cook, where my grandmother would help me with my Spanish homework, and where I felt the safest. He took that away from me, from us, just like he's taken everything else we've ever had."

Wolf's hand resumes rubbing my back, having stopped as soon as I started my tirade. Gathering me closer, his other arm bands around my body, hugging me to him. It's meant to give comfort, solidarity; there's nothing sexual about the move, yet it warms me all the same.

"Your dad sounds like an asshole."

I bark out a laugh, grateful for the blatant honesty. "He is. But I haven't been able to make it home in the last few weeks, so my mom has been doing everything by herself, though she swears she doesn't want me there anyway. Part of me believes her since this is more difficult for her than it is for me, but I still wish I would have been able to help."

He hums in response, squeezing me one last time before shifting me off him and standing from the bed. Moving to his closet, he grabs a pair of gray sweatpants, a black T-shirt and matching hoodie, a pair of briefs, and white socks. "Give me five minutes, and then I'll bring you to your apartment, okay?"

Swallowing any disappointment down by his lack of response, I nod my head and push the comforter off of me. Grabbing my ruined jeans from the floor, I slide them on and thank God that Wolf's ridiculously long shirt covers my vagina and all potentially offending parts of my body. I push my feet into my shoes, pull on my jacket, and then straighten up Wolf's bed. Wolf's place is almost uncomfortably neat, and

319

I know from my experience in my apartment that he hates any form of disorganization or things out of place. I fluff the strangely high number of decorative pillows before arranging them in size order.

True to his word, Wolf walks back into his room five minutes later, fully showered and dressed. "You ready to go?"

"Yep." I nod, picking my bag up off his dresser and following him out the door.

—

Wolf pulls his truck in front of my apartment complex and shifts it into park, idling at the curb. "Go up and change; I'll wait down here for you."

Whipping my head to Wolf, I shout, "What?"

He gives me a bored look like I should have known that he was coming with me to my mother's house. "What kind of dick would I be if I let you pack shit up by yourself after you just told me how upsetting today was going to be for you?"

Furrowing my brow, I replay the words spoken earlier. "I never said today would be upsetting."

"Princess, you cried on my chest when you spoke about your mom moving. You think packing up your bedroom is going to be a fucking laugh fest? Please." He rolls his eyes, not hiding his opinion. "You're wasting time. Go," he orders, leaning over me to pop open the passenger side door.

"You don't want to come up? I'll be a few minutes; I need to shower."

"Absolutely fucking not. If I go into that apartment, I'm either fucking you or rearranging your pantry. Probably both. We don't have time for that, so go."

"I—uh. Okay." Hopping down from the truck, I race across the pavement, relieved that it's early on a Sunday and not many people are out. Rushing up the stairs and into my apartment, I give myself a body shower and don't bother washing my hair. After putting on a light coat of makeup, I survey my appearance. Normally, I love how short my hair is, but on days when it needs a wash, not being able to pull it up into a ponytail is annoying. Unfortunately, today, it needs a wash.

Power walking to my room, I throw on leggings, a tank top, and an oversized sweatshirt before grabbing a baseball cap and pushing it over my head. Grabbing my purse that I discarded on the entry table, I look at my phone and pride myself on taking less than twenty minutes to get ready. I may have created a small flood in the bathroom and a tornado in my bedroom, but I'll just clean that when I get back this afternoon.

Throwing my front door open, I race out of the apartment building and into Wolf's waiting truck. I'm ashamed to admit that I'm winded from my rush out the door.

"Okay," I pant. "My mom lives fifteen minutes away. Give me the phone, and I'll plug in the address."

"Calm down, Serena. You sound like you're out of breath."

"Shut up, Wolf. Give me the phone." I hold out my hand, waiting for him to deposit it in my palm. He shakes his head at me but hands over the phone. In no time, I have my mom's address programmed into the phone, and we're on the road.

I don't let myself dwell on introducing Wolf and my mom, nor do I think about how Wolf will react to some of the very juvenile things in my room, like my old One Direction poster. Instead, I watch the trees pass by and try to silence all

321

thoughts.

Wolf's throat clears, eviscerating my hopes of a thought-free ride. Though his eyes are on the road, I can feel him watching me through his peripheral.

"What?"

"We're exclusive."

I squint at him, unsure of what he's saying. "What?" I ask again.

"There are no other men. There are no other women. Boyfriend, girlfriend, whatever fucking name you want to call it, we're exclusive."

He's not so much asking me as he is telling me. "I didn't think there were other people, but okay. Thanks for clarifying."

"Good."

"Good," I repeat. I turn my head back toward the window, thinking about the bizarre way he just confirmed the status of our relationship. A hand trails over my wrist, pulling one of my hands off my lap and resting it inside his atop the center console. I turn my head and stare forward at the road. From the corner of my eye, I can see a smirk flit across Wolf's mouth, and I can't help the one that breaks across my face.

35

Wolf

Despite all my prior thoughts, Serena's hand feels right nestled in mine, like it's exactly where it's supposed to be. It may sound cliché or like a stupid line from a movie from the eighties, but there's a sense of rightness that envelops me at the pressure of her palm. I'm trying to contain the smile that's attempting to break out across my face, but it's hard.

I was up until the early morning hours watching her as she lay across my chest like a starfish. It felt good having her there, on top of me and in my bed, and I knew that this morning, I'd confirm with her what we are to each other. I squeeze her hand, relishing how her fingers feel in mine.

I'm saved from having to think about it too much as the GPS signals that we've arrived at her mother's place. It's a modest white ranch-style house with lots of flower beds and trees in the front that look like they've been planted with care and consideration. I turn to Serena, about to ask her if this is the right place, when I realize that her face has gone unusually pale, and her mouth hangs open.

"Serena, what's wrong? Is everything okay?" I unclick my

seatbelt and release her hand, cupping her jaw to bring her eyes to mine. "Hey, talk to me. What's going on?"

"What the hell is he doing here?"

"What?" I follow her gaze and stare at the Porsche Macan in the driveway next to a Honda Civic; it seems out of place in the neighborhood. Looking back at Serena, I ask a question I already know the answer to. "Whose car is that?"

"My father's."

"Is there any reason why he would be here?"

That seems to snap her out of her stupor. She glances at me and shakes her head. "No. I don't think so. Wolf…" Her voice trembles. "We need to go inside. What if he's hurting her?"

"Serena, we need to call—Goddammit," I sigh. Serena doesn't wait for me to finish my sentence and throws open the door, bolting toward the house with surprising speed.

I fling open my door, slamming it behind me, and race after her, stopping her just before she opens the front door. "Serena, you need to wait. Let me go in first. If your mom is in trouble, or if he has a fucking weapon, I'm not letting you walk into the line of fire."

"I will not wait out here—" she starts, but I cut her off with a squeeze of her hand.

"And I'm not asking you to. But you need to stay behind me until we know that everything is safe."

"Fine."

Nodding, I drag her behind me and step up to the front door, easing it open to loud yelling from my left. Turning in the direction of the voices, I grab Serena's hand and walk forward, trying to keep my steps as light as possible. The closer we get to the voices, the louder and more distinguishable they become.

324

"How dare you come into this house like I owe you something. You are a disgrace of a man, a joke of a father. I hope you burn in hell for what you have put our daughter through."

"It's sad that an educated woman is prone to fits of hysteria. The best thing I ever did was leave you." My eyes widen at the cruel tone of Serena's dad, and I hear her suck in a breath behind me. Squeezing her hand, I peek around the corner, verifying that there are no weapons. A petite woman with dark hair stands with her back to me, while an older man with gray hair and a matching beard perches against a kitchen table, arms crossed like he's owed something.

Turning back to Serena, I whisper, "It looks like they're just talking. No weapons, and your mother doesn't appear hurt." She pulls away from me, storming into the kitchen like a woman possessed.

"What the fuck are you doing here?"

"Serena," her mother gasps. "You're early."

"Daughter," her father replies coolly. "I see you brought company."

Serena's fists clench, and I can see the tension spread throughout her body. "I will ask you one more time: what the hell are you doing here?"

"Such dramatics. You get that from your mother. I am picking up my last payment for the house."

"What?"

"I—"

"Stephen, for once in your sorry excuse for a life, just stop."

"Mom, what is he talking about?"

Her mother sighs, shaking her head at Serena's dad before turning around to Serena. Her pretty face is washed in concern and weariness. "For the last ten years, I've had to pay your father a monthly rent to stay in this house."

"But-but, you pay the mortgage." Mrs. Castillo nods, shooting daggers toward Mr. Castillo. "And he made you pay on top of that?"

"My signature wasn't free, Serena," her father adds, fueling the tension in the room.

"Are you fucking kidding me?" Serena storms up to him, going toe-to-toe with her father. Striding over to her, I pull her back. I would never interfere with what she needs or wants to say, but putting herself in physical danger is not happening. I don't know shit about her dad other than that he's a horrible person.

"Wolf," she growls, turning her furious golden gaze to me. I just shake my head, stepping back but keeping a hold on her arm to prevent her from rushing forward again. "Fine," she mumbles, turning back to her dad. "You piece of shit; you made her pay back the alimony through rent, didn't you? You horrible, egotistical, selfish bastard. I hope you're happy in your perfect house, with your perfect family. Stay the fuck away from us, stay away from my mother, and live your miserable life far away from where I can see it. You have never, not once, considered how this would impact me, not to mention this is probably illegal. Mamá." She turns to her mother, tears streaming down her face. "Why did you give him money?"

"He wanted full custody, *Muñeca*; it was the only way to keep him from taking our arrangement to the courts. I would give up everything I own to keep you safe. I already failed you by letting you miss out on your adolescence, and I refused to allow him to have more say over your life."

"Mamá, I'm so sorry," Serena cries. "I can't—your savings.

Did he take everything?"

"Of course not, *hija*, I'm fine. I don't care about the money; I care about you." Mrs. Castillo walks to us, throwing her arms around Serena's frame. I release Serena's arm and use the distraction to size Mr. Castillo up. He's a slender man, small in stature and no more than one-hundred-sixty pounds; I've bench-pressed more than he weighs. He senses my appraisal and offers a toothy smile as though he has a right to be here.

Fuck that, and fuck him. Walking around Serena and her mother, I approach him, not stopping until I'm leaning over him and breathing in his air. "Get the fuck out of this house."

"It's my house—"

"Good for you. Do you like harassing women while they're in their home, their fucking space, and threatening them? What the fuck kind of person does that?"

His eyes narrow, and he opens his mouth, but before he can say anything, Mrs. Castillo skirts around me and slaps an envelope against his chest. "Here is your money, Stephen. Now get the hell out."

His fingers grip the white envelope, and he sneers. He must sense how close I am to pummeling his face because instead of responding, he storms past us and slams the door behind him. We all stay silent as the sound of his engine rattles the house, maintaining our stillness until the car gets far enough away that his presence is no longer felt.

"So, *hija*, who's your friend?"

Laughter and tears bubble out of Serena, and before I know it, she's hysterically crying into her hands. Instinctually, I go to her, wrapping my arms around her and pulling her into my body. I let her sobs soak my shirt as I look at her mother and offer an awkward smile.

"Hi, I'm Wolf. Serena's boyfriend."

36

Serena

"Princess, are you sure?"

"I'm fully healed, and after the day I've had, I am not taking no for an answer," I threaten, dragging Wolf into Ink and Needle. "I need these butterfly penises off of me, now."

"Hey, guys. Wolf, you're supposed to be off today. Why are you here?" Aubrey asks as soon as we enter the shop.

"He's giving me a tattoo," I respond, weaving Wolf through the design tables and toward his room. I release Wolf's hand as soon as we walk into his space. "I would close the door if I were you. I'm going to take off my shirt now."

Wolf stares at me, a raised eyebrow and smirk adorning his features. "You sure you're ready to sit for an hours-long tattoo?"

I unzip my sweatshirt and throw it on one of the green chairs. "Wolf, I have so much adrenaline right now, I doubt I'll even feel the prick of the needle."

He sighs, reaching behind him to close the door. "Fine. But if it gets to be too much, then you need to tell me."

"Wolf, I can promise you, I need this." I strip off my shirt and bra, throwing them in the same direction as my sweatshirt. "Pants, too?"

He nods. "I'm going to have the stems and flowers come up from your hip."

"Fine." I bend down and strip off my leggings, too. Unlike the last time I was here, I feel no awkwardness at Wolf seeing my body. "Set up the station thing."

"Okay, Serena, you need to slow down. Don't rush me, princess. I'm going to prep the table and get all my equipment set up, but I need to make sure everything is good before we start, so sit down, get comfortable, and don't interrupt my process. Okay?"

I nod, dropping down to the chair without my clothes on it, and lean back.

—

It takes fifteen minutes for Wolf to set up the station; I'd know—I watched the clock the entire time he readied his equipment. When he finally motions for me to come to the bench, I breathe a sigh of relief.

"Finally," I mumble as I climb onto the paper-lined tattoo bench and lie down. My quip earns me a sharp smack on my ass.

"Smartass."

"Grandpa."

"Serena," he warns, spraying cool liquid on my skin before wiping me down with a paper towel.

"Fine, sorry."

"Good, now stay still. I need to place the stencil on your skin and then see if I need to add any additional elements."

"Will you have to redraw the stencil?" I ask, curious about

330

the process.

"No, the stencil is fine. But I may add a few things to the piece freehand. Give me a minute to apply this, and then I'll see what it needs."

I shut my mouth and stay perfectly still as he lays a large paper over my back, pressing it down with gentle force. He peels the sheet from my back and stays quiet for long minutes, seemingly considering his next move.

Finally, he breaks the silence. "I'm going to add a few things. Do you trust me?"

"Of course," I don't hesitate to respond.

"Good, then I'm not going to tell you what I'm doing. You'll see it when you're done." A cool tip presses against my skin, and I fight a shiver at the contact. Minutes bleed into each other as Wolf modifies the tattoo, adding to the drawing at the center of my back and right hip. I don't know how long I lay there as he draws on me, head down and eyes closed, but I startle at the sound of his voice. "Okay, you ready, princess?"

"Yeah, I'm ready."

"Let me know if it gets to be too painful, okay?" he instructs, phrasing it as a question but meaning it as a demand. Tucking my arms under my head, I nod, shutting my eyes and letting the buzz of the tattoo gun mute everything else.

Wolf:

If I couldn't see the rise and fall of her back from her breathing, I would think that Serena was a corpse or a sex doll. Unlike some of the largest, most tattooed men I've worked on, she doesn't move a goddamn muscle, doesn't twitch as I work through the design I have. Starting with the outline, I took my time to make sure that every part of the tattoo was

331

flawless. I also ensured that the flying cocks on her back were no longer existent. I asked her a few times if she was okay, and she hummed her response, almost like she was in a trance.

Applying the last of the ink for today's session to her back. I sit up, set my tattoo machine down on my tray, and admire the design gracing Serena's back. Just like in the drawing in my bedroom, multiple strelitzias are painted on her back, starting from her right hip and traveling up to the center of her back. The lines are feminine and strong, a testament to the potency of the stem and the unique beauty of the flower. Colored in shades of green, orange, blue, and purple, the design is bold and stunning against the curve of her spine. When I placed the flowers, I realized that after everything she'd gone through with her dad, with so many people in her life, she deserved to have the butterflies she desperately wanted. I added three Blue Morpho butterflies to the piece: one at the bottom to symbolize the past, one resting on the center flower to symbolize the present, and one flying independently toward her left shoulder blade to illustrate the freedom she has in her future.

"You ready to see it, Serena?"

"You're done?" she asks, sounding surprised.

"It's been five hours. We're done for today," I laugh, spraying her back again and wiping off the excess ink. "We will need a couple more sessions to finish, but before you see it, I have to ask, are you okay?"

"Am I okay that my dad is the biggest asshole on the planet? Not really. But I have a mom who loves me, friends who have become family, and a boyfriend"—she pauses, scoffing at the designation—"who gives me tattoos. So, all things considered, I'll survive."

"Serena, I'm serious."

She sighs, letting out a long breath before answering. "I know you are, Wolf. But really, I'm okay."

I accept her answer and help guide her up and onto her legs. "We'll go over the aftercare—and this time, you'll listen—after you see it. Spinning her around so that her back faces the floor-to-ceiling mirror, I hold up a smaller mirror, allowing her to see her reflection. I watch her face closely, praying that I don't see any disappointment or sadness when taking in the work. I'm relieved that only awe is present.

"Oh my God, Wolf," she gasps, bringing a trembling hand to her mouth. "How did you—I can't—Wolf," she breaks off, her watery eyes meeting mine. "I love it. I love it so much. I-I can't believe you designed this for me."

"Did you see the butterflies?"

She nods, working her throat as she swallows down the emotions I see building in her chest. "Thank you, Wolf. This is everything to me." She throws herself at me, wrapping her arms around my waist and tucking her head into my chest. I'm careful to grip her by the shoulders.

"I know, princess. I know."

37

Epilogue

Five months later

Serena:

"Are you sure this is a good idea?" I ask, shaking while I hold the tattoo gun.

"Yes, Serena," Wolf sighs, sitting shirtless and upright on the tattoo chair.

"But what if I hurt you?"

He raises his eyebrow, and I am so tempted to wipe the smug look off of his face. "Princess, it's a tattoo; of course it's going to fucking hurt." When I got home from my summer class this afternoon, Wolf called, asking me to come to the tattoo shop. He never told me that he wanted me to tattoo something on his damn chest.

"But what if you bleed?"

"Again, it's a tattoo. Why are you so nervous about this?"

"Wolfric, I am nervous because I am permanently inking something on your skin, which is a collection of art and beauty and detail. Have you seen my pottery? The vase I made in my class last week looks like an anus."

I watch as Wolf's forehead wrinkles and his eyebrows pull down. "That was a vase? I thought it was a fruit bowl."

"Why would I put flowers in a fruit bowl?"

"Fuck if I know. I still can't figure out how you organize half the shit in your apartment." He scowls, shaking his head at me. "Okay, princess. Now, can we do this tattoo? I don't have all night." Wolf twists his body and reaches for me, grabbing my waist and hauling me onto his lap. My legs fall on either side of him, and I straddle him while my right hand is still gripping Wolf's tattoo machine.

"I can't tattoo like this," I complain, freaking out even more now that I can feel the obvious erection beneath me. How am I supposed to pay attention to what I'm doing if every time I shift my clit rubs against his dick?

"You had your chance to tattoo normally, but you're being a wimp. All you have to do is trace the lines; it's not like you're performing brain surgery or rocket science."

"Fine." Sticking my tongue between my teeth, I bite down, concentrating on the instructions Wolf gave me on how to use the tattoo gun. He attached something to the gun called a trigger switch, making the foot pedal unnecessary for the application. "Okay, I'm doing it. Here it goes," I narrate, lowering the gun to his chest. Before I even touch his skin, he yelps.

"Ow, fuck, shit."

"What? Oh my God, what happened?" I rear back, hunting for the source of the pain. Wolf's face cracks into the biggest, dumbest-looking grin. "God, I hate you."

"No, you don't. You love me, princess. But sorry, I couldn't help myself." He shrugs like he didn't just take ten years off my life.

"Not funny. I hope this hurts." Bringing the gun to his chest, I press lightly against his skin and begin tracing the small butterfly that rests over his left pectoral. The design is simple, nothing more than a few curves and lines, but I know that it means something. When he first told me that I was going to tattoo him, I balked and told him, under no uncertain terms, that it wasn't happening. However, when he told me that he wanted a butterfly over his heart to symbolize me and our relationship, I couldn't help but cave in.

"Is this even sanitary? I'm straddling you while I tattoo your skin."

"Should I bury my dick inside you while you do it? Would that make you less anxious?" he asks.

Lifting the gun from his chest, I glare down at him. "Again, not funny."

"I wasn't trying to be." His hands move from my thighs to my ass, pressing me further against his erection. "Something about you with a tattoo gun is hot as fuck."

Squirming on top of him, I suck in a breath as he rubs against my clit. "Let go of my ass, Wolf. I will transform this butterfly into a penis with wings if you don't let me concentrate."

"Fine," he sulks, dropping his hands to his side while I finish the tattoo. Not even five minutes later, I pull back and set the tattoo gun on the tray table beside the chair.

"Okay, that's the best it's going to get," I sigh, keeping my eyes trained on the shaky lines and imperfect curves of the butterfly. "You would have done better tattooing it yourself."

"I don't care what it looks like, just as long as I know you did it. You have my markings on your body, and I wanted something from you." He reaches up, cupping my jaw in his hands. "I love you, princess. I don't know how the fuck we got here, but we're here. It's you, me, and these tiny little butterflies, Serena."

I don't try to hold back the smile that tugs at my lips. We've been trading "I love yous" for the last month, and each time he says it, my heart swells. "I love you, too," I respond, pecking him on the lips. "Now, is it my turn for a tattoo? I think I'm owed something after this traumatic session."

His hands clamp down on my ass, squeezing hard before pulling me forward. Capturing my lips in a hard kiss, he lines the seam of my lips with his tongue before working it inside my mouth. Licking into me, I shift against him, grinding into his erection before he wrenches his mouth from mine, breathing heavily.

"You're a pain in my damn ass, princess."

38

Bonus Epilogue

Lincoln

I don't want to be here, staring at happy-as-fuck couples in our backyard while I try to pretend like everything is okay.

Of course it's not okay; Seraphina brought Mitch the Dick to this party, despite crying to me on the phone for months, telling me how much she hates him. We became friends the first night we met, almost a year ago, and have spent hours on the phone like fucking saps talking about our problems, our dreams, our fucking hopes. She confided in me everything that Mitchell had done to her: the emotional abuse, the total disregard for her feelings, the callous way he's treated her. It's pathetic, it's juvenile, and it's disgusting.

I made her swear that she wouldn't get back with him, not necessarily because I wanted her for myself, but because no woman should be constantly belittled. I'm not blind; she's stunning, with her dark hazel eyes and long brown hair, but she's about to start her freshman year, while I'm graduating in the fall. I'm not looking for anything, yet I can't deny the ache in my chest each time I look over at Sera perched in Mitch the Dick's lap.

Sure, he's not a bad-looking guy, but he's a goddamn snake. I see the way he clutches her thigh every time she speaks, the way he not-so-subtly corrects her when she doesn't agree with what he's saying. He's a controlling asshole at eighteen, and I can't imagine how much worse he'll be the older he gets.

Focusing back on the conversation in front of me, I hear Sera's soft, lyrical voice explain, "I don't think I'm going to do the summer experiential education program. I'd like to work in the library for a few more months while I'm home instead of spending the summer at a camp in Pennsylvania with people from high school I don't want to see anymore."

"No, Fin, we're doing the camp. My parents got us a cabin with Rich and Cory, remember?"

Her name is Seraphina, so just the fact that he's shortening it to "Fin" pisses me off. I watch Sera wince as she turns to Mitch. "I already accepted the position at the library."

"You'll have to tell them you can't do it then."

"No, I—"

"Fin, my parents sent a large donation to make sure we were all in the cabin together and placed in the same research group. We owe it to them," he says, shutting her down.

She swallows, nodding her head. "Of course."

"Fuck this," I mumble under my breath and throw my bottle of beer into the fire. The sound of the glass hitting the logs makes a loud popping sound, but I don't give a shit. Stalking across the yard, I throw open the glass door and walk inside the house, desperate to get away from everyone.

I round the corner of the kitchen and approach the stairs, stopping my progress at the softly whispered "Lincoln" that

339

bounces off my back. Sighing, I turn to Sera, bathed in artificial light and looking more beautiful than she has a right to.

"Why aren't you talking to me?" she asks, worrying her lip between her teeth.

I scoff, gifting her with a sardonic chuckle. "I didn't know if I was allowed to. Mitch the Dick seems to be making all the decisions for you." My chest aches as hurt blooms on her face, but I'm not wrong, and she needs to fucking hear it.

"That's not fair."

"Not fair? Seraphina, he's answering every question for you. You can't even work at a goddamn library this summer because his mommy and daddy paid for a cabin in the woods, which sounds like the start of a fucked-up horror film. What the fuck are you doing? Why are you with him?"

"Lincoln, it's not that simple."

Stepping forward, I cup her face in my hands, cradling it gently with the reverence she deserves. "It is that simple. Why is he here?"

She swallows and opens her mouth like she's about to say something when the back door slides open, and Mitch the Dick calls out, "Fin, where are you?"

Seraphina tears her face from my hands and looks over her shoulder. "Just finding the bathroom. Be right there." Looking back at me, she whispers, "I'm sorry, Lincoln."

Shaking my head, I sigh, "Me too, Sera," and walk up the stairs and out of her life.

Made in United States
North Haven, CT
24 August 2024

56525231R00196